THE
JERUSALEM
ASSASSIN

Also by Avraham Azrieli

Fiction:

The Masada Complex – A Novel

The Jerusalem Inception – A Novel

Christmas for Joshua – A Novel

Non-Fiction:

Your Lawyer on a Short Leash

One Step Ahead – A Mother of Seven Escaping Hitler

www.AzrieliBooks.com

THE
JERUSALEM
ASSASSIN

A NOVEL

By Avraham Azrieli

Printed in the United States by CreateSpace, Charleston, South Carolina.

This book is a work of fiction. The characters, incidents, and dialogues are products of the author's imagination and are not to be construed as real. Other than the known historic events and political figures, any resemblance to actual events or persons, living or dead, is entirely coincidental.

ISBN: 1460906551
ISBN-13: 9781460906552
Library of Congress Control Number: 2011902342

For my mother, Ruth, for many years of love and encouragement.

Part One
The Chase

Wednesday, October 11, 1995

The flight from Damascus landed at Charles De Gaulle Airport at lunch time—an opportune time for long lines and lax immigration scrutiny. The Hawaiian shirt stuck to Al-Mazir's sweaty back, but he counted on the flowery design to convey the vacationer's image he aimed to fake. He walked down the drab hallways and joined the queue of mustachioed men in striped suits, elders in checkered kafiyas, and veiled matrons clutching droopy children. Progress was slow, paced by the thumping of stamps on passports. He breathed deeply, calming himself. He had no reason to worry. The French consul general in Damascus had personally handed him this passport, which belonged to a recently deceased Frenchman but carried Al-Mazir's own photo.

The butterflies in his stomach fluttered urgently as he stepped up to the counter and placed the passport before a uniformed woman. His French was barely conversational, and if she made any inquiries…

"*Bonjour.*" She browsed the passport, hit a few keys on her computer keyboard, and found a vacant spot to land her stamp. *Thud!*

He let the air out of his lungs in a slow, soundless whistle.

"*Bienvenue à Paris, Monsieur.*"

"Merci beaucoup." Al-Mazir took the passport, shouldered his overnight bag, and walked by the two gendarmes and through the automatic glass doors. He circled the luggage carousel and headed for the exit. The trickiest part was behind him, but he feared it would not take long before busy tongues reached the wrong ears. He must return to the safety of Damascus as soon as a three-way agreement was concluded with Abu Yusef and the Saudi prince for funding the fight against Arafat and his traitorous Oslo Accords with the Jews.

Entering the Arrivals Terminal, Al-Mazir passed through a crowd of expectant relatives and cabbies looking to hook a passenger. He scanned the terminal for Abu Yusef's men. A group of passengers peered at a large electronic display of flights information. A couple labored to pacify an irate baby. And a punk in black leathers tinkered with his motorcycle helmet. Off to the right, three young men stood near a currency-exchange booth. They returned Al-Mazir's glance with intense, dark eyes. One of them stepped forward. *"Salaam Aleikum."*

"Salaam Aleikum," Al-Mazir replied.

"Allah's blessings upon you." The young man kissed Al-Mazir on both cheeks. "I am Hassan Gaziri."

"Abu Yusef's nephew? By Allah, you were a toddler last time I saw you!" Al-Mazir embraced Hassan, detecting a gun in a shoulder holster. For a moment he hesitated. Was this a trap? Was Abu Yusef's invitation nothing but a ruse to eliminate a competitor?

Outside, a green Peugeot 605 waited at the curb. Bashir, Abu Yusef's long-time enforcer, sat behind the wheel. But Hassan steered Al-Mazir to the left and opened the rear door of a second car, a black Renault Safrane. The driver was a young man in a suit, who kept both hands on the steering wheel and gazed forward. Hassan ran around to the other side, and his two companions joined Bashir in the green Peugeot. The doors slammed and the two sedans took off.

Al-Mazir was relieved. If they wanted to kill him, they would make him sit by the driver, vulnerable to a quick knifing from behind. And the use of two cars showed Abu Yusef's concern for his guest's safety. Al-Mazir sat back and exhaled in relief.

All was going well. Their old partnership had given birth to the Munich Olympics spectacle, which had put Palestinian resistance at the top of world news. Now, after years apart, they would join forces again to deliver an even greater catastrophe unto the Zionist enemy.

Gideon had noticed the Hawaiian shirt as soon as the middle-aged passenger emerged from the passport-control area. At first he dismissed the possibility. A terrorist travelling under a false identity would rather emulate a gray sparrow than a peacock. But a reverse strategy could be at play—deflecting suspicion by defying expectations. Gideon glanced at the photograph stuffed inside his helmet. Even though Al-Mazir had gained considerable weight since the snapshot had been taken, his facial features were yet to completely melt into his pudginess. And the reception by the Arabs confirmed his identity, especially the extended embrace he used to pat down his host for weapons.

Gideon slipped on the full-face helmet and said, "The Frogs let him in. He's in the second car."

The built-in speakers inside his helmet crackled with Bathsheba's voice. "I see him."

"Go!" He exited through the sliding doors just as her BMW K1 motorbike took off with a hushed exhaust rumble.

In the padded back seat of the Renault, Hassan pulled a silver thermos from a pouch, unscrewed the top, and poured coffee into a porcelain cup. The rich aroma filled the car.

"Ah!" Al-Mazir sniffed at the edge of the cup. "The real thing!"

"Abu Yusef brewed it especially for you," Hassan said. "Black, twice-boiled, no sugar."

He sipped and smacked his lips. "Perfect!"

"My uncle told me it was your only luxury back in Beirut, when the PLO fought a holy jihad for Palestine."

"I'm still fighting." Al-Mazir glanced at the young man. "I've kept alive the spirit of Beirut, continued to spill the Jews' blood."

"You have been wise. We all see it now, after the Oslo treachery of Arafat—"

"Don't mention that name!" Al-Mazir took another sip and held the thick brew in his mouth before swallowing. "So how is my dear comrade?"

"Abu Yusef is eager to see you. He prays that you join us soon."

"With my courageous followers, yes?"

Hassan blushed. He straightened the lapels of his tailored suit. "*Insha'Allah.*"

Al-Mazir noted the young man's embarrassment with satisfaction. In the eleven years between 1972 and 1983, starting with the Munich Olympics attack, the string of extravagant airline-highjack operations, and the buildup of PLO forces in southern Lebanon for an invasion of Israel, Al-Mazir and Abu Yusef had worked ceaselessly under Arafat to achieve the dream of a free Palestine. But rather than leading an invasion, Arafat needled the Galilee with a constant barrage of Katyusha missiles until Israel sent troops into Lebanon. PLO forces quickly collapsed, and a 1983 ceasefire agreement sent Arafat and his men on a safe passage to Tunisia. But not Al-Mazir. He broke away from the PLO and went to Syria, where he had formed the Nablus Liberation Force, whose defiance resonated with disillusioned young Palestinians.

Abu Yusef, on the other hand, had spent ten years with Arafat in Tunisia, only to splinter from the PLO in protest of the 1993 Oslo Accord with Israel. And now, after two years and a second Oslo agreement, Abu Yusef's underfunded group could take credit for only a single attack on a Jewish school in Marseilles, while Al-Mazir claimed eighteen attacks on Jewish and Israeli targets, including a magnificent bus explosion in Tel Aviv that had almost derailed the recent Oslo II signing ceremony in Washington. It was no wonder, therefore, that his old partner had reached out to renew their alliance and had arranged for this clandestine trip to Paris. Tonight they would dine with a Saudi donor, whom Abu Yusef had cultivated to sponsor a militant Palestinian opposition to Arafat.

Hassan poured more coffee into Al-Mazir's cup.

"Thank you." Al-Mazir took a sip and looked out the window. This was his first trip out of Syria since 1983. He had missed Europe's colors, sounds, and smells. But while his mind was still occupied by the pleasing sights, he noticed Hassan's right hand slip under his jacket toward the hidden gun.

Betrayal!

His shoulders tensed up for action as he prepared to lob the steaming coffee into Hassan's eyes, shove a heavy elbow into his ribcage, and take possession of the gun.

Gideon mounted his own K1, started the engine, and released the clutch. The heavy motorbike leaped forward. A startled porter swerved a luggage cart, and a pile of suitcases cascaded onto the curb. Gideon leaned sharply, avoiding the luggage and the angry porter, and raced off.

He caught up with Bathsheba and slowed down to match the pace of airport traffic. An Avis shuttle bus separated them from the two cars ahead. The green Peugeot took the ramp onto the highway, followed by the black Renault.

"They are heading north," he said into his helmet, "away from Paris."

In his side mirror he saw her black helmet tilting as if saying: *So what?* But Gideon was alarmed by this development. Their operational assumption had been that Al-Mazir, if he actually showed up, would be driven to a safe apartment in Paris, where Abu Yusef would be waiting. After the meeting, he would become an easy target. Inner-city assassinations were quick and uncomplicated—a red stoplight, spraying the target with bullets, disappearing into traffic. End of story. But the highway was tricky, even on powerful motorbikes. Shooting at high speed could lead to cars flipping over, a multi-vehicle pileup, and innocent casualties, followed by police barricades at the highway exits. On the other hand, trailing the two cars to their destination carried its own risks. A suburban setting would make the two K1 motorbikes stand out like black flies on a slice of cheesecake.

Their orders for this scenario had been clear: Once they're off the highway, eliminate Al-Mazir at the first opportunity. Tracking down Abu Yusuf's hideout would have to wait.

"As soon as they exit," Gideon said. "I'll go first. You finish off."

Her black helmet nodded once.

Hassan's hand emerged with a mobile phone, not a gun. Al-Mazir slouched back in the seat. He accepted the proffered phone, pressed it to his ear, and heard Abu Yusef's unmistakable voice. "*Ya habibi!*"

"*Ah-Salaam!* Allah's blessings upon you!"

"Hearing your voice is like hearing the prophet Mohammed himself!"

Al-Mazir laughed. "Your slick tongue is still anointed with the olive oil of Palestine."

Abu Yusef's laughter was hoarse with static. "In my dreams I still chase you among the ancient groves of Nablus."

"Me too, my friend. Me too." Al-Mazir chuckled with pleasure. The intervening years of estrangement had failed to diminish their childhood bond. He had been foolish to harbor suspicion.

"The excitement has kept me awake all night. You'll be awed by my plan. It is grand! More impressive than Munich, more spectacular than Entebbe, more stunning than a hundred *Achille Lauros*. And we'll soon have the money to do it!"

"And where will we meet your generous friend?"

"I have arranged a dinner right here, at our villa. A tender lamb is roasting over red embers—just like home. The scent alone will get you inebriated."

"Ah! You know me too well!"

Gideon leaned right and rolled the throttle, accelerating after the cars, which cut through three highway lanes toward an exit ramp. The motorbike responded with explosive power, rapidly closing the gap between him and the cars. "Here we go!" He glanced at the mirror by his right hand and registered her headlight close behind.

The green Peugeot approached the turnoff to the local road. It stopped at a red light, its right taillight blinking. The Renault stopped behind it.

His right hand let go of the throttle and reached into his coat for the mini-Uzi. He kept a grip on the handlebar with his left hand, two fingers extended over the clutch lever. His left foot downshifted while his right foot tapped the brake to decelerate, coming to a full stop behind the Renault. He saw Al-Mazir in the back seat, pressing a mobile phone to his ear. The younger man was sitting behind the driver.

Bathsheba's motorbike stopped a few feet behind, slightly to the left.

Boots planted on both sides of the K1 to balance it, Gideon drew the mini-Uzi and cocked it. With both arms extended over the small windshield, he aimed the weapon, but suddenly his left boot slipped, likely on an oil stain, and the motorbike began to tip sideways. He grabbed the handlebar and fought to keep from falling over.

The traffic light turned green, and the Peugeot moved instantly, making a sharp right turn onto the local road. The Renault driver glanced in his rearview mirror, noticed the weapon, and slammed the gas pedal. The engine uttered an angry roar, followed by the high pitch of spinning wheels.

His left boot found a dry foothold, and Gideon pulled the motorbike straight up. He aimed the mini-Uzi to the right, where he expected to find the Renault following the green Peugeot, but it turned left, skirted the stationary cars lined at the red traffic light, and raced away on the local road. Gideon cursed and corrected his aim, but by then the Renault was sheltered by the line of waiting cars.

He stashed the weapon back under his coat. His left foot hit the gear shift into first, his hand twisted the throttle, and the motorbike took off. He leaned all the way to the left, executing the sharpest turn possible, his head as low as the headlights of a station wagon waiting at the light. He prayed there was no more oil on the road.

A l-Mazir gripped the door handle and yelled into the phone, "Assassins! Help!" Abu Yusef's reply was drowned in the screeching tires and roaring engine.

The large Renault weaved from lane to lane through traffic. It passed a delivery van and cut back in to avoid a collision, causing the van to run off the road.

Looking back over his shoulder, Al-Mazir saw the headlight of a motorcycle. "Allah's mercy! Shoot him down!"

"Get down!" Hassan drew his gun, released his seat belt, and lowered the window. He extended his arm out, but the driver swerved sharply, and Hassan fell back. He cursed and got back to the window. His shots popped in a rapid succession.

G ideon bent forward, ducking behind the tiny windshield. A moment later, the shooting stopped. He twisted hard on the throttle and aimed the motorbike at the solid white line, passing a bunch of cars. The Arab driver was very good, and the top-of-the-line Renault had ample power, but no sedan could outrun a BMW K1.

He switched hands, his left reaching across to hold the right-side handlebar grip, keeping the throttle at a steady pace behind the Renault. With his right hand he drew the mini-Uzi, aimed it at the rear window, and pulled the trigger. The glass disintegrated into a thousand shards, which pelted him like hail. The Renault spun around, slid across the opposite lane and into a ditch.

Gideon kept his motorbike on a straight line, down-shifted, and stopped on the right shoulder. In his rearview mirror he saw Bathsheba slow down and cut across the opposite lane in front of an oncoming car. She couldn't stop in time, and her K1 slipped and fell over.

He cursed, pulled on the throttle, and made a U-turn, heading back.

She was already on her feet, running to the Renault.

There was a lull in traffic, and no sign of the green Peugeot.

She aimed at the car. A long burst of bullets exploded into the side windows, crushing bones and flesh, splashing red blood. The empty magazine fell to the ground, and she shoved in a new one. Aiming forward, she pulled open the back door.

"Hurry up," Gideon said, but the speakers in his helmet brought back only the sound of her breathing.

Inside the Renault, crouched forward, Al-Mazir recited verses from the Koran. On top of him, Hassan's body spewed blood in slowing spasms. A phone on the floor let out a distant voice.

Bathsheba cracked open her eye-shield and met Al-Mazir's eyes. "Greetings from Jerusalem," she said and pulled the trigger.

He was dead before the last bullet made its short way into his torn chest.

Gideon pulled a brown envelope from his inside pocket and tossed it to Bathsheba. She tore it open and flung a bunch of photos into the car, covering the bodies with images of naked youths utilizing sex paraphernalia.

A couple of cars came down the road, slowing to a crawl, windows rolling down, voices shouting in French. Behind them, a little blue Porsche arrived at high speed, honking to hurry them along. But Gideon could only think of the green Peugeot, racing over with three armed Arabs ready for battle amidst all of these French civilians. "Let's go," he said. "Now!"

In a country villa surrounded by tall hedges and old pecan trees, Abu Yusef slammed the receiver and looked at a room full of men. "Battle stations! Go!"

They grabbed their weapons and ran out to their assigned positions—twelve around the perimeter of the property, four on the roof, and three pairs patrolling the road through the village.

A few moments later, Bashir appeared. He was a muscular native of Hebron, who had been with Abu Yusef for many years.

"Two motorcycles," he said. "Hassan went in the other direction to escape the assassins—"

"He's dead. They're all dead."

Bashir's face darkened. "I should have turned back to help them."

"You should have noticed the tail from the airport!" Abu Yusef struggled to control his rage. "You should have driven *behind* the Renault, not rush ahead like a mindless dog!"

"I didn't expect Arafat's people to find out—"

"It was the Israelis. I heard a woman's voice. *Greetings from Jerusalem.*"

"The Israelis? How?"

"They must have a snitch in Damascus, or in the French foreign service. Are you sure they didn't follow you here?"

"Impossible."

"Go, check our defenses. And keep the men in position until tomorrow, just in case you made another error!"

Bashir left.

Abu Yusef stepped outside to a wide patio decorated with fresh roses and sprinkled with mint leaves. A long table had been set, the plates patterned with the Palestinian tri-colors, the silverware shining to perfection. A giant outdoor grill stood at the edge of a sparkling swimming pool. A steel skewer impaled a lamb over the red embers. A handle attached to the skewer dangled unattended. The man assigned to turn it must have run to his assigned battle post.

The belly of the limp animal dripped fat, producing a hissing sound and a flare-up below. The aroma of roasting gave way to the stench of burning fat. Abu Yusef stepped forward and kicked the grill. It tipped over and fell into the swimming pool with a huge splash of water and steam.

Bathsheba closed the distance in long steps. Gideon moved forward on the saddle, making room. Her almond-shaped eyes glistened through the helmet eye-shield. "Did you see his—"

"Climb on! Quick!"

She mounted the motorbike behind him, breathing hard. "*Wow! Wow! Wow!*"

The earphones rang in his ears. "Don't shout."

"The terror! You should've seen his eyes!"

Distant sirens sounded.

Gideon made another U-turn and headed in their original direction, away from Ermenonville. The surge of power propelled the motorbike forward. In four seconds, they were moving at sixty miles per hour.

"He knew!" She slipped forward on the short saddle, her hands around Gideon, her panting loud in the tiny speakers inside his helmet. He felt her thighs pressing against him on both sides. She groaned. "He watched me! Terrified! Knew he was about to die!"

"Every dog has his day."

"He got it alright! *Pow!*"

The thin hand of the RPM gauge rolled clockwise and crossed the red line. The engine's buzz flowed through the saddle, and Gideon heard Bathsheba utter a grunt as her thighs closed on him again, her body molded against him like a spoon. As he passed the blue Porsche and the other two cars, his foot kicked into second gear. The engine pace dropped, its shuddering subsided. He felt the tension in her body loosen, her thighs parting.

"He saw the bullets hit his chest. *Splash!*"

The engine revs peaked again, high-pitched buzzing, transferred through the saddle. Gideon felt her arms tighten around him, her body cling to his back. Her thighs squeezed inward rhythmically. The motorbike moved fast on the local road, leaning deep into each turn.

He released the throttle. "Stop it!"

"No!" Her voice came deep through the earphones. "Keep going!" Her breathing grew more rapid. "His face! His eyes! *His fear!*"

"Stop it!"

Her right hand dug under his leather jacket, forcing its way under his shirt. Her glove was gone, her fingers cold against his skin. "Go faster!" Her body moved back and forth.

He leaned forward, trying to separate from her.

"The bullets tore him up! He felt them!" Her body pressed against Gideon's back, her fingernails plowing his stomach.

"Enough!" Gideon used his right hand to try to pull her hand out from under his jacket while holding on to the handlebar with his left, keeping the motorbike balanced. He cried in pain as her fingers hooked into him.

"Go! Go! Go!" Her voice was filled with urgency, her body not ceasing from its constant jerking. "Give it gas, damn it!"

Gideon's hand closed around the throttle, pulling it violently. Her crotch hit him repeatedly from behind as she rubbed herself back and forth on the quivering saddle. The engine screamed, rising to the highest pitch. Her body moved faster and faster. Her thighs closed on him like a vise, opened and closed, again and again. Her breathing turned into moans while he kept the throttle open all the way, the engine revs well into the red. The shuddering intensified, buzzing through the saddle into their bodies. She slid back and forth, her moans becoming short, rapid whimpers. Gideon twisted his face in pain as her thighs clamped on him. He kept the motorbike zooming in a straight line, thankful for a gap in traffic, and gasped as she clung to him in a final, violent spasm—thighs and arms tight around him, fingernails digging into his chest. She cried out, and a moment later her body slackened.

He shifted to a higher gear. The engine revs declined. He felt Bathsheba begin to tremble. His hand found the small switch on the right side of his helmet and turned off the communications system. He wished he could wipe the sweat from his face.

At his bedroom in the rear of the villa, Abu Yusef shut the door and locked it. He called the Hilton Hotel in Paris and left word for Prince Abusalim az-Zubayr that dinner was cancelled.

Latif put his slim arms around Abu Yusef. "I'm so sorry."

"I can't believe Al-Mazir is dead." He sat on the bed, and tears emerged from his eyes. "Why did I bring him here? To see him? To hug him? To celebrate with my beloved friend?

It's my fault. I should have gone to see him in Damascus. His blood is on my hands!"

"Allah took him for a reason." Latif caressed Abu Yusef's thinning gray hair and kissed his forehead. "So that you can take over. His men will now follow you."

"And Hassan? What will I tell my sister?" Abu Yusef wept. "Allah has deserted me!"

"Allah loves you." Latif's embrace tightened. "He will help you take revenge, kill a hundred Jews for each of our martyrs."

They crossed the Seine River at Pont de la Concorde, circled the Obelisque, and sped up the Champs Elysees. Gideon kept the motorbike in the left lane, glancing at the side mirrors, his ears pricked for sirens that would break the constant hum of the widest avenue in the world.

Halfway to the Arc de Triomphe, he pulled to the left and parked between two cars along the center divider. They dismounted and ran between moving cars to the opposite sidewalk, still wearing their black helmets, scanning the flow of people and automobiles for any irregularity, any change of pace, any indication that someone had spotted them.

Nothing.

They slowed down and removed their helmets. Bathsheba's tall figure, cropped hair, and sculpted face never failed to draw men's eyes, which right now was a disadvantage.

At the Café Renault, where tourists sipped coffee in booths resembling cars, they turned left onto Rue Pierre Charron and passed by the window displays of Iran Air. Bathsheba motioned at the Iranian flag. "Do you have any bullets left?"

He walked faster.

On Rue Francois they turned right.

Near the end of the block, a short, thin man wearing a dark wool cap leaned against a white Citroën BX. He drew once more from his cigarette, dropped it, and put it out with the sole of his shoe.

Bathsheba got in the back, Gideon behind the wheel, and Elie Weiss in the passenger seat. The car smelled of cigarette smoke. They drove off.

Elie looked forward, not turning his head.

"Your source told the truth," Gideon said. "Al-Mazir was on the Damascus flight. Abu Yusef's men picked him up, but drove north to the suburbs, not to the city. They split up. We chased the car he was in and shot him."

"Any problems?"

"Not with the Arabs." Gideon glanced at Bathsheba through the rearview mirror.

"We had fun." She leaned forward and ruffled his hair. "We're a good team."

Elie coughed in a slow, deep rumble that sounded as if it should emerge from a much larger man. He pulled the tight-fitting wool cap down over his ears. It gave his head a conical shape. His face had a sickly hue.

Gideon drove fast, passing other cars whenever possible, taking turns with sudden jerks of the wheel. In Paris, slow driving drew attention.

Heading east on Rue La Fayette, he slammed on the brakes and made a tight U-turn. A quarter-block back, he turned into Rue Lamartine, a narrow one-way street with little traffic, and took a swift left turn into Rue Buffault, where he stopped at the curb.

They waited a few minutes.

Elie opened the door. The air was cold and moist. He led the way across the street and down the opposite pavement, past the municipal office building. Next was number 32, a public elementary school, where a marble plaque commemorated twenty thousand Parisian Jewish children deported to Auschwitz between 1942 and 1944. A bouquet of dry flowers rested in a metal ring under the plaque, wrapped in the French red, white, and blue flag.

The next building, number 30, was a synagogue. Its three mahogany doors were embraced by ornate marble pillars resembling palm fronds, and a Biblical quote on top: *Blessed are you in coming, and blessed are you in leaving.* A temporary wall of plywood, supported by police barriers, separated the sidewalk from the street, shielding the forecourt and doors from passing cars. The synagogue had been the target of a terrorist attack a decade earlier.

Gideon pushed open the heavy door at number 28 and held it for Elie and Bathsheba. The old apartment building had an elevator, but they took the stairs.

On the third floor landing, Elie was out of breath. He coughed hard and spat into a handkerchief. Gideon entered the apartment with his weapon drawn. He checked the bedroom, which had one bed and two thin mattresses on the floor, and the workroom, where a large metal desk carried a telephone, a computer, and a small TV. Electrical wires crisscrossed the floor.

Elie sat at the desk and pulled off the wool cap. He opened a file, took out a small photograph, and showed it to them.

"That's the one who shot back at us," Gideon said.

"Hassan Gaziri." Elie tapped the photo with his finger. "A nephew. Abu Yusef must be very upset. And nervous. He's hunkered down in a secluded house, difficult to access, lots of hiding spots for his men to wait in ambush for foolhardy attackers."

"So what?" Bathsheba kicked the leg of the table. "We give up?"

"We plan ahead," Elie said. "Let him stew in grief and anger and dread. Let him experience what he has caused so many others to experience."

"That's never going to happen," Bathsheba said. Her father, a judo champion, had represented Israel in the 1972 Olympic Games in Munich. At his funeral near Tel Aviv, three-year-old Bathsheba had held a red rose. The next day, her picture was picked up by news outlets worldwide. "He's a murderer," she said. "He doesn't experience the feelings we experience. Right now, all he's thinking about is how to kill more Jews."

"That too," Elie said.

"Then we should go now, drive around Ermenonville, ask people. Someone might have noticed a bunch of Arabs living in a house."

"My father," Elie said, "may he rest in peace, was a *shoykhet*, the only kosher butcher within a week's mule-ride from our shtetl. He taught me that a successful act of slaughter requires meticulous preparations—for both the *shoykhet* and the animal."

Bathsheba laughed, but Gideon didn't. He had once seen Elie work with a long blade on a former SS prison guard, an elderly man who had spent decades evading the consequences of his crimes. Since then, despite Elie's small stature and worsening health, Gideon had felt apprehension in his presence.

"Driving around could draw attention to you," Elie said. "We need an observation point. Show me the layout."

With a roadmap flat on the desk, Gideon's finger traced Charles de Gaulle Airport, the highway north, and the exit ramp. "That's where the green Peugeot turned right. We can wait at this gas station." He pointed at the intersection off the highway. "The Peugeot 605 is a pricey car. They'll use it again."

"Start on Friday," Elie said. "Give them a day to calm down."

"Calm down my ass," Bathsheba said. "They're going to strike back."

Elie glanced at his watch. "I have a flight to catch." He raised his hand to stop Gideon, who started to rise. "Stay here. I'll take the train to the airport."

———

Part Two
The Momentum

Thursday,
October 12, 1995

"Do you hear them?" Prime Minister Yitzhak Rabin peered through the window shutters at a group of demonstrators on the opposite sidewalk. "They're praying for my early death!"

"I didn't know you believe in the power of prayers." Elie Weiss sipped from a cup of tea, which the prime minister had fixed for him.

"It depends who does the praying." Rabin sat down. It was the same sofa Elie remembered from past visits to the official PM residence in Jerusalem. He had reported to each of the previous occupants—Levi Eshkol, Golda Meir, Yitzhak Rabin himself during his earlier tenure, Menachem Begin, Yitzhak Shamir, and Shimon Peres. And now, with Rabin back in office, the place had a stale, museum-like quality, contrasting with the boisterous chants across the street.

"My wife moved back to our apartment in Tel Aviv. Can you blame her?"

"Not really."

Prime Minister Rabin's eyes had remained blue and steady, but he wore large glasses from a bygone fashion. His reddish hair had turned gray, and his firm jaw had slackened. "We've been through a lot, Weiss."

"But not much has changed." Elie lowered the cup to the saucer.

"I disagree." The previous week, Rabin had signed the second phase of the Oslo Accords at the White House, moving forward with the land-for-peace deal with the Palestinians. "Arafat has changed. The PLO has changed. And the balance of hope has changed."

"The balance of risk, also." Elie took out a pack of cigarettes, but didn't light any. The chanting outside stopped, and a single voice yelled, "*Rodef!*" It was a Talmudic term, referring to a "Pursuer," a Jew who was a menace to his fellow Jews.

The prime minister shifted—quickly, as if something had stung him. "Can you believe these Talmudic ayatollahs?"

A chorus outside joined in chanting, "*Rodef! Rodef! Rodef!*"

A burst of coughing tore through Elie's chest. He struggled to control it. "Sorry," he managed to say, "tail end of a bad cold."

"You should quit smoking."

"After you." Elie wiped his lips with a handkerchief. "My sources tell me there are widespread doubts about the Oslo process, even among moderate Israelis. They don't share your trust in Arafat."

"You think I trust that murderer? No! I'm relying on his opportunism. And his grandiose view of himself. We're giving him a Palestinian state on a silver tray."

"Some say he's still dedicated to the dream of greater-Palestine, that he accepted Oslo's partition concept as a temporary phase."

"Oslo doesn't forbid dreaming. But the momentum of peace will take everyone to a better reality."

"Most of his new Palestinian policemen are PLO terrorists."

"*Former* PLO terrorists."

"You're gambling with Jewish lives."

"Me? The Knesset approved Oslo!"

"It approved the first Oslo agreement two years ago with sixty-one to fifty-nine votes, and only because of payoffs and bribes to tie-breaking members. Hardly an enthusiastic endorsement."

"That's democracy. I'll keep going even with a one-vote majority. And these ayatollahs," Rabin jerked his head at the window, "can have their free speech, blowing air like propellers!"

"There's some validity to their anger. Palestinian terror hasn't stopped."

"It's a process! What do they want? Miracles? We're making progress. The PLO renounced violence and recognized Israel. Arafat is governing Gaza and much of the West Bank. And the Palestinian Authority is starting to work. For the first time in Israel's history, we have a partner for peace."

"Like you said at the Nobel Prize ceremony: *Enough of blood and tears! Enough!*"

"That wasn't the Nobel speech. I said that when we signed the first Oslo agreement at the White House in 1993."

"But the blood and tears haven't stopped."

"It's the price of peace. Do you have an alternative?" Prime Minister Rabin glared at him.

"Yes. Let the blood and tears come from the veins and eyes of Arabs, not Jews."

"Ah, there you go again." He rolled his eyes. "We can't kill all of them."

"It's them or us."

"It's hope or despair!" Rabin's voice rose in anger. "And the agreement I just signed gives Arafat full control of the main West Bank cities—Jericho, Nablus, Hebron, Bethlehem. Let him rule over a million angry Palestinians! Let him deliver clean water, run health clinics, and haul off the trash! Let him fight Hamas!"

"And if you lose the next elections?" Elie toyed with the cigarette pack. The conversation was going in the direction he had hoped for. "The peace process has damaged your popularity."

"Leadership is not a popularity contest." Rabin tilted his head, smiling in a way that was almost shy. "Look, peacemaking is just like conducting a war. There's a main thrust. And there are pinpoint attacks on secondary targets. Our main thrust is the Oslo Accords, leading to two states living peacefully side-by-side. Our secondary targets are the all-or-nothing opponents on both sides. For Arafat, they are the *Right of Return* diehards, his PLO dropouts, who call him a traitor for recognizing Israel. For me, they are the right-wing *Eretz Israel* politicians, who'd rather forgo peace than concede a few biblical tombs in the West Bank."

"The West Bank is our backbone. Without it, Israel will be eight miles wide."

"The Palestinians will not have an army. Arafat knows my red lines."

"Arafat doesn't have to worry about an electoral defeat."

"I'll win the next elections," Rabin said. "The opposition offers no hope. Israeli voters want more than doomsday prophesies and personal attacks."

"You're having me kill Arafat's opponents. Do you want me to help with yours?"

"Are you offering this help on behalf of the Special Operations Department or just as Elie Weiss?"

"SOD and I are one and the same. I can do more for you than pollsters and campaign consultants. I know how to deal with Jewish insurgents." Until 1967, Elie had run a network of informers in ultra-Orthodox yeshivas in order to monitor seditious elements who posed an existential risk to Israel, just as fundamentalist Jewish groups had destroyed Jewish kingdoms in ancient times. But the dramatic victory of the Six Day War, which many viewed as divine intervention, had ended the siege mentality in Israel and diffused the ultra-Orthodox anti-Zionist fever. Subsequently, Elie shifted his base of operations to Europe. "I still have some local assets," he said.

"To do what?"

"The hothead fringe of the settlers' movement could be used to tarnish Likud. Guilt by association."

"That's your mistake," Rabin said. "Arik Sharon and Bibi Netanyahu are not hotheads or insurgents. They're my political opponents. I'll beat them at the voting booth."

"Current opinion surveys predict you'll lose."

"They can't predict tomorrow's weather, how can they predict the election results a year from now? A lot can change."

"The tide's against you. A few more terror attacks could cause your coalition partners to quit, topple your government, and force early elections in ninety days."

"Then I'll win on the issues."

"Voters might find it difficult to hear your rational arguments against the backdrop of ambulance sirens and wailing mourners. But my strategy would make your right-wing opponents seem even less appealing than you."

"I'm a soldier. I fight fair and square."

"Fair to whom? If you lose, the Oslo process will lose. And your supporters will lose."

"We won't lose the elections." Rabin paused, his silence filled by the chanting voices from outside. "I know how to win a battle."

"With words? My strategy entails action, not words. Bundle up Bibi and Arik with the radicals, show the public that all those who oppose the peace process are dangerous fanatics."

"Shin Bet is handling the fanatics."

"Our domestic security agency is not a political outfit. Shin Bet has no understanding of public opinion and shifting ideologies."

"They're doing a good job protecting me."

"That's the point. Their posture is defensive. You need someone with a proactive approach."

"Someone like you?"

"Someone capable of orchestrating bold actions—from local disturbances to spectacular events that will shock public opinion. The goal should be to cause the majority of Israelis to despise all right wingers, detest them, ostracize them."

"How?"

"By branding the whole political right—including Likud—as a violent fringe."

"Easier said than done."

"I'm working on it already," Elie said. "Your victory would require a two-stage plan. First my agents are setting up ugly skirmishes that create an association in voters' minds between the violent, extreme-right fringe and mainstream Likud. Then a dramatic event will totally demonize the whole right-of-center political spectrum."

"Sounds too good to be true. What are the risks?"

"The risk is this: You've lost the premiership once, and it took you years to return to office. Do you want to lose it again? You're too old for a comeback."

Yitzhak Rabin's jaw tightened. "What kind of a dramatic event?"

Elie hesitated. He looked around the room.

"Don't worry. The Shin Bet sweeps this house for listening devices daily. What you tell me stays here."

"I hope so," Elie said. "Remember what we tried with Prime Minister Eshkol? A credible assassination attempt can prop up even the most pathetic politician."

"I'm not Levi Eshkol!" Rabin looked away, as if embarrassed by his outburst.

"And this isn't nineteen sixty-seven. I can deliver the elections to you. I already have most of the pieces in place. Give me the green light, and I'll do the rest."

"What's the plan?"

"That's my business. I'll secure your victory, and you'll reward me with an appointment."

"There we go again." Rabin chuckled. "You still want to run the Mossad?"

"A good politician's supposed to forget his broken promises."

"I remember those more than the ones I fulfilled."

Almost three decades ago, on the eve of the Six Day War, IDF Chief of Staff Yitzhak Rabin had promised to appoint Elie Weiss to run Mossad—if Rabin ever became prime minister. But the appointment never came despite Rabin's ascendance to the pinnacle of political power in 1974 and again in 1992. During those years, Elie had operated in Europe, where he hunted down elderly Nazis and performed unique tasks for successive prime ministers, who occasionally needed to bypass the Mossad for political, legal, or financial reasons.

Elie's semi-independent Special Operations Department had its own funding sources, known only to him. And with the political winds shifting against the Oslo peace process, he saw his chance again. It was now or never. "My reward will be an appointment as intelligence czar. I'll be your point man for Mossad and Shin Bet."

"Both of them?"

"Yes."

The prime minister removed his glasses and examined Elie, as if questioning his sanity. "You want to run Mossad *and* Shin Bet?"

This was a crucial moment. Should Rabin take the bait, Elie would control the most powerful spy apparatus in the world.

"They'll have their own respective chiefs," Elie said calmly. "They'll continue to report to you—through me. As part of your Prime Minister Office, I will coordinate all clandestine activities, including intelligence gathering and covert operations—domestic and overseas."

"I'm an elected leader, you're not. I can't vest so much power in one person. We're a democracy. There's a reason Shin Bet may only operate within our borders and Mossad only overseas."

Elie gestured in dismissal. "It's a meaningless distinction. An imitation of the American FBI and CIA. We're a small country under siege, facing chronic existential risks. For Israel the line between domestic and overseas security is irrelevant."

The demonstrators outside broke into a new chant: "*In blood, and fire, Rabin will expire!*"

The prime minister tilted his head at the window. "Bizarre, isn't it? One day I'm signing a peace agreement in Washington to the tune of worldwide cheers, and the next day I'm sitting in my Jerusalem home and hear my countrymen call for my death." The chant grew louder. "*In blood, and fire, Rabin will expire!*"

In Paris, Gideon was soaping himself under a warm shower when he heard the bathroom door open. "Bathsheba?"

"Who else?" She dropped the toilet seat. "What are you using? It smells great!"

He made sure the curtain was closed. "Can I have some privacy?"

"Almost done."

A moment later he heard her flush, which sent the water temperature spiking in the shower. "Ouch!" He stepped out of the stream. "Do you mind?"

"Sorry." She laughed behind the curtain. "Need help scrubbing your back?"

"Don't—"

Bathsheba stepped into the shower. She was naked but for her peace-sign necklace. "Worry not. I'm here for hygienic purposes only." She snatched the sponge from his hand, made him turn around, and started scrubbing his back.

Gideon lifted his leg to step out of the shower. "This is totally unprofessional!"

"We're not professionals." She blocked his way. "We're rogue gunmen for an old butcher who suffers from a Holocaust complex."

"You underestimate Elie."

"And you underestimate me." She used round motions, pressing the sponge to his skin at just the right force, leaving a fire that was a notch below actual pain, but high enough to make him groan. He leaned with both hands against the tiled wall, surrendering to her capable hands. She worked on his shoulders, treating his muscles to a soapy massage, scrubbed his neck up to his hairline, then traveled down his spine. "Nice ass," she said.

"Hey!"

"Relax," Bathsheba's breath tickled his nape. "You're in good hands."

"I'm not interested."

"We'll see." The sponge dropped by his foot. Her hand descended through the crease between his buttocks, pushed forward between his thighs, and collected his erection in a tight grip. "At least someone here is telling the truth." She nibbled his arm while her other hand reached around his hip. "Let's finish cleaning you up."

Prime Minister Rabin shifted on the sofa as if he couldn't find a comfortable position. "Look, Weiss, it's not a bad idea to have someone in my office coordinate all Israeli intelligence operations. It's practical. But you're too old for such responsibility."

"I'm a year younger than you and have fifty years of experience in clandestine activities." Elie knew the prime minister couldn't refuse a deal that guaranteed he would stay in power. This was mere posturing. "Any other issues?"

"You're not a team player."

"You mean, I won't convene committees to ponder every operation long enough to make it obsolete?"

Rabin laughed. "That's how the government works."

"Would you trust a committee to devise a secret plan to ensure your political survival?" Elie used the word *survival* to drive home the point. "And when you lose, what's the future of your peace agenda under a Netanyahu government?"

"Oh, please." Rabin shook his head. "There will never be a Netanyahu government. He barely made it to major in the army. The voters won't put him in power."

"The polls tell a different story."

"I don't believe trickery would sway the voters. And I don't fight dirty."

"My plan is fail-safe. And there's no prize for an honest loser."

"Are you calling me a loser?" Rabin's smile was lopsided, more hurtful than humored. "Tell me about the Paris situation."

Elie swallowed his disappointment and responded in a measured tone. "With Al-Mazir out of the way, we'll soon move on Abu Yusef and his Saudi sponsor."

"Arafat will be delighted." Rabin looked at Elie for a moment, as if contemplating whether to say something. "Tanya Galinski was here the other day."

"Ah." Elie was immediately concerned. "We go a long way back."

"So I've heard. She's doing an excellent job running Mossad's Europe desk."

"Is she?" He wondered whether Rabin mentioned Tanya as a possible opponent to his appointment as intelligence czar.

"She was concerned," Rabin said. "The spectacle of crashing cars and flying bullets so close to Paris seemed excessive. She said you're better with a blade."

"The Munich Olympics massacre was also a spectacle. Al-Mazir's death required equivalence."

"Tanya is upset with me." The prime minister smirked, as if this was a personal tiff. "She gave me a little lecture about how only Mossad may operate abroad."

"Fine with me."

"Technically, that's the law."

"Do you want Mossad to take over the Abu Yusef situation?"

Rabin sighed. "Mossad has more lawyers than agents these days. I'll be waiting for analysts to investigate, bureaucrats to exchange memos, accountants to authorize budgets, lawyers to issue caveats about the Geneva Convention—"

"It will be different under me. How would peace survive if not by fear and intimidation of its opponents?"

"That's a twisted approach. Peace will succeed through prosperity, through momentum of positive results. The Arabs wouldn't fight us if they had a good life."

"Illusions. Anti-Semitism is deadly bacteria, which have kept mutating over three thousand years into worse forms of cruelty toward Jews. It's a brand of hatred that has thrived among rich and poor alike."

"That's why I'm making peace!"

"Peace won't extinguish the most resilient germs in the history of human wickedness."

"So what? You want to kill a billion Muslims?"

"Only the carriers who spread the contagious disease of anti-Semitism." Elie suppressed a cough. "Your Oslo Accords will only work with a serious dose of antibiotics—an army of Jewish assassins, hunting down every opponent of Israel, every plotter of attacks on Jews, every mosque preacher who calls for jihad—"

"How will you pay for this army of assassins?"

"I have enough funds." Technically he was lying. The Nazi fortune held by the Hoffgeitz Bank of Zurich was still out of his reach. But not for long. The mole he had managed to insert into that secretive private bank was getting close to the top. "Money will never be a problem for me," he added.

"Money is a problem for Mossad and Shin Bet." Rabin stood. "Anyway, go back to Paris and take care of Abu Yusef and his Saudi sponsor so that I can seal a final deal with Arafat."

Elie went to the door. "I'll get it done."

"I know." Yitzhak Rabin returned to the window and squinted through the slats at the nightly vigil across the street. "I have complete trust in you."

"Unfortunately I cannot reciprocate the sentiment."

The prime minister laughed. "Sometimes I wonder, Weiss, whether you intend to be funny or scary."

Rabbi Abraham Gerster observed the group of demonstrators from the rear of the sidewalk. They yelled hoarsely, "With blood, and fire, Rabin will expire!" Across the street, the windows in the prime minister's three-story residence were shuttered. A wall separated the forecourt from the street, which was illuminated by floodlights.

A stout young man with a freckled face and a large knitted skullcap silenced the group with a raised hand and recited from Psalms, "*So shall all your enemies perish, O God, lost and destroyed!*"

Rabbi Gerster pulled down the brim of his black hat. His photo occasionally appeared in news articles about Neturay Karta, the ultra-Orthodox sect that he had led for decades before handing the reins over to his protégé, Rabbi Benjamin Mashash.

One of the demonstrators, a skinny youth with dark skin and a colorful skullcap, walked up and down with a cardboard sign: 1936 BERLIN = 1995 OSLO.

Rabbi Gerster asked, "What does it mean?"

"They're the same." His face was more mature than his slimness suggested. "Adolf Hitler and Yitzhak Rabin. Pursuers of Jews!"

The intense hate shocked Rabbi Gerster. Unlike the theological objection to Zionism, which ultra-Orthodox Jews held because only God may bring Jewish sovereignty back to the Promised Land, these demonstrators focused on the prime minister personally.

The nationalist camp saw the handover of territories to the Palestinians as a handover of Jews to be killed by Gentiles. Until now, their rage had been expressed only with words and threats, but could it evolve into physical violence? Could this be the revival of the old menace of Jewish internecine bloodshed?

"The sinner shall have no hope," the demonstrators chanted. *"The traitor's path shall end in demise!"*

Across the street, a steel gate opened and a guard stepped out of the prime minister's courtyard. He surveyed the street, glancing left and right, and beckoned a white sedan that was idling nearby. Its headlights came on, and it advanced along the curb until its rear door lined up with the open gate.

As if expecting their voices to reach the prime minister more easily through the open gate, the demonstrators increased the tempo of their chanting, practically shouting each word that King David had written three millennia ago. *"God's enemies... shall have neither seed...nor issue!"*

A small figure wearing a dark wool cap emerged through the gate, crossed the curb, and got into the sedan. The face was visible for only a second or two, but Rabbi Gerster recognized Elie Weiss by his aquiline nose.

The chubby leader switched from Psalms to a familiar song of Jewish defiance. *"Scheme your evil plot, and it shall be blotted!"*

The rest of them immediately joined him. *"Utter your curse, and it shall not stand, because God stands with us!"*

The white sedan moved off the curb slowly while the rear window rolled halfway down. The interior was illuminated by the floodlights, and Rabbi Gerster locked eyes with Elie Weiss.

"Scheme your evil plot, and it shall be blotted," the demonstrators sang again, pushing against the barricades.

Inside the car, Elie's hand rose in a subtle greeting.

Rabbi Gerster responded with a curt nod, but then he noticed the leader of the demonstrators returning Elie's gesture with a quick thumbs up while chanting, *"Because God stands with us!"*

Friday,
October 13, 1995

Wilhelm Horch, vice president at the Hoffgeitz Bank in Zurich, adjusted the contrast knob on his computer screen. It showed a live video feed from the hidden camera in the office of the bank's president upstairs. Satisfied with the picture quality, he put his feet up on the desk and watched his father-in-law dictate the next letter.

"To the Association of Swiss Banks, chairman of the board, address, greetings, etcetera." Armande Hoffgeitz tilted his chair backward and gazed at the ceiling. "We are in receipt of your recent inquiry about wartime accounts opened between nineteen thirty-five and forty-five. We commend your initiative to pacify the concerns of the last remaining victims of Nazi aggression. We are thus pleased to report that our records show no inactive accounts from said years—"

"Perhaps we should use a different term." The voice belonged to his assistant, Günter Schnell, who was sitting with his back to the hidden camera. "Something more...vague."

Wilhelm listened intently. He knew that at least one dormant account existed—a huge account, opened during the war by SS General Klaus von Koenig—which likely constituted a major part of the bank's assets. How would they get around it without lying?

"Let's see." Armande Hoffgeitz contemplated for a long moment. "Technically Klaus's account has been inactive, which would require disclosure."

"But there was one instance of activity, when he sent a messenger to attempt a withdrawal—"

"That little Nazi with the long nose, who didn't know the account number or the password?"

Günter looked at his notes. "Untersturmführer Rupert Danzig. He tried to make a withdrawal in May, nineteen sixty-seven."

"That's twenty-eight years ago!"

"He presented appropriate credentials," Günter insisted. "And he had General Klaus von Koenig's ledger showing all of the deposits made to the account."

"He could have found the ledger in a ditch somewhere."

"But he showed familiarity with Herr General. He clearly knew him well."

"Not well enough to know the account number and password."

"He claimed to have forgotten."

"But he never came back."

"Not yet."

"Not ever." Herr Hoffgeitz knuckled his desk three times. "My old friend Klaus is dead. I'm sure of it. He must have perished in a bombardment or on the voyage to Argentina. By that time, the Allies were sinking most U-boats within three days of sailing."

"Banking regulations require us to assume a client is alive, unless a death certificate is presented to us by the executor of the estate."

"Fifty years has passed since we last saw Klaus at the border. Half a century! And twenty-eight years since that creepy little imposter showed up with Klaus's ledger, trying to steal from us." Armande Hoffgeitz pointed to the dictation pad. "Write this down: We are thus pleased to report that our records show no accounts in which the owners or their representatives have made no contact with the bank, directly or indirectly."

One floor below, Wilhelm laughed. His father-in-law was a clever man.

"That's better," Günter said, writing it down.

"Honesty is the best policy!" Armande grinned. "And finish with: Please let us know if we can further assist you in your worthy endeavor. With best personal regards. Armande Hoffgeitz, President."

Günter stood. "I'll have the letter ready for your signature in a few moments."

"We must indulge the association." The banker pushed up the gold-rimmed spectacles that had slipped down his nose. "My poor colleagues have to pacify the damn Jews with a show of a diligent inquiry."

"I'm more concerned," Günter said, "with the new computer system. My hard-copy records are locked up safely. But how can we keep our clients' secrets when the information is stored as electronic signals? Wires everywhere, computer terminals on every desk—I'm very uncomfortable!"

"With the computers or with Wilhelm?"

Günter didn't answer.

"Look, my son-in-law is forcing us to adjust to the information age." Herr Hoffgeitz smiled. "It's uncomfortable, old hands that we are, but—"

"I meant no disrespect, but he's not one of us."

"Look, you remember that I also had my doubts. A young man without kin, not of Swiss ancestry, wants to marry my Paula? I was very concerned. But our investigation showed nothing but the tragic circumstances of his parents' death."

Günter nodded.

"And he did graduate from Lyceum Alpin St. Nicholas with honors." Armande Hoffgeitz tapped his ring, which bore a serpent intertwined with the letters *LASN*. For two centuries, every man in the bank's employ had worn the same alumni ring, a prerequisite to hiring.

"Yes, but—"

"His professional record was impeccable, and Paula loved him. Still does. How could I deny her this happiness?" The banker didn't wait for an answer. "And he has proven himself. A hard worker, excellent with clients. And Klaus Junior is growing so nicely."

"I don't—"

"Wilhelm has been with us for how long?"

"Thirteen years."

Herr Hoffgeitz nodded. "Let me speak with him about the computer situation. I'm sure the two of you can find common ground."

The assistant, himself not young anymore, bowed stiffly. As he walked to the door, his bespectacled face grew, filling Wilhelm's computer screen. The edge of the door appeared for a second at the bottom, just below the camera, and disappeared as Günter exited.

At the far end of the office, Armande Hoffgeitz got up and maneuvered his heavy girth between the chair and the desk. He turned to the window and looked out. Despite the distance from the miniature video camera above the door, the pleasure on the banker's pudgy face came through. He loved his Zurich, where the Hoffgeitz Bank had operated for 216 years at the same stout building on the corner of Bahnhofstrasse and Augustinergasse, managed by a long line of Hoffgeitz males. The neighboring buildings housed other private banks with understated facades and long family traditions. A hundred feet under the neatly swept Bahnhofstrasse, thick walls of steel and concrete protected massive vaults that contained the formidable fortunes entrusted to Armande Hoffgeitz and his colleagues. They, and the institutions they ran, had made Zurich a financial mecca.

Like the building in which his bank resided, Armande Hoffgeitz had weathered the years gracefully. At eighty-four, he was one of Zurich's most respected private bankers, personifying the mystic aura surrounding the bank and its anonymous international clients. The bank's investments in select private and public corporations were rumored to add up to several billion dollars. Diversifying among major industrial, agriculture, retail, construction, energy, and shipping companies, the Hoffgeitz Bank had refrained from accumulating a controlling position in any single public company, making it impossible to trace its investments.

A minute after his head had disappeared from the computer screen, Günter Schnell knocked on Wilhelm's door. With a single keystroke, he made Armande Hoffgeitz vanish from the screen, replaced by columns of numbers, and pressed the button under his desktop, unlocking the door.

"Herr Horch?" Günter leaned in through the half-opened door. "Herr Hoffgeitz wishes to see you."

"Hey! Open the door!" Bathsheba knocked and tried the handle again. "I'm going to wet my pants!"

"I'm almost done." Gideon dried his face on a towel and turned the key. "All yours."

"Don't leave." Bathsheba held the door as he exited the bathroom. "I like sharing."

"I don't." He realized she was about to slip out of her nightgown and turned away. "What happened yesterday should never happen again."

"Never? Then you'll be in a lot of pain. I heard men have to ejaculate at least once a day to maintain—"

"We're colleagues, not lovers!" He reached back without looking and shut the bathroom door.

"Fine," she said behind the closed door, "go ahead, play hard-to-get, I'll play along if it makes you feel better."

"I'm not playing. I mean it."

"How about a cold shower then?"

"If you continue, one of us will have to resign from the service."

"The service?" Bathsheba started the water in the shower. "What service? We're working for the Elie Weirdo Freak Show."

Gideon struggled to control his anger. "The Special Operations Department reports directly to the prime minister's office, and Elie Weiss is a great mentor—"

"Weirdo!"

"He might be different, but he's very powerful. We're not the only team working for him undercover—"

"Weirdo!"

"He hired us when Mossad wouldn't. Where is your gratitude?"

"Weirdo!"

"L emmy!" Armande Hoffgeitz waved him in. "Did you make it back from Paris okay?"

"Why not?"

"Driving that little toy of yours?" The banker shook his head. "I'll never understand why you'd rather drive an old Volkswagen all the way there instead of taking a short flight in first class."

"It's a Porsche, not a Volkswagen."

Armande waved in dismissal. "A Beetle is a Beetle even with a low roof and a fancy name."

"And a much higher speed."

"It should, considering all the time and money you have put into it. How was Paris?"

"Very productive. I took a Saudi client to see *Madame Butterfly* at the Paris Opera. Maria Teresa Uribe played Cho-Cho-Sun. Incredible performance!"

"Not my cup of tea. And how are Paula and Klaus Junior?"

"Your grandson insists on a Saturday-morning sailing. I told him it's going to be chilly, but he wouldn't give it up."

"He's a true Hoffgeitz, just the way his uncle was." Armande glanced at the photo of his late son in a black frame on the desk. Klaus V.K. Hoffgeitz had died in a freak skiing accident in 1973. "Tell Junior that I'll join him at the bow. We'll face the wind together!"

"Bring your coat and hat."

"I will." He patted a pile of computer printouts filled with numbers. "Look, I'm too old to learn new tricks, and so is Günter. We've always kept records with pen and paper—"

"It's not the computer system. It's me. I failed to earn Günter's trust."

"Nonsense. He respects you greatly." Armande Hoffgeitz pushed up his glasses. "But he's accustomed to the safety of physical records and steel doors, not wires and keyboards."

"Let me propose," Lemmy said, "that Günter will enter new transactions into the computer database and at the same time continue to update his paper records."

"Why can't we let him keep only paper records for my clients while the rest of the bank transitions to the electronic records?"

"We need all the numbers in the computer system in order to maintain a correct daily balance of the bank's total assets, reflecting deposits and withdrawals in all the accounts without exception. Every bank in Zurich will soon be automated the same way. The Banking Commission set the new accounting regulations, and compliance would be impossible without a computerized system."

Armande Hoffgeitz raised his hand. "I'm familiar with the regulations."

"But it won't change the fact that only Günter has the account numbers and passwords for your clients. Only he can look at individual records—paper files *and* computer files. We bought the best equipment, with top security features and redundancy. It's better than the systems used by Credit Suisse, UBS, and all the other banks."

"Still, it feels too...intangible...unprotected, you understand?"

"That's a common misperception. Imagine the computer as a large filing cabinet with a separate drawer for each account, made of steel that's thicker than our underground vaults. Each drawer is equipped with two keys—account number and password. No one except Günter will be able to look up specific records of your clients' accounts. The only accessible data is the total financial positions at the end of each day, including net assets after deposits and withdrawals. I covered all this in my presentation last year, but if you want me to suspend the project—"

"No. No. Keep going, but make sure Günter is comfortable, yes?"

Gideon and Bathsheba left the Paris apartment and drove to Ermenonville. From the parking area beside a gas station they had clear views of the intersection connecting the local road with the highway. Other than single-lane roads hampered by slow farming machinery, this was the only way for Abu Yusef's men to reach Paris.

Bathsheba opened yesterday's evening paper, *Le Parisien.* Al-Mazir's bloody corpse was splashed across an inside page, his faced blurred, under a headline: *Three Palestinians Shot in Turf War over Underage Prostitution*

"Phew," Bathsheba said. "Profiteering from kiddie sex. These Arabs would do anything for a buck."

"You're really twisted," Gideon said.

"Do you want to straighten me out?" She fluttered her eyelids. "Will you spank me?"

"Just watch the road." He had bought an audio edition of Frederick Forsyth's *The Day of the Jackal.* With the first tape playing on the cassette player, he settled to scan passing cars for the green Peugeot 605.

Back in his office, Lemmy's eyes rested on the wooden model of *The Paula,* her mainsail and jib full with wind. Klaus Junior had carved it out of a pine log as a school project recently. At the stern of the boat stood tiny people—Paula, flanked by Lemmy and her father. Klaus Junior stood at the helm, adorned in a miniature blue-and-white sailor suit resembling the one Lemmy had brought from Monaco for his birthday last year.

"Herr Horch?" It was his lanky assistant, Christopher, bowing his head to avoid the top of the doorframe. "Any news from upstairs?"

"I think Günter's ulcer is bleeding again."

Christopher laughed. "That bad?"

"Worse." He had hired Christopher Ditmahr two years earlier. The young man had an ideal résumé—a graduate of Lyceum Alpin St. Nicholas and Zurich University, followed by internship at Chase Manhattan bank in New York. His application had come in just as Lemmy was ready to hire. Christopher was smart, diligent, and devoted to his boss in the unspoken camaraderie shared by non-Swiss living among Zurich's uppity purebreds.

"I think Günter is paranoid," Christopher said. "I showed him how to sign in with his personal pass code, activate the program, key in each account number and password, and enter the amounts of deposits and withdrawals. He insisted that we practice with fictitious accounts. I couldn't believe it! What did he think? That I'd memorize his secrets?"

"That could be useful."

"Sir?"

"Just kidding." Lemmy sat back, placing his feet on the desk. "I sympathize with the poor fellow. Günter has been with Herr Hoffgeitz since—"

"Nineteen forty-one."

"Correct. Imagine working for the same boss for fifty-four years."

"He thinks Herr Hoffgeitz is God."

"And bank secrecy is the Ten Commandments." Lemmy chuckled. "By the way, has there been any activity in Prince az-Zubayr's account?"

"All quiet on the Saudi front," Christopher said. "Nothing since the transfer to the private account of the French Consul General in Damascus."

Like every Friday night during the bitter Jerusalem winter, only the male sect members attended prayers in Neturay Karta. Their wives prepared the Sabbath meals and watched the young children at home. At the conclusion of the prayers, Rabbi Abraham Gerster recited the mourners' Kaddish. He paused, took the required three backward steps, bowed toward the Torah ark, and chanted the last line: "*He, who brings peace to Heaven, shall bring peace upon us and upon all His people of Israel, and we say, Amen.*"

Everyone answered, "Amen."

Rabbi Gerster put on his black coat and wrapped a scarf around his neck. He watched as Rabbi Benjamin Mashash, who had succeeded him as leader of Neturay Karta, walked down the aisle to the door and stood there to shake each man's hand and wish them a good Sabbath.

When the synagogue was empty, Rabbi Gerster joined Benjamin and his three teenage sons, who had their father's dark eyes and their mother's light complexion. The oldest, Jerusalem, was named after Rabbi Gerster's son and Benjamin's best friend, who had died during the Six Day War, almost three decades ago. Jerusalem Mashash already showed the start of a beard, and his dangling side locks swung back and forth as he reached to open the door.

"So, Jerusalem," Rabbi Gerster said, exiting the sanctuary to the chilly air outside, "what do you know tonight that you didn't know this morning?"

Benjamin's sons were accustomed to Rabbi Gerster's daily query. They spent every day studying Talmud and were eager to share their knowledge with the elderly rabbi.

Jerusalem said, "Today we studied a Talmudic rule: *Where there are no men, be a man!* One interpretation is that the rule applies to prayers. In other words, even in a place that has no minyan of ten Jewish men to pray together, one must pray alone."

"That's a convenient interpretation," Rabbi Gerster said.

"Convenient?" The boy wasn't afraid to argue, just like his dead namesake. "To pray is a duty. A task. The rule creates a chore where there wasn't one. What's convenient about that?"

"To pray is a chore?"

"Easier to be free from the duty to pray, right?"

"Praying is a ritual," Rabbi Gerster said, "which gives men comfort, peace of mind, and a sense of fulfillment. It's a privilege, isn't it?"

"Couldn't a privilege be also a chore?"

"Telling a Jew to be a man where there are no men sounds more serious than a mere technicality about prayer quorum, don't you think?"

"One commentator suggests that the rule imposes a duty to be a Jew where there are no Jews."

Rabbi Gerster rested his arm on the youth's shoulders. "But isn't a Jew still a Jew, whether he's with other Jews or alone?"

"The rule isn't about technical hereditary Jewishness. It's about being a good Jew when no one else *behaves* like a Jew."

"Behaves like a Jew? What's that?"

"To observe God's laws, like keeping the Sabbath, eating only kosher food, and so on."

"Then the rule should have said: *Where everyone else is a sinner, be righteous!* But Talmud said to be a man even where there are no other men. What does it mean to be a man?"

"To do the right thing?"

"Do we need a special rule for that?" Benjamin spoke for the first time since they had left the synagogue. "Shouldn't we always do the right thing, whether we're alone or not?"

Jerusalem tugged on his payos. "If everyone else says that wrong is right, a man must still follow his conscience and do what's right without fear of others."

"Very good!" Rabbi Gerster winked at Benjamin, who smiled with fatherly pride.

They climbed the stairs to the second-floor apartment and entered the small foyer, taking off their coats and hats.

Benjamin's wife, Sorkeh, appeared from the kitchen, her round face glistening with sweat. "Here you are!" She wiped her hands on her apron. "Come, let's start. The little ones are starving."

In the dining room, Benjamin's younger children—another boy and three girls under ten years old, sat at the table, chattering with careless innocence. Rabbi Gerster lingered alone in the foyer in front of a small frame on the wall. A military photographer had snapped the photo twenty-eight years ago. It showed the youthful chief of staff, General Yitzhak Rabin, shaking hands with a fresh paratrooper who had graduated with the highest honors from basic training. Clean-shaven and bright-eyed, his red beret was tilted to the right with a sharp crease. A strip of brass was glued to the bottom part of the frame: PRIVATE JERUSALEM ("LEMMY") GERSTER 1949–1967

Rabbi Gerster touched the face in the photo and kissed his fingertips. "Good Sabbath, my son."

Lemmy punched in a series of numbers on a pad, and the steel door clicked open. The data center, set up in a converted underground vault, held the massive computer system the bank had purchased last year.

"Gentlemen!" He approached Christopher and Günter, who sat together at a terminal. "This has been a productive week, hasn't it?" He watched Günter expectantly.

"Of course, Herr Horch." The elderly man grimaced, as if his words tasted bitter.

"I'm glad the two of you are working together so well."

"It's a pleasure," Christopher said, playing along. "We're making great progress with these fictitious accounts."

"Very good. Be sure to cover all the security features."

"Of course," Christopher said. "We'll stay here as long as it takes."

"At least you won't get cold," Lemmy said. Unlike the other subterranean vaults, this one was warmed up by the computer servers, electrical boards, and thick bundles of colorful wires. He glanced at his watch. "I should be going. Herr Hoffgeitz is joining us for dinner. Paula's cooking his favorite—crock-pot Swiss beef with mashed potatoes and cheese fondue."

"Yum." Christopher smacked his lips, and Günter turned to him with raised eyebrows.

Lemmy chuckled. "Have a good weekend."

Gideon replaced each audio tape with the next while the Jackal cleverly evaded his pursuers and got closer to his target. A few Peugeot sedans passed by during the afternoon, one of them green, which caused a brief excitement until they saw the driver, an old Frenchwoman who could not possibly belong to Abu Yusef's group.

Traffic on the local road grew sparse as the sky darkened. They consumed tuna sandwiches and Coke for dinner. An hour later, Bathsheba relocated to the back seat, curled up, and fell asleep. Gideon donned night-vision goggles and watched the road while the audio novel played on.

It was near midnight when the Jackal's bullet missed De Gaulle by a hair, and the indefatigable Inspector Lebel kicked in the door and killed the assassin. Gideon pressed the eject button on the cassette player, turned on the ignition, and headed back to Paris. On the radio, the news included an update on the shooting near Ermenonville. One of the bodies was identified as that of Al-Mazir, a Palestinian rumored to have taken part in the PLO's 1972 Munich Olympics massacre. In Gaza, Yasser Arafat announced a day of mourning for "our fallen comrade" while anonymous sources expressed embarrassment at the former guerilla's involvement in juvenile sex trade. In Jerusalem, the prime minister's office denied Israel's involvement in the assassination, stating, "Our energies are totally dedicated to peacemaking with our willing partners."

Saturday, October 14, 1995

The Paula left the dock early on Saturday, its sails taut in the steady breeze. Lemmy steered the boat—a Beneteau Oceanis 510—away from shore, cutting a path in the fuzzy layer of white caps. The sky was clear, and the biting air forewarned of a cold winter.

Armande Hoffgeitz stood with his grandson at the bow, rising and sinking against the tree-covered hills on the opposite bank of Lake Zurich. Klaus Junior held a monocular, tracing the sights that his grandfather pointed out. The boy shifted his aim to a flock of geese heading south across the bow. One of the birds dropped a glob, barely missing them, and they burst out laughing.

"They're like two peas in a pod," Paula said. "I haven't seen Father this happy since my brother died."

He kissed her honey-colored hair. "We're blessed. And the wind is good too."

"Aye, aye, Skipper." Paula sipped from a glass of merlot. "I should have let it sit another year."

He took a swig from his nearly frozen Heineken bottle. "This one's properly aged."

"Like me?" She banged her hip against his.

Her cheerful nature had put him at ease since the first time he approached Paula in the fall of 1967, on his first day at Lyceum Alpin St. Nicholas. The plan required him to carefully implement each phase in their relationship—an initial approach as a new student seeking advice, follow up with seemingly coincidental run-ins, develop a circle of mutual friends to maximize time together at school and on vacations, and only a year later, clinch their relationship as lovers. He had also nurtured a friendship with her young brother, Klaus V.K. Hoffgeitz, ensuring a loyal ally close to her heart.

After graduation, Paula had studied art at the University of Zurich, living at Hoffgeitz Manor on the hills overlooking Lake Zurich. Lemmy worked evenings and weekends at the accounting department of Credit Niehoch Bank while studying at the Zurich School of Economics. She had insisted on keeping their relationship secret for fear of upsetting her father, who had planned for her to marry the scion of another Swiss banking dynasty. The tragic death of Klaus V.K. made her even more reluctant to upset her father. Finally, in 1979, when Lemmy was already a rising star at Credit Niehoch, he asked Herr Hoffgeitz for Paula's hand in marriage. The aging banker reluctantly gave his blessing and walked her down the aisle at the Fraumünster church. Over the subsequent year, the two men got to know each other, discussing economics, finance, and the emerging deregulation of the banking industry. The father's prejudicial displeasure with Paula's choice gave way to grudging respect for Lemmy's intelligence and knowledge. In 1982, Armande invited him to join the Hoffgeitz Bank.

He had started as an account manager, one of twelve men who constituted the core of the private banking operation, each handling a group of clients. After several years, on the day following Klaus Junior's baptism, Lemmy became chief accounts manager. And last year, Armande had promoted him to vice president. These promotions had been earned with hard work and successful client development, especially with Mideast oil sheiks. In addition, the presumed succession to a young and capable son-in-law projected long-term stability and continuity to the clients of the Hoffgeitz Bank. And lately Lemmy's control over the bank's technological metamorphosis placed a great deal of power in his hands, bringing him ever closer to the ultimate goal of the mission that had brought him into this family in the first place.

Paula kissed his neck. She avoided his cheeks as he had not shaved this morning. Between weekdays at the bank and Sunday's church attendance, Saturday was the only day he could dress casually and skip shaving. He had joked with Paula that the skin of his face needed a break, though in truth this habit was his private tradition—a link to a distant, secret past of observing the Jewish Sabbath.

"Coming about!" He turned the wheel, and the boat changed course into the wind. The waves slapped against the hull. Paula helped him lower the mainsail and drop anchor.

They sat in the back of the boat around a table that was bolted to the deck, and Paula served sandwiches of brie and smoked ham. She and her father shared the rest of the merlot.

Lemmy sliced his son's sandwich in half. "Did you tell Grandpa about the new technology lab at school?"

Klaus Junior shook his head while drinking orange juice.

"What new lab?" Armande cut a corner from his own sandwich and forked it.

"We got a whole room full of computers. We're going to sand the Internet."

"*Surf* the Internet," Paula corrected him.

Lemmy laughed. "You don't want any sand in those computers."

"Computers everywhere." Armande sighed. "No escape. What about books, writing—"

"But Grandpa, you gave them to us!"

"Don't talk, Junior," Paula said. "Finish eating first."

He chewed faster.

Armande stroked his grandson's hair. "Patience. Patience."

When he finally swallowed, Paula handed him a napkin. "Now you can talk."

"My teacher said that the computers were a gift from you. He made everyone sing a song about generosity."

"I arranged it with our Dutch suppliers," Lemmy said. "A donation to the school. It cost us very little, especially with the tax credit the bank will take on it. I made it in your honor, Father. I hope you don't mind."

Seeing his grandson's pride, Armande Hoffgeitz glowed. "Why should I mind? Our family has supported education for many generations. It's our tradition!"

After a few hours of sleep, Gideon and Bathsheba left the Paris apartment and drove to the gas station near Ermenonville. He brought an audio edition of Ken Follett's *Eye of the Needle*. They settled down to wait, the narrator's voice filling the car.

Shortly after noon, while biting into a tuna sandwich, Bathsheba spotted a green Peugeot 605, identical to the one they had been looking for, the darkened windows rolled up. "Go!" She tossed the sandwich out the window and pulled a handgun from the glove compartment. "It's them!"

"Put away the gun." Gideon turned on the engine.

He stalked the Peugeot for ten miles in dense highway traffic until the driver rolled down his window. "Take a look," Gideon said, accelerating. "*Only* a look!"

Bathsheba tilted the visor so that the makeup mirror reflected the view from her window. As they passed by the Peugeot, she said, "Bummer."

Glancing sideways, Gideon saw the occupants of the car—a couple in their eighties and a large schnauzer.

She dropped the handgun back in the glove compartment. "Cost me that lousy sandwich. I'm starving!"

He took the next exit and drove back to the gas station.

Elie Weiss walked to a nearby café and settled to read the *Financial Times*, sip coffee, and nibble at a croissant. On his way back to the apartment, he paused to watch people go around the barriers into the synagogue. It was Saturday morning, he realized, the time for Sabbath services. On a whim, he entered the synagogue.

The sanctuary was cavernous, with beautiful wooden seats, painted-glass windows, and stone arches carved with biblical scenes. A cantor stood at the podium in a bejeweled prayer shawl and top hat, his deep baritone reaching every corner as he sang *Adon Olam*, Master of the Universe. The congregants, in formal suits and skullcaps, repeated each line in a chorus of singing voices, the ancient Hebrew words pronounced with a French accent. The women behind the see-through lace partition sang as well.

This was very different from the little synagogue of his childhood in rural Germany, near the Russian border, where Rabbi Jacob Gerster, Abraham's father, had led the service in a pleading voice, his head covered in a black-and-white prayer shawl. In the shtetl, the windows had been small and opaque, the benches roughly hewn, and the congregants bearded and hunched as they begged the Master of the Universe to protect them and their families from the cruelty of the anti-Semitic gentiles. There had been no colors at his childhood synagogue, only black and white. Mostly black. And not much singing either.

He opened a prayer book, but his eyes were misted, blurring the square letters and tiny vowels. And despite decades of loathing God, who had allowed the Nazis to kill his family, Elie's lips pronounced the words, *"Be'yado afkid ruchi – In His hand I entrust my soul, asleep or awake, God is with me, I have no fear."*

The black 1942 Rolls Royce waited at the dock. Günter held the door for his boss. Armande Hoffgeitz kissed Paula on both cheeks, hugged Klaus Junior, and shook Lemmy's hand. "See you tomorrow at church," he said before Günter shut the door.

Paula's Volvo rattled over the cobblestones as it crossed the Limmat River over the General Guisan Quai. Lemmy glanced at his son through the rearview mirror. "Nice sailing, Junior."

Klaus Junior saluted.

Paula said, "That was a nice initiative, donating those computers."

In the back seat, the boy asked, "Can I also tell Grandpa about the baby?"

They looked at each other, and Paula said, "What baby?"

"I heard you talking yesterday."

"There's no baby," Lemmy said.

"Not yet." Paula blushed.

Their home sat on a grassy knoll in the Eierbrecht suburb of Zurich. Armande had bought it for them when Klaus Junior turned two. It had five bedrooms, a swimming pool in the back, and a six-car garage.

As soon as the Volvo stopped, the boy ran to the Porsche. "Papa! Come!"

"I promised him," Lemmy said. It was a classic 1963 Porsche 356 Speedster in dark blue. The insurance company had recently appraised it at a price equivalent to a modest home in a good neighborhood. Lemmy had bought it two years earlier from the widow of a deceased client. The original engine enjoyed a new life with a set of dual Solex carburetors. It had a new soft top and a powerful Burmester sound system. The elaborate anti-theft alarm had been installed by a Dutch specialist from Amsterdam, an old friend who was also responsible for the security measures surrounding the new computer systems at the Hoffgeitz Bank, as well as the secret video surveillance cameras, which Lemmy alone could access.

He was about to get into the Porsche when Paula gripped his arm, pulled him closer, and kissed him on the lips. "Don't be long. You have important work to do."

"On the old lady?"

"*Hey!*"

"I meant her!" He gestured to the back of the garage at his next restoration project. It was an odd looking Citroën, whose Maserati engine was exposed under the missing hood, and whose existence was all but a rumor among a niche of classic cars collectors who referred to her as the *Missing Third*. Only two known examples existed of the SM Presidential—an extended body version of the Citroën SM, with four-doors and a folding soft top, which Henri Chapron had built for the 1972 official visit of Her Majesty Queen Elizabeth II—and both were parked safely at the *Palais de l'Élysée* in Paris. But when Lemmy had visited an African dictator to personally collect a substantial deposit in diamonds, he discovered that the rumor had been true. The *Missing Third*, a working prototype stolen from Chapron's workshop and sold to the Francophile predecessor of Lemmy's client, had been wrecked a decade earlier during the coup d'état that had elevated him to power. Having noticed Lemmy's interest in the rusting Citroën, the grateful dictator shipped it to Zurich in a wooden crate marked USED BOOKS.

"You better be in my bedroom in thirty-minutes," Paula said, "or I'll find someone else to do the job."

He got behind the wheel. "I'll be back!"

The Porsche engine started with a deep gurgling sound, settling into an even rumble. Klaus Junior released a lever above the windshield and pushed the top down.

"Buckle up, little man." Lemmy pumped the gas pedal, making the engine growl. "We're taking off."

Fifteen minutes later, they were driving along the east bank of Lake Zurich. The water to their right was blue, dotted with a few brave sailboats. A cool breeze came in through the open roof.

Klaus Junior tinkered with the radio. "Did your papa like to drive fast?"

"My father?"

"Did he also drive a Porsche?"

Lemmy slowed down. "No."

"Why?"

"He wasn't into fast cars."

"Were you good friends?"

He had shunned those memories long ago, lest they reignite the blinding rage, which would interfere with his mission. But his own son deserved answers. "When I was a young boy, my father was very affectionate. But later on, we grew apart. He was very strict."

"And then he and your mama died?"

Lemmy hesitated. His father, Rabbi Abraham Gerster, might still be alive—that is, if you considered an insular, ultra-

Orthodox sect to be a form of life. "As it happened," he said, "a terrible autumn afternoon was the last time I saw them."

"It's okay, Papa." The boy leaned over as close as his seat belt would allow and put a small arm around Lemmy's neck. "Now you have us."

That night in Jerusalem, when the Sabbath was over, Rabbi Abraham Gerster left the neighborhood unnoticed. The city was coming back to life after the day of rest, with renewed bus service and pedestrian traffic. Twenty minutes later, he arrived at the King David Hotel. An armed guard stood at the entrance—a new phenomenon after a recent spate of Palestinian suicide bombings. Rabbi Gerster greeted the guard and entered the hotel.

He settled in a corner of the main lobby, where a TV set was showing a program about a new medical device invented by scientists at the Weitzman Institute. He ignored the furtive glances of hotel guests, who probably wondered why an elderly ultra-Orthodox rabbi with a white beard and long, dangling side locks would sit alone in a hotel to watch TV. And they would be correct. Not a single member of Neturay Karta owned a TV—an appliance that imported sin and promiscuity into one's home and caused men to neglect the study of Talmud. But he had a good reason to come here, having noticed an item in Friday's edition of the religious daily *Hamodiah* about a TV report to be aired after the Sabbath. He had to watch it.

The nightly news show started with a story about the preparations to transfer control of Ramallah to Arafat's Palestinian Authority. Answering a reporter's question at the entrance to the Knesset, Prime Minister Yitzhak Rabin said, "If Israel is to survive as a Jewish state, we must defuse the demographic bomb. Let the Palestinians establish their own state in the West Bank and Gaza and live in peace alongside Israel."

The story Rabbi Gerster had come to watch appeared next. According to the reporter, Itah Orr, she had agreed to be blindfolded and driven to an unknown location in the West

Bank for the swearing-in ceremony of new members of the Jewish underground ILOT—a Hebrew acronym for Organization of Torah Warriors.

The film was taken at night with poor lighting. A handful of young men, faces masked with bandanas, held pistols and copies of the Bible. They recited an oath: "I hereby join the ranks of the Organization of Torah Warriors. I swear, by all that's dear to me, and by the honor of the Jewish People, that I will fight against the evil government until my last breath."

The leader, a stocky figure who wore a large knitted skullcap, declared behind his mask, "The only law is the law of God and His Torah! No more Oslo Accords! No more sinful land-concessions! No more treason!"

Rabbi Gerster recognized the voice. It was the freckled, twenty-something stout man who had led the demonstration in front of Rabin's residence and had furtively returned Elie Weiss's greeting.

The camera zoomed in on one of them. Short, with a thin, boyish voice, his eyes peeked out through crude holes in the black fabric, blinking nervously.

The group sang *Hatikvah* in voices so off the mark that it bore little resemblance to the national anthem.

At the end, the leader raised a fist and declared, "We are the warriors of Torah! We will enforce the law of *Rodef!* Death to the pursuers of Jews! Death to the traitors!"

———

Monday,
October 16, 1995

The first business day of the week was always busy at the Hoffgeitz Bank, as clients sent in transaction instructions after a weekend of deal making. This Monday was no exception. Lemmy lingered in the trading room, which the account managers shared. Phones rang, telex printers buzzed, and fax machines hummed. He stopped to greet each man. They ranged in age from forty to seventy, and he inquired about their children, wives, or an ailing parent. He had worked for years to earn their respect and loyalty, making sure none of them begrudged his early seniority. They knew it had not been only marital patronage that had propelled him upward in the bank. He had a gift for cultivating foreign clients whose cultures were vastly different from the Swiss. Oil-rich Arabs and African strongmen needed a safe place for their money, away from the political instability of their region, and they expected a level of personal service that few bankers in Zurich were capable of providing. Herr Wilhelm Horch often visited Saudi Arabia, Kuwait, and the Gulf states to spend leisure time with his clients. He marveled at their oasis compounds, rode their camels, and raced their Ferraris. And they trusted him with their money and secrets.

Christopher was at his desk outside Lemmy's office. "Good morning, Herr Horch!"

"And to you. Any news?"

"Prince Abusalim's account just received a deposit of two-and-a-half million dollars from the Wall Street branch of Citibank."

"Nice. Total account balance?"

"Almost seventy-seven million U.S. dollars." Christopher followed him into his office. "All from undisclosed depositors."

"He needs money, but receives none from his father." During a visit to their desert oasis, Lemmy had met Sheik Da'ood Ibn Hisham az-Zubayr, a cousin of King Fahd. The sheik was a powerful tribal leader, who earned fat commissions on food and equipment purchases for the kingdom. His son, Prince Abusalim az-Zubayr, at thirty-eight was continuously travelling around the world to close huge deals, but his only personal asset was the secret account at the Hoffgeitz Bank.

"What about the prince's own family?"

"His two wives and nine children live with the rest of the extended family back in Saudi Arabia. When I first met Prince Abusalim last year, I told him that a man without money is a man without power, and hidden money is hidden power, which is tenfold mightier." Lemmy pointed downward in the direction of the bank's subterranean vaults. "And I told him that, when it comes to secret money, Zurich is the Haram El-Sharif."

"The *what?*"

Lemmy pulled a book from a shelf above his desk. He opened it to a page flagged with a blue sticker and showed Christopher a full-page photograph of a walled city crowned by two domes—one silver, one gold.

"That's Jerusalem." Christopher pointed to the golden dome. "I was a volunteer at a kibbutz once, and they took us to all the tourist attractions."

"Really?" Lemmy was alarmed. His assistant had never mentioned it before. "What made you go to Israel, of all places?"

"You know," Christopher blushed, "I was a bit rebellious, wanted to piss off my parents. They were old-fashioned Germans, hated Jews, so that's why I went there."

Lemmy examined his assistant's face, but saw no signs of deceit.

"Didn't Mohammed ascend to heaven from this location?"

"For us Christians, it's the biblical holy temple of the ancient Israelites, where Elijah's carriage took off in an explosion of fire and smoke." Lemmy returned the book to the shelf. "A smart banker can benefit from studying clients' faiths, notwithstanding your personal religion, because there's always a business opportunity when a rich man's mind is possessed by spiritual beliefs that cloud his logic and reason."

Christopher laughed.

"According to my research, the az-Zubayr tribe has a historic aspiration to rule Haram El-Sharif. Just like the Saudi clan is the *Kharass al-Hameini*, Guardians of Mecca, the tribe of az-Zubayr claims to be the *Kharass El-Sharif*, Guardians of the Dome of the Rock."

"Isn't Jerusalem the capital of Israel?"

"The Israelis unified Jerusalem during the Six Day War, but they gave control of Temple Mount to the Muslim Wakf, which is an independent religious council of mullahs. Later, King Hussein of Jordan was pressured by the PLO to give up his rights in the West Bank and Jerusalem. Now Arafat is getting ready to negotiate the final phase of the Oslo Accords, hoping to obtain East Jerusalem as capital of Palestine. But other powers are at play."

"The prince?"

"Correct. Even though his father has pledged loyalty to the Saudis, Prince Abusalim harbors ambitions to recover the status of *Kharass El-Sharif.* He must choose who to support— Arafat and the Oslo peace process or the militants committed to destroying Israel."

"How would he choose?"

"Arafat is already getting billions from the Europeans and Americans. His opponents, on the other hand, need money for their anti-Oslo jihad. Prince Abusalim can make a deal with them. When Israel is gone, they'll anoint him *Kharass El-Sharif,* Guardian of the Dome of the Rock, restoring the hereditary birthright for the tribe of az-Zubayr."

"Sounds like a dangerous fantasy."

"Clients' fantasies are a major force in the banking business. What is wealth but a fantasy?" Lemmy sat back in his chair. "He has gotten several deposits through Citibank in New York, right?"

"Yes."

"Does he maintain an account there?"

"No. It's a conduit."

"But Citibank knows where each deposit came from, correct?"

Christopher nodded.

"Will they tell us?"

"Not directly, but when I worked in New York, I noticed a weakness in the system." Christopher took a piece of paper and scribbled a diagram. "Citibank sent us electronic funds for Prince Abusalim's account. If we reject the transfer, it would bounce back to Citibank, which in turn would bounce it back to the original bank, which would issue an electronic receipt for the returned funds. Usually the acknowledgment bears the account's information."

"So if we ask on behalf of the client that Citibank provides a copy of the acknowledgment, we'll see the source of the money?" Lemmy thought for a moment. "Let's do a partial rejection, a hundred dollars from each deposit, and see what comes back."

Christopher hesitated. "Without client authorization?"

"It's in the prince's interest that we know his affairs, even if he doesn't realize it."

"Still early in New York City. We could get a confirmation today, unless they smell a rotten fish and call the prince directly."

"It's a risk I'm willing to take." Lemmy watched Christopher reach the door. "By the way, which kibbutz?"

"Excuse me?"

"That summer you spent in Israel, which kibbutz was it?"

"Oh, it was in the north, near the Lebanese border." He hesitated. "I'm not sure about the name."

Lemmy wasn't going to let him off the hook so easily. "Was it Haifa?"

"No, Haifa is a city." Christopher's forehead creased in a show of mental effort. "I think...it was called...Gesher."

Shortly after two p.m., Bathsheba noticed another green Peugeot 605. It came from the direction of Ermenonville and made a left turn onto the highway ramp.

Gideon followed. "Get the camera. Elie wants photos. He thinks they might be using decoys to check for tails."

Bathsheba kept her head straight, looking forward through the front windshield, but positioned the vanity mirror on the sun visor diagonally to give her a clear view through the side window. The green Peugeot passed a group of slower cars and returned to the middle lane. Gideon pressed the gas pedal, changed lanes, and passed it. Bathsheba held the Polaroid camera just below the window sill on the passenger side, raised it briefly, and snapped a photo.

Gideon returned to the middle lane ahead of the Peugeot. He glanced at the rearview mirror. "Driver looks Arab, about forty. Didn't look at us. I think he's the same guy who drove this car at the airport. There's a second man in the back, wearing a fur hat."

"Abu Yusef!"

"We don't know."

"The same car, the same driver, and Abu Yusef is getting the same treatment as Al-Mazir!"

"We follow and watch. Elie said to do nothing more."

"Screw Elie." Bathsheba opened the glove compartment and took out the handgun.

"It worked!" Christopher waved a sheet of paper like a flag. "I got acknowledgements with the names of the sources. Here, I listed each one with the amount transferred."

Lemmy examined the list. An $11 million deposit had come from J.C. Jameson & Co., an international wheat dealer in Kansas. An additional $7.5 million from Seattle Air and Jet Inc., a manufacturer of replacement parts for fighter jets. And $13 million from F. Lucas and Sons, a canned foods processer in Virginia. It went on—a list of leading corporations in the various industries. "This is incredible," he said. "Great job!"

His assistant was grinning with pride.

"I'll keep this." He patted the list of companies that had bribed Prince Abusalim az-Zubayr. "Needless to say, don't mention this to any of our colleagues."

G ideon snatched the handgun from Bathsheba. "Abu Yusef isn't stupid. He won't use this car himself after it's been seen."

"Maybe he's out of money. He can't *walk* to Paris."

The sign showed an exit for the Peripherique, the beltway that circled Paris. Gideon slowed down and let the green Peugeot pass him two lanes away. It took the exit, merged onto the Peripherique, and headed west. They followed. A couple of minutes later, the Peugeot took the exit for Avenue de Saint Ouen.

Bathsheba said, "Where the hell is he going?"

"Have you regained your sanity?"

"Don't patronize me. This man killed my father."

"Abu Yusef killed your father. This man might be a retired CEO or a gynecologist. We need a positive ID before we take a life."

"Give it back."

Gideon threw the gun in her lap. "You may shoot only in self-defense, understood?"

She pushed the gun under her leather waistcoat. "If it's Abu Yusef, I'm not waiting for him to shoot first."

He followed the green Peugeot, letting two or three cars separate them at all times. Mossad procedure required taking side streets in coordination with two other vehicles in order to avoid detection by the target. But they were not Mossad, and there were no other vehicles to assist them. Gideon tried to minimize the risk of detection by dropping farther behind.

At La Fourche, the green Peugeot bore left onto Avenue de Clichy, circled the square, and continued on Rue d'Amsterdam. Evening traffic was dense, moving with the typical Parisian briskness. At Place de Havre the green Peugeot suddenly sped forward, taking advantage of a gap in the traffic. When Gideon tried to follow it, a stream of cars emerged from Boulevard

Haussmann on the right. He accelerated, but a small Fiat cut into his lane. He slammed the brakes, skidded on the cobblestones, and barely missed the Fiat. For a moment he thought he had lost the Peugeot, but Bathsheba spotted it farther down, turning into a side street. Gideon closed the distance quickly and made the same turn.

There was no trace of the green Peugeot. He drove slowly along Rue de Provence, a narrow, one-way street.

Nothing.

They looked down the first side street.

Clear.

The second.

Clear again.

At Rue de Mogador, a one-way street going south, the green Peugeot was parked at the curb. Gideon made the turn and pulled over.

Bathsheba brought the binoculars to her eyes. "He's dropping off the passenger. Fur hat and a long coat. I can't see his damn face!"

"Even the coat is green," Gideon said.

"I'm going after him." Bathsheba took out her gun and screwed on a silencer.

"Don't shoot!"

"If it's Abu Yusef, I'll give him my father's regards."

Gideon knew he couldn't stop her. He shoved the camera into her hand. "If it's not him, take a picture. Maybe it's one of his men. Elie would know."

Café Atarah on Ben Yehuda Street in Jerusalem was almost empty. "I am Rabbi Abraham Gerster," he said, joining the lone woman at a corner table. "Thanks for agreeing to meet with me."

"How could I decline?" Itah Orr, a veteran reporter for *Channel One TV,* held the note he had left for her at the office that morning. "I tried to do a story about you years ago, on the tenth anniversary of the Six Day War. It would have been a good story."

Rabbi Gerster smiled. "There are many stories that are far more interesting than mine."

"More interesting than the leader of the anti-Zionist Neturay Karta sect, who sacrificed his only son for Israel's greatest victory?"

"The *former* leader. Rabbi Benjamin Mashash took over my duties a long time ago."

"You were still Neturay Karta's leader when you sacrificed your son."

"I didn't sacrifice him. Jerusalem rejected our faith and joined the army without my blessing."

A waitress brought two cups and poured black coffee. The reporter added cream and sugar, mixing it in. "Lemmy, wasn't it?"

"His nickname, yes."

"He graduated paratroopers training first in his class and went on to serve courageously on the Golan Heights."

"While ignoring his mother's desperate letters until she killed herself!" Rabbi Gerster immediately regretted his outburst. Temimah's despair had been caused by his own behavior no less than by Lemmy's silence. "Please. These are old wounds. My son and wife deserve to rest in peace."

"So why did you contact me?"

Rabbi Gerster glanced over his shoulder. The few patrons in the café did not appear to pay attention to him. "I watched your report on Saturday night."

"I thought you people don't watch TV."

"Those boys, taking the oath, were they for real? Or was it some kind of a show, a make-believe piece of propaganda?"

"Wait a minute." Itah Orr jerked her head, clearing away shoulder-length gray hair. "What do you care about those kids? Or about Israel? You people live in your ghetto in Meah Shearim, don't pay taxes, don't serve in the army, don't even recognize the State of Israel—except for its social security checks, of course."

"We object to Zionism, but we study Talmud every waking moment to make up for all the Jews who neglect their sacred duty."

"And how exactly would your Talmudists feed their hordes of children without Zionist tax money?"

"Questions, questions." Rabbi Gerster sighed. "You're like a vacuum cleaner for information. I need a peek inside your dustbin, that's all."

She laughed. "Fair enough."

"About that swearing-in of ILOT, tell me what you think. Please."

"Tit for tat. First tell me why you—a lifelong anti-Zionist rabbi—are suddenly concerned with a tiny nationalist militia? What's going on?"

Rabbi Gerster stood up and buttoned his black coat. "I was mistaken in approaching you. May God bless your day."

"Wait!" Itah Orr stood. "I'm sorry. I guess I'm still angry about my story getting killed."

"Twenty years ago?"

"I had enough material for a great piece. Your son was very popular with his boot camp buddies, an excellent soldier and loyal teammate. And there was a mysterious woman he was carrying on a relationship with, much older than him and very attractive. Petite, black hair, pale face. She came to the base once, caused quite a stir."

He kept his face straight, hiding the storm that Tanya's description whipped up inside him. "Are you fishing for information?"

Itah smiled, looking much younger. "Just curious. I can't do anything with it now. It's too old a story."

"Why didn't you publish it back then?"

"Because a little creep from some secret service came to the studio and threatened me and my editor with immediate arrest on trumped up charges. He took all my drafts and notes and all the roughs we had filmed. It was as if I had touched a live wire."

"Perhaps you had." He chuckled. "But that's ancient history. I didn't contact you to speak about my Jerusalem, may he rest in peace. Now will you grant me the respect of answering my questions?"

"Will you answer mine?"

"When a time comes for me to tell my story, I promise to speak only to you."

"Give me something now."

"Okay. How about this: I don't believe in God."

The reporter's eyebrows rose almost to her hairline.

"It's true." He placed a hand against his heart. "I swear."

"Okay, Rabbi Gerster. You don't believe in God, and we are in business." She offered her hand.

He glanced around furtively, making sure no one was watching, and shook it. "Tell me about the ILOT ceremony."

"They were young," she said, "late teens or early twenties. Almost like boy scouts, except that the pistols were real and the vows were sincere."

"Why did they allow you to attend?"

"In my profession, you don't argue with a good source. Their leader is a true Jewish fascist."

"The chubby guy?"

"Yes. Freckles. That's his moniker. He's very clever in using the media, has given me great stories—the type of stories any journalist would grab and run with."

"Do you believe these boys are for real?"

"Absolutely. Classic right-wing extremists. A few months ago they incited a riot and beat up Arabs in Hebron, turned over market stalls, and destroyed produce. They set up fake military checkpoints in the West Bank and body-searched Arabs. They went into Old Jerusalem with clubs and broke windows and a few bones, forced Arab merchants to shut down their stores."

"All this was done by Freckles' group?"

"Oh, ILOT isn't the only one. There are several other militias just like it—Kahane Chai, EYAL, Geva'ot. Each group numbers a handful of youths. They engage in violent attacks on Palestinians in order to scare the Arabs out of the West Bank and ensure Jewish control over biblical Israel. They're not deadly like the Palestinian attacks on Jews. I mean, these kids don't shoot and bomb innocent civilians, but they engage in harassment, and they're aggressive enough to draw attention."

Rabbi Gerster picked up a teaspoon and turned it around in his hand, using the curved back as a mirror to scan the view behind his back. "But their anti-Arab activities, distasteful as they are, could be a prelude to something worse." He put down the spoon. "Violence against fellow Jews."

"It's a natural progression. Take a look at this." She handed him a stapled stack of papers. The cover said: *ILOT – Member Manual – Top Secret*

He browsed the pages. "Can I keep it?"

She nodded.

"Anything else about that ceremony? Any leads?"

She hesitated. "I noticed their backpacks. It was really dark out there, but I could see the university logo—"

"Which one?"

"Bar Ilan Law School."

G ideon saw a gendarme signaling the green Peugeot to move forward, which it did. A taxicab picked up a heavy matron with hefty Galeries Lafayette shopping bags. The department store spanned both sides of the street, each wing taking up a whole block. A glass-walled overpass connected the two buildings, and Gideon saw the man in the green coat and fur hat walking from left to right. Seconds later Bathsheba glanced down at him, swung a finger under her chin, and disappeared to the right. A sense of doom began acidulating in Gideon's stomach.

The minutes passed slowly. Too slowly.

He turned off the engine and got out of the car.

As he began to cross the street, Bathsheba showed up, trotting toward him. "Shot him in the nuts," she said. "He's a screaming soprano in menswear upstairs."

"Shit!" Gideon jumped back into the car.

"It's quite a scene." She slammed the door. "You should go look."

"Damn!" He started the engine. "I told you not to—"

"Relax," Bathsheba laughed. "I didn't shoot anyone."

He took a deep breath, exhaling slowly.

"It wasn't him."

"You're sick." He motioned at the green Peugeot, still waiting for its passenger down the street. "Did you take a photo?"

"He's just a boy. Fourteen or fifteen. And he's from Jordan."

"How do you know?"

"I got close enough to hear his conversation with the salesman. And to smell his Cacharel. He must've bathed in it—a typical teenage faggot."

"Here he is."

The passenger with the green coat, fur hat in hand, approach the Peugeot. Bathsheba snapped a photo.

"We'll follow them," Gideon said.

"Waste of time. He's just a rich boy."

"How do you know?"

"He bought two Pierre Cardin suits for a small fortune, plus alteration charges. You were right—not every Arab in a green Peugeot is Abu Yusef." Bathsheba leaned over and kissed him on the cheek. "See? I can admit a mistake when I make one."

"You're an angel." He glanced at his watch. It was too late to drive all the way back to Ermenonville.

In the apartment on Rue Buffault, Elie was taking a nap on the cot when he heard the front door being unlocked. He sat up and reached for the sheathed blade, but Bathsheba's voice sounded in the hallway. They were back early.

He listened to Gideon's report and looked at the photos. The driver was in profile, shown through the open window. "That's Bashir Hamami, Abu Yusef's deputy."

"Can't be!" Bathsheba's face turned red. "Who would take such a risk for shopping?"

Elie picked up the other photo. "Abu Yusef's boy toy."

"Expensive toy," Gideon said. "I thought he's short on cash?"

"Not just a toy," Elie said. "Remember the bomb at the Jewish school in Marseilles? Nineteen kids dead, almost thirty injured. The investigators found video footage of an unidentified youth entering the school ten minutes before the explosion. His face was turned away from the security cameras, but he had dark skin and short hair, just like this kid. And he wore a skullcap, even carried a Hebrew prayer book, but police later verified he wasn't a student." Elie fingered the photo. "This must be the guy who planted the bomb in Marseilles."

"He'll be back on Wednesday," Bathsheba said, "to pick up the suits. I heard him give his name to the salesman. Latif."

"Good," Gideon said. "We'll follow them back to Ermenonville."

Elie considered it. "Bashir is a fox. He'll notice you, if he hasn't already. Maybe you should just kill the boy at the store."

"Just like that?" She clicked her fingers. "What if he's not the bomber from Marseilles? Maybe he's just a skinny teenager who bends over for Abu Yusef?"

"Doesn't matter," Elie said. "Clearly the boy is Abu Yusef's soft spot. Why else would he allow a shopping spree at a time like this? This boy's death would shake up Abu Yusef, cause him to make mistakes."

She glared at him. "What kind of a monster are you?"

Gideon got up. "Bathsheba!"

"Have you considered the possibility of pushing Abu Yusef over the edge? What if he throws caution into the wind and runs out to kill a bunch of Jews?"

"Unlikely," Elie said. "But I sympathize with your sensibilities. You don't want to kill the boy? No problem. Wait on Wednesday at Galeries Lafayette, follow the green Peugeot to Ermenonville, and find out where they're hiding." He collected the photos and put them in his pocket. "Let's get something to eat."

Tuesday, October 17, 1995

Across Paris, at his clinic near Gare du Nord, Dr. René Geloux moved his stethoscope on Elie's bony back. He listened to the crackling sounds that accompanied the movement of air while his eyes glanced at the x-ray prints on the illuminated board.

"So," Elie said, "am I still alive?"

"You may put on your shirt, Monsieur Weiss." Dr. Geloux was even older than his patient, but long summer weekends at his estate south of Paris had kept him slim and tanned. "Your emphysema is getting worse, and there might be something worse going on. You need to carry oxygen, that's for sure. I'll prescribe it."

"I can't walk around with a tank." Elie pulled on his shirt. "And other than my father, whose life was cut short by the Nazis, the men in my family always lived to a hundred."

"Did they smoke for fifty years?"

Elie shrugged.

"You need a breathing test and a specialist to take a look inside your airways with a bronchoscope. How's tomorrow?"

"I'm busy." Elie buttoned his shirt. "Give me something for the pain."

"That's not a solution. Low oxygenation, combined with excessive exertion, could be fatal."

"We're old pals, the grim reaper and I." Elie's laughter was dry, scratchy. He grabbed the physician's hand. "Come on, I have a job to do."

"Don't tell me about your jobs. I've taken the Hippocratic Oath. And you should be in a hospital!"

"Not yet." Elie coughed into a tissue. "This is a crucial time. Important things are happening, long-term efforts finally coming together. But in a few weeks I expect to relocate back to Jerusalem. The doctors at Hadassah will fix me."

"They might need to give you new lungs." The old physician took a small bottle from the glass cabinet. "One tablet every three hours. It'll take the edge off the pain."

They walked through the empty waiting room and down the hallway, which was lined with books on glass-fronted shelves. Dr. Geloux handed Elie his coat and unlocked the door.

Two-thirds of the way up the doorjamb, nailed to the wood, was a silver tube shaped as a thick cigar. Rolled inside was a parchment bearing Hebrew letters that a righteous scribe had inked with a quill. Dr. Geloux took Elie's hand and made him touch the mezuzah. "You need all the help you can get, my friend."

Indulging his old doctor, Elie kissed his fingers. He crossed the sidewalk and got into a waiting taxi. "To the airport," he told the driver. "Departures terminal. Swissair."

"Christopher?" Lemmy held down the intercom button. On the computer screen, the video feed from a hidden camera showed his assistant swivel in his chair toward his desk.

"Yes, Herr Horch?"

"I just filled out a withdrawal order for one of my clients— Rupert Danzig. You'll see it on your screen in a moment. Kindly draw up a cashier check for seventy-five thousand U.S. dollars for him."

On the screen, Christopher's face seemed tense as he leaned over the phone, speaking directly into the microphone. "Will Herr Danzig come here in person?"

"No. I'll deliver the check personally over lunch."

"Should I draw it to the order of Herr Danzig or *To Bearer* without a name?"

"Make it *To Bearer.* He can endorse it to himself if he so chooses."

Gideon sat on the wide windowsill and marked an orange with a knife. Halfway through peeling it, he noticed a woman cross the street three floors below and approach the building. Her hair was pulled up in a bun, dark against her pale face. She wore a heavy coat over plain winter boots and seemed like any other petite Parisian woman returning home from work, elegant in a subdued, graceful style. But Gideon saw the slight twist of her head, left and right, as her eyes quickly scanned Rue Buffault up and down before she pulled open the heavy door at number 34. Her escorts were even less obvious—a delivery guy on a scooter, pretending to tinker with the motor, and a woman in a pay phone booth at the corner.

He went to the hallway, unlocked the front door, and opened it. He could hear her coming up the steps.

"Good morning, Gidi'leh."

"Shalom, Tanya." He shut the door behind her. "Elie didn't say you were coming."

"How would he know? I'm a spy, remember?" She pinched his cheek. "Your mother sends her love. We met for coffee last week."

The half-peeled orange slipped out of his hand and fell to the floor. Gideon picked it up and brushed off the specks of dirt. "How is she?"

"How should she be, with her only son throwing away his life?" Tanya Galinski, whom he had known since childhood as his mom's elusive friend, now ran the Europe desk at Mossad. She controlled a network of agents and informants, spoke several languages with a variety of regional accents, and had developed a thorough understanding of the EU's economic and political life. But she still treated him as a kid. "Hasn't your mother suffered enough?"

A guilt trip, all over again. "Please, I've heard it a thousand times."

"Hearing isn't the same as listening." Tanya passed by the window and gestured subtly with her hand, signaling her escorts. "Your mother is a widow without a grave to visit, only a medal in the drawer. If you die like your father, she won't survive it."

"Is this the reason you blocked my application to Mossad?"

In the cluttered room, Tanya looked for a place to sit, changed her mind, and remained standing. "The rules exclude children of bereaved families from serving. No exceptions."

"Punishing me because my father got himself caught?"

"Shush!" Her porcelain-like face reddened. "Your father took the worst personal risk in order to defend Israel from its greatest national threat."

Gideon knew the basic facts: Over two decades ago, the KGB had caught his father taking photographs inside a nuclear installation near Leningrad. That night he banged his head on the floor repeatedly until he fell unconscious. He died of a brain hemorrhage before the Soviets managed to interrogate him. Israel couldn't even ask for his body—the KGB was convinced he was a West German agent. His corpse was buried behind the Lubyanka prison.

Tanya sighed. "Why don't you go back home, Gidi'leh? Working for Elie Weiss is a dead end. The Special Operations Department is a one-man show. Once he's gone, it's the end."

"What do you know about SOD?"

"Who's going to take over?"

"I'm sure Elie has designated a successor."

"Has he ever spoken with you about his other agents? His finances? Any operations beside what you're involved in?"

"No, but that doesn't mean—"

"Elie Weiss is finished. Mossad will no longer allow him to operate. We've made it clear to the top authority in Jerusalem."

Gideon was shocked. "Mossad is challenging SOD? What's next? You'll challenge Shin Bet?"

"That's ridiculous. Shin Bet and Mossad are the two spy agencies set up by Israeli law—for domestic and overseas operations respectively. Elie Weiss created SOD without legal authority."

"And you guys do everything according to the law?"

Tanya shrugged.

"Elie doesn't need your permission to operate. He has direct authority from Rabin and independent financial resources!"

"Those funds belong to the State of Israel, and by law only Mossad may conduct clandestine operations abroad. We're determined to enforce this principle."

"Don't you think Elie has prepared for such confrontation? You, of all people, know how dangerous he is."

Tanya took off her coat. "I've told you too much already. For your mother's sake, leave now. Go back to the university, find a lovely Israeli girl, get married—"

"You never married."

"How can you compare? I'm a member of the Holocaust generation. We survived to do a job, not to pursue personal happiness. It's a totally different situation with us."

"Why? You were young when the Germans lost the war. Couldn't you fall in love?"

Tanya looked away, grimacing.

"I'm sorry," he said. "That was rude."

"I'll tell you." She took a deep breath, exhaling with a sigh. "His name was Abraham. Near the end of the war, I was seventeen, and he was eighteen. For a short time, a few months, despite the cold and hunger and violence, our passion was endless. It was like a glorious dream in the middle of the worst nightmare. But then we lost each other."

"How?"

"We each thought the other one had died. We were deceived."

"By whom?"

"By Elie Weiss."

"*What?*"

"It doesn't matter anymore. Fifty years have passed. Hard to believe." She patted his cheek. "I'm sharing this so you understand how devious Elie can be. You're still young. Go back to Israel, live a normal life, raise kids. Your poor mother deserves a bit of happiness. I can tell you that for me, as busy as I am with my work, the little time I spend with my daughter and her family is the only time I feel happy."

Was she lying to make him distrust Elie? He wanted to question Tanya about her old love and Elie's involvement, but he could see on her face that she would not answer.

"With all my achievements at Mossad," Tanya said, "Bira is my greatest pride."

"Is she still digging out old bones and broken clay with her students?"

"What else?" Tanya laughed. "She's working on a Jewish cemetery at Gamla, on the Golan Heights. It dates back to the Great Revolt. Every other day a bunch of black hats come by to chant curses at her team for the *desecration* of those stupid old bones."

"Those stupid bones are archeological evidence of the Jewish past on our land."

"You see?" Tanya's face lit up. "You're still passionate about that! Bira said you should return to archeology."

"Tell her I'm more interested in fresh corpses."

"That's morbid. And where's Elie?"

"We expect him back later today." Gideon glanced at the desk, making sure nothing revealing was left on it. Tanya was the only outsider Elie allowed in the apartment, but her comments about shutting down SOD would change that.

"I'm just off a red eye from Washington," she said, "and we didn't stop working, takeoff to landing. The second Oslo agreement requires careful implementation. We're working with other countries to drum up support for the Palestinians' effort to build government institutions."

"Including secret services?"

"It's a necessary evil." Tanya rubbed her eyes. "I could use a good nap."

"There's a bed in the other room. What about your escorts?"

"What escorts?" She removed a plain clasp and her hair fell around her face, well below her shoulders. Threads of silver lightened up the black. She brushed it with her fingers and rolled it around itself, tying it together. Under the heavy coat she wore a wool dress that revealed a slim, youthful body. She had long passed sixty, but the skin of her face bore no hint of aging. He wondered whether she found time for lovers.

The voice on the speakerphone said, "How is my favorite banker this morning?" Prince Abusalim az-Zubayr spoke with an impeccable British accent, which he had acquired at Oxford.

"I'm delighted to hear you, Excellency!" Lemmy's mind brought up the tall, dark man, the intelligent eyes under a groomed mane of hair. "Are you well?"

"*Insha'Allah,* my friend." The prince's voice was even, lucid, showing no hint of impatience as he moved on to business. "How is my six-one-nine El-Sharif?"

By providing the password and account number—chosen for the 619 AD mythological journey of the Prophet Muhammad to Jerusalem—Prince Abusalim gained access to his account with the Hoffgeitz Bank, including discussion of confidential financial information on the telephone.

Lemmy pulled up the account on his computer screen. "Current balance is near seventy-seven million U.S. dollars."

"That sounds correct." The prince's voice remained calm despite the size of his fast-growing fortune. "I'd like to make a transfer."

"Of course. Will you be investing or acquiring a pleasure motorcar?"

"Making a donation."

"Your generosity will be rewarded by Allah." Lemmy pulled up a blank form on the screen and typed in the prince's name in the space for the account's owner. "The amount?"

"Two hundred thousand dollars."

"Recipient?"

"Monsieur Perez Sachs. He'll pick it up in cash at the local branch of Banque Nationale de France in Senlis, France."

Lemmy's fingers danced on the keyboard. "We'll execute the transfer today."

"My warm gratitude, Herr Horch. Please visit Paris again soon. I've discovered another cabaret—beautiful girls, every one of them!"

Prince Abusalim az-Zubayr put down the receiver. The rays of the sun illuminated the deep colors of the rug at the foot of the canopy bed. The pile of leather belts, pointy hoods, and studded collars brought a grin to his face, reminding him of the three teenage girls from last night. Unlike the submissive Arab females, the French gave as much as they took, wielding their alluring physique in the battle over peaks of volcanic pleasures.

Out on the balcony, he tightened the waistband around his silk bathrobe and leaned against the railing to watch the French capital's own phallic symbol, the elevators ascending and descending through the Eiffel Tower's enormous web of iron beams.

Back inside, he poured a cup and browsed the front page of the *Financial Times*. The British pound was falling again. Muammar al-Qaddafi announced the expulsion of thirty thousand Palestinians from Libya in protest of Arafat's signing of the second Oslo agreement. Iraqis went to the polls to obediently reelect Saddam Hussein. And Israel prepared to hand over control of West Bank cities to the PLO.

Pierre arrived on time. "*Bonjour,* Monsieur Abusalim," he said in his clipped, hurried French.

The bathroom was equipped with a barber chair that could turn and recline toward the sink. The prince sat down, surrendering to Pierre's experienced hands. It was Tuesday, which meant only shampoo and a shave, but no trimming, which was just as well. He needed a nap after such a night.

At noon, Lemmy walked out the front door of the Hoffgeitz Bank for his daily lunch. He strolled down Bahnhofstrasse, enjoying the crisp air and beautiful shops. A pretty woman smiled at him, and he smiled back. He passed Credit Niehoch Bank, where he had worked years ago, and the massive building shared by Grieder and Bank Leu. Turning left, past the armory, he paused in front of St. Peter Kirche—the church of Old Zurich. Paula had once explained that the copper bells atop the tower were the largest in Europe, built to warn the neighboring citadels of Germanic or Mongol invaders.

The Limmat River was just around the corner, and despite the cashmere coat, he felt the cold draft from the lake. He walked faster.

The Orsini Restaurant kept an open account for the overpriced lunch he regularly shared with Zurich's most successful bankers. But today he passed by the iron gate and continued down the narrow alley.

At the corner was the clock store, where he had bought Paula the five-foot-tall grandfather clock that rang hourly in their living room in perfect synchrony with the chimes of St. Peter Kirche. The alley curved to the left, and he slipped into the service door in the rear of the Bierhalle Kropf.

The dining hall smelled of cigarette smoke, fried sausages, and potatoes baked in butter. Lemmy unbuttoned his coat, loosened his tie, and stepped into the clutter of voices and laughter. The long wooden tables and hard benches were occupied with the usual mix of bank clerks, blue-collar workers, and off-season tourists. He negotiated his way down the center aisle until he reached the far end. The last table was partly occupied by four elderly men, chewing on fried sausages and sauerkraut. He squeezed through and sat all the way in the corner, his back to the wall.

A voluptuous waitress waved cheerfully from the aisle. He pointed at his neighbors' beers and plates, then held up two fingers and gestured at the empty seat across the table.

The lead article in *The Economist,* which he had brought with him, questioned the viability of the Swiss private banking industry should Switzerland join the European Community.

Two overflowing glasses of beer were passed down from the aisle, followed by two plates loaded with sausages and *Apfelkochli*—sugary apple slices, fried in cinnamon and butter. Lemmy winked at the waitress, nodded at his neighbors, and returned to *The Economist.*

Halfway through the meal, he heard coughing from across the table.

Elie Weiss blew his nose into a paper napkin, which he squeezed into a ball and put in his coat pocket. He kept his wool cap on.

Lemmy leaned forward and spoke German with minimal movement of his lips. "You look awful."

"You, on the other hand, look prosperous," Elie said. "How's your father-in-law?"

"Fine for eighty-four, but the next heart attack could be fatal."

"It's about time. By the way, good tip about Damascus." Elie held the beer glass with two hands and sipped.

"I saw the salacious photos in the papers. Quite a scene."

"A public execution scares other Oslo opponents. Rabin hopes the benefits of peace will calm the Palestinian street." Elie smirked. "And swords shall be forged into scythes."

"Ploughshares."

"Yes, those also."

Lemmy glanced at their table mates, who were engaged in argument over a soccer game lost to a Spanish team the previous weekend.

"What about the Koenig account?"

"Günter needed goading, but he's cooperating now. In two or three weeks, all of the accounts will be on the system."

"Finally. It's been a long road."

"I'll still need a password to take any action within the account itself."

Elie nodded. "Letters and numbers. Something related to Tanya Galinski. That Nazi truly loved her. You can relate, yes?"

The comment needled Lemmy, even after all these years. "I'm not my father."

"There's no shame. She was irresistible."

"Is my father still alive?"

"For you, he's dead." Elie's lips twitched as if he tried to smile, but couldn't. "Rabbi Abraham Gerster disavowed you, sat shivah after you, even though you were still alive, just because you decided to leave his holy sect. A real father wouldn't do that. What do you care if he's dead or alive?"

"I cannot understand him, especially now that I have a son of my own. Nothing could make me stop loving Klaus Junior. It's against nature—"

"What's not to understand? He's a religious fanatic. And you denounced his God. For him, you died the day you chopped off your side locks and threw away your black hat. And your mother became a sinner when she killed herself. That man is nothing to you."

"Still, I can't imagine anything that could cause me to disown my son."

"Don't forget who you really are." Elie was whispering, but the hoarseness in his voice gave it a tone of hushed rage. "That family of yours? Just part of the job!" He slipped a brown envelope across the table. "Your wife and son are Gentiles. *Goyim!*"

"That's irrelevant—"

"They're your cover, nothing more!"

It was no longer the case, but neither was it something he could actually discuss with Elie—not at this time and place, anyway.

"Our destiny," Elie said, barely audible, "is about to arrive. Money and power to launch *Counter Final Solution*."

Lemmy nodded.

"I'm banking on you!"

"Of course." Lemmy understood. It had been Elie's lifelong project—to take possession of the enormous fortune SS Oberstgruppenführer Klaus von Koenig had deposited with Armande Hoffgeitz fifty years ago and use it to finance a worldwide network of Jewish assassins who would eliminate every enemy of the Jewish people. "I'll gain control over the account very soon. It's a lot of money. Will you transfer it to Paris?"

Elie shook his head. "Up to you. You'll be in charge."

"What do you mean?"

"As my successor."

"Me?" Lemmy pushed aside the half-full plate and leaned forward over the table. "I'm a Swiss banker. I've never communicated with anyone but you. I don't know anything!"

"The information will be available to you when it's time for a transition."

"Not interested. It's too dangerous!"

Elie clacked his tongue.

"My life is complicated as it is. You don't know—"

"I know more than you think." A hint of a smile passed over Elie's thin lips. "All in good time. Have a pleasant day, Herr Horch."

Lemmy folded his coat over his arm and made his way to the aisle. Their table mates lifted their beers in greeting. Glancing back, he saw Elie examine the cover of *The Economist*, his thin body rocking back and forth as if in prayer.

In his alcove off the foyer of the synagogue, Rabbi Abraham Gerster took out the stapled booklet Itah Orr had given him and placed it on the small desk. *ILOT – Member Manual – Top Secret*. The second page carried typed text that resembled the oath recited at the swearing-in ceremony he had seen on TV. The third page had the *Table of Contents*:

1. TIGHT LIPS – HOW TO KEEP YOUR TRUE IDENTITY SECRET FROM FRIEND & FOE;
2. FALSE IDENTITY – HOW TO SELECT, MAINTAIN, AND CHANGE YOUR ALIAS;
3. PASSWORDS – HOW TO CREATE, OBTAIN, AND USE THEM;
4. COMRADES' PERSONAL INFO – WHAT YOU DON'T KNOW YOU CAN'T REVEAL;
5. FIELD SECURITY – HOW TO DETECT AND SHAKE OFF A TAIL;
6. SURVEILLANCE – HOW TO CONDUCT BASIC TRACKING, SCOUTING, AND WATCHING;
7. SABOTAGE – HOW TO MAXIMIZE DAMAGE WHILE USING EVERYDAY MATERIALS;

8. STREET WARFARE — HOW TO START A RIOT, TRIP LAW ENFORCEMENT, AND SLIP AWAY;

9. FIRST AID — HOW TO TREAT FOR TEAR GAS, BATON STRIKES, HORSE KICKS, AND BULLET WOUNDS;

10. LIGHT WEAPONS — HOW TO OBTAIN A LICENSE, PURCHASE, AND MAINTAIN GUNS;

11. TARGET PRACTICE — BASIC RULES, SECRET LOCATIONS, STANDARDS OF PROFICIENCY;

12. SURVIVING CAPTURE — HOW TO RESIST PHYSICAL/ PSYCHOLOGICAL PRESSURE BY THE AUTHORITIES;

13. READINESS TO SACRIFICE — GIVING UP YOUR LIFE FOR TORAH, LAND, AND PEOPLE OF ISRAEL!

Rabbi Gerster proceeded to read each page of the ILOT manual with growing concern. The loud, constant hum of hundreds of Neturay Karta men studying Talmud in the synagogue filtered through his door, providing none of the calming effect he usually found in the familiar noise. Some of the pages provided detailed instructions, which appeared to have been copied from military manuals more suitable for urban warfare than an illegal militia. The pages dealing with passwords, aliases, and surveillance tactics contained details and procedures that had clearly originated in professional secret service training manuals, not in the mind of an amateur right-wing activist.

A knock came from the door. Rabbi Gerster folded the ILOT manual and stuck it in his coat pocket. "Yes?"

Benjamin's eldest son, Jerusalem, poked his head in the door. "My father asked if you would like to hear today's lecture."

"Ah, yes." Rabbi Gerster rose slowly from the chair. "I can't wait to hear how Benjamin explains the sage Elazar's comment about the lawyers."

"You mean, how *not* to be like the lawyers?" Jerusalem held the door. "I told my father that maybe the sage Elazar was joking."

Rabbi Gerster laughed. "You're a clever boy."

The synagogue greeted them with cigarette smoke and the intensity of voices arguing over Talmudic quandaries.

"Most of our friends here," Rabbi Gerster waved at the rows of scholars, "would never assign humor to our ancient sages. Why is it, Jerusalem?"

"Perhaps they forgot," Benjamin's son intoned in the traditional singsong of Talmudic studying, "that the sages were flesh and blood, like us."

"Precisely!"

At the Hoffgeitz Bank, Lemmy entered his office and made sure the door was locked. On the way from the Bierhalle Kropf he had reflected on the conversation with Elie. *You'll be in charge...as my successor.* It must have been a joke. Running SOD required skills and knowledge he did not possess. He had been an undercover agent for twenty-eight years, slowly growing roots as a reputable banker in Zurich. His Mideast clients had been a fountain of useful intelligence for Israel, and every year Elie had sent him on jobs that sharpened his deadly skills. But he had never worked directly with other SOD agents, had not been privy to the organization's structure or composition, and had never interacted with any Israeli official. To the best of Lemmy's knowledge, only Elie Weiss knew who Wilhelm Horch really was and that Jerusalem Gerster had not died in battle on the Golan Heights in 1967. This total anonymity enabled him to do his job in relative safety while protecting his family. There was no way he could take over command of SOD from Elie Weiss. It would put everything he possessed and everyone he loved at an unacceptable risk.

But then he remembered another thing Elie had said. *I know more than you think.* Another joke? Another mind game? How could Elie watch him?

He pulled the envelope from his coat pocket and tore it open. It contained a photo of a youth in a long green coat, holding a fur hat. He was in profile, too far to show exact facial features. On the back of the photo, in Elie's familiar handwriting, was a short note:

WEDNESDAY, 3:00 P.M., PARIS, RUE MOGADOR, GALERIES LAFAYETTE, WEST BUILDING. WATCH FOR A GREEN PEUGEOT. TARGET IS THE BOMBER OF THE MARSEILLES SCHOOL. HE'LL GO TO MENSWEAR DRESSING ROOM. SECOND TEAM WILL WATCH THE DRIVER ON RUE MOGADOR.

Lemmy looked at the small photo for a long moment and memorized what little details it gave. He reviewed the operational instructions one more time and slipped the photo into the paper shredder.

Elie Weiss left the Bierhalle Kropf through the front entrance and waved down a taxi. Zurich's train station was only a few blocks away, and the elderly Swiss cabbie wasn't happy as he collected the minimum fare and no tip. "I'm not a bus driver," he said in German.

"*Arbeit macht frei,*" Elie said as he got out.

He took the escalators down into the underground station. As the train left for the airport, he opened *The Economist* and found an envelope glued onto page 67, which carried an article titled: MIDEAST LEADERS TALK BUSINESS – CAN RABIN AND ARAFAT QUELL THEIR MILITANT OPPOSITIONS WITH ECONOMIC PROSPERITY? Elie read it quickly. Typical European wishful thinking held that terrorism will disappear if western nations subsidize a nice middle-class lifestyle for the Palestinians. It was like expecting hyenas to forgo their natural malice in exchange for free meals. Elie had no doubt that the editors at *The Economist* knowingly twisted the truth because, just like the Palestinians, their hostility to Israel was not rooted in political causes or economic circumstances, but in anti-Semitism, manifested temporarily as anti-Israelism.

Inside the envelope he found a cashier's check for $75,000, made *To Bearer*. The funds in his account at the Hoffgeitz Bank had come from dozens of former Nazis he had tracked down over the years, many with the help of Lemmy's banking skills. Invariably, they were easy to terrify, like a bully facing someone worse. They paid handsomely for their sins, and the cash supported on-going SOD operations while he pursued the real prize—Koenig's fortune, which awaited its destiny in a dormant account at the Hoffgeitz Bank.

Also inside the envelope were two sheets of paper. The first provided a list of the bribes paid to Prince Abusalim az-Zubayr, which totaled $76,750,000. The second sheet was a copy of an electronic transfer of $200,000 from the prince's account at the Hoffgeitz Bank to a bank in Senlis, France, dated today.

As soon as the train reached the airport, Elie walked to a pay phone. It was two thirty p.m. He inserted a phone card and punched in the number.

The phone at Rue Buffault rang three times, and Gideon answered, "Yes?"

"Get a roadmap," Elie said, "and find Senlis. It's a small town, maybe a village."

After a moment of paper shuffling, Gideon said, "Senlis is about twenty miles north of Paris."

"Near Ermenonville?"

"Correct."

Elie coughed and held his other hand to his chest until the pain eased. "Our man will pick up a large sum today at Banque Nationale De France at thirty-eight Rue Philippe. He won't trust anyone else, but he'll bring guards. Watch from a distance, take photos, but nothing else."

"Your old friend is here. She's napping."

Elie considered the situation for a moment. Tanya must not learn of these developments. "Get lovebird and leave quietly. If our guest wakes up, tell her you're going to buy food. Go to Senlis and watch the bank."

"Follow him?"

"No. There will be more transfers. I want to confirm it's really him, but our main target is his sponsor. We have to hold off until we can get both of them together." Elie hung up and walked to Gate 24A, where the next Swissair flight to Paris was already boarding.

Gideon parked the Citroën halfway up the street from the two-story, glass-fronted building. Bathsheba propped a black-and-white photo of Abu Yusef on the dashboard, and they settled for the wait with an audio version of Frederick Forsyth's *The Fourth Protocol*. An hour into the story, John Preston brought the stolen documents to the Yard, and a technician dusted them for prints. Gideon remembered Preston, played by Michael Cain, wearing his nonchalant expression that communicated so much to truly discerning Michael Cain fans.

"He's not coming." Bathsheba hit the stop button on the cassette player. "Or it's not him at all."

"The bank closes in nine minutes," Gideon said.

"Let's go for a drink." Her left arm rested on the back of his seat, then slipped down to his shoulder.

He pretended not to notice.

Bathsheba's mouth was close to his ear. "You smell so clean." Her fingers slid under the curls at the back of his head. "I was thinking—"

"Don't start." Gideon pushed her hand away.

Bathsheba sat straight up in her seat and saluted.

He laughed despite his best efforts. The absurd contradiction between her girlish clowning and her womanly beauty was too funny to resist. She was a performer, both in her irreverence and on the job. Men never refused Bathsheba. He had seen her lure men who recklessly surrendered to the powerful lust she ignited. He sensed that she despised their submission. Did she despise all men because her father had died, leaving her orphaned when she was so young?

"Look!" Bathsheba pointed.

A green Peugeot stopped in front of the bank and a man sprang out of the passenger side. He looked up and down the street and tapped on the roof of the car. Both rear doors opened and two other men came out. They all wore dark suits and had thin mustaches, and the driver, Bashir, awkwardly hid a machine gun under his jacket.

She aimed the Polaroid. "Come out, come out, wherever you are."

Abu Yusef emerged. He was older than the others, his hair gray and thinning on top. He crossed the pavement carrying a briefcase to the door of the bank.

The camera clicked. "I'd rather shoot bullets," she said, "than photos."

"He's too well protected."

A few minutes later Abu Yusef reappeared and hefted the briefcase into the back seat. The Peugeot drove off. Gideon waited a few minutes before heading back to Paris.

Elie Weiss sat on the edge of the bed. Tanya's face was peaceful, almost happy. Finding her asleep was an unexpected pleasure—it had been three hours since he had called from Zurich. She must have been very tired. He enjoyed this rare opportunity to gaze at her without being regarded with cold hostility. For decades they had coexisted in the clandestine trenches of the war against Israel's enemies, but neither her beauty nor her loathing of him had abated.

He pulled off his gloves and carefully rested his hand on her cheek. Tingling warmth reached up through his arm to his chest. His eyes misted up and he leaned closer, taking in her unique aroma.

Her eyes opened. She pushed his hand away and sat up.

"Shalom, Tanya."

"Shalom."

"You look well."

"What's wrong with you?"

"Nothing." Elie rubbed his bald head. "I saw Abraham last week. A chance encounter. I barely recognized him. His beard is totally white."

"He's not seventy yet." Tanya stood, her hair came loose, and the past fifty years fell off. She was again the girl sitting in the snow on the first day of 1945, wrapped in a fur coat, her Nazi lover's warm corpse beside her. Elie had fallen in love with her right there, a passion that would forever go unrequited. Instead she fell for Abraham, but her love had fared no better—Elie had made sure of that.

"We haven't spoken in years," Elie said. "He shirked his duty when he passed the leadership to that fatherless disciple of his, Benjamin Mashash."

"A leader without an heir is a failed leader. What's your succession plan?"

"People like us never retire. We must work to prevent the next Holocaust, use whatever skills and resources we possess. Abraham grew up as the rabbi's son, so he should use the skills he acquired preparing for the pulpit. And I was the *shoykhet*'s son, so I use the skills which I was groomed to practice."

"Slaughtering animals?"

"Precisely, whether they walk on two legs or four. And you, Tanya? Are you still using your *female* skills?"

"What's left of them."

"You're too modest." Elie smirked. "What you had achieved by your seventeenth birthday was enough for a whole career—an irony, really, that thanks to you the stolen riches, which your dearly beloved Klaus had stashed away until he could rebuild the next Reich, will instead finance the defense of a Jewish state *to last a thousand years*."

"I'm home!" Lemmy entered the house from the garage, and Klaus Junior leaped into his arms. "How was school?"

"Great!"

"You're early." Paula appeared in the kitchen doorway, wearing an apron. "What happened? The bank burned down?"

He kissed her on the lips. "I missed you guys, so I came home."

"There's no dinner yet. I just started—"

"Turn off the oven. Let's go out for pizza."

"Wait a minute!" Paula stuck a finger in his chest. "What's the catch?"

"You know me too well." He laughed. "I need to go to Paris in the morning."

"I knew it!" She pulled off her apron and tossed it at him. "Paris again—without me?"

"A quick business meeting, back tomorrow night." He raised his hand. "Scout's honor."

"Papa!" Klaus Junior was already putting on his shoes. "When you were little, were you a scout leader?"

"Not exactly." Lemmy pulled off his tie. "We didn't have scouts in the neighborhood where I grew up."

Abu Yusef dropped the briefcase on the bed and opened it. "Look!" He picked up a bundle of bills and threw it to Latif. "You were right! Allah still loves me!"

"And I love you too!" Latif rushed into his arms.

They collapsed on the bed together, and Abu Yusef yelled, "I'll show the damn Jews whose God is bigger!"

Latif's white teeth glistened. "You will show the whole world."

Abu Yusef felt the heaviness, which had weighed on him since Al-Mazir's death, lift up. Not only could he now afford the supplies needed for an extravagant revenge, but this money signaled the Saudi prince's commitment to the cause.

"All of Al-Mazir's men will flock to you." Latif unbuttoned his shirt. "You will unseat Arafat and become the leader of Palestine!"

Elie lit a cigarette. "You didn't come here to rummage through old memories, did you?" He watched Tanya's face carefully.

"We're concerned. The little war you've started here could spread."

"What war? The one over underage prostitution?"

"Those photos didn't fool Abu Yusef. He must respond. What will it be? The El Al terminal? Another Jewish school?"

"The Arabs don't kill Jews in response to what we do. They've been killing us long before we did anything to them."

"Here we go again." Tanya sighed. "Times are changing, politically and diplomatically. Our Jewish state is almost fifty. It's time we think and act not only as Jews, but as a state. Mossad is the government agency for overseas espionage. Let us take over the Abu Yusef situation."

"This isn't a job for bureaucrats."

"Neither is it a job for an old man and two cute amateurs."

Elie ignored her sarcasm. It was useful to be underestimated. "The prime minister asked me to handle this. He didn't ask Mossad, did he?"

"Rabin wants deniability, because it's illegal to assassinate targets without compliance with the appropriate procedures."

"Are you questioning Yitzhak Rabin's authority?"

"He's a soldier on a campaign," Tanya said. "He has staked his reputation, his political future, and his legacy on the Oslo process. He thinks that eliminating Arafat's opposition will pave the way for the final status agreement."

"Pipe dreams," Elie said. "Unlike you and me, Rabin didn't experience the Holocaust. Otherwise he would know that Arafat, like all Gentiles, cannot stop hating Jews. They'll never live in peace with us. We must continue to fight—or die."

"Then why has Arafat signed two Oslo agreements? Why is he implementing those agreements?"

"It's the 'salami method.' Arafat is negotiating in phases to get more and more slices of land without any real concessions on the 'final status' issues—the Palestinian refugees' right of return, final borders, and the sovereignty over Jerusalem."

"Rabin believes the Palestinians will ultimately keep the peace, even if their current intentions are cynical."

"Illusions. Once we stop giving him pieces of land, Arafat will use the land and weapons he's gotten under Oslo to resume fighting—this time from a position of ruler of the West Bank and Gaza, a short distance from Jerusalem and Tel Aviv."

"Is that what you told Rabin?"

Elie shrugged. "He thinks the fruits of peace would be too sweet for the Palestinians to spit out. He calls it *momentum*."

"And you're removing obstacles from his path."

"Look, I do what the prime minister asks even when I disagree with his strategy. With time, he will come around to seeing things my way."

"*Nekamah? Revenge?* That's a better strategy? Endless, useless bloodshed?"

"Revenge is useless?" Elie paced back and forth across the small room. "That's the thinking that caused King Saul to spare the Amalekites and lose his kingdom!"

"Enough with this biblical demagoguery."

"The past is instructive." He could barely speak now, his scarce resources of energy almost depleted. It was time to gain her sympathy. The last thing he needed at this crucial time was open war with Mossad. He sat on the bed and dropped the cigarette on the floor, putting it out with the sole of his shoe. "Let me finish this last job. I'm very tired. This is it for me."

"I'll give you a week. But if Abu Yusef spills Jewish blood, all bets are off. We'll come after you, shut you down."

Elie understood. This was the message she had come to deliver. "You'll enjoy that, won't you?"

"Yes!" Tanya's serious expression suddenly broke into a smile. "I will!"

He watched, reluctant to even blink, afraid to miss the transformation of her features, the arch of her lips, the faint creases in her cheeks, the way she moved with efficient, quick agility, full of grace. Even as she mocked him, Elie wanted this moment to last so he could take in every detail, memorize her every gesture, savor every bit of emotion he had managed to rouse in her.

"Haven't you had enough of this?" Tanya came closer. "For fifty years you've begrudged me for loving Abraham instead of loving you. But how could I—or anyone else—love you? You're consumed by hate, by death, by killing our enemies, real or imagined. Even Yitzhak Rabin knows that yesterday's worst enemy could be today's best partner."

Was she speaking of Rabin and Arafat or of the two of them, facing each other in this Paris apartment after a lifetime of rivalry? For a moment, Elie's mind was consumed by hopes. Was there a chance for the two of them, after all these years? Would she take him in her arms, kiss him, caress him, tell him that she loved him? Because if she did that, he would give her everything—the job, the Nazi fortune, the life he had lived in secrecy, even his single-minded dedication to the cause. One hug, one kiss, one demonstration of true feelings, and he would give up everything that his life had stood for until this moment.

"We're not going to let you go on killing," she said. "Don't force me to shut you down. Quit voluntarily, and you can go home to live in peace for the rest of your days."

Her words burst the bubble of his pathetic dream. Elie coughed a few times, intentionally causing the pain in his chest to spike, knowing his face would become ashen. He had to make her believe his deceit. "You're right. I'm worn out. After Abu Yusef is done, I'll go to Jerusalem."

"And you'll hand over all SOD operations to Mossad."

"Not much to hand over," he lied.

"Including Klaus's money? I want his bank ledger back."

Elie gave her his hand, and she shook it. He held on, gazing at their joined hands, savoring the moment. Clearly she was fishing for information about her lover's fortune, trying to find out whether Elie had ever been able to put his hands on it. "On one condition," he said.

"What?"

"Will you take care of Gideon and Bathsheba?" The question implied that the two were his only agents. To give credence to his deception, he met her eyes. "I'll give back Koenig's deposits ledger. To you, personally, so you can use it for a worthy purpose."

"It's a deal." Tanya hesitated. "You're not playing games again, are you?"

"With you? How could I?" His hand let go of hers and rose to her face. Barely touching, his fingers caressed her hair. "My beautiful Tanya."

Wednesday, October 18, 1995

Abu Yusef woke up early. Through the window he watched the bare tree branches sway in the wind. He heard Latif shift under the covers and turned to look at him. Settled back into sleep, hugging a body pillow, Latif's smooth face was peaceful. Abu Yusef smiled. The boy was an angel, a heavenly gift sent to ease the loneliness of the long struggle for Palestine.

There was a knock on the door. Bashir entered with a pitcher of orange juice and a thermos of black coffee.

"Assemble the men in the dining room," Abu Yusef said. "We have work to do—and the money to do it with."

"Of course." Bashir glanced at the sleeping Latif and left the room.

Lemmy's favorite border crossing handled traffic between Paris and Dijon to the west, Strasbourg and Stuttgart to the north, Basel and Zurich to the east, and Bern and Lucerne to the south—thousands of cars and trucks bearing license plates from France, Luxembourg, Germany, Austria, Switzerland, and Italy, in addition to many EU, NATO, and UN vehicles. The inconvenience of using a stick shift in slow traffic was a small price to pay for reliably lax border inspections. He had estimated the delay at no more than one hour, which would enable him to reach Paris by early afternoon at the latest. He could also push the Porsche harder, which was even more fun.

At the French side of the border, a customs officer beckoned him to stop. Lemmy lowered the window, turned down Stravinsky's *The Rite of Spring*, and handed his passport to the officer. "*Bonjour!*"

The officer glanced at the Swiss passport and handed it back. "Anything to declare?"

Lemmy smiled. "Nothing at all."

The officer gave the car an admiring look. "*Bon voyage.*"

Abu Yusef walked into the large dining room with Bashir. The twenty or so men stood at attention. "I lost my beloved friend," he said. "May Allah accept Al-Mazir's soul with open arms."

Some of the men touched their foreheads in devoutness.

"Like me, he was a boy from Nablus, who dedicated his life to fight for our land." Abu Yusef lowered his head and placed his right hand on his chest. "Al-Mazir was a hero of the Palestinian revolution. We must avenge his blood."

They grunted in agreement.

"We are few, but we will grow. Our Palestinian brothers will soon realize that the PLO is selling out, that Arafat is whoring away our land to the Zionist enemy. He calls it peace, but we know it's capitulation and shame. They will join us from Syria's refugee camps, from Tunisia and Lebanon, and even from the slums of Paris." Abu Yusef shook his finger in the air. "We will lead the Palestinian jihad. Off with Arafat and his gang of pork-eaters and vodka-drinkers! Off with the Jews!"

Abu Yusef embraced each of his men. Back at the head of the table, he opened his arms to Bashir. "May Allah's blessing accompany us on the path to victory."

"*Insha'Allah!*" Bashir embraced Abu Yusef.

They exited the dining room together.

"You spoke well," Bashir said. "The men's morale is renewed—"

"The hell with their morale. You think I don't know my men?" Abu Yusef snorted. "They would rather drink vodka and lay with prostitutes than risk their lives to liberate Palestine from the Zionists."

"A strong leader can inspire the meekest of soldiers. They want to believe in you, but they see this." Bashir gestured down the corridor, toward the bedroom.

Abu Yusef felt his face turning hot. "Latif is a good soldier."

"I can send him into the synagogue with explosives and use a remote detonator."

"No!"

"He won't even know what happened to him. It's the best way to get rid—"

The door to Abu Yusef's bedroom opened. Latif appeared wearing only his white briefs. The olive skin of his chest was hairless, his shoulders straight and bony, his arms long and slim. His boyish face flushed under Bashir's hard glare. "Sorry," he said and closed the door.

Bashir said, "Allow me to take care of him."

"Not yet." Abu Yusef placed his hand on Bashir's shoulder, which felt as hard as a rock. "When we win Jerusalem, I'll marry a good woman and give Palestine ten brave sons."

Bashir's expression was neither blank nor hostile, but all-knowing. "As you wish."

Shortly before one p.m., Lemmy drove into the underground parking garage at the Societe Generale building, across from the Paris Opera, and parked the Porsche in a corner spot far from the stairway. He sat in the car and waited to see if anyone was following. The garage was quiet.

Using the point of a pocket knife, he popped out the cover of a storage compartment built into the steel dashboard. A wooden box filled the space. He opened it and removed the Mauser handgun that rested in a perfectly matched depression.

Etched along one side of the barrel, it read: K.v.K. 1943 DEUTSCHLAND ÜBER ALLES

On the other side was the Hebrew word for revenge: NEKAMAH

He wiped off the excess oil and cocked it. The clanking of steel sounded louder in the tight confines of the car.

A t one thirty p.m., Abu Yusef gave Latif a thick bundle of cash. "After you pay for the suits, give the rest of the money to Bashir."

"I can't wait for you to see them!"

Abu Yusef patted his behind. "Go, quick, before Bashir loses his patience."

Latif put his arms around Abu Yusef's neck. "You're so good to me."

"That's right." He breathed in the scent of shampoo from the boy's hair. "Go, go. We'll have plenty of time when you come back."

W ith well-practiced motions, Lemmy screwed on the silencer. He put an extra magazine in the breast pocket of his jacket and replaced the cover over the dashboard storage compartment. Standing by the car, he quickly put on the trench coat and brown fedora. The Mauser fit in a special pocket sewn into the coat at the right hip, easily accessible through a zippered slit. He buttoned the coat and locked the Porsche. The red alarm light next to the steering wheel started blinking. He bent to look in the side mirror and pressed on a fake salt-and-pepper goatee.

Once outside the parking garage, he took the corner around the opera, crossed the street, and headed down Avenue Haussmann, away from the Galeries Lafayette department store. He paused at shop fronts and pretended to examine the displays. Some had already put up their Christmas decorations, hoping to elevate shoppers' spirits more than two months before the holiday. He took more than an hour to make sure no one was following him before he headed back to the Galeries Lafayette. It was time to get acquainted with the operational landscape.

Before Gideon and Bathsheba left the apartment, Elie repeated his instructions. They were to watch Abu Yusef's boy toy go in, wait until he came out, and follow the green Peugeot back to the Arabs' hideaway. But under no circumstances were they to raise any suspicions. If there was any disturbance, they must return to the apartment immediately.

"If you think he noticed you," Elie said, "drop the tail and return here. We'll get him on his next visit to the bank in Senlis."

Gideon was curious to know what made Elie so certain about future money transfers, but kept the question to himself. He had learned from experience that Elie Weiss divulged only the information he absolutely had to share.

Lemmy kept on the coat, fedora, and gloves. He scouted the enormous store, up and down the escalators, across each wing, in and out through different entrances. Avenue Haussmann, a six-lane road with heavy traffic and no legal parking, offered four pedestrian entries into Galeries Lafayette, with hundreds of shoppers coming and going continuously. Rue de Mogador was a side street that passed between the two blocks of the store. It was lined with cars in which husbands and chauffeurs waited. He spent a few moments examining a wall map of the store to memorize several alternative escape routes through various fire exits and loading docks.

Standing inside the store behind the glass doors, Lemmy watched customers being dropped off and picked up on Rue de Mogador.

At 2:43 p.m., a white Citroën arrived. Lemmy recognized Elie's young agents—the man with a head of curls and the woman with sharp, beautiful features and close-cropped hair. They remained in the parked car.

The minutes passed quickly. By 3:12 p.m., Lemmy was concerned. He would not wait for the green Peugeot more than thirty minutes beyond schedule.

Inside the white Citroën, the driver kept watching the street in his side mirror.

Another ten minutes went by. Lemmy felt the Mauser through the side of his coat. Was Elie's information wrong? Could this be a trap?

The couple in the Citroen began arguing. The man shook his head repeatedly. The woman suddenly bolted out of the car and ran down the street to the corner of Avenue Haussmann. Lemmy stepped closer to the glass doors to watch her. She glanced left and right over the railing that separated the sidewalk from the traffic. As she turned, her expression changed, her pace slowed to a casual stroll, and she stopped at a window display. Lemmy looked the other way and saw a green Peugeot coming down Rue de Mogador. It stopped at the curb near the entrance.

The driver was a Middle Eastern man, about fifty. He unfolded a newspaper and began to read. There was no passenger in the car, and Lemmy realized the target had been dropped off at the main entrance on Avenue Haussmann. He was already inside!

A flight of stairs led to the main level. Lemmy passed the counters displaying Chanel, Estée Lauder, OrLane, Shiseido, and Monteil. He circled the line of women at the cashier and took the escalators up, two steps at a time.

Crossing the ladies' shoes area, he noticed Paula's favorite— Lundi Bleu.

Another set of stairs to the right.

Menswear.

He passed Yves Saint Laurent, and turned left.

Red-and-white sign: *Pierre Cardin.*

The salesman at the counter smiled.

Lemmy slowed down, looked away, pretended to browse through a rack of shirts, and approached the far end. A few customers pecked at the long racks of suits in shades of gray.

Around the corner was a line of dressing rooms. One curtain was shut.

His right hand slipped through the slit and gripped the ivory handle. He aimed the Mauser under the coat, barrel forward, pressed to the hip, the silencer parting the coat lapels. His finger slipped into the trigger slot.

Shifting the curtain with his left hand, Lemmy saw a fur hat on a hook, a green coat, and a thin man in white briefs, his back to the curtain, his leg raised, poised to slip into the pants.

Lemmy's finger started pressing the trigger.

The target must have sensed the movement behind him. He straightened and turned. "*Pardon*," he said in a voice surprisingly soft. "I'm almost done." His body completed the turn, and he looked at Lemmy, no more than a foot separating them, smiling with shiny teeth against olive skin. It was a familiar smile, but there was no stopping now. The Mauser coughed twice.

The target's smile crumbled into a mask of terrible fear, which soon slackened into the familiar paralysis of approaching death. Two bullets, aimed to pass through the heart and lodge in the spine, instantly disabled the capacity for physical reactions, including the ability to expel a final scream. His body lost its firmness. He collapsed on the small bench and dropped to the side, resting against the wall, his eyes open wide.

Lemmy shut the curtain, collected the two casings from the floor, and walked along the racks to the back stairway. Down one floor, he turned left at the sign *Sortie – Reserve Au Personnel* and pushed through a fire door. Down a set of gray-painted service stairs, left again, he jogged through a long, dim corridor. A pair of steel doors let him out onto a loading dock on Rue de Provence, a few steps from the bustle of Avenue Haussmann.

The target's smile flashed in Lemmy's mind. A ghost from the past.

No past! You're Wilhelm Horch! A banker!

He paused at the corner. No sirens. No screams. No fools trying to give chase.

A moment later he was across the street and inside the door to the parking garage. He took the stairs down.

The Porsche waited where he'd left it.

His body began to shake. He doubled over. His knees grew weak. He took a few deep breaths, waiting for the sick feeling to pass. The image of the teenager's face stayed with him, switching between smiles and death masks. The dark eyes glistened, then went blank.

Back in the car, he unscrewed the silencer, repacked the Mauser in the storage compartment, and tapped the cover back into place. He took off the trench coat and fedora, removed the fake goatee, and stuffed everything behind the seats.

As he drove out of the parking garage, two police vans raced toward the Galeries Lafayette, sirens whining. He merged with traffic in the opposite direction, slipped Stravinsky into the CD player, and with the first tunes of *The Rite of Spring*, his breathing slowed down.

He lowered the window and cold air filled the car. It had been a fluke of nature—the target's eerie resemblance to Benjamin Mashash, whose face Lemmy had not seen in decades, whose face by now must have matured greatly from the face of the eighteen-year-old Talmudic scholar, Lemmy's study-companion and best friend, back in the Neturay Karta sect in Jerusalem, a divided city on the eve of a great Mideast war.

He stopped at a traffic light and shut his eyes, recalling Benjamin, whose eyes squinted in laughter, teeth white against the olive skin, ringlet side locks dangling on both sides of his earnest face.

Oh, Benjamin!

"You're early." Elie Weiss pointed to his watch. "What happened?"

Gideon slumped in a chair. "A bunch of police cars appeared, a whole swarm of them, and Bashir split."

"You followed him?"

"He drove too fast. We couldn't keep up without being noticed."

Bathsheba paced back and forth. "We should have waited right there. Bashir has to return to pick up the boy. He has to!"

"With all that police activity," Gideon said, "we couldn't stick around."

"Was there a fire in the store? Or an accident?" Elie lit a cigarette, keeping a straight face even though he knew what the arrival of police cars had meant. The job had been executed—successfully, no doubt, because Jerusalem Gerster never failed.

"Whatever it was," Bathsheba said, "we're back to square one."

"We'll catch them soon enough." Smoke petered out of Elie's lips with each word. "The next transfer to Senlis is our hook."

Abu Yusef wasn't happy when Bashir returned without Latif, reporting that the Galeries Lafayette was surrounded by police. With several guns and a few hand grenades in the Peugeot, Bashir had to get away in a hurry, but he was confident that, as the huge department store was filled with thousands of shoppers, Latif would easily melt into the crowds. "He knows the drill," Bashir said. "He'll walk around and check out some stores until the emergency is over. He'll call, and I'll drive back to Paris to get him. Don't worry."

But a few hours passed, the phone didn't ring, and Bashir fell asleep on the sofa in the living room, snoring lightly. The rest of the men, other than the sentries on duty, were in the pool house, watching an action movie with Jean-Paul Belmondo.

By ten p.m. Abu Yusef was pacing in the patio outside, wrapped in an oversize wool coat, a small radio glued to his ear, tuned to an all-news French channel. With time his mind wandered, and the anchor's chattering became mere background noise. But suddenly the words *Galeries Lafayette* popped out. He paused and listened, his mind translating each French word into Arabic: *Victim. Dressing room. Algerian or Moroccan. Age fifteen to twenty. Cash. No papers. Shot twice. Police investigating.*

Amidst the shock and pain, Abu Yusef saw Bashir through the window, slouched on the sofa, his legs crossed, his mouth slightly open. A terrible realization came to Abu Yusef. He ran to the pool house to alert the men, but stopped halfway around the water. What would he tell the men? *Bashir killed my pretty boyfriend!* They would laugh—or worse. They looked up to Bashir, trusted him, and obeyed his orders. In a conflict between them, who would the men choose?

He changed direction and crossed a patch of grass to a storage shed. Inside, leaning against the wall, was the long skewer they had used to roast the lamb. The cook had cleaned the skewer, and it shone in the dark, its sharp point near the pitched ceiling. Abu Yusef grabbed it and returned to the patio. Through the window he saw Bashir in the same position, fast asleep.

It took all of Abu Yusef's self-control not to stab him through. He gripped the metal rod and aimed it at Bashir's thick throat, just under the chin, and pricked the skin.

The snoring ceased, and Bashir's eyes opened. He didn't move. Even his calm expression remained unchanged despite the sight of the long skewer, which had easily pierced a whole lamb from rectum to jaw.

"Say your prayers," Abu Yusef said.

Very slowly, Bashir raised his hand. "I swear. I didn't kill Latif."

"Then how do you know he's dead?" Abu Yusef laughed bitterly. "How?"

Avoiding sudden moves, Bashir's forefinger pointed at the steel rod. "What else...could come between us?"

"You killed him!"

"Must be...the Israelis."

"Impossible!" Abu Yusef pressed a little harder, and a trickle of blood ran down the side of Bashir's throat. "You did it! Murderer!"

With blinding quickness, Bashir's hand flew at the skewer and flipped it sideways, its point trailing blood. At the same time, Bashir's leg bent sideways, his knee pounding Abu Yusef's thigh. The pain was sharp and debilitating, his leg muscles drained of sustenance. And while Abu Yusef collapsed, Bashir jumped to his feet, the skewer in motion, spinning like a parade stick.

Abu Yusef found himself flat on the carpet, the red point of the skewer in his ear.

"How dare you," Bashir groaned, panting hard, "doubt my loyalty?"

Abu Yusef felt a drop of Bashir's blood leave the point of the skewer and fill his ear. He tried to move and realized that Bashir's foot was pinning him down. But the fact that he was still alive proved Bashir's innocence. "Okay. I believe you."

Bashir dumped the rod on the carpet. "I serve under you to fight the Zionists, not to chauffer your bottom boy on shopping trips. But I didn't kill him."

"How did the Israelis find Latif? How did they know where, when?"

"They must have followed us. It's the only possibility." Bashir pressed his hand to the bleeding wound under his chin. "I failed to notice them, but they are clever."

"I will avenge him!" Abu Yusef stood, choked with hate. "And Al-Mazir!"

Thursday, October 19, 1995

According to the TV newscast, police had been unable to identify the murder victim at the Galeries Lafayette. The large amount of cash found on the youth suggested he was involved in narcotics or prostitution activities, both controlled by Arab immigrants. The camera showed a gurney roll out of the store with a zipped-up body bag, followed by footage from recent police crackdowns on criminal gangs in Paris.

"If you wait long enough," Elie said, "these Arabs end up killing each other."

"A convenient assumption." Bathsheba stared at him. "It wasn't one of your hit men, was it?"

"Don't be ridiculous," Gideon said. "Abu Yusef got bored with the boy and had him killed."

Elie opened a drawer in the desk and took out a large folder. He searched through a pile of newspaper clippings and dug out a one-page article from the *New York Times*. It was less than a year old.

Bathsheba came behind Gideon and rested her chin on his shoulder.

He finished reading and looked at Elie. "So?"

"Summarize it, will you?"

"It's about Prince Abusalim az-Zubayr, son of Sheik Da'ood Ibn Hisham az-Zubayr. Their company, Transport International al-Saud Inc., holds a virtual monopoly on food and machinery purchases for the kingdom. That's billions of dollars." Gideon's eyes went quickly through the lines. "The prince is an Oxford graduate, lives in a suite at the Hilton Hotel in Paris, many sisters, one half-brother, Salman."

"How exotic," Bathsheba said. "And why do we care about this prince?"

"Go on," Elie said.

"Their oasis north of Riyadh is home to the extended family, including Prince Abusalim's wives and children. The old sheik owns everything." Gideon scanned the rest of the article. "The interviewer asked the prince what he thought about the Mideast peace process. Answer: Oslo is a sham, because Palestine is part of the land of Islam, and the Jews are usurpers. Question: What about Arafat? Answer: A leader must be a true believer, someone willing to fight a jihad for Jerusalem."

"That's odd," Bathsheba said. "I thought the Saudis support the Oslo peace process."

"They do," Elie said, "but Prince Abusalim dreams of becoming *Kharass El-Sharif,* keeper of Haram el-Sharif." He lit another cigarette, holding it between a thumb and yellow forefinger. "That's why we targeted him. Now he's collecting bribes from vendors to finance the Palestinian jihad. Remember the tip about the French consulate in Damascus arranging a passport for Al-Mazir?"

"You have someone watching the prince's bank account?" Bathsheba suddenly seemed interested. "Talk about holding someone by the balls!"

"Follow the money," Elie said, "and you'll find your enemy."

"This prince," Gideon said, "is a bigger threat to Israel than Abu Yusef. He can bankroll a hundred more terrorist groups."

"Correct." Elie pulled a sheet of paper from the file. "This is a list of bribes the prince has collected. Use the fax machine at the central post office to send it to this number."

Gideon looked at the number scribbled on the sheet. "What country has prefix 966?"

"Saudi Arabia," Elie said. "A country where thieves get their right hand chopped off without anesthetics."

Lemmy wiped the mist off the bathroom mirror and leaned closer. He kept his sideburns to a minimum, always in a straight line with the upper part of his ear. He had once let his sideburns grow longer, but it reminded him of the payos he had worn so many years ago. Elie had trained him well. *Think of yourself as Wilhelm Horch. Forget Jerusalem Gerster. His memories died with him. Gone.*

But despite his complete dedication to the mission, his mind was not immune to the past. Over the years, a familiar tune would trigger a memory of dancing with the righteous men of Neturay Karta, a passing scent from a restaurant would whet his appetite for one of his mother's dishes, or a familiar face on the street would make his heart skip a beat—like the target in Paris yesterday, reminiscent of Benjamin's smile.

During the long drive in the Porsche, and through the short night beside Paula, the face from the Galeries Lafayette had pestered him like a nagging fly.

Enough!

He placed the blade carefully and slid it down. He did the same on the other side, compared both sides in the mirror, and continued shaving, clearing wide swaths in the foam on his cheeks and chin.

As he got out of the bathroom, Paula opened her eyes. The bright rays of the morning sun came through the blinds, illuminating her golden hair, spread on the pillow like a halo. "Wilhelm Horch." She opened her arms. "No middle initial."

He leaned over and kissed her.

She pulled off his towel.

"It's late," he said.

She lifted the blanket. "Into my cave! Procreate!"

"Junior will be late for school."

Her hands clasped his shoulders, pulling him down. "Then we must hurry."

Lemmy's chest felt cool against her warmth. She scrunched up the nightgown, and her legs parted, rising to encircle his hips. They kissed, tasting each other, their eyes open.

She led him in with her hand and sighed as he penetrated. Her fingernails sank into the flesh of his back, urging his movements. He buried his face in her hair, taking in her loveable scent.

His breath grew faster, her body responding in sync, her whispering sweet, growing urgent, until she whimpered and he froze, paralyzed by the impending burst of pleasure, and pushed into her one more time, as deep as he could, letting go, inseminating his wife.

Paula caressed his back while their panting slowed down. "This one felt like a girl."

"You think so?"

"No question. A passionate, athletic, bright girl."

He leaned on his elbow, his face an inch from hers. "I'm sorry we waited so long."

"You've come around. That's what counts."

He saw no blame in her happy face and felt guilty. He had objected to a second child since Klaus Junior had been born, citing a variety of reasons, none of them sincere. Elie Weiss had allowed him one child—to cement the marriage and the position in the bank. *You hold the key to the future security of the Jews. Your success will ensure the safety of our people for generations. Counter Final Solution!*

Paula had respected his objection despite her craving for a baby. She had assumed his reluctance was rooted in a hurtful family history at which he hinted. He had avoided speaking about his childhood, only providing her with the scant details of the false identity Elie had arranged. He had arrived at Lyceum Alpin St. Nicholas in late 1967 as a recent orphan from a fire that had killed his parents near Munich. The burn scars on his back had turned to mild scars between his shoulders and buttocks.

"I should have come around long ago." He was referring to that Tuesday, the previous month, when he had accompanied her to her annual checkup. Paula's long-time gynecologist, Dr. Linser, joked that soon she would no longer need to take the pill, and for a brief second Paula's usual cheerfulness gave way to something approaching grief. Without allowing logic to intrude, Lemmy had said, "Let's try for a girl while there's still time."

He kissed her again—not with lust, but with tenderness of gratitude, for she truly loved him, even with his secrets, which she must have sensed. She was forty-three, still capable of a pregnancy and the rigors of child rearing. The experience at the doctor's office had triggered something powerful inside Lemmy, as if his life as Wilhelm Horch had finally edged out the dark past, the secret assassinations, and the great mission itself, allowing him to truly be a partner to Paula.

She touched his cheek. "Are you okay?"

"I'd love to have a daughter," he said, surprising himself at how complete he felt with the statement. "Or a boy. It'll be a joy either way."

Rabbi Abraham Gerster took the bus from Jerusalem to Ramat Gan, then a taxi to Bar Ilan University. The campus surprised him with its greenery and modern architecture. He had assumed that the only religious university in Israel would be more like a yeshiva, a large building crowded with male scholars and aging, bearded professors. But Bar Ilan University was nothing like a yeshiva. The lawns were filled with young men and women, who sat together and chomped on lunch sandwiches, chatting animatedly. Most of the women wore their hair loose, only a minority wearing scarves or hats over their natural hair. The majority of the male students revealed their religious observance with only a small knitted skullcap, while some heads were bare altogether in the manner of secular Israelis. Only a few wore the black garb of Talmudic scholars.

He was the subject of curious glances, with his white beard and payos, the black coat and hat. He still felt as young as any of these students, but in truth he was old enough to be their grandfather.

He followed the signs for the law school. The building was named after the late Prime Minister Menachem Begin. He browsed the directory.

PROFESSOR GABRIEL LEMELSON – JEWISH LAW – ROOM 305

On the third floor, the office door was open. A man sat at a small, round table with three female students. They were discussing recent legislation that gave civil courts jurisdiction over the financial aspects of divorce, while rabbinical courts maintained exclusive jurisdiction over the dissolution of the marriage itself.

The professor noticed him through the open door, removed his reading glasses, and stood up. "Oh, goodness!" He beckoned. "Please, it's an honor."

The students took their bags and left.

Professor Lemelson shut the door. "How can I help you, Rabbi Gerster?"

"You know who I am?"

"Of course! I wrote my dissertation on the abortion law." He pulled a soft-bound book from a shelf. "Some scholars, myself included, believe that nineteen sixty-seven could have become famous for a different war—a Jewish civil war—if not for your Talmudic ruling against violence and rioting."

"That's an exaggeration."

"I respectfully disagree. It was truly a paradigm change in ultra-Orthodox ideology. Your ruling marginalized the literal traditionalists' advocacy of biblical stoning and burning. In essence you sanctified study and worship as preferable to violent enforcement of God's law."

"I only spoke to my community."

"But your ruling, even though it was issued to the relatively small Neturay Karta sect, radiated calming rays to every black-hat yeshiva in the country. You launched singlehandedly the inward-looking, insular culture as the righteous way of life. Your vision has since become the modus operandi for all ultra-Orthodox communities in Israel. As a result, we have avoided large-scale religious violence over secular-religious conflicts, such as abortions, Sabbath violations, pork selling and consumption, restaurants serving bread during Passover, and the continuous trimming of rabbinical courts' jurisdiction—not to mention the controversies over archeological digs."

"You give me too much credit."

"On the contrary. The mostly amicable coexistence with the ultra-Orthodox, which secular Israelis today take for granted, has been a direct result of how you diffused the abortion protests." Professor Lemelson patted the book. "Perhaps you'd like a copy?"

"I already have one."

"You've read my book?"

"When it was first published. Your conclusions were all wrong."

"Wrong? Why?"

"You assumed that the ultra-Orthodox culture is homogeneous. It's not. And violent fundamentalism could grow from modern orthodoxy, as the settler movement is proving."

"Against the Arabs, yes, but they're not engaged in internecine violence. Since your sixty-seven ruling, there has not been a single case of Talmudic advocacy for Jews to attack Jews. Not one!"

"That's precisely why I'm here. What do you know about ILOT?"

The professor's face registered no interest. "Just what I saw on TV. It seemed like a bunch of kids playing pretend—"

"They carried Bar Ilan Law School backpacks."

"So do thousands of students, alumni, and their family members. These ILOT kids are a fringe minority."

"I thought you'd be interested, considering your work on the abortion conflict."

"Oh, I've moved on." Professor Lemelson laughed. "Religious violence is dead, academically speaking. Completely passé. Jews fight each other with words, not weapons. My research focus has shifted to legislative conflicts. Grant money is plentiful, and students are interested in politics."

"What about our history?"

"That's the reason studies of intra-Jewish violence are conducted in the archeology department. And I'm allergic to dust." Professor Lemelson chuckled. "I now study overlapping Jewish laws and modern Israeli legislation. It presents a more acute intellectual conflict."

"And what if you learned that your students are among the Torah warriors of ILOT? Wouldn't that present an acute intellectual conflict?"

Professor Lemelson got up and paced back and forth across his small office. "Are you speculating or are you in possession of factual indicia requiring further study?"

"Have your students raised the question of *Rodef* or the legitimacy of attacking other Jews for their political positions? Or for any reason?"

The professor seemed shocked. "We discuss many topics in the classroom."

"And this particular topic—killing a Jew who's endangering another Jew?"

"Yes, in fact we recently discussed it. The issue was raised theoretically as a proposition for debate. But that's the whole point of free, intellectual exchange in an academic setting, isn't it?"

"Who raised it?"

"I can't give you names! My students shouldn't be persecuted for discussing ideas!"

"Who's talking of persecution?" Rabbi Gerster smiled at the much-younger professor. "Do you take me for a member of the Zionist police?"

The comment caused Professor Lemelson to laugh. "I'm sorry. I should have realized your interest is merely Talmudic."

"Exactly. It's an intellectual interest. I'm sure your student wouldn't mind chatting with a harmless old rabbi."

Sitting at his computer, Professor Lemelson searched his students' list. "I can give you a name, but no contact information." He scribbled on a piece of paper. "Leave a message with your phone number in the office downstairs. One never knows with these students. You might get a call back."

———

Friday,
October 20, 1995

Prince Abusalim az-Zubayr reclined in the wide chair with the *Wall Street Journal.* The Lear jet crossed the southern tip of the Sinai Peninsula, and the Red Sea filled the round window with deep-blue water. Tiny oil tankers left white wakes, pointing to the Suez Canal.

At the sight of the approaching Saudi coastline, he finished his scotch. Holding the glass up against the sun, he examined his fingernails. Pierre had brought a manicurist with him that morning, a cute little Korean with perfect little hands. He would have kept her for the rest of the morning if not for the unexpected phone call that summoned him for a meeting with his father. Perhaps the king had granted them additional contracts for imports? It could mean millions more for his secret account!

The Lear entered Saudi airspace and banked its wings to the right, veering south. An attendant came into the cabin with a silver tray. He placed a cup of black coffee next to Prince Abusalim and reached for the half-full scotch bottle.

"Wait!" Prince Abusalim filled the glass and emptied it in a few gulps. As the servant was leaving with the forbidden alcohol, the white-stucco sprawl of the holy city of Medina appeared in the distance. The prince lowered the back of his seat and closed his eyes. He had an hour to kill while the Lear flew over Hejaz into the Najd region.

Touchdown was barely felt. The long runway bordered the north side of the family oasis, ending in a giant hangar. The doors slid open to welcome the Lear. It was dwarfed by the sheik's personal Boeing 747.

A Mercedes limousine took him down the paved road, shaded by rows of palm trees. Tribesmen in white robes and kafiyas opened the gates, and a moment later the main house appeared.

Hajj Vahabh Ibn Saroah, the sheik's loyal deputy, descended the marble steps in his traditional white galabiya, which touched his sandals. A checkered kafiya was secured to his head by the two black bands that symbolized his religious status.

They embraced and kissed.

Hajj Ibn Saroah had been with the sheik all his life. He had commanded the sheik's nomads through fierce fighting for the establishment of a position of power in the king's court and had continued to command the sheik's personal security guards, to communicate the sheik's orders, and to mete out punishment to sinners. Under his belt the hajj kept a shabriya—a crooked blade that could slice a man's hair lengthwise.

"How is my beloved father?"

"His Highness is in good health. As you are, I hope." Hajj Ibn Saroah walked quickly, his head slightly bowed.

"Indeed. Allah has been good to me." He wanted to ask for the purpose of this urgent summoning but was reluctant to show a weakness to this man who, despite his pretences, was only a notch above a slave.

A marble-tiled hallway led them to a pair of gold-plated doors.

"Abusalim!" The sheik put aside the worn volume of the Koran, which he had been reading, and rose slowly. "I am so happy to see you!"

"Father." Prince Abusalim bowed and kissed the lapel of his father's long galabiya, its white cotton embroidered with gold.

The sheik embraced his son, planting a kiss on each cheek. "It's been almost three months since your last visit."

"I've been working very hard."

"And you did well. Our revenues have doubled this year." The sheik smiled. "I'm very proud of you, Abusalim."

"May Allah preserve your health for many years. I am nothing without your guidance."

Sheik az-Zubayr had just celebrated his seventieth birthday and, as his three wives could testify, had maintained his youthful virility. "But what good is my guidance if you live in Paris, among all the infidels?"

"I would come more often, Father. But I have many responsibilities."

"Indeed you do." The sheik caressed his goatee. "Have you lost interest in your wives? Maybe you should take a new one?"

"Not yet. Maybe next year."

"You only need to ask, yes?"

"Thank you, Father." Prince Abusalim wondered if that was the reason for calling him home. Had one of his wives complained about his long absence? The younger one was pregnant, so it must be his first wife. He would visit her tonight, satisfy himself, and rough her up as a lesson in the virtue of silence.

Hajj Ibn Saroah cleared his throat.

"Ah, yes." The sheik's hand pointed vaguely. "I'm sure it's nonsense, but do you remember the deal we made about a year ago with Jamson, the American wheat dealer?"

"Yes. Thirty million, I think."

"Exactly! You always had a good memory for numbers. Anyway, Vahabh was told that you asked them for a reward."

Abusalim stood up. "*What?*"

"A bribe," the hajj said.

"Who told you this lie?"

Sheik Da'ood put a hand on Prince Abusalim's shoulder. "We know it's a lie. But Vahabh recommended that I ask, that we hear it from you, that's all."

The hajj picked up the sheik's Koran. "Swear that the accusation is false."

Prince Abusalim turned to his father. "This is outrageous!"

"Swear!" The hajj held the Koran forward.

Sheik Da'ood looked at his son expectantly.

"Fine!" Prince Abusalim rested his hand on the holy book. "I swear in Allah's name that—" He tried to continue, but his throat became parched like the desert outside. He coughed, but his voice was gone.

The hajj put the Koran aside.

The prince knew he had to come up with an explanation. But how much did they know?   "Abusalim?" Sheik az-Zubayr sounded bewildered. "Why don't you swear it?"

"Because he took the bribe," the hajj said. "And whatever he demanded, they added to the price we paid."

Prince Abusalim considered arguing, but remained silent.

"My son is a common thief." The sheik's voice shook. "In Allah's name, why?"

The hajj asked, "What did you do with the money?"

Prince Abusalim was relieved. It appeared that they didn't know about the Swiss account or the other vendors. "I gave it away. For you, Father."

"To whom?"

"The Palestinians."

"Which Palestinians?"

"Abu Yusef, leader of the opposition to Arafat."

"You stole money from me to sponsor a terrorist?"

"He's not a terrorist. He's the leader—"

"They already have a leader!"

"Arafat sold out. Abu Yusef will soon emerge as the new Palestinian leader. He'll inspire a new intifada that will drive the Jews away. And when he takes Jerusalem, he'll restore us to our throne."

"What throne?"

"Abu Yusef promised to make you mufti of Jerusalem. The *Kharass El-Harem*." That was inaccurate. Abu Yusef had promised to appoint Prince Abusalim, not his father. "We will be the equals of the House of Saud—"

"You are a fool!" The sheik spoke with rage his son had rarely witnessed before. "A filthy murderer promised to make me mufti of Jerusalem? Me? The father of a thief?" He paced across the room and leaned against the wall as if he were going to faint.

"It's our destiny," Prince Abusalim insisted. "We must help the Palestinians in their war against the Jews."

"Don't preach to me! I've given millions to ease their suffering! In Gaza, the West Bank, the refugee camps—a worthy charity for a man righteous enough to be *Kharass El-Harem*. I give them food and fresh water, I build schools and underground sewers. But I don't fill the pockets of murderers who fornicate with other men!"

Hajj Ibn Saroah took the sheik's arm. "Calm down, Your Highness."

"I know what I'm doing, Father."

"You're an imbecile! Abu Yusef is on the Munich list. The Israelis will kill him sooner or later, and maybe they'll kill you too."

"The Israelis don't assassinate Palestinians anymore. The Oslo Accords granted complete amnesty to all PLO veterans."

"Enough!" The sheik pointed a trembling finger at Prince Abusalim. "You will remain here with your wives and children, pray and study the Koran until I decide your punishment."

"But I cannot stay." He bowed to his father. "Please, forgive me. The company's business requires my presence in Paris."

"The company is *my* business." Sheik Da'ood az-Zubayr picked up his Koran and left the room.

In the morning, after Gideon and Bathsheba left for Ermenonville, Elie swallowed one of Dr. Geloux's pills. It took the edge off his pain but also interfered with the clarity of his mind, which he found frustrating. He stayed in bed, hoping for a few hours of sleep, but soon the phone rang. It was Tanya. Mossad had received information that a Palestinian group was buying weapons from a dealer in Paris.

"Thanks for the tip," Elie said. Was it a lie? Another Mossad manipulation? Or was Abu Yusef using the money he got from Zurich? No. He wouldn't spend the first cash infusion on buying weapons in the overpriced French black market. Rather, he would spend it on food and booze to keep his men happy and use the next transfer to send Bashir to Algiers to buy cheap guns and explosives, which he would smuggle back into France. "It's not Abu Yusef, but at any event we're going to take care of him in the next few days."

"Let us assist you."

"I'll contact you if I need help."

"For your sake, I hope you do that."

He hung up and thought about Tanya's offer. The stakeout at the intersection near Ermenonville was useless if Abu Yusef had already acquired a different car. The best chance to catch him was at the next bank pick-up in Senlis. The fax to Saudi Arabia should have caused a crisis in the prince's relationship with his father, which should provoke the ambitious young man to speed up his scheme by increasing his sponsorship of Abu Yusef. But what if the old sheik locked up his wayward son in the family oasis, away from phones and jet planes? Without another transfer to Senlis, Abu Yusef might not be stopped until it was too late. Elie wondered for a moment: Should he accept Tanya's offer? Should he trust Mossad?

No!

If he let them in, they would try to take over SOD at the very moment of its maturity and success. Many years had passed since Tanya had surrendered to him the ledger detailing the fortune that General Klaus von Koenig had deposited with the Hoffgeitz Bank. But she had never told her superiors about it, probably afraid that Elie would kill her if she did. Not that he would ever hurt Tanya, but she didn't know that. And now Lemmy, the Israeli youth Elie had transformed into a Swiss banker and the Hoffgeitz heir-apparent, was about to fulfill his ultimate mission within one of the most secretive financial institutions in the world.

Obtaining access to the Nazi fortune was the key to Elie's plan—the money to finance his grand vision. And soon Prime Minister Rabin would make the only rational decision and accept Elie's offer of help. Rabin would regain his popularity and win the next election, and Elie would become Israel's intelligence czar, gaining control of both Mossad and Shin Bet—a combined clandestine force with a worldwide infrastructure and highly trained personnel. He would have the money, the power, and the means to launch a potent network of assassins, ready to strike down the next Hitler, the next Arafat, Khomeini, or Gaddafi, the next Eichmann, Nasser, or Stalin. Multiple teams would burrow under the social fabric of every country, ceaselessly working to identify, pinpoint, and eliminate every agitator who spewed hatred of Jews. For the first time in their painful three thousand-year history, the Jewish people would wield a global weapon capable not only of eliminating contemporary enemies, but also of eradicating altogether the sturdy germs of a chronic, murderous mental disease called anti-Semitism. And considering what was at stake, the risk of another Abu Yusef terror attack seemed irrelevant.

When Lemmy went downstairs, Klaus Junior was already in the kitchen, eating cereal with milk. "We're late, Papa!" He snatched the keys to the Porsche and sprinted out.

Lemmy rinsed the cereal bowl in the sink, collected a bottle of water from the fridge, and went to the garage. He found the boy in the passenger seat, the engine already working. "How did you manage to turn off the alarm?"

"It's easy!"

"Is that so? Then why don't you just drive yourself to school, smarty?"

"Can I?"

The Porsche sped down the winding road, tires screeching with each curve. On the right, Lake Zurich was covered by a thin layer of morning mist. Klaus Junior, buckled up in the passenger seat, fiddled with the radio, changing stations. "We're going to be late. I hate to be late."

Lemmy glanced at his son. "Nothing wrong with a little tardiness."

"I'll tell my teacher it's your fault."

"Now I'm really scared."

The boy laughed and banged on the dashboard with his hand, causing the rectangular storage cover to pop out. Lemmy reached across and tapped it back in. He had not yet returned the Mauser to the safe deposit box at the bank, where it would stay until the next job.

The car phone rang. Lemmy pulled the receiver from its cradle. "Yes?"

"Good morning, Herr Horch." It was Christopher. "I have Prince az-Zubayr on the line."

"Put him through."

The familiar voice came on the line. "Wilhelm?"

"Excellency! How are you?"

"Been better, my friend." The British accent was not as smooth, the vowels abrupt. "I had to fly home. My private dealings have been compromised."

Lemmy steered the Porsche onto the shoulder and stopped. Klaus Junior pointed to his watch.

"My father's slave has been snooping around."

"Where?"

"A wheat vendor. Those Americans have big mouths. No business ethics whatsoever."

"They're unscrupulous cowboys. How can I help?"

"My father ordered me to stay here. I expect his anger to subside soon, but if not, I might need your assistance."

"Not a problem. We have a standing charter arrangement with Swissair. I'll come for you personally."

"Your loyalty is exemplary," the prince said. "I'll be in touch."

Lemmy put down the phone. The call had not surprised him. It was typical Elie Weiss methodology—jarring the target, who made hasty moves, precipitated exposure and defeat.

"Papa, was that a real prince?"

"Yes," Lemmy said. "He's the first-born son of an important Saudi sheik. They consider themselves royalty."

"Why did he call you?"

"I'm his banker, probably the only person he can trust." Lemmy turned on the engine, glanced over his shoulder to find a gap in traffic, and drove on.

"Does he need money?"

"He needs his father's forgiveness."

"What did he do?"

"He lied."

"That's bad." Klaus Junior brought his knees to his chest, resting his feet on the seat and hugging his legs. "Do you ever lie?"

"Well, I must keep secrets. For the bank, I mean. Our clients expect it, you understand?"

Abu Yusef stood outside, letting the sun soothe his face, and watched Bashir back up a dark-blue BMW 740iL sedan. The men unloaded wooden boxes of Kalashnikov machine guns, pistols, ammunition, and hand grenades. In all, the car and weapons cost almost everything the prince had given them. But soon their group would headline every news report in the world, and there would be more money, men, and power. He was sure of it.

Abu Yusef pulled Bashir aside and asked him to remove Latif's clothes from the bedroom. He wanted them in the car when they drove to Paris to punish the Jews.

The bus to Efrat, a West Bank settlement that had grown into a town, dropped its passengers at a shaded strip mall, where many women and a few men were shopping for the Sabbath. Rabbi Gerster asked for directions to the address he had written on a piece of paper. The reporter, Itah Orr, had run the name of Professor Lemelson's student through her sources and obtained the address. He hoped it was correct.

The apartment building had an elevator, but he took the steps to the fourth floor, finding the family name scribbled above a doorbell button. He pressed it.

The woman who opened the door looked at his black garb, reached into the pocket of her apron, and handed him a few coins. "Here. Shabbat shalom."

"No, thank you." Rabbi Gerster bowed slightly, declining the charity with a quick gesture. "I'm looking for Ayala. Is she home?"

"My daughter hasn't arrived yet. What do you want with her?"

"Professor Lemelson from Bar Ilan suggested that I speak with her. It's nothing serious."

Two little boys peeked at him from behind their mother. She tightened her head covering. "Well, I don't—"

"Hello there." Rabbi Gerster extended his hand to the older boy, who looked about ten. "My name is Abraham. What's yours?"

The boy shook his hand. "I'm Amos." He pointed at his brother. "This is Chaim."

"Hi, Chaim." Rabbi Gerster shook the little one's hand. "And do you boys know this week's Torah chapter?"

"I do," Amos said. "*Zachor.* Remember what Amalek did when we escaped from Egypt."

"Correct!" Rabbi Gerster smiled at the mother, whose face softened. "And who were the Amalekite people, Chaim?"

"They were really bad goyim," the boy said. He was not older than seven. "And they hurt the Jews and even killed some. Even that!"

"Correct. And you, Amos, do you know why God gave Amalek, an evil Gentile nation, the honor of dedicating a whole Torah chapter to them?"

"Please." The mother moved aside. "Come in."

The room had a sitting area on the left and a dining table on the right, with little space left to move around. The smell of cooking was heavy, even with the windows open.

Rabbi Gerster sat on the sofa.

The boys shared an armchair, squeezing together.

"A whole Torah chapter is a big deal, right?"

They nodded.

"So there must be a reason for this honor, yes?"

"Maybe they weren't all bad," Amos said, glancing up at his mother, who shrugged and went to the kitchen.

"But they killed Jews," Chaim protested. "That's a big sin!"

"True," Rabbi Gerster said. "But maybe the story is such an important lesson that—"

"I know!" Chaim raised his hand, as if he were in class. "To make peace!"

"That's stupid!" Amos elbowed him. "They didn't make peace! God told them to kill all of Amalek, even goats and cows!"

"Boys?" The mother reappeared, a towel in her hand. "Are you behaving?"

"You're both right," Rabbi Gerster said. "God named the chapter for Amalek because they taught us an important lesson—the difference between a real enemy and a temporary rival. An enemy we must fight to the end. But a temporary disagreement we must resolve peacefully. Do you understand?"

"To make shalom?"

"Correct." He looked at Amos. "Now, is your brother an enemy?"

Amos looked at his shoes and shook his head.

"So even when you boys fight, you still must make peace, yes?"

Both of them nodded, and Amos said, "Sorry."

"But if you see a snake about to bite your brother, do you try to make peace with it?"

They yelled in unison, "No!"

"That's the lesson of Amalek. We fight if there's no chance for peace. But with everyone else, we must give a chance to shalom. Especially between brothers, right?"

The boys looked at each other and giggled.

"Hey, guys!" A young woman carrying a backpack and a guitar came in.

"Ayala!" The boys ran to their sister and hugged her.

The mother took the bag and the guitar. "You have a visitor."

Rabbi Gerster stood.

Ayala had a kind smile and large, brown eyes that radiated intelligence. "I'm sorry but...have we met?"

"Please." He gestured at the armchair. "Only a moment of your time."

They sat opposite each other, while the mother took the boys to the kitchen. Ayala tugged at her denim skirt, making sure it covered her knees.

"I'm Rabbi Abraham Gerster."

"From Neturay Karta?" Her face expressed surprise but not hostility. As a modern-Orthodox, educated young woman, she would know about the ultra-Orthodox sect that viewed Zionism as a form of blasphemy. "What are you doing here, among us Zionist usurpers?"

He laughed. "Spoken like a future lawyer. And speaking of law, I understand you have questions about the concept of *Rodef,* yes?"

Her face paled.

"Don't worry. I'm not here to cause trouble. I've dedicated my life to keeping shalom among Jews. That's why the subject of *Rodef* interests me."

"I'm no longer interested in this subject."

"Was there a boy?"

Her cheeks flushed. "We went out a few times. He's very smart, but after a while, I got a little—"

"Scared?"

She thought for a moment. "Uncomfortable."

"Yes?"

"He's a good person, really. And very smart." Ayala looked toward the kitchen door, as if nervous that her mother would hear. "He's Sephardic. His parents came from Iraq. We're from very different backgrounds, you understand?"

Sephardic, as the inexact term was used inclusively, referred to the almost two million Jews who had been forced to escape from Lebanon, Syria, Iraq, Iran, Yemen, Egypt, Tunisia, and Morocco after the 1948 war. The Arab regimes, bitter over their failure to annihilate the new Jewish state, fanned the flames of anti-Semitism against the ancient Jewish communities that had lived among the Muslim populations for many centuries. They arrested Jews, confiscated businesses, and burned Jewish homes. The Ashkenazi Jews, who originated in Europe and were first to embrace Zionism and settle in Palestine, had taken in the huge numbers of Sephardic refugees and absorbed them into the young state of Israel. But the perception of inferiority had been slow to fade away. Ayala's parents, like many other Ashkenazi Jews, would not delight in their daughter marrying a Sephardic man.

"They would respect my choice." Ayala shrugged. "For a while, I really liked him. His ideas were intriguing. But in the end I decided to break up. It's over."

"And the idea that intrigued you most? Was it the duty to kill a person who endangers the life of another Jew?"

"The duty is not in doubt. Only the scope of it." Ayala hesitated. "Of course you should stop a person who's intentionally endangering a Jew. Torah's *Rodef* is a murderer in hot pursuit of his victim. The same goes for *Moser,* a Jew who hands over other Jews to be killed by the Gentiles. But some people argue that the rule applies more widely." She drew a large circle in the air with her hands.

"To include someone who's not actually pursuing or handing over other Jews, but who persists in actions that endanger Jews?"

"Maybe."

"Like a politician who pursues policies that imperil Jewish lives?"

"Or hands over Jewish land," Ayala said. "I mean, you could argue that the Land of Israel is as sacred as a Jewish life, so the same concept applies to land concessions, correct?"

"Are you saying that the *Rodef* and *Moser* rules require killing a Jewish leader like Prime Minister Rabin, for example, who's handing over parts of biblical Israel to the Palestinians?"

"In theory, it's a valid line of reasoning, a logical conclusion, don't you agree?"

"Was that your boyfriend's conclusion?" Rabbi Gerster leaned forward, narrowing the distance between them. "Is that why you became uncomfortable?"

"With Yoni?" She laughed. "Oh, no. Ideas don't scare me. I love to argue about ideas. I mean, no one's going to kill anyone. He was just theorizing, you know?"

"Are you sure?"

"Of course! We're law students, and Jewish law is a big thing at Bar Ilan University. We always compare modern Israeli law to the law of Talmud, okay?"

"Then what scared you about him?"

"I didn't like his friends."

"The one nicknamed Freckles?"

She nodded, surprised. "You know Freckles?"

"A lucky guess." He smiled. "I've heard of him."

"Oh." Ayala looked at the window, her face contemplative. "Yoni was secretive. I can't waste my time on someone who doesn't share, right? How can we get married if we don't know everything about each other?"

"Such as?"

"Money and stuff. Yoni has nice clothes, a new handgun—"

"He carries a gun?"

"We all do. I got a Beretta twenty-two. It's cheap, but you can't travel in the territories without a gun." She patted the pocket of her long skirt.

"What kind of a gun does he carry?"

"Also a Beretta, but bigger caliber. He let me shoot it when we went hiking in the desert. It's nice. I mean, we had fun together. Like, we drove to the Galilee and to Haifa, ate at nice restaurants. But I know his parents don't have money, so *how?*"

"He must have told you something."

She rolled her eyes. "Some story about an old Jew who likes Freckles, kind of a sponsor, wants to help religious-nationalistic young men who are dedicated to the Land of Israel."

"Did you meet this sponsor?"

"No." She laughed. "He supposedly lives in Paris."

"Did Yoni mention a name?"

"No, but I didn't believe it anyway. Why would a rich old Jew from Paris give money to some Israeli students to buy stuff and take their girlfriends to restaurants? It made no sense."

"But the money must have come from somewhere." Rabbi Gerster tugged at his beard, pondering what she'd said and whether to push any further. "It must be very frustrating for you."

"Not anymore." Ayala smiled, looking very young. "I met someone else. Really nice."

"May God bless your new relationship."

"Amen."

"Would you mind telling me Yoni's last name?"

"Yoni Adiel." She jotted down a number. "Please don't mention my name."

After sunset, when Gideon and Bathsheba returned to the apartment, Elie took Gideon to bug the phones in the prince's suite at the Hilton. On the street, Elie noticed police signs along the barricades by the synagogue: No Parking!

"Must be a big function here this coming Sabbath," Gideon said.

"This is useless." Elie stopped and leaned against one of the metal barricades. "To effectively prevent a car bomb, they must block off the street completely, ban all vehicles, and frisk pedestrians. Do they really think a terrorist cares about getting a parking ticket?"

At the Hilton, it took Gideon less than thirty seconds to bypass the cardkey system and enter the suite. He drew his gun and checked the rooms. No one was there, but it clearly served as someone's permanent living quarters.

One corner of the living area was taken by a desk and a filing cabinet. Gideon started working on the phone. Elie browsed through the files, which contained copies of contracts between Transport International El-Saud and its vendors.

"Look at this!" Gideon called Elie to the bathroom. It was vast, including a makeup station that accommodated a full-size barber chair. Inside the cabinet, arranged on shelves, were chains, hooks, nooses, studded leather straps, handcuffs, and a horse whip.

Elie shut the cabinet doors. "How stimulating."

The bathroom phones—one on the counter, another by the toilet—kept Gideon busy for a few more minutes. All bugs were voice-activated and set for the same frequency. The signals could be picked up within a quarter of a mile.

Eleven minutes later they were back in the car. Elie swallowed another pill.

———

Part Three
The Diversion

Saturday, October 21, 1995

They dressed in suits and ties, their black shoes shining. Outside the villa, it was quiet and chilly. Bashir opened the door, and Abu Yusef got into the back seat of the BMW. As they drove out the gate, he looked back over his shoulder and wondered if he would survive the day to sleep here another night. This morning's attack would be a needle prick compared to what he was planning for the Jews, a sample intended to whet Prince Abusalim's appetite and reassure him that their group had the competence to shake up the world and shoot down the Oslo Accords. But if Abu Yusef died today, his plans would die with him. Bashir had tried to convince him to assign the job to the younger men, but he had insisted that age was an advantage. The police would stop young Mideast-looking men, whereas two gray-haired gentlemen would likely be allowed to pass through uninspected. Besides, he felt an irresistible urge to take this revenge with his own hands and watch the Jews die with his own eyes.

On the radio, a French woman sang about love. He thought of Al-Mazir and Latif, both of whom he had loved and lost. Now it was the Jews' turn to lose those whom they loved.

Tanya rang the doorbell at Andre Silverman's art gallery on Avenue Junot, and the lock clicked open. She nodded at her escorts, and they drove off while she took the stairs up to the duplex above the gallery, where Andre lived with Juliette and their son, Laurent.

Andre hugged and kissed her. They had known each other since she had acquired the small bookstore on the ground floor, next to the gallery. The location in the heart of Paris, only a few hundred yards from Moulin De La Galette, made it an ideal front for a Mossad station.

Today was Laurent's Bar Mitzvah, and Andre had insisted that Tanya come over for breakfast before the synagogue service. The stately house was full of guests, who did their best to avoid collision with the myriad antique treasures, which Andre had found in estate sales and rural markets. Tanya introduced herself to Juliette's parents and widowed sister, who had flown in from Lyons the previous night, and to Andre's brother, who had driven from Antwerp with his wife and three daughters.

The large table in the dining room on the second floor was loaded with fresh baguettes, scrambled eggs, and an assortment of French cheeses. The guests gathered noisily, piling food on their plates.

A few minutes later, Laurent appeared in the dining room. His round face flushed as everybody circled him and patted his shoulders. "Mazal tov! Mazal tov!"

Andre clapped his hands. "Time to go!"

They walked to the synagogue along the quiet avenues. The men carried zippered bags made of soft blue velvet that contained their folded prayer shawls and prayer books. The women held shopping bags filled with candy. Tanya walked with Juliette, who shared in detail the difficulties she had endured to conceive and carry Laurent through a horrendous pregnancy.

The synagogue on Rue Buffault had been restored to its original, pre-war glory through the efforts of several patrons. Andre Silverman had been a pivotal force in the restoration project, especially in the details of craft and decoration. Now the names of his parents, who had died in Auschwitz, were displayed on the Wall of Memory by the entrance, along with thousands of other victims.

A police car and a black Citroën limousine were parked in front of the synagogue. Two uniformed gendarmes stood in the forecourt, chatting with a chauffeur in a visor hat. They glanced at the group entering the foyer of the synagogue, where Rabbi Dasso greeted Andre and his guests. Coats and scarves were discarded, the men entered the crowded prayer hall, and the women climbed the stairs to the second-floor mezzanine. Tanya sat next to Juliette near the railing and looked below, where the congregants shook Andre's hand and patted Laurent's shoulder. All the big names in the French art scene were here, many of them Gentiles, including Charles Devaroux, a fellow art dealer who was now minister of art and culture under President Jacques Chirac.

The rows of seats faced east, filled with men and boys in suits, ties, and colorful skullcaps. Laurent sat next to the rabbi on the dais by the Torah ark, facing the congregation.

Tanya tried to follow the prayers in the book. She had not been inside a synagogue in many years.

After an hour of silent prayers and joyous singing, the rabbi took the Torah scroll out of the ark and passed it to Laurent, who carried it to the dais. Andre Silverman joined his son, who rolled open the parchment and read the Hebrew words in a thin voice with a heavy French accent.

The Torah chapter was divided into seven, and for each part a male relative was called up to recite a blessing. For the last portion, Laurent recited, *"Blessed be God, king of the universe, for choosing us from all the nations to receive the Torah."*

He proceeded to read aloud, "Remember, O Israel, what Amalek did when you escaped from Egypt, weary and famished, how Amalek cut you down and killed your weakest. Therefore, you shall erase the nation of Amalek and leave no trace of it under the sky. You shall never forget!"

Abu Yusef watched the Jews put their holy scroll back in the ark. Their rabbi went up to the pulpit, bringing with him the chubby boy, who held a sheet of paper. Abu Yusef glanced at Bashir.

"Dear family and friends," the boy said in a trembling voice, his eyes on the paper. "Thank you for sharing this important day with us. This morning we read how God orders us to remember what Amalek did to us and take revenge, *Nekamah*, of our enemies."

Abu Yusef leaned over and whispered to Bashir, "That's us!"

Bashir placed a calming hand on Abu Yusef's knee. They were seated in the last row, all the way to the side, dressed formally like the men and boys around them. They wore skullcaps on their heads, and the prayer shawls around their necks were white with blue stripes, like the Israeli flag. But unlike everyone else, the soft blue velvet cases in their laps were not empty.

The boy looked up and smiled at a woman in the mezzanine. "We ask a question," he continued. "Why did God order King Saul to kill every Amalekite man and woman, baby and child, ox, lamb, camel, and ass without mercy?"

Abu Yusef realized he was sweating. He glanced back over his shoulder and was relieved that the doors remained shut. The gendarmes stayed outside during the service. He heard noises from above, looked up at the mezzanine, and saw the women passing around bags of candy. He took a deep breath. *Everything according to plan.*

"Amalek attacked the Israelites after God split the Red Sea for them and drowned the pursuing Egyptians. By attacking us, Amalek challenged God. That's why it was singled out for total and eternal revenge."

Bashir unzipped his blue velvet case. Abu Yusef did the same.

The boy cleared his throat. "But other than Amalek, even enemies deserve a chance to repent their cruelty and become friends. Forgiveness and peace should always prevail between Israel and its neighbors."

Abu Yusef almost sneered. *Peace! Right!*

Bashir's hand slipped into his velvet case.

"In conclusion, dear family and friends, God wishes us peace, shalom. And today, as I become a man, I thank my beloved parents for bringing me up to this occasion, and Rabbi Dasso for helping me prepare my Torah reading. Sabbath Shalom!"

Everyone stood and tossed sweets at the boy. "Mazal tov! Mazal tov!"

In the back of the prayer hall, Abu Yusef and Bashir pulled the hand grenades from their velvet cases, drew the rings from the fuses, and hurled the grenades through the rain of candy toward the podium. They dropped to the floor and covered their heads with their hands.

The explosions followed one another in rapid succession. An instant later, the two Arabs got up and ran through the rubble toward the front of the synagogue, away from the doors.

The wooden benches had smashed into one another as if hit by a giant fist, taking the congregants down, flesh and wood gritted together into a mass of red and brown. Smoke filled the air, descending slowly. The floor was strewn with body parts. Abu Yusef's shoes squeaked in the puddles of blood.

A woman up in the mezzanine shrieked, "Laurent! Laurent!"

The explosions had shattered most of the wooden dais. The boy sat upright, his back to the Torah ark. The sun shone on him through the blown windows. At the foot of the dais, a white-haired Jew slumped, his chest open. Spasms of dark blood burst out between his ribs, which protruded from the flesh like broken sticks. He didn't move. Nearby, another Jew tried to push up from the floor, his head rocking up and down. But he had no legs anymore, only stumps that oozed blood. He tried to reach down and stem the gushing blood. Slowly his head stopped rocking, and the stream of blood slowed to a trickle.

The woman in the mezzanine kept shrieking, "*Laurent!*"

The boy's eyes opened.

Abu Yusef followed his gaze and saw, through the descending smoke, the woman lean over the railing above. She cried again, "*Laurent!*"

"*Oui, Mama?*" His voice was clear, but a moment later his head bowed, his chin rested against his chest, and his gaze froze.

"Get one of them!" Bashir's voice tore Abu Yusef from momentary paralysis. He bent down and collected the Jew with no legs. With the corpse pressed to his chest, Abu Yusef followed Bashir, who was carrying a toddler with a split skull and a severed forearm.

The doors opened and the gendarmes peeked in cautiously.

The explosions tore Elie out of deep sleep. At first he thought the noise belonged in his dream. Using the wall for support, he made his way to the window. He pushed the curtains aside. Three floors below, people were running in the street.

He bent over the windowsill and looked to the right at the forecourt of the synagogue. A cloud of smoke was rising, and a small crowd formed a semi-circle around a pavement strewn with pieces of glass and wood.

His mind was maddeningly slow.

An explosion? In the synagogue? How?

It's not Abu Yusef. Couldn't be. Had no time to plan, to scout, to infiltrate.

Must be another group.

Hamas? Hezbollah? Al-Qaida? The Iranians?

More screaming!

A man with a colorful skullcap emerged from the smoke, carrying a bloody child.

Another man followed, also carrying a child. *No. Not a child. An old man without legs!*

The wounded were laid down on the pavement. A faraway siren sounded, and another one. More people ran from both ends of Rue Buffault toward the synagogue.

But against that tide of curious spectators, the two men who had carried out the first wounded walked toward Rue Chateaudun. Their suits were stained with blood, but they seemed composed and purposeful. As they passed across from his window, Elie recognized them.

Abu Yusef and Bashir Hamami!

A groan escaped his lips, and it must have been loud enough to overcome the clamor, because Abu Yusef's head turned and his eyes met Elie's.

For a brief moment, the world stood still around them.

Abu Yusef's hand went under his suit jacket, reaching for a gun, but it came out empty. He moved a thumb under his throat and hurried after Bashir.

Elie watched the two Arabs until they disappeared around the corner. He stepped back into the room and found himself on the floor, gasping for air.

The blue BMW 740iL waited with its engine on. They jumped in. Bashir barked at the driver to go. They drove for five minutes, taking sharp turns, verifying that no one was following.

"There!" Bashir pointed to a pay phone near a metro station.

The driver stopped at the curb and Bashir stepped out. Abu Yusef joined him. They put their heads together as the phone rang at the newsroom of *Paris-1*. Like all incoming calls, Abu Yusef knew it would be recorded, and he had instructed Bashir in advance what to say.

"*Paris-Une. Oui?*"

"This is the Abu Yusef group." Bashir spoke English.

"Yes?"

"We attacked the synagogue on Rue Buffault. Our freedom fighters committed this brave attack under the command of our leader, Abu Yusef, the future president of Palestine."

"Wait a minute! Who are you?"

"Our leader is Abu Yusef, the future president of Palestine. We will continue our struggle until Palestine is free again! Long live Palestine!"

Bashir hung up, they got back in the car, and the driver hit the gas, merging back into traffic.

The first wave of ambulances departed with the bloodied victims to several Paris hospitals. Under gathering clouds, uniformed gendarmes loaded black plastic bags into the hearses. The only sound was the crackling of glass fragments under their boots.

Gideon and Bathsheba returned from Ermenonville after hearing the news on the radio. They found Elie in the crowd, a small man in a gray coat and a wool cap pulled down over his ears. He looked the same as the other Parisian spectators, ogling the scene of disaster, memorizing the ghastly details to be shared with friends in the local café. But at a closer look, Elie's gray face showed no curiosity. The black eyes narrowed to hateful slits, the lips pressed together tightly.

When the last body bag was gone, a fireman rolled a hose off a fire engine and began washing the pavement.

"Seventeen dead," Elie said. "Let's go."

As soon as they entered the apartment, Bathsheba exploded. "I told you we should shoot Abu Yusef in Senlis! It's your fault!"

"Your assumption is wrong." Elie looked at her coldly. "This bombing wasn't done by Abu Yusuf. And if you disapprove of my command, you may leave. Reapply to Mossad, see if they take you now."

"She has a point," Gideon said. "We should have—"

"Abu Yusef didn't have time to plan something like this," Elie said. "This was done by someone else, maybe even the PLO itself, trying to jack up the price for the next phase of the Oslo negotiations."

"Didn't you hear the news?" Bathsheba followed him into the room. "Abu Yusef took credit!"

"You believe the news?"

Gideon watched Elie's face. Was he lying?

"Taking credit means nothing," Elie continued. "Abu Yusef was first to call a TV station. An Algerian group also took credit, claiming they targeted the minister of art and culture. Others will follow. You'll see."

Bathsheba seemed unconvinced.

"We're leaving," Elie said. "This apartment is no longer safe for us." He gathered his papers into a small pile, topped by his heavy copy of the Bible, a decorated edition that was bound between two plates of carved wood.

They packed their clothes, equipment, and weapons—two mini-Uzis and three handguns with silencers.

Gideon drove. On Rue de Rivoli, across from the public gardens, Elie told him to park at the curb.

No. 4 Palace de La Concorde had once been a hotel, but in the sixties an American law firm had turned it into its Parisian branch office. Now it had a wood-paneled lobby, which was bustling with men in business suits and strained faces. Elie led the way to a bank of pay phones in the back and ran a phone card through the slot. Gideon noticed the first numbers he was punching. Forty-one for Switzerland. One for Zurich. Then Elie moved and blocked the view.

Paula started working on a beef stew for dinner. The pot was hissing on the stove while she sliced a large sweet onion. The telephone rang. "Can one of you gentlemen get it?"

Klaus Junior moved the white knight to B-4. "Check!"

"What?" Lemmy examined the board. "Are you trying to kill my queen?"

The phone on the kitchen counter rang again.

Paula said, "Guys?"

"Sorry," Lemmy said, "but we're at war here!"

She dropped the kitchen knife on the cutting board and picked up the receiver. "Hello?" She listened for a moment. "Herr Horch will be right with you."

Lemmy got up. "Don't move anything. I've memorized the battlefield, and I'm winning."

"You're dreaming, Papa!"

He twisted his face at Paula, who picked up the knife threateningly. He circled her at a safe distance and snatched the receiver. "Yes?"

"Are you watching the news?" The voice was meek and scratchy, but Lemmy recognized it instantly.

"Excuse me?"

Paula gave him a curious look.

Elie Weiss coughed. "Turn on your TV."

Lemmy's hand tightened around the receiver. Elie had never called him at home.

"Watch the report from Paris."

"What is this about?" Lemmy glanced at Paula, whose eyes moistened from the sliced onion.

Elie said, "Here's what I need you to do. First—"

"I beg your pardon." Lemmy tried to keep his voice formal, professional. "Please call my office on Monday morning. I'm sure we can assist you."

"Shut up!" Elie's voice was still hushed, but the rage came through clearly. "Security is not important anymore."

Lemmy wiped the sweat off his forehead with the sleeve of his shirt. He could feel Paula and Klaus Junior watching him.

"Listen carefully. First, as soon as the prince contacts you, call me at the Hilton Paris under the name Rupert Danzig. Second, you must take over the bank ASAP. We're out of time."

Lemmy almost choked. He couldn't believe Elie was saying this on an open line. "This is highly irregular—"

"Get rid of your father-in-law. Tomorrow. It's an order!"

"Who is this?"

"Remember who you are! *Nekamah!*"

The line went dead.

"Is everything all right?" Paula asked.

"An odd duck. Some clients are just…weird."

"Papa? What's your next move?"

"Coming." Lemmy could hardly believe what had just happened. Elie's voice on his home phone, with Paula and Klaus Junior a few feet away. Such an invasion was never supposed to happen. Complete separation was the only way things worked. Otherwise Wilhelm Horch's life would collapse like a tower of cards.

Get rid of your father-in-law. Tomorrow. It's an order!

Was Elie losing it? Armande Hoffgeitz as a target? A job inside the family? It was madness! Why the sudden urgency?

The news!

"Papa? Are you playing? *Check!*"

Lemmy advanced a pawn, an irrelevant move.

Klaus Junior moved in for the kill and announced, "*Check mate!*"

"Great game." Lemmy got up and walked out of the kitchen, not looking at Paula. He could not face her.

In the living room, he turned the TV on to CNN.

Klaus Junior followed him. Lemmy put his arm around the boy's shoulders, and they watched the broadcast from Paris, a procession of injured people and body bags moving across the screen.

Everything was white—the walls, the ceiling, the door, the sheets that covered Tanya. Even the curtain hanging from a circular rail around the bed was white. A woman appeared, her coat white, hair white, face white, only her lips were red as rose petals. "Ah! Madame is awake!"

Tanya tried to sit up. "Am I dead?"

"Not at all," the woman said matter of fact, as if responding to a normal question. She pointed to an embroidered logo on her coat: *Saint Antoine Hospital.*

The pain appeared suddenly, as if someone hit her head with a hard object. Tanya groaned and touched a bandage on her right temple.

"Careful." The nurse held her hand. "You had a concussion. Do you remember?"

It took a moment for the memory to surface. "The synagogue!"

"Yes, terrible. The detectives would like to speak with you when you're ready."

As soon as the nurse left, Tanya got out of bed. She was dizzy from the pain in her head, but this was no time for self-pity.

The cabinet doors were not locked. Her dress, which was dark enough to hide the bloodstains, was draped over a hanger, and her shoes rested on a shelf next to her purse, which contained false identification papers and a credit card that could not be traced. Tanya got dressed, rinsed her face in the white basin, let her hair down over the bandage, and left.

———

Sunday,
October 22, 1995

Prince Abusalim spent the night in a sparse room with only a prayer rug to cushion the concrete. At dawn, he was brought to his father's chamber, and they prayed together. No words were exchanged, and Abusalim figured this was his punishment—a night of seclusion, discomfort, and repentance.

Within an hour of sunrise, the air was already warm and dry, the palm trees still, and the servants hushed with dread. Sheik Da'ood az-Zubayr kneeled, his forehead on the carpet, and completed his prayers. Hajj Ibn Saroah helped him rise.

Prince Abusalim touched his forehead down once more and got up. The long galabiya covered him as a cloak, reaching down to the plain sandals. He could smell his own body odor and longed to soak in a foam bath, sit on the balcony in view of the Eiffel Tower, and sip chardonnay while browsing the *Wall Street Journal*. He took his father's hand and kissed it. "Thank you for making me realize my errors—"

The sheik pulled his hand away and left the room with the hajj.

Prince Abusalim followed, puzzled by his father's behavior. Two limousines waited at the foot of the marble steps. The first had already departed when Prince Abusalim got into the second. It drove in silence down the road toward the airstrip.

He twisted his face at the bittersweet smell of smoke and animal manure that drifted over from the tribesmen's huts.

They climbed into the Boeing 747, and the doors were shut. The front sitting room was paneled with gold and thick cushions. He went upstairs to the miniature mosque on the upper-deck and sat with an open Koran. The carpeted floor floated on a swivel to allow it to turn toward Mecca no matter where the plane was heading.

The engines roared and the pilots began taxiing. The plane was less than two years old, equipped with state-of-the-art flight instrumentation, including a live link to the command center at the main Royal Saudi Air Force, enabling the pilots to view air traffic in every part of the region, including neighboring Kuwait, Iran, Iraq, and the Gulf Emirates.

After takeoff, they turned west toward the Red Sea. The prince pushed aside the silk curtain and looked out the window. The yellow desert was vast, stretching through the horizon, its monotony disrupted only by an occasional nomads' encampment, a handful of camels and sheep grazing on a faded stain of greenery.

The hajj appeared at the door. "Your father wishes to see you."

On the main level, in the rear suite, a large TV was playing. At first the screen was red. Then the camera zoomed out from a man's open chest and shifted to his face, which was twisted, mouth open in a last scream. It moved across a demolished hall, resting briefly on a shattered body, a severed hand on a bed of charred prayer books, a woman kneeling by a boy who sat upright, his head slumped forward, unresponsive to her pleas. In the background, a recording of a short conversation was played:

"*Paris-Une. Oui?*"

"This is the Abu Yusef group."

"Yes?"

"We attacked the synagogue on Rue Buffault. Our freedom fighters committed this brave attack under the command of our leader, Abu Yusef, the future president of Palestine."

"Wait a minute! Who are you?"

"Our leader is Abu Yusef, the future president of Palestine. We will continue our struggle until Palestine is free again! Long live Palestine!"

The TV screen again filled with red, focusing on a stained sheet over a dead body.

Prince Abusalim felt his knees go soft. This was the reason his father had ordered him into seclusion last night! He kneeled and bowed, his forehead to the carpet. He remained in this position until the plane landed near Mecca.

Two Mercedes sedans waited at the end of the runway. Again the sheik and the hajj went in the first, Prince Abusalim in the second. The sun was high already, the yellow desert surrounded by dark peaks—in the east, Jabel Ajyad and Jabel Qubays, in the northeast, Jabel Hira, where Mohammed had once found seclusion. They drove down the Al-Mudda'ah Avenue, which was crowded with pilgrims. Ancient Mecca had been the oasis on the caravan route connecting the Mediterranean coast with Arabia, Africa, and Asia. But since Mohammed had returned here in 630 AD, it had become a city of religious fervor. How he missed Paris! But not the bloody sights from Abu Yusef's synagogue attack. What unfortunate timing, just as his father was going to forgive him!

Prince Abusalim knew he must convince his father that the attack was part of a holy jihad. The Jews had brought it upon themselves. Unlike Arafat, Abu Yusef had the stomach to continue fighting. One day the Jews would tire of death and sorrow, leave the Middle East to its rightful Arab owners, and go to America or Canada, where many of them already lived safely among the Christians. And Abu Yusef would rule Palestine, with the power to appoint the new mufti of Jerusalem.

Confident in his grand plan, Prince Abusalim was ready to grovel before his father in this holy place and put on a show of solemn penitence—a small price to pay for the glory awaiting him down the road.

The cars stopped at the gates to the vast courtyard of the el-Harem Mosque. They were greeted by a group of az-Zubayr tribesmen, who led the way across the huge courtyard, through the noise and dust, toward the black Ka'abah.

The sheik stood in front of the giant singed cube. He looked up at the holiest shrine of Islam—the building that Ibrahim and Ishmael, his son by Hagar, had built together as a replica of God's house in heaven.

Hajj Vahabh Ibn Saroah beckoned Prince Abusalim to his father's side. The prince knelt in the dust. He prepared to bow for prayers, but paused. Something was wrong.

The sheik nodded at the hajj, closed his eyes, and began whispering verses from the Koran.

The hajj drew his crooked blade. "Extend your hand forward, thief!"

Prince Abusalim froze with fear. He could not comprehend this terrible turn of events. He had expected his father to demand that he prayed, maybe even crawled in the dust to beg forgiveness. But to suffer the fate of a common thief? "Father! I beg you!"

"You stole. You pay." Hajj Vahabh Ibn Saroah raised his shabriya, its blade pointing to the sky. "Your right hand!"

"No!" Prince Abusalim tried to rise, but two of the men held him down. "I need my hand," he cried. "Father! Don't do this to me!"

The only response from the sheik was more verses, recited in a louder voice.

The hajj reached down, grabbed Prince Abusalim's wrist, and pulled it forward, holding it tightly.

The prince could barely breathe. He imagined his severed hand dropping to the yellow sand, twitching with remnants of life. "Father! No!"

The sheik's voice grew even louder, the verses uttered in quick succession, drowning out his son's pleas.

The sun reflected in the crooked blade as Prince Abusalim felt his wrist pulled forcefully, extended before him, his open palm facing up, pale as a fearful face.

Tanya stood at the window while a group of Mossad agents searched the apartment on Rue Buffault. Elie and his two agents must have departed in a hurry, leaving behind food, towels, linen, and a few audio books. The street below was quiet. The synagogue forecourt had been cleaned up, but orange tape still blocked access to the building. A police car parked at the curb with two officers inside.

Tanya touched her forehead, still tender. She had searched her memory repeatedly, but could not remember any suspicious person or unusual behavior prior to the explosions. She had not even seen the grenades fly, because at that moment she was reaching down into a bag of candy. The darkness had lifted only when she woke up in the hospital.

"We're done here," one of her agents said. He pointed to the dismantled box of the computer. "They ripped out the hard drive."

"Pack up everything. I want hair samples, gun residue, prints, anything you can find."

She was already in the hallway when another agent stopped her. He held up an empty pill bottle. "Found it behind the bed. Pain killers. No patient's name, though. It's from a pharmacy near Gare du Nord."

"Go see the pharmacist," Tanya said. "Samples go to doctors who do regular business at the shop. This could be our lead."

The hajj sliced downward with the crooked blade. It sank into the flesh of the open palm. Prince Abusalim flinched and let out a cry. The hajj pulled the shabriya sideways, carving the flesh, and let go of the prince's wrist. He wiped the blade on his galabiya and slid it into the sheath.

Prince Abusalim pressed his hands together and fell forward, his face in the sand. His hand was on fire, wet with blood, but the pain was mixed with relief. His father could have ordered the hand severed completely, as done to ordinary thieves, but instead his palm was cut symbolically, the wrist unharmed, the fingers working normally.

Sheik az-Zubayr knelt in the sand and bowed before Allah. The men around them did the same, and for a few moments the small group was an island of stillness in the midst of a bustling sea of pilgrims.

The hajj helped Sheik az-Zubayr to his feet. Prince Abusalim remained bowed, more out of feebleness than of devoutness. The kafiya fell from his head, and his unkempt black hair turned gray from the dust. One of the men bandaged the wound while the prince fought back tears of pain and relief.

In Zurich, the pastor spoke about gratitude for God's gift of life on earth. The old church of the Fraumünster, with its towering stained-glass windows, glowed on sunny days, and this Sunday was especially glorious. Lemmy sat in the front row with his wife, son, and father-in-law. The church was almost full, though most were tourists. Every Zurich guidebook recommended the Fraumünster for its Chagall windows, whose incredibly vivid biblical figures dominated the sanctuary in bold colors. Lemmy was tickled by the irony—a Christian place of worship, glorified by the creations of a Jewish artist.

He felt Klaus Junior squeeze his hand as they stood to sing a hymn. Looking up at the impossibly high window depicting Jesus, he wondered what Chagall had been thinking as he painted the man whose life and death had inspired two millennia of Christian anti-Semitism, of bloody crusades, riotous burnings at the stake, a torturous inquisition, deadly pogroms, and a Holocaust perpetrated by Nazis bearing a swastika—a version of Christ's cross with twisted tips. Illuminated by the unseasonal sun, the face of Jesus glowed as if it had an internal source of energy. The primary colors signaled joy, but on closer inspection Lemmy saw no happiness in the face of Chagall's Jesus. His expression was severe, almost angry, glaring down at the full church, as if the hymned prayers were nothing but distasteful banter. Had this been Chagall's private joke—to accept the hefty fee raised by Armande Hoffgeitz and his colleagues back in the sixties for the beautification of the ancient church, only to deliver a towering portrait of their savior as an angry Jew, his face expressing revulsion at their misuse of his name to justify mass murders of his kin?

Lemmy realized his father-in-law was watching him. They smiled at each other and continued to sing. Klaus Junior stood between them, holding both their hands, his thin voice sounding over the adults' chorus. He was secure in his world of church and school, of doting parents and a loving grandfather. How would he react when told of Armande's death? How well would a ten-year-old recover from the shock of hearing that his grandfather was shot by an assassin? And it could be worse! Every assassination on Lemmy's secret record had been accomplished under the cover of anonymity, a quick jab of violence in a faraway location, followed by immediate departure, leaving no trace. He was a professional, his training was excellent and his preparations meticulous. He had never before feared capture, even when Elie had sent him on uniquely dangerous jobs. In his mind, the survival of the Jewish people was more important than the fate of one man, including himself. But what about the fate of one boy? What, Lemmy wondered, if he got caught this time, exposed as Herr Hoffgeitz's killer? After all, being the next in line to lead the bank, he would automatically become a suspect. And this was Zurich, the place where he lived and worked and possessed a wide circle of acquaintances, which would make the scandal even worse. How could Klaus Junior survive the loss of both his father and grandfather at the same time in such horrific, outrageous circumstances? This was a risk Lemmy could not take. He would not chance breaking his son's heart!

Elie's admonishment rang in Lemmy's ears. *Your wife and son are Gentiles. Goyim. They're your cover. Nothing more!*

The Boeing 747 brought them back to the az-Zubayr oasis. The sheik's personal physician sewed up Prince Abusalim's hand. He changed into a clean galabiya and went to bid his father farewell.

The sheik embraced his son. "I now understand that Allah wanted me to see my own error in allowing my son to live among the infidels, where evil temptations led you to stumble."

"Don't blame yourself, Father. It was my error. But don't worry. It won't happen again."

"We must remove you from the den of sins. Go back to Paris and wrap up our business there. Have all the files and your personal possessions packed up and ready. I will fly over next week in person to bring you home."

Home! All he could do was bow so that his father couldn't see the disgust on his face.

"You will live right here by my side, with your wives and children and our tribesmen. It's where you belong, Abusalim."

The prospect nauseated the prince, and he struggled to control his voice. "That would be...wonderful."

Hajj Ibn Saroah escorted him through the long hallways. "Do not disappoint your father again."

Prince Abusalim did not respond.

"I haven't told him everything."

"Everything?"

"The bribes from other vendors. I trust you will return the money to each one—"

"Stay out of it!" The prince's sharp voice hid his panic. The situation was worse than he had imagined. "How dare you spy on my affairs?"

The hajj held the door for the prince, and they stepped outside into the bright sun. A black limousine was waiting at the bottom of the steps to drive him to the plane.

"Have a safe trip, Excellency. May Allah—"

"Don't mention Allah!" Prince Abusalim shook a fist in the hajj's face, realizing too late that it was his injured hand, which now pulsated with pain. "You're a slave who forgot his place!"

Hajj Ibn Saroah bowed and walked back to the house.

As soon as the Lear jet began taxiing down the runway, Prince Abusalim pulled off the kafiya and galabiya and threw them on the floor. He sat in his underwear on the wide chair and yelled, "Come here!"

An attendant walked in and blushed at the sight of the prince.

"Jack Daniel's!"

"Excellency, we are not out of Saudi airspace yet—"

"On the rocks! And bring the bottle!"

In Jerusalem, the day of study for Neturay Karta men didn't end until close to midnight. The last group left the synagogue, still arguing about a Talmudic question of animal sacrifice, which had occupied them since that morning: Would one cow satisfy the collective sacrificial obligations at the temple on the Passover holiday or was each pilgrim required to bring his own animal for slaughter at the altar?

Along in the silent synagogue, Rabbi Gerster turned off the lights, locked the front doors, and went out into the cold night. He walked down to the gate and turned right. Halfway up Shivtay Israel Street, a car flashed its headlights. He got in.

"Almost gave up on you." Itah Orr wore a scarf over her head, tied loosely under her chin.

"I didn't want anyone to notice me leaving."

"How did it go with Ayala?"

"Very well. She's a lovely young woman. We need to take a look at former boyfriend, Yoni Adiel, also a law student at Bar Ilan. Apparently he suggested that the Talmudic law of *Rodef* applies to politicians who hand over parts of the land of Israel to the Arabs."

"That's all? He's not the only one making this argument. I don't have time to go around engaging right wingers in theological debates. It's a waste of time."

"The girl says he's got money to spend but no regular job and no family support. He hinted that the funds came from a rich sponsor who likes Freckles."

"Who's the sponsor?"

"She only knew that he was an elderly man living in Paris." Rabbi Gerster suspected Elie Weiss was that sponsor, but that was not a name he would mention to anyone. "But the combination of cash and know-how in guerilla resistance, such as the ILOT manual you gave me, indicates a high level of competency. Go to your sources and find out everything possible about Yoni Adiel."

"If you're right," Itah said, "this story might be much bigger than a group of right-wing youths harassing a few Arabs."

"Follow the money. That's the key." He opened the door to leave, but shut it when the interior light came on. "Have you heard from Freckles? Anything going on with ILOT?"

"He told me to attend the large Likud rally at the Zion Square on Saturday night."

"If these guys have money for girlfriends, restaurants, and handguns, they could afford more serious weapons."

"I'll make some calls and let you know."

"Good. Once we have the facts, I'll corner Yoni Adiel."

"Why would he talk to you?"

"He's a fundamentalist Jew. You think he would pass up an opportunity to talk shop with Rabbi Abraham Gerster of Neturay Karta—"

"—who doesn't believe in God?" Itah grinned in the darkness.

"Shush." He put his finger to his lips. "That's our secret."

———

Monday,
October 23, 1995

At the Hilton in Paris, Elie took the elevator down to the lobby and found a bank of pay phones near the restrooms. He called the Hoffgeitz Bank in Zurich and asked for Günter Schnell.

"*Guten Morgen, Herr Schnell,*" Elie said.

"Who is this?"

"Untersturmführer Rupert Danzig. Remember me?"

The sound of air sucked in a shocked inhalation was followed by a long silence. "Please hold."

After a few minutes, two clicks sounded, and another voice came on. "Armande Hoffgeitz speaking. What is this about?"

"Herr President?" Elie waited for a couple of hotel guests to pass by on their way to the restrooms. "This is Untersturmführer Rupert Danzig."

"Who?"

"It's been a long time, but here I am again, calling on behalf of your old friend, Oberstgruppenführer Klaus von Koenig." Elie spoke German with an eastern accent, an area until recently under Soviet communist control.

"That's impossible!" The banker's voice was shaking. "I don't know who you are!"

"I think you do, Herr Hoffgeitz."

"Do not call here!"

"But surely you want to hear from dear Klaus, yes?"

"I will summon the police! This is Zurich, not some lawless East German province!"

"The police?" Elie chuckled. "Perhaps you should consult your lawyers before contacting the authorities. Even Swiss law forbids misappropriation of clients' funds. It's a serious felony."

"How dare you! This bank has never lost a deposit from any client—"

"Including Klaus von Koenig?" Elie didn't expect a response. "If anyone should call the police, it should be me, don't you think?"

There was a loud bang as if someone hit the desk in frustration.

"Very good," Elie said. "Please make sure the records are in good order for my inspection. I will see you soon. *Auf Wiedersehen!*"

After dropping Klaus Junior off at school, Lemmy drove to the bank. As he climbed the stairs, Günter was coming down, his face ashen. "Günter? Are you feeling ill?"

"Ah, Herr Horch." He paused, looked up toward the next floor, and continued on his way down, mumbling something incoherent.

Christopher was at his desk. "Prince Abusalim az-Zubayr called. He just landed in Paris. He'll call from his hotel."

Lemmy went into his office and shut the door. "Here we go," he said out loud. He called the Hilton in Paris and asked for Rupert Danzig's room.

After a few rings, a woman answered. "Who is this?" She said it as an Israeli, and he assumed she was the agent he'd seen by the Galeries Lafayette.

"I'd like to speak with E.W. please."

"E.W. is out right now," she said, switching to English with an even sharper Israeli accent. "A message?"

"Tell him that the prince has landed."

"Thank you." She hung up.

The computer completed its boot-up process. After two separate pass codes, the live video menu appeared with the list of the cameras: On the third floor, the interior of Herr Hoffgeitz's office and the anteroom with Günter's desk, on the second floor, Christopher's desk just outside Lemmy's door, and on the first floor, the large room where the account managers worked. Each camera was smaller than a fingernail, built into a smoke detector, together with a pin-sized microphone. His computer was set up by the Dutch specialist to operate all cameras remotely.

He selected Herr Hoffgeitz's office.

The chair at the desk was vacant, the office quiet. Lemmy used the arrows on his keyboard to turn the camera left and right.

No sign of his father-in-law.

As his finger reached to hit the escape button, Lemmy heard an odd sound, like an abrupt whizzing. He moved the camera again, searching the empty office. At the bottom of the screen a black object appeared. It grew as he aimed the camera lower, closer to the door.

A shoe.

The whizzing sounded again.

Lemmy made the camera shift to the right. A face appeared. Armande Hoffgeitz was on the floor, his eyes closed. He breathed with a whizzing.

This would be Armande's fourth heart attack, Lemmy thought. A few more minutes and he would be dead of natural causes—no need to plan and execute a job or fight Elie over it.

He closed the video program, and Armande Hoffgeitz's face disappeared from the screen. All he had to do was sit tight for a few more minutes, let the old man take his last few breaths.

Lemmy's gaze wandered to the desk and met Paula's laughing eyes in a photograph, standing with Klaus Junior. She loved her father, and the boy loved his grandfather. Lemmy imagined them crying at the news, sobbing by the open coffin, kneeling at the gravestone—

"Damn!" He ran out of his office, startling Christopher, and sprinted upstairs. The door was slightly open. Herr Hoffgeitz was lying behind it. Lemmy pushed until there was enough space to squeeze in.

Christopher followed him.

"Call an ambulance!" There was no pulse, or it was too weak to detect. Lemmy shoved his fingers into Armande's mouth and pulled on the tongue. With the airway clear, he began resuscitation.

G ideon watched Elie walk into the suite, find a chair, and sit down, panting heavily.

"Someone called," Bathsheba said. "A man with a very nice voice."

Elie pulled off his wool cap. "The message?"

"The prince has landed."

Black rings circled Elie's eyes. He pressed his chest and coughed again.

"I'm listening to his phones," Gideon said, pointing to the equipment. "Nothing yet."

Bathsheba pulled a juice bottle from the fridge. "I hate waiting like this. We need to take the initiative. What if Abu Yusef drops another bomb?"

"*Another?* He didn't attack the synagogue," Elie said, "and he won't act until he gets more money."

Bathsheba was unfazed. "How do you know the prince will contact Abu Yusef? Maybe they've already arranged it or maybe he'll call from a public pay phone, like you do all the time to hide things from us—which is insulting, by the way."

"You miss the point," Elie said, ignoring her gripe. "Prince Abusalim is no passive donor, but a businessman with an ambitious agenda. And he's too spoiled to be inconvenienced by pay phones. Especially now, after he almost lost everything, he'll be even more eager to secure his birthright. He will lead us to Abu Yusef, and we'll take them both down."

"What birthright?" Bathsheba laughed. "He's a rich Saudi with a taste for rough sex."

"Not so simple," Gideon said. "The last Quraysh to rule Mecca was Abd Allah ibn az-Zubayr—a direct ancestor of Prince Abusalim, who's next in line to lead this old and bitter dynasty."

"That's right," Elie said. "His dreams of prominence have deep roots in history. He won't wait for another quarrel with his father." Resting his hand on the carved wooden cover of his bible, Elie added, "It's a story as old as time."

"I think we should break into his suite as soon as he arrives," Bathsheba said, "and start chopping off his toes one by one until he tells us where to find Abu Yusef."

"You're so eager to inflict pain." Elie twisted his face, the skin as taut as wax paper over his facial bones. "Pain is a fine tool for the right occasion. In this case, inflicting pain on the prince is like using a screwdriver on a nail. He doesn't know Abu Yusef's hiding place, and therefore he'd be useless to us without his toes."

Gideon laughed, but Bathsheba pressed on. "So that's it? We wait for another transfer to Senlis and follow Abu Yusef home? And then what? How are you planning to get through all those men protecting him?"

The medics arrived within minutes and took over the resuscitation effort. Lemmy sat down and watched them work with efficiency and skill until they brought back a pulse.

When they rolled Herr Hoffgeitz out of the building, a few spectators stood on the pavement by the waiting ambulance.

"Call Paula," Lemmy told Christopher. "Tell her I'll meet her at the hospital." He climbed in after the gurney, the doors closed, and the ambulance sped away.

Armande Hoffgeitz was admitted to the cardiac ICU at Zurich University Hospital. Paula arrived moments later, and so did Armande's long-time physician, Dr. Spilman, who went in to consult with the hospital staff.

An hour later, Dr. Spilman came out to speak with them. He hugged Paula, who had known him since childhood. "It's not good," he said. "His condition has stabilized, but it's too early to predict the chances of recovery."

"He's a strong man," Paula said. "Look, he's still alive, right?"

"Only because of this young man." Dr. Spilman patted Lemmy's shoulder. "Another minute or two, and he would have left us forever."

Paula stayed with her father, and Lemmy took a taxi back to the bank. Christopher was waiting for him. They hurried up the stairs.

Günter stood in front of Herr Hoffgeitz's door. His lips trembled.

"It's touch and go," Lemmy said. "He's very ill."

Günter did not move from the door. He took off his glasses and began shining them nervously with his tie.

"Dr. Spilman and Paula are with him." Lemmy took a step closer. "I'd like to check his office, in case he took some medications before—"

"I've already checked. No medications in there."

"I must insist."

"But Herr Hoffgeitz left instructions for such an event." Günter pulled a sheet of paper from his breast pocket. "I am responsible for all his accounts. Me alone!"

"For up to thirty days—while I run the bank's affairs on behalf of the family."

"Maybe longer. The board of directors shall meet and decide."

"Their job is to appoint a qualified person to take over. Do you feel qualified to run this bank?" Not waiting for an answer, Lemmy turned to go.

"Would you like to see the instructions?"

"I have my own copy." Halfway down the stairs, Lemmy paused. "Were you in Herr Hoffgeitz's office when he collapsed?"

Günter stepped back as if physically assaulted. "Of course not! I would have called for help!"

"You seemed upset when I came in this morning."

Günter hesitated. "We received a phone call. Very disturbing."

"Why?"

He clearly did not want to say any more, but the desire to defend himself tipped the scales. "A man called, pretending to represent someone else."

"Who?"

"He has done it before. Many years ago."

"Done what?"

"Pretended to represent someone else."

"Who?"

"An old friend of Herr Hoffgeitz."

"Let me see if I get it straight." Lemmy blew air in feigned frustration. "Many years ago a man called—"

"Visited. In person."

"When?"

"In sixty-seven."

"Twenty-eight years ago?"

Günter nodded. "He had the signed ledger that recorded all of the deposits, but he didn't have the account number and the password."

"So he went away, and after all these years, he called again this morning, claiming to speak for an old friend of Herr Hoffgeitz. I assume that friend still has an account with us, yes?"

"It's complicated." Günter seemed ready to collapse. "Herr Hoffgeitz was very angry."

Bathsheba brought Chinese takeout. Elie wasn't hungry. He stayed in the bedroom, reading his bible with a cigarette in hand. The two of them ate outside on the balcony, Gideon with a paperback edition of Robert Ludlum's *The Bourne Identity* and Bathsheba with the binoculars, examining every detail on the imposing structure of the Eiffel Tower. Below, heavy traffic snarled across the Seine River on Pont de Bir Hakeim.

When the sun went down, Gideon went inside and lay on the sofa to read.

Close to midnight, the lights blinked on the eavesdropping equipment. He grabbed the headset and listened. Bathsheba called Elie from the bedroom.

When the conversation ended, Gideon took off the headset. He shook his head. "Unbelievable! Just unbelievable!"

"Play it from the beginning," Elie said.

The prince said, "Hello?"

"Allah's blessings, Excellency." The caller spoke with an Arabic accent.

"*Insha'Allah.*"

"Your generosity was put to good use. The Palestinian revolution is indebted to you forever."

Prince Abusalim hesitated for a moment. "The suffering of our Palestinian brothers is a bleeding wound in the heart of every Arab."

"Indeed, indeed." Abu Yusef exhaled audibly. "May Allah open the eyes of our more fortunate brothers so they follow your example."

"Your courage is certain to break through their hardened souls. Though next time you should care not to hurt the French, our hosts."

"Indeed it was unfortunate." Abu Yusef sighed. "But when you cut wood, chips fall. We are fighting for the Haram El-Sharif, which deserves your guardianship, as destiny has prescribed, to spread the rule of Allah under the Koran."

"*Insha'Allah.*"

"Our operation last week was just the beginning. Allah will bring us victory. And he will bless you with fortunes ten times your generosity."

"Yes," said Prince Abusalim, "I think He will. How much do you need?"

"The fight is long and costly. Very costly."

"Truth is, I'm having some difficulties right now."

"I understand." Abu Yusef paused. "Can we help?"

"There is a man who stands in my way. He will be in Paris soon."

"We shall be honored to remove that man from your way."

"Five million dollars."

"Excellency!" Abu Yusef uttered a strange chuckle, probably out of shock at the size of the reward. "Your friendship alone is a sufficient gift. But of course, we accept!"

"Good. I'll arrange to transfer half the amount. Call me on Wednesday morning for the details. The other half will be paid after you remove him."

"Agreed! And who is that dog, that filthy infidel, who dared to stand in your way?"

Elie pressed the stop button. He took a piece of paper, scribbled on it, and showed it to Gideon. "Is this the target?"

"Correct." He looked at Elie with astonishment. "How did you know?"

Elie put his hand on the thick bible. "There are no new stories. It's all in here." He pointed at the recorder. "Make a copy of the tape."

"Hey," Bathsheba said, "I want to hear the end!"

"The end is near." Elie went back to the bedroom. "Wake me up at eight."

———

Tuesday, October 24, 1995

The three of them waited outside until the doctors completed morning rounds in the ICU. Paula explained to Klaus Junior what had happened to his grandfather and how the doctors were trying to help him recover.

The room was painted light blue, with framed posters of greenery and water. Armande Hoffgeitz's eyes were closed and various tubes entered his body. Steady beeps came from the heart monitor above the bed.

"Hi, Grandpa." The boy touched the hand that rested on the sheet. "I have to go to school now. Get better so I can see you later, okay?"

Paula and Lemmy followed him out of the room.

"Is Grandpa going to die?"

Lemmy kneeled, his face level with his son's. "We don't know yet. But he's very ill. Will you pray for him?"

The boy nodded.

Paula smiled through her tears.

Lemmy took him to school and drove to the bank. Christopher had summoned the staff to a conference room. Lemmy gave them a brief update on his father-in-law's medical condition and prognosis.

Herr Diekman, the most senior account manager, stood up. "All of us pray for Herr Hoffgeitz's quick and full recovery. In the meantime, we have complete confidence in your leadership."

"Thank you. Paula and I appreciate your support and friendship at this difficult time."

Everyone was silent for a moment.

"Being one of the oldest institutions in this city," Lemmy continued, "the Hoffgeitz Bank is a symbol of stability. We take pride in our superb and uninterrupted client service. As vice president, I have assumed all administrative and managerial responsibilities for the bank. Any and all account transactions that exceed the equivalent of ten thousand dollars, cumulative for a single day, require my signature—including the accounts owned by Herr Hoffgeitz's clients, which are under the supervision of Herr Schnell."

Günter, who was standing against the wall, nodded. The other men exchanged glances around the table, but no one questioned the instructions.

"If you have any concerns, please come to me. Our message to our clients and the banking community is that business continues as usual at the Hoffgeitz Bank."

He returned to his office and spent an hour returning phone calls and answering mail. Before lunch, he summoned Christopher. "I was wondering, has Günter completed entering the data into the system?"

"Yes. I've followed his progress on my computer. He has inserted numbers for all of the accounts that Herr Hoffgeitz handles personally, which amounts to less than thirty accounts actually. Is there a problem?"

"My father-in-law had a heart attack right after a mysterious phone call regarding an account of an old friend. Why?"

"Maybe your wife knows who it is?"

"I won't drag Paula into the bank's business." Lemmy rocked in his chair. "It's my responsibility to find out what's going on before the bank's reputation could be damaged. You agree?"

Christopher nodded. "You want me to ask Günter again?"

"He won't talk. But the computer now holds all the records of deposits and withdrawals in each of the bank's accounts since the beginning of this year, correct?"

"Yes, but because Herr Hoffgeitz's accounts are segregated from the clients managed by you and the account managers, I can only see the total turnover for his clients' accounts as a combined group, not individually."

Lemmy played with the pen. "What's the total value of all the deposits currently with the bank?"

"Calculated in U.S. dollars, our total holdings in all the accounts add up to about forty-two billion." Christopher rose. "I can find the exact number—"

"And what part of it is held in the accounts of Herr Hoffgeitz's clients?"

"As a group, almost sixty percent."

"About twenty-four billion dollars?"

"Yes."

"Good. What I need from you are two numbers. First, the total turnover—deposits and withdrawals—in Herr Hoffgeitz's clients' accounts as a group during the month of September. Second, the total turnover in the rest of the bank's clients' accounts as a group, also during the month of September. Can you do that?"

"Easy." Christopher left to run the numbers.

Lemmy brought up Herr Hoffgeitz's office on his computer screen. Günter was sitting in the president's chair on the far side of the room, surrounded by the light from the window behind him. Using the arrows on his keyboard, Lemmy zoomed in. The face drew closer, filling the screen, the lips trembling, the eyes shut tightly, the tears flowing.

A moment later, Christopher knocked on the door.

Lemmy punched the escape key and unlocked the door.

Christopher placed two pieces of paper on the desk.

The numbers were shocking. Lemmy examined them carefully, calculating in his mind, and then sat back in his chair, struggling to keep his feelings from showing on his face. On the desk before him was the reason for Elie Weiss's lifelong obsession with the Hoffgeitz Bank.

"Herr Horch? Anything wrong?"

"Don't you see?" Lemmy grabbed a pencil and jotted down a few numbers, then turned the page. "I rounded up your numbers for simplicity. Herr Hoffgeitz and Günter manage accounts for a small group of clients. We don't know who they are, but we do know there's a total of about twenty-four billion dollars, right?"

Christopher nodded.

"During September, the total turnover in his clients' accounts was about twenty-one million dollars. That's about—"

"Less than one-tenth of one percent of the total balance of all his clients' accounts combined."

"Correct." Lemmy wrote the number down. "Now, in the rest of the bank's accounts, including those that I manage and the accounts handled by the others, we have total balance of about eighteen billion dollars altogether, correct?"

Christopher nodded.

"And according to your numbers, the total turnover in and out of these accounts during the last month was four hundred and seventy million dollars, which is a little more than—"

"Two-and-a-half percent."

"Correct!" He threw down the pencil. "See?"

"How strange." Christopher stared at the numbers in astonishment. "Herr Hoffgeitz's clients barely move their money. Why?"

"Good question!"

"Maybe some of his clients are not active at all?"

"Bingo!" Lemmy picked up the pencil. "If Herr Hoffgeitz's clients are divided into two groups—active accounts and inactive accounts—how much would each group hold?"

"You mean, if we assume that Herr Hoffgeitz's active clients behave like the rest of the bank's clients?"

"Correct."

"We could extrapolate the turnover amount in Herr Hoffgeitz accounts—twenty-one million dollars—by the normal turnover percentage of two-and-a-half percent."

"In other words, take the turnover amount in his accounts and multiply it by forty, which comes to—"

"Eight hundred and forty million."

"That's right. So out of twenty-four billion dollars in the accounts that Herr Hoffgeitz manages exclusively with Günter's help, only eight hundred and forty million dollars are in active accounts."

Christopher thought for a moment. "And the rest is sitting in inactive accounts—"

"Or a single account."

"With a total balance of over twenty-three billion dollars!"

"Based on September's figures," Lemmy said. "But even if the numbers fluctuate a bit, we can safely assume that a huge part of Herr Hoffgeitz's clients' holdings remains inactive."

"That's incredible!"

"*Interesting* may be a better word. But also logical, because he would normally assign the routine handling of clients to one of the accounts managers. Herr Hoffgeitz would only keep special accounts under his own management."

"Special in what way?"

"That's what we need to find out." Lemmy walked around the desk and stood by the door. "Great work, Christopher. You'll make an excellent assistant to the president."

"Thank you!"

"Now try to sniff around Günter, but don't frighten the old guy, okay?"

Christopher disappeared behind the door, but a moment later buzzed Lemmy on the intercom. "Prince Abusalim az-Zubayr is on the line. He wants to talk to you."

At the Hilton suite in Paris, the lights blinked on the eavesdropping system. "Outgoing call," Gideon announced.

"Put it on the speakers," Elie said.

"What happened?" Bathsheba clapped. "No more secrets?"

Gideon hushed her, and a man's voice came from the speakers. "Welcome back, Excellency. How is Paris treating you?"

"It's good to be back, Herr Horch. Six-one-nine, El-Sharif."

"How can we help you?"

"I know this voice!" Bathsheba pointed at the machine. "That's the man who left the message earlier."

Elie put a finger to his lips.

"Another transfer," the prince said, "to the same bank in Senlis."

"Of course. How much would you like to give Monsieur Sachs this time?"

"Two-and-a-half million dollars. And there will be another transfer of the same amount in a week or so, after he completes a certain job for me. I'll let you know."

"It's an honor to serve you. The transfer will take place tomorrow, Wednesday, the twenty-fifth. It might take the French a few hours to get the cash ready. Should be available for pickup in the afternoon."

"Perfect. Be well, my friend."

Gideon turned off the speakers. "We're back in the game."

"It's not a game," Bathsheba said. "And who's Herr Horch?"

"This is it," Elie said. "Tomorrow afternoon. We must prepare well. We won't have a second chance."

"Wasn't Horch a carmaker?" Gideon reset the recording device.

"This guy doesn't make cars." Bathsheba looked at Elie. "How the hell did you manage to turn a Swiss banker into an Israeli agent?"

"Don't worry about that."

"I do worry! What if he's a double agent? What if he's sick of you blackmailing him or whatever you're doing to make him work for you? What if he's setting us up for Abu Yusef?"

"She's right," Gideon said. "We need to know if Horch is reliable."

"He's more reliable than the two of you put together." Elie lit another cigarette and opened his bible. "Better start to prepare. Everything will depend on your performance."

Prince Abusalim rang room service for a bottle of iced champagne and an assortment of sweets. He went to the bathroom and watched his naked image in the wall-to-wall mirror, taking pleasure in his muscular body as it produced a healthy stream of urine.

Wearing nothing but a bandage on his hand, he returned to the bedroom, where a voluptuous blonde was spread out on the bed, supported by a mound of pillows, eating square bits of chocolate from a silver bowl nestled between her breasts.

He wondered if he should let her stay the night.

The book of Koran rested on the night stand. He opened the drawer and dropped the Koran out of sight. "You eat too much chocolate, my little Rubens." He squeezed the flesh of her thigh.

She giggled, reaching for his groin. "Maybe I'll eat *this* chocolate."

"That's my girl." He grabbed her hair. "*Bon appétit.*"

Paula served tender pork chops and sweet potato fries for dinner. Klaus Junior nibbled at the food as he listened to Lemmy reading aloud get-well cards sent by bank employees, clients, and a few of Armande's old friends.

While Paula served cheesecake for dessert, the phone rang.

Lemmy got up. "I'll take it in the study."

He shut the door and picked up the phone. "Wilhelm Horch here."

"I gave you an order," Elie said. "Have you finished off the old man?"

"And I asked you not to phone me at home." Lemmy covered his mouth as he spoke into the receiver. "I have a family!"

"Silence!" Elie launched into a series of coughs, followed by spitting. When he spoke again, his voice was weak. "Do not interrupt me again, or I'll visit your home in person and practice my father's trade on your Gentile wife and your little Nazi namesake."

The threat was so extreme that Lemmy could not speak.

"I need you to change the prince's money transfer instructions. Write it down."

Lemmy jotted Elie's instructions on a pad and hung up. He sat there for a long time, unable to return to the kitchen and face Paula and Klaus Junior as if nothing had happened. Had Elie spoken merely out of rage? Or had it been a valid forewarning of real intentions? There was no way to know what Elie would do to ensure the realization of his grand vision. It had been a terrible mistake to give Elie the impression that his feelings for Paula and Klaus Junior could in any way hinder his complete dedication to the cause of Counter Final Solution. Elie would not hesitate to send a hit team to Zurich. What's a couple of dead Gentiles in the context of obtaining twenty-three billion dollars to combat global anti-Semitism?

The door opened and Paula entered the study. She closed the door and came around the large desk. Gently she wiped the sweat from his forehead. "Are you going to leave us?"

"What?" He looked up at her. "Hell, no!"

She kissed the top of his head.

He hugged her, his ear against her stomach. "I'll never leave you."

"Good. Very good."

"It's something else." He stood, facing her. "I should have told you long ago."

Paula put a hand on his mouth. "I know who my husband is. You are a wonderful man and a terrific father. The rest is work stuff. I don't want to know."

He held her tightly. She truly, unconditionally loved him. And he felt the same, which meant that Elie had a valid reason for his deadly threat, because if Lemmy had to choose, Paula and Klaus Junior would come first. He had no qualms about killing to protect Israel, and he would have no qualms killing to protect his family!

They descended to the floor, kissing each other on the way down. They lay on the carpet. He nibbled at her neck, his left hand around her nape, his right hand pulling up her skirt. He mounted her, his knees parting her thighs. Paula quivered, breathing rapidly.

———

Wednesday, October 25, 1995

"My father will recover." Paula sat in front of the vanity in the corner of their bedroom. "He won't give up. I know him."

"Armande is strong," Lemmy agreed while tying his shoes.

Paula started her morning makeup routine. "I should have convinced him to work less, to spend more time with Junior. Maybe now he'll agree to work part-time. You could run the bank day-to-day, right?"

"I'm not his son."

Any reference to her dead brother, even indirectly, made Paula's eyes moisten. She no longer cried, and most people would not even notice it, but Lemmy saw her reaction and regretted it. She smiled, which was her way of telling him it was okay to discuss this painful subject. "You're like a son to him."

"Not exactly. He doesn't mind it when I go skiing, but when Junior wanted to learn how to ski, your father flipped."

"We're going to do it this year. We have to."

"That's right. I mean, what kind of a Swiss kid doesn't ski?" Lemmy watched her face, which lit up when discussing their son. "The winter is coming. Should I make reservations?"

"As long as it's not Chamonix."

The Alpine ski resort had taken the life of Klaus V.K. Hoffgeitz in the twilight hours of a sunny day in the winter of 1973. He was found in a crevasse near an easy blue-diamond slope. An expert skier, he must have taken a wrong turn, confused by the shadows so typical of the western face of the mountain. Autopsy revealed that his injuries had not been severe, except for a stab wound, likely caused by the unlucky fall on a sharp icicle, which entered his brain through the throat, melting away long before the body had been found.

"I miss my brother," Paula said. "He was fun."

Lemmy held her hand. "I'm sorry."

"I've accepted it. God wanted him by His side." She wiped her eyes. "And my mother's real illness, what really killed her, was a broken heart, which I also understand. But for my father, losing Klaus V.K. has been the tragedy of his life—not just the grief over a wonderful, loveable son, but the loss of his heir. I think it's like the world went out of order for him. It was the breaking of continuity, an end to generations of family tradition. My father feels that he failed in his hereditary duty to groom a male heir."

"It's tragic."

"I tried to convince him it wasn't like this anymore. It's the twentieth century. Families hire professional managers to run inherited businesses. No one cares about bloodlines any longer. It's so old fashioned."

"Your father is not easy to convince. He takes everything very seriously." Lemmy had not told Paula about the phone call that had instigated her father's heart attack or about the huge sum in the inactive account. She was safer not knowing. "I think he was hoping to run the bank until Junior is ready to take over."

"He's ten!" She laughed, and the light from the window glistened in her eyes.

"It will take twenty years before—"

"Not necessarily. If we expedite his schooling, he could graduate university at twenty, while spending each summer at the bank to learn the ropes. Theoretically, in twelve or thirteen years he could take over as president. And I'll be there to help him."

"That's ridiculous!" Paula brushed her hair. "My father is already eighty-four."

"He's as sharp as a young man, and if he recovers from this heart attack—"

"Our son is not the banker type."

"What's that supposed to mean? He's good with numbers."

"Klaus Junior would be miserable as a banker. It's too boring."

"Am I miserable and boring?"

She laughed. "You're delightful and fascinating."

"In what way?"

"I can show you." She came into his arms, smelling fresh and enticing. "If you want."

"I'll be late to work. But if you won't allow Klaus Junior to become a banker, then we have to—"

"Make a banker."

"It's our hereditary duty." Lemmy began to undress. "A matter of generational traditions. The board of directors expects no less from us!"

Paula's body shook with laughter. "We're going to make the rabbits jealous—"

Pop! The window exploded, raining slivers of glass all over them.

Lemmy pushed Paula down and lay on top of her, sheltering her with his body. He glanced up at the ceiling and saw a bullet hole. His mind digested the incredible fact: Elie had acted on his threat!

Gideon listened as Prince Abusalim called room service to order breakfast for two. A half-hour later, Abu Yusef called. The prince put the Palestinian terrorist on hold and, after a moment, picked up one of the phones in the bathroom. "The money is ready," he said without a preamble. "It will arrive at the bank in Senlis later today."

"The freedom of Palestine shall belong to you!"

"*Insha'Allah.* Call me in three days. I'll give you the time and place for the job. Make sure you have enough firepower. He will be well protected."

"Don't worry, Excellency. It will be executed successfully."

"Don't underestimate your target. In Saudi Arabia we have a saying: A man whom the desert failed to kill is immortal."

"We also have a saying," Abu Yusef said. "A man who feels immortal is easier to kill."

L emmy expected a second bullet, but none came right away. He heard the Porsche's alarm whining and recalled leaving it out in the driveway last night. "Stay down! I'll get Junior."

Paula tried to rise. "I'm coming—"

"Down!"

Staying low, he headed for the door. The bullet had come through the front of the house. Why had the shooter aimed at the window, when he could have shot them later outside? Was it a diversion while another assassin broke down the front door? Or the rear patio glass? Or was a lone sniper hiding in the woods across the street, waiting to take a second shot when a face appeared in the window? But the angle was too steep, as if the shooter was close to the house!

He ran downstairs, reached the kitchen, and crouched under the counter. "Klaus! Where are you?"

No response.

A sense of terror flooded Lemmy. Was the boy injured? Was he bleeding? But there had been only one shot, and the bullet was stuck in the bedroom ceiling. The boy must be listening to music with headphones.

"Klaus!"

Nothing. Where was he?

The Mauser! Lemmy knew he had to get it from the car and shoot back. By now he was doubting that this attack was Elie's doing. It was too imprecise, even illogical considering that Elie's threat had been directed at Paula and the boy. Elie would not have sent a shooter to attack while Lemmy was in the house, ready to defend them or get killed himself. Without him, how would Elie gain control of the Nazi funds at the Hoffgeitz Bank?

All these thoughts rushed through his mind while the professional assassin within him coldly planned the run for the Mauser and the ensuing shootout. It would be hard to take proper aim at the sniper, but mounting a counter-attack was the best defense. He crouched by the front door, focusing on the task at hand. The Mauser had been in the car since the Paris job. It had taken two bullets to finish off the Arab. Nine left. He would have to run to the Porsche, break the windshield, pull the storage cover, get the gun out of the box, load it, cock it, aim, and start shooting. Even with the car between him and the sniper, Lemmy knew he'd likely get hit at least once. But there was no other way to scare off the attacker before Paula or Klaus got hurt.

He grabbed the knob and realized the front door wasn't locked. Why? Had Junior gone outside?

He threw the door open and sprinted to the Porsche in the driveway, expecting the pop of a shot and the jolt of a bullet hit.

Nothing. The sniper must have been focused on the windows, not expecting someone to run out. He was adjusting his rifle right now. Lemmy sped up. Ten yards to go. He lifted his arm over his head, ready to elbow in the windshield.

Five. Four. Now—

The windshield was already shattered. Like a spider-web, thousands of tiny cracks spread like rays from a finger-size hole in the upper part.

A bullet hole!

Lemmy glanced up at the broken bedroom window on the second floor of the house. The bullet had come from inside the car!

Through the windshield he noticed the open storage compartment.

Klaus Junior was in the passenger seat. His face was white, his eyes wide open. Lemmy opened the door and removed the Mauser from the boy's hand. He held the warm barrel and pulled the small forefinger out of the trigger slot. Aiming at the sky, he released the magazine and cocked the Mauser to dispose of the bullet in the chamber, which he picked up and put in his pocket with the gun.

As he lifted his son from the car, Paula ran out of the house.

"He's okay," Lemmy managed to say, his voice choking. "He's not injured."

Christopher jumped to his feet. "Good morning, Herr Horch!" He seemed surprised to see his boss in so early.

"Prince Abusalim called me last night," Lemmy lied. "A small modification in the transfer instructions. The recipient name will change to Grant Guerra."

"Okay."

"Send the order as soon as business opens. Such a large amount in U.S. dollars might require them to order extra cash."

Christopher took the sheet and turned to his computer. The altered order would travel on telephone lines electronically through two inter-European clearing centers to the local branch of Banque Nationale de France in Senlis.

Lemmy wondered how Elie was planning to do the job. Was he sending in his agent to receive the money and wait to shoot Abu Yusef? The Arabs would be armed and alert. The bank probably had security cameras and push-button alarms, possibly even an automatic lockdown feature, which could be a disaster. And even if the assassination was successful, the subsequent investigation could lead to the Hoffgeitz Bank. The Zurich police department would never attempt to obtain the identity of his client—bank secrecy laws were sacred—but the French might tip the media, which would attract unwanted attention. A hit inside a bank was too risky, even in France. What was Elie thinking?

Paula called to report that Klaus Junior was watching TV and eating pancakes but refusing to discuss with her what had happened. She had told him that his father would take him to a shooting range to have proper training in gun safety and usage, which made the boy excited. Lemmy apologized again for making such a foolish mistake—he should not have left a weapon in the car. Paula didn't ask why he had the gun in the first place—most Swiss men served in the national army reserve and owned personal firearms.

He pulled the Mauser from his pocket and placed it on the desk. He recalled holding it for the first time in his father's study, back in Jerusalem. So much had happened since then— the abortion riots, his excommunication from Neturay Karta, paratrooper service in the IDF, and the mission into Jordanian-occupied East Jerusalem to destroy the UN radar, which had prevented detection of Israel's preemptive strike and led to the victory of the Six Day War. And then, alone in the world, he had accepted Elie's offer of clandestine service, spent a summer in intense German-language study, attended Lyceum Alpin St. Nicholas, courted Paula, and turned himself into a successful Swiss banker, a family man, and a secret agent. The key to his long career was careful planning and meticulous execution to minimize risk of exposure. The exception was his continuous use of the Mauser for killing Israel's enemies. The barrel had been honed to prevent ballistic tracing of the bullets, and he had taken pains to keep it out of sight and utilize generic ammunition. He knew that the repeat use of the same weapon was hazardous, but this Mauser was the single object of continuity in his life, the only physical possession going all the way back to the city of Jerusalem—and a boy named Jerusalem.

When Abu Yusef walked into the dining room, the men stopped talking and gathered around the large table. "We achieved a great victory on Saturday," he declared. "The Zionists are bleeding badly. We must hit them again and again until they scatter to the four corners of the earth or die!"

The men cheered, raising clenched fists.

He turned to a map of Europe, which Bashir had pinned to the wall. "With our donor's generosity, we are ready to launch a historic campaign that will blow away the Oslo Accords." Abu Yusef paused, looking around. "Who in this room speaks Italian?"

Two of the men raised their hands.

"Spanish?"

Three hands came up.

"Greek?"

One hand.

"Dutch?"

No hand came up. Abu Yusef shook his head. "Pity. The Dutch are all Zionist bastards. Danish?"

A hand came halfway up. "I get by," the man said.

Abu Yusef nodded. "Swedish?"

Another hesitant hand.

"Good." He noticed two men whispering. "What?"

One of them said, "I speak good German."

Abu Yusef shook a finger. "We're not going to Germany. We won't fall into that trap again. The world doesn't like to watch Jews getting killed in Germany. It's counter-productive."

He realized they didn't understand.

"Munich was an unusual opportunity," he explained. "The Olympics, the media. And I admit that even Munich might have been a mistake. When the Nazis exterminated the Jews, the Americans or British could have easily bombed the German rails and silenced the death camps. That's why, after the war, everybody felt guilty and let the Jews steal our land. Jews know a lot about guilt, and if we kill them in Germany, they'll cry *Holocaust!* Everybody will forget about us and feel sorry for the Jews again."

Some of the men mumbled curses.

"But you can go to Austria," Abu Yusef said to the German-speaking man. "There are plenty of fat Jews in Vienna—an excellent target." He looked at his list. "We still need Flemish and Portuguese."

"I have a few recruits," Bashir said. "They'll be in later."

"Good." Abu Yusef turned to the map. "The blue pins stand for El Al stations and terminals. Red pins for Israeli embassies and consulates. And yellow pins for synagogues and Jewish schools. We'll hit all these targets on the same day. Forty-seven targets representing the forty-seven years since the United Nations allowed the Zionists to declare their state!"

The men clapped.

"That's right!" Abu Yusef held up a fist. "We'll rock the world!"

When they quieted down, Bashir stepped forward. "Listen carefully. The money is coming in today. This evening you'll receive your individual assignments, including maps, blueprints of the target buildings, and escape routes. Also, each team will receive enough cash to purchase vehicles, weapons, explosives, timer fuses and everything else you'll need to successfully destroy your targets. Tonight you'll pack up your personal belongings and be ready to head out in the morning, each team travelling separately. After the simultaneous attacks, we'll reconvene in a new location."

"Think of the international impact!" Abu Yusef looked each man in the eye. "Forty-seven years of shame will be redeemed by delivering forty-seven unforgettable lessons to the Jews. We're getting enough money to do what no one has ever dared before—a barrage of attacks at the same time, synchronized to maximum shock and awe. On a single glorious day, we'll flood Europe with the blood of the Jews, just as the valleys of Palestine are flooded with the Zionist pests."

He paused to give them time to absorb the enormity of the operation. They seemed excited. And nervous.

"This time next week, the Oslo process will be derailed by your daring and unprecedented accomplishment. Your spirit will revive our people's hopes. And soon you'll lead them back to Jerusalem!"

He turned and left the room, hoping his words had inspired them. He had spoken as if a whole army was lined up in front of him, not merely two dozen men. More were joining, though. And when forty-seven Jewish targets blew up simultaneously all over Europe, every Palestinian man would leave his family and join their ranks. There would be an army of warriors waiting for his orders. The peace process would collapse into accusations and counter-accusations, and soon after that, he would see Palestine again as a victor, sailing his armada into the Haifa Bay through water dotted with the bobbing heads of dead Jews.

Bashir joined him. "It won't be easy. We're taking on the whole Oslo peace process. They'll be pissed off—Arafat, Rabin, Clinton. Everybody will be after us."

"No," Abu Yusef said. "Everybody will respect us."

"That also," Bashir said. "Many of Al-Mazir's men are ready to join. After the operation, we'll set up recruiting networks all over."

"But first of all, we need our best two men to do the job for the prince. We can't afford to disappoint him." Abu Yusef opened the door to his bedroom. It was dark except for a lamp near the empty bed.

Bashir turned to go.

"Latif was a good boy," Abu Yusef said. "I miss him. Maybe one day, after our victory, I will marry a woman. Like Arafat."

"That's right." A rare smile appeared on Bashir's face. "A woman like Arafat."

Gideon wore a navy-blue suit and a gray tie. He stuck on a thin, black moustache. The small leather briefcase completed the image of a young businessman. Bathsheba had brushed his curly hair back, smoothed it down with gel, and sprayed him with Cacharel. Before he left the car to enter the bank, Elie said, "Put your hook deep into him and give him no reason to suspect you."

"Show him," Bathsheba said, "how deep you can bend over."

Gideon slammed the car door and walked down the street to the bank.

The manager, Monsieur Richar, put down his pen and stood up. "*Oui?*"

"Grant Guerra." Gideon extended a hand. "I believe you have funds awaiting me?"

"Oh, yes!" The bank manager beckoned a bespectacled clerk. "We're ready for you. It's an honor!"

"Much obliged."

"Would you like to open an account with us? Our investment department can assist you with devising an appropriate strategy for growth. We'd like to earn your business."

"Perhaps in the future. Today's transfer is earmarked for a joint venture that requires a substantial cash transaction. I will require a meeting room to conduct it."

"Of course." The bank manager seemed a tad disappointed. "We ordered additional bills as soon as we saw the wire. We normally don't carry that much in U.S. dollars."

"Excellent."

They led him to a vacant office. An electrical counting machine rested on the table. The manager examined Gideon's driver's license, a fake that matched the particulars on the transfer from Zurich, and asked him to sign a receipt. A few moments later, a clerk brought in the money in a sack—twenty-five thousand $100 bills.

As the manager was leaving the room, Gideon said, "My associate, Monsieur Sachs, should arrive within the hour."

"Certainly, Monsieur Guerra. Would you like some coffee while you wait?"

The street outside the Banque Nationale de France buzzed with afternoon shoppers. The white Citroën drew no attention. Bathsheba sat behind the wheel, Elie in the passenger seat. It was four o'clock p.m., and there was no sign of Abu Yusef.

Bathsheba turned on the radio and searched the dial until she found music. Her head rocked with the drumbeat. "What if he doesn't show up?"

Elie shut off the radio. "Abu Yusef has been waiting all his life for something like this. Arafat has always managed to squeeze heaps of cash from donors, who liked and feared him at the same time. Today Abu Yusef will step out of Arafat's shadow, financially speaking."

"And he'll cast his own long shadow, if we don't stop him."

Elie nodded. "They'll be edgy with so much cash on board. You must be very careful following them back to the nest. If they notice us, bad things will happen."

Bathsheba used a piece of cloth to shine the binocular lenses. The minutes passed slowly with constant traffic along the street. Customers visited the retail shops and clients frequented the bank. Closing time approached fast.

"Here we go." Elie pointed.

A blue BMW sedan stopped in front of the bank, followed by a red Mazda RX-7. Bashir Hamami got out of the BMW and looked up and down the street, his right hand under his coat. Two younger men emerged from the red Mazda and joined Bashir. One of them opened the rear door of the BMW, and Abu Yusef stepped out with a large briefcase.

"Nice cars." Bathsheba reached into a tennis bag on the back seat and took out a handgun with a silencer. She cocked the gun and put it on the floor between her legs. She repeated the process with another gun, which she kept in her lap.

"You're a pessimist," Elie said.

"Wasn't plan B your idea?"

"For me, redundancy is a necessity, not an aspiration."

Gideon was on the move as soon as he saw the cars through the glass front of the bank. He took off his jacket, straightened his tie, and hurried to the front door, reaching it just as one of Abu Yusef's men opened it from the outside.

He flashed a wide smile. "Monsieur Sachs?"

Abu Yusef looked at him with surprise and shook his hand.

"Welcome to Banque Nationale de France. I'm Grant Guerra—foreign currency desk. I'm sorry we missed each other last week."

"Then how did you recognize me?"

Without missing a beat, Gideon gestured at the men and cars. "We don't handle many transactions of this size in our branch."

Abu Yusef's eyes measured him up and down. "It's a pleasure, Monsieur Guerra."

"Please, call me Grant."

"Grant. A strong name." He signaled to his men to stay outside and followed Gideon through the bank.

As they passed by Monsieur Richar's office, the bank manager glanced over his spectacles and started to get up. Gideon waved and continued to walk. These few seconds were the weakest link in the sequence of planned events. An interaction with Richar could blow his cover. Abu Yusef would realize he was dealing with someone pretending to be a bank employee and try to draw a weapon. Gideon was ready for plan B. He would kill Abu Yusef quickly with a knife, but the way out of the bank would require a public shootout with the Arabs outside. Even with Bathsheba and Elie attacking them from the rear, Bashir and his men presented a formidable force, and such a battle would have uncertain consequences.

They entered the office before Monsieur Richar managed to join them, and Gideon shut the door. "A few formalities, if you don't mind?"

"Of course," Abu Yusef presented a Belgian passport under the name of Perez Sachs.

Gideon examined it carefully and compared it to a copy of a false transfer order he had brought with him that carried the name Perez Sachs as recipient. He smiled at Abu Yusef and handed him the form and a pen. "Please sign here, Monsieur Sachs." He pointed and rested his hand on the Arab's shoulder.

Abu Yusef recognized the scent. Cacharel. It reminded him of Latif, and the memory at once saddened and aroused him. He signed *Perez Sachs* and looked up at the young man, who was standing over him. Their faces were only a few inches apart, and Abu Yusef took in the sweet scent, leaning slightly closer. His nostrils quivered. He returned the pen. For a moment, their hands connected, and Abu Yusef felt a wave of heat in his groin.

"Would you like to count the money now?" Grant's gaze was direct and unwavering, bright with excitement.

"I trust you."

"We have time. It's no problem." Delicate wrinkles adorned the corners of his glistening eyes. The white, tailored shirt fit perfectly on what was clearly an athletic, masculine body. "I'm at your service, in every way you should require."

"I might be a demanding man." Abu Yusef chuckled.

"I'm accommodating by nature."

"You work out regularly?" He moved a finger down the clerk's shirtsleeve.

"Yes." His face became a little red, but he kept smiling. "I like to break a sweat."

"It shows." Abu Yusef felt doubly aroused by the young man's discomfort. He opened the large briefcase, packed up the money, and closed the lid. The handsome bank clerk remained close, smiling, inviting. Didn't he mind the age difference, the belly, the receding hairline? His body language communicated undeniable interest. Was it the money? Did it matter? Abu Yusef took a deep breath and asked, "Perhaps we could chat later?"

"If you'd like to, sure." Grant scribbled a number on a piece of paper and handed it to Abu Yusef. "Call me at eight tonight, okay?"

Abu Yusef followed him to the front door. It was obvious Grant was anxious to usher him out of the bank lest his boss noticed there was more going on between the two of them than a banking transaction. "Until later then."

"*Au revoir,* Monsieur Sachs." The young banker's hand touched Abu Yusef's back, gently prodding him out to the street. He winked and closed the glass door.

Bashir had the men facing away in all directions, alert to any sign of trouble. Abu Yusef got in the back seat of the BMW, the briefcase on his lap. "Allah is great," he declared. "Let's go!"

The Arabs kept to local roads, avoiding the highway. Rush hour slowed everything down and provided plenty of vehicles to blend in. Bathsheba stayed well behind, while Elie kept the binoculars trained on the red RX-7. Twenty minutes later, they reached Ermenonville. The two cars turned into a narrow street. Bathsheba passed the turn and stopped. She got out, ran to the corner, and peeked through the shrubs. An iron gate opened, and several armed guards stood aside to let the cars enter.

Back in the Citroën, Bathsheba said, "This is it. The snake pit." She drove off while Elie wrote down the name of the street: *Boulevard Royale.*

After ten minutes, the manager came to check on Gideon. "Monsieur Guerra, I was hoping to meet your associate."

"I'm so sorry," Gideon said. "He was anxious to get going. It's a large sum to carry around."

"Of course. I assume the arrangements were satisfactory."

"Superb." Gideon put on his coat. "Thank you again."

The bank manager bowed. "At your service."

As they headed back to the front door, Gideon was relieved to see the vacant curb. He stepped out into a chilly evening, walked down the street, and turned right at the next corner. Halfway down the block, he leaned against the wall and vomited.

Rabbi Gerster joined hundreds of mourners at the Sanhedriah Cemetery in Jerusalem for the funeral of the rabbi from Paris, whose body had been flown to Israel that morning on an El Al jetliner. He had never met Rabbi Dasso, but felt an urge to show his respect to a man who had literally given his life to the pulpit. Besides, Rabbi Gerster was quite certain that the funeral would attract political activists, possibly even a few ILOT members.

A Paris-born Knesset member took the microphone to deliver a eulogy. "Rabbi Maurice Dasso was devoted to his congregation and to God. He died while praying, while celebrating a Bar Mitzvah with a Jewish boy, who also died. Those evil hands killed Rabbi Dasso in the middle of the holy Sabbath, a day of spirituality and peace, but not for the Jews of Paris. The murderers descended on the righteous! Cut short the prayers! Turned the joy of a Bar Mitzvah into grief! Snatched away Sabbath's peace and turned it into blood and death and grief!" He raised his hands at the sky. "*Oy! Oy!* How the righteous have fallen!"

Rabbi Dasso's wife and children, standing by the coffin at the open grave, began crying. Many others cried with them.

"Our enemies never rest." The Knesset member wiped his eyes. "I want to ask them: Why do you hate us so? Why does your hatred of Jews thrive with every generation?"

Many in the crowd yelled, "Why? Why?"

"Why does your thirst for Jewish blood never languish?" He looked up, shaking his head. "What have we done to deserve your venom? Is it the faith in one God, which we have gifted to mankind?"

The mourners cried, "No!"

"Is it the justice of the Ten Commandments and the civil law of Talmud's thousand pages, which has inspired laws of fairness and equality in every country in your so-called civilized world?"

"No!"

"Is it the wisdom of philosophy and ethics that we have shared with humanity? Or the beauty of music and literature, scribed by Jewish quills to pleasure the ears of all nations?"

"No!"

"Is it the scientific leaps that improve the lives of millions? Or the cures we've invented for fatal maladies?"

"No! No! No!"

Taking a deep breath, he cried, "Then why do you hate us, Gentiles?"

There was no response. Even the French ambassador, standing in a section reserved for dignitaries, bowed his head—perhaps in agreement, perhaps in shame. The morning newspapers had reported that the French government had known of Abu Yusef's activities even before his deadly attack on a Jewish day school in Marseilles the previous month. An anonymous source at the Quai D'Orsay, enraged over the death of the minister of arts and culture in the synagogue bombing, had told the Associated Press that Yasser Arafat himself had asked the French to look the other way while he attempted to deal discreetly with his estranged deputy.

After the burial and prayers, as he was leaving the cemetery, Rabbi Gerster saw a group of women holding a huge placard:

PRIME MINISTER RABIN: HERE IS YOUR "PARTNER FOR PEACE"
ARAFAT'S RÉSUMÉ:
FOUNDER OF PLO, FATAH, BLACK SEPTEMBER, TANZIM,
AL-AKSA BRIGADE: 1965-PRESENT;
ATTACKS ON FARM COMMUNITIES IN THE SOUTH AND NORTH,
HUNDREDS DEAD, 1965-70;

BOMBING OF SWISSAIR FLIGHT 330,
47 PASSENGERS DEAD, 1970;
BOMBING OF SCHOOL BUS NEAR MOSHAV AVIVIM IN ISRAEL,
9 CHILDREN DEAD, 1970;
HIGHJACK OF TWA, PAN AM, AND
BOAC PASSENGER PLANES, 1970;
ATTACKS ON MULTIPLE CIVILIAN TARGETS IN
JORDAN, THOUSANDS KILLED, 1970;
ATTACK BY GUNS AND GRENADES AT LOD AIRPORT
IN ISRAEL, 1971;
ATTACK ON THE MUNICH OLYMPICS,
ATHLETES MASSACRED, 1972;
ATTACK ON US EMBASSY IN SAUDI ARABIA,
CIVILIANS DEAD, 1972;
MURDER OF US AMBASSADOR TO SUDAN, CLEO NOEL, 1972;
MURDER OF 11 CIVILIANS IN AN APARTMENT BUILDING IN
KIRYAT SHMONA, ISRAEL, 1974;
MURDER OF 21 CHILDREN AND 5 ADULTS IN
A SCHOOL IN MA'ALOT, ISRAEL, 1974;
MURDER OF 4 CIVILIANS IN BET SHE'AN, ISRAEL, 1974;
ATTACK ON HOTEL SAVOY IN TEL AVIV,
NUMEROUS DEAD, 1975;
ATTACK ON BUS ON COASTAL HIGHWAY IN ISRAEL, MANY
CIVILIAN DEATHS, 1978;
INCITING CIVIL WAR IN LEBANON THAT KILLED
THOUSANDS OF CHRISTIANS, 1979-82;
LAUNCHING THOUSANDS OF KATYUSHA MISSILES
INTO N. ISRAEL, MANY DEAD, 1979-82;
HIGHJACK OF ACHILLE LAURO, WHEELCHAIR-BOUND
OLD MAN SHOT, THROWN OVERBOARD, 1985;
BOMBING OF BUSES, TRAINS, BEACHES, SCHOOLS,
THOUSANDS DEAD & INJURED, 1986-TODAY;
SIGNING OSLO "PEACE," CONTINUING TERROR VIA PELP,
ISLAMIC JIHAD, HAMAS, 1993-TODAY;

Another sign read: PRIME MINISTER RABIN: HOW CAN PEACE BE MADE WITH A MASS MURDERER?

An elderly woman held a sign that showed Arafat in a leopard skin with a subtitle: WILL A LEOPARD CHANGE ITS SPOTS?

Across the street, Rabbi Gerster saw another group. They held a long banner made of cloth and colored in blue and white. It said: GIVE PEACE A CHANCE!

Gideon sat on the floor in the corner of the hotel room, surrounded by tools and wires. He picked through the bag of Jaffa oranges and chose a small one, not much bigger than a nectarine. He marked the skin with a knife and peeled it, placing the pieces of skin in a neat row.

"Can I help?" Bathsheba sat crossed-legged next to Gideon.

"You can watch."

"I'd like to watch you later with your new friend."

"Jealous?"

She stretched her legs. "Abu Yusef isn't my type."

"Unfortunately you're not his type either."

"Let him work," Elie said.

Gideon added a few drops of gasoline to a small container of explosive powder and mixed it. He scooped out the paste, shaped it into a ball, and inserted a miniature fuse. Bathsheba held a square of aluminum foil in her palm, and he placed the black ball in the center, wrapping it and smoothing out the creases. Using liquid adhesive, he glued the pieces of peeled skin to the foil, forming a fake orange, marked by a knife to ease its peeling.

"It won't kill him," Bathsheba said. "It's too small."

"Depends where it explodes," Gideon said. "Location, location, location."

Abu Yusef walked into the villa with Bashir. The men gathered around them. He held up the briefcase and declared, "In the name of Allah, we're in business!"

The men cheered.

"The world is about to hear us! Forty-seven lessons on one day! And then again, another forty-seven! And another! Until blood spews out of their ears!"

Everyone cheered again.

Bashir stepped forward. "Now to practical details. We received word from our French hosts. They prefer that we leave the country as soon as possible." He looked at his watch. "You have until midnight to pack up and be ready to go. I will have operational instructions and cash ready for each team. Allah's blessings upon you, heroes of Palestine!"

Abu Yusef shook each man's hand as they left the room. He would follow them out of France after completing the job for Prince Abusalim and collecting the second half of the money.

He carried the briefcase to his bedroom. He placed it on the bed, opened it, and marveled at the green bills. He wished Latif could be here to celebrate this new beginning. He sighed, and thought of the foreign currency manager at the bank. Why not? Better to celebrate with an attractive stranger than alone.

The piece of paper had a Paris number on it. He sat on the bed, picked up the phone, and dialed.

At 8:07 p.m., the phone attached to the outside line rang. Gideon let it ring twice before answering. Elie heard the conversation through the speaker. Abu Yusef suggested meeting Grant at the corner of the Champs Elysees near the Obelisque.

Elie stubbed his cigarette in a cup of stale coffee. "Let's get ready."

"Party time," Bathsheba said. She pulled on a pair of leather boots with high heels, which made her buttocks stick out under the black miniskirt. Her legs seemed endless in their mesh-black stockings. She put on a black jacket over a red tank top. A chain of glass pearls and a pair of gold coins as earrings completed the look.

In the car, she pulled off the boots in order to drive. Traffic was heavy, but they reached Place de La Concorde a few minutes early and parked on the south side. Gideon got out and shouldered a knapsack. He waited for a brief break in traffic and crossed the square, careful not to slip on the cobblestones. Past the Obelisque, he reached the north corner of the Champs Elysees, where he leaned against a street lamp. He was dressed in gray slacks and a blue jacket, and his red tie flapped in the breeze.

The blue BMW sedan sped around the square and stopped at the curb. Gideon got in, and the car drove off.

"There we go!" Elie cracked his window and tossed out his cigarette. "Don't lose him!" The tension demanded more oxygen from his ailing lungs, and his chest felt as if a porcupine had moved in.

Bathsheba engaged first gear and looked over her shoulder in search of an opening in traffic.

"Go!"

"I'm trying." She released the clutch, but a car raced by, causing her to hit the brake. The engine died. "Damn Frogs!" She restarted and pulled into traffic without a glance, tires screeching. A man shouted something in French through his open window, and she yelled back, "Asshole!"

The BMW was out of sight. Elie leaned forward, his nose almost touching the windshield, and searched through the river of cars that flooded the Champs Elysees. A passing car's headlights shone on him, and he saw his reflection in the glass—a narrow face and two hollow, dark eyes under the black wool cap.

Bathsheba gripped the steering wheel with two hands and raced up the Champs Elysees. She swerved left and right to get ahead, cut cars with barely room to spare, and earned a lot of honking.

"You lost him," Elie said, peering ahead. "Not good!"

Abu Yusef was relieved to see the young man waiting at the appointed place and time. His worries of a last-minute change of heart now put to rest, he settled back and relaxed, his left arm resting on the black briefcase that held his fortune, his right hand in Grant's lap. The back seat of the BMW 740iL felt like a tranquil island amidst the intensity of city traffic, but the young man's hand was cold, a sign of nervousness. It was understandable, a bank clerk of modest means on a date with a very wealthy suitor—who was really a dangerous guerilla fighter! Abu Yusef chuckled at the thought.

Grant smiled in the dark.

It would be a thrilling tryst, a fitting conclusion to the most successful day in Abu Yusef's life. Money to spend, loyal men to implement his synchronized, Europe-wide attacks, and thousands of potential recruits to join his group. Munich had been a modest success compared to what awaited the world. His chest was too tight to contain all his pride and excitement. He felt alive!

Bashir steered the large car effortlessly among the crazy French drivers. His eyes occasionally left the road and checked the rearview mirror for a tail. He had objected to this rendezvous, pacified only by the argument that it would be months, maybe years, before Abu Yusef again would have the opportunity to pursue a chance encounter with a willing, alluring companion without fear of detection.

After a series of sudden turns and aimless cruising, they were back at the circle around the Arc de Triomphe. Reassured that no one was following them, Bashir seemed calmer, driving with one hand as he turned down Avenue De Friedland. Abu Yusef trembled with excited anticipation. In a few minutes, secluded in the privacy of a hotel room, they would be free to go at each other, and this young man would give himself completely, surrender without resistance, do as he was told!

They had lost Abu Yusuf's BMW on Champs Elysees, and had circled the Arc De Triomphe several times, scanning each avenue and boulevard to no avail. Elie decided to wait, reasoning that Bashir would return to the huge circle once he was satisfied that no one was following. Bathsheba found a place to linger at the corner of Avenue Kleber, and they watched the hundreds of cars that drained into the circle from all directions. As Elie had predicted, the BMW eventually reappeared.

"I'm impressed," Bathsheba said, "you called his next move."

"Bashir had to come back here to reorient himself. Now he'll go straight to a cheap hotel that rents rooms by the hour."

This time, Bathsheba stuck to the BMW with only a few cars separating them. She counted on Bashir's false sense of security.

Abu Yusuf felt his pulse rising, accompanied by a happy lightheadedness. Avenue De Friedland became Boulevard Haussmann. They were getting closer. At Chaussee D'Antin, Bashir waited for a green light and took Rue La Fayette all the way to the Gare du Nord—the city's railway station for all northbound travelers. He eased into an alley and parked under a yellowish neon sign: PINNACLE MOTEL.

They got out of the car. It was quiet except for the music from a bar at the corner.

Bashir grabbed Grant's knapsack.

"It's okay." Abu Yusuf put a calming hand on Grant's arm, and they watched Bashir empty the bag on the hood of the car. His callous hand sorted through the objects—a book, a wallet, a magazine about motorcycles, and an orange. Bashir threw the book into the bag, then the wallet and the magazine. He held up the orange and examined it against the street light. The shining skin had been marked by a knife. Bashir turned the orange and put his thumb under the stamped word: JAFFA.

Abu Yusuf said, "My friend's family once owned a citrus grove in Jaffa."

The bank clerk nodded, and Abu Yusuf realized how alien their political grievances must appear to this young Frenchman.

Bashir dropped the orange into the bag and quickly frisked Grant's body. "I called your bank's headquarters," he said. "In Paris. They never heard of Grant Guerra."

"I'd be surprised if they did," the answer came without hesitation. "We have over four hundred branches and seven thousand employees. But they'll know my name when I'm chairman of the board."

Even Bashir smiled at this response, and Abu Yusuf breathed in relief. He had high expectations for tonight and didn't want the mood spoiled before the pleasure began. He tilted his head at the car, signaling Bashir to watch the briefcase, which rested on the passenger's seat.

Bathsheba parked the car around the corner from the Pinnacle. Elie got out and peeked. He could see Bashir's head through the rear window.

"It's getting cold," she said.

"It was colder in the attic," Elie said, "when I watched a bunch of German soldiers kill my siblings. They used the knives my father sharpened daily for the ritual slaughter of kosher animals. I heard my brother explain to my baby sister that it wouldn't hurt—a quick nick and she'd fall asleep, just like the lambs. But one of the Germans heard him so they cut her belly open and laughed as she screamed."

For the first time since she'd join SOD, Bathsheba was speechless.

"They're beasts." Elie pulled the wool cap down over his ears. "The Germans. The French. The Arabs. All of them. Beasts. Don't forget it. They're the beasts and we're the lambs."

"Get back in the car," she said. "Gideon can manage by himself."

"Redundancy is the key to success." Elie touched the handle of the blade that was sheathed against his thigh. The pain was gone from his chest. The net was suspended above his prey, ready to drop. He felt like the fearless youth he had once been, kneeling in deep snow by an Alpine road with Abraham Gerster, ready to take revenge on another Nazi.

The room on the third floor smelled of hashish and unwashed bodies. The plastic shade over the lamp on the night table was painted with red leaves and green flowers, which threw bleak shadows on the walls. A stained quilt covered the bed. A fan turned slowly above.

Gideon put his knapsack on the bed. Before he could turn, Abu Yusef's hands encircled his waist, and the soft belly pressed against his back. He shuddered in disgust as moist lips slurped his nape.

"Ah, Grant!"

An overwhelming tide of nausea swept Gideon as Abu Yusef's hands grabbed his crotch. The room rolled around him, and he took a deep breath, exhaling loudly. This brought about a series of lustful sighs from behind, and Gideon raised his hands to absorb the impact as he was thrown facedown onto the bed, the Arab atop him, thrusting, breathing faster. A tongue stuck deep into his ear.

In panic, Gideon rolled aside, pushing him off.

Abu Yusef was panting hard. He slipped his fingers into Gideon's curls, clutching hard. "You're just so sexy!"

He forced a smile. *"Merci."*

Abu Yusef seemed bothered by something. He reached into the pocket of his jacket and took out a round object. As he placed it on the bed, Gideon realized it was a hand grenade.

A ny feelings of inadequacy evaporated when Abu Yusef saw Grant's apprehension. He had planned to impress the young banker with the grenade, and the effect was magical. Overweight and out of breath after a few minutes of lustful physical exertion, he was still a warrior, a brave man, who inspired awe in young men. It had been the same with Latif, may he rest in peace.

"Is this a real bomb?"

Abu Yusef sat up on the bed. "Don't be afraid. It's not going to explode—unless I make it go off."

Grant nodded, but his face remained tense, and he glanced at his knapsack on the bed. He must be thinking of leaving, Abu Yusef realized. "I'm experienced with weapons. It's very safe if you know what you're doing."

"Really?"

Abu Yusef held up the grenade. "If you pull this ring and the pin comes out, it's four seconds." He made a sudden motion with his hands and yelled, "Boom!"

The laughter brought them closer, but clearly the bank clerk was not yet ready to take off his clothes. Abu Yusef got down from the bed, placed the grenade on the floor, and pushed apart Grant's knees. They parted reluctantly, so he pushed harder, which excited him even more. "Let me pleasure you. Don't be afraid."

"Okay…but go slow."

"Sit back, and I'll take care of you." Abu Yusef leaned forward and kissed the rough cloth of Grant's trousers, his hand reaching down to unzip his own fly.

The hardest part was not to vomit. Gideon's hands rested on Abu Yusef's shoulders. He wished he could just strangle the Arab. He could try. He was younger. But Abu Yusef was bigger and heavier.

Stick to the plan!

He looked down at the Arab's head digging in his groin, heard the sounds of slurping and groaning. From above, the sight of the thinning, oily hair made him convulse. Abu Yusef reached for the grenade on the floor, held it, rubbed it against himself, while his kissing lips searched through Gideon's trousers for a trace of an erection. It would not be long before he realized this was a one-sided affair.

Gideon swallowed to push down a tide of sickness. He reached into the knapsack with one hand and found the orange. He tore off the skin with the underlying foil and held the small ball in his fist.

His face still buried in Gideon's groin, Abu Yusef lifted the grenade and pressed it to Gideon's chest. The sight of the live grenade in the Arab's hand was unsettling. Would Abu Yusef manage to pull out the fuse in the last minute and take Gideon's life with his own?

There was no time for contemplation. Gideon brought the tiny bomb to his mouth, and closed his teeth on the head of the tiny fuse. At the same time, he placed the palm of his right hand on Abu Yusef's forehead. The Arab shook with lust, his motions intensifying, biting into Gideon's crotch, his teeth plowing the pants. Gideon pushed on the sweaty forehead, tilting back the head, and Abu Yusef's face turned upward, the mouth gaping, dripping with saliva, the eyes wide and partly blinded by the light. Gideon's left hand pulled the small ball, the fuse pin remaining between his teeth, and dropped the ball into the Arab's gaping mouth, shoving it deeper with his thumb until it slid far down the back of the mouth into the throat.

Abu Yusef gagged. He tried to breathe. His mustachioed face stricken by incomprehension, his hands—the right one still holding the grenade—reached for his throat.

"Swallow!" Gideon forced the Arab's jaw to close and slapped him across the face. "It's good for you."

There was a sound resembling a hiccup, and the ball of explosives slid down into Abu Yusef's stomach.

Gideon kicked him in the chest, sending him to the floor, and rolled over the bed to the opposite side, landing behind it.

Elie passed by the BMW, a little old man in a winter coat and a wool cap, hunched and slow, drawing no attention from Bashir Hamami, who sat inside with the engine running. Up the three steps, he was gone through the wood-and-glass doors into the motel.

The night manager asked, "*Que veux tu?*"

Elie handed him a few bills. "Two men came in a little while ago, one much younger."

"Room thirty-two." He pointed at the stairs. "Third floor on the right."

Elie climbed up the stairs. Reaching the third floor, he paused on the landing to catch his breath. A door cracked open, and Gideon beckoned him in.

Abu Yusef was lying on the carpet, red foam dripping from his mouth. His eyes glared, frozen in horror. His pants were bundled around his ankles, and bloody feces piled by his naked buttocks.

"You used too much explosives."

"Next time I'll use a fake grape."

Elie leaned over the dead face. "*Nekamah,*" he said quietly. "Revenge." He handed Gideon a Polaroid camera he'd carried under his coat.

The camera ejected each photograph with a buzzing sound as it recorded Abu Yusef's humiliating end.

"The money is in the car," Gideon said as they stepped out of the room. "A black briefcase."

Downstairs, Elie went out first. He ambled past the BMW, his collar pulled up against the cold. At the corner he told Bathsheba, "Be careful. He's clever and vicious."

"He's a pig." She strolled down the street, her heels knocking on the cobblestones.

Elie watched from behind the corner. He saw Bashir's head turn, following Bathsheba as she walked by the car, her long, sculpted legs in black stockings, the leather miniskirt swaying.

She paused by the Pinnacle and pulled a cigarette from her cleavage. She stooped and looked at Bashir through the car windshield.

His window slid down. He flipped on a lighter and reached out with both hands, shielding the small flame.

"Nice car," Bathsheba said. "Are you German?"

He grinned.

She put the cigarette between her lips and leaned on his hands. The tip of the cigarette entered the flame, and she drew in, blowing the smoke in his face. Her fingers closed around his right wrist, weighing down on it. Her grip must have been firmer than he had expected, yet her smile was disarmingly lurid. Elie was impressed by her coolness.

The burning cigarette fell from her mouth. "My father died in Munich."

She was taking too long. Elie started toward the BMW while reaching under his coat for the blade.

Bashir dropped the lighter and pulled his hands back in. But Bathsheba was ready. Her right hand rose, and the black barrel of the handgun, lengthened by a silencer, pointed at Bashir's chest. It coughed twice, and his body jerked with each shot. She brought the end of the silencer to her lips and blew on it.

Gideon emerged from the motel and approached the BMW while Bathsheba was walking back toward Elie, slow in high heels over the cobblestones. Elie sheathed the blade, relieved. He beckoned them to hurry up as a group of Frenchmen emerged from the bar up the street, blabbering loudly.

The BMW's white reverse lights came on.

Gideon reached under his coat for a gun he didn't have. Elie opened his mouth to warn Bathsheba, but the engine roared and the tires screeched.

She turned abruptly and lost her balance, falling down. Gideon was on the pavement within reach of the BMW, but there was nothing he could do as the large car leaped backward. Bathsheba tried to get up, but she was too slow. Her hands rose in futile defense as the rear bumper hit her. The car continued, the right wheels running over Bathsheba's extended legs, crushing her bones in a series of sickening crunches. The car jumped the curb and hit the wall of a building.

His perforated chest dark with blood, Bashir turned slowly and looked at Elie through the passenger-side window, his face a mixture of pain and satisfaction. Up the street, the bar patrons yelled, and a few of them approached what seemed like a drunk driver running over a prostitute. Elie crossed the street, leaned on the car, and inserted the blade just above Bashir's collarbone, sliding it downward into his chest cavity. For a second he felt the Arab's heart muscles flutter against the blade. He twisted and pulled it out, while Bashir uttered a last groan.

Gideon sprinted to Bathsheba. He grabbed her arms, pulled her up over his shoulders, and hurried to the Citroën. They laid her on the back seat, legs folded up.

Pulling Abu Yusef's hand grenade from the knapsack, Gideon ran back to the BMW. He snatched the heavy briefcase from the passenger seat, tore out the fuse from the grenade, and tossed it in.

As they raced away, a ball of fire exploded behind them.

Gideon made a sharp turn, and in the back seat Bathsheba cried, "*Daddy!*"

A moment later she became quiet. Glancing back, he saw her open eyes, not moving.

Dr. Geloux took a while to get downstairs from his living quarters. He unlocked the front door and let them into the clinic. Gideon lowered Bathsheba on an examination table. Her face was gray and blank. He closed her eyelids.

There was a telephone in the outer office. "Make the calls," Elie said.

Gideon called the police station in Ermenonville. He told the attending officer that he lived on Boulevard Royale and was hearing explosions and the staccato of automatic weapons from the direction of a villa surrounded by a brick wall. He made similar calls to the police stations in neighboring Senlis and Chantilly.

Dr. Geloux joined them a few minutes later. "Terrible shame," he said. "Such a beautiful young woman."

Gideon dropped into a chair. He felt cold and empty.

Elie handed Dr. Geloux an envelope with the photographs they had taken of Abu Yusef's dead body. "We have to leave Paris immediately. Please take this to the nearest TV station. Tell them it's Abu Yusef. His body is at the Pinnacle Motel near Gare du Nord, room thirty-two."

Dr. Geloux put the envelope in his pocket.

Elie opened the black briefcase and took out a bundle of bills. "Hide this briefcase. We'll come back for it."

The doctor pushed it into a closet.

"Let's go," Elie said.

Gideon stood. "What about Bathsheba?"

"She made a mistake and paid for it. Nothing we could do." Elie turned to Dr. Geloux. "Call the Israeli embassy, leave word for Tanya Galinski. She'll make the arrangements to ship the body to Israel for a proper burial."

"Tanya Galinski?" The doctor scratched his chin. "Is she a petite woman, with dark hair, a porcelain face, and the bearing of a princess?"

"Yes," Elie said, "that would be Tanya. Why?"

"She was here yesterday, looking for you."

"*Here?*" Elie gripped Gideon's arm. "We must leave! Now!"

When they opened the door to exit the clinic, several quiet men pointed guns at them.

Tanya appeared from the shadows. "Shalom, Elie."

Thursday, October 26, 1995

The El Al jumbo jet stood on the tarmac far from the main terminal at Charles De Gaulle Airport. Several armored police vehicles guarded the plane. The first group of passengers crossed the short distance from the bus to the stairs. Gideon watched them through the window on the upper deck. A Mossad agent guarded the door, occasionally whispering to his wristwatch.

Some of the first-class seats had been removed to make room for Bathsheba's coffin and Elie's hospital bed. He was asleep. His skin was almost transparent, and his facial bones gave him a skeletal appearance. A nurse attended to his IV bags and the heart monitor.

While the flight attendants downstairs recited the emergency instructions for use of exits and oxygen masks, Tanya Galinski showed up with a small entourage. She greeted Gideon with a nod. He turned away, adjusted the small pillow against the fuselage, and closed his eyes.

Pierre was ready for Prince Abusalim in the bathroom with a jar of warm lather and soft music on the radio. He fastened the cape around the prince's neck, lowered the back of the barber chair, and laid a steamed towel over his eyes. He applied the lather to the prince's cheeks and chin while on the radio Jacques Brel sang *"Regarde Bien Petite."*

The blade was like a musical instrument in Pierre's hand, hovering near the skin so lightly that Prince Abusalim barely felt it. Pierre worked slowly, patiently, humming with Brel as he stretched each plot of skin and slid the blade.

His eyes closed under the soothing facecloth, Prince Abusalim thought about the dramatic events that would unfold in the next few days, paving the path to the restoration of the family's greatness and his own eternal fame. Pierre was done with the left side, and the prince heard him shuffle around the chair. Brel continued singing, but Pierre stopped humming.

The prince began to wonder. He pulled the warm towel off his eyes and tried to sit up, but strong hands held him down.

The barber was gone. Hajj Vahabh Ibn Saroah looked back from the mirror, his brown skin and white hair oddly out of place in the dark business suit that replaced his robe and kafiya. He held Pierre's blade. His sun-beaten face radiated raw power. Two men stood by the chair, holding the prince down.

The hajj took out a pocket-size cassette player and placed it on the counter among the toiletries. He leaned over Prince Abusalim and brought the blade to the skin, moving it down, marking a dark path in the white lather. When the hajj placed the blade for a second take, the voices came from the small cassette player:

"Our operation last week was just the beginning. Allah will bring us victory. And he will bless you with fortunes ten times your generosity."

Prince Abusalim recognized Abu Yusef's voice and tried to rise, only to be pushed down. He heard his own voice reply: "Yes. I think He will. How much do you need?"

"The fight is long and costly. Very costly."

"Truth is, I'm having some difficulties right now."

"I understand." Abu Yusef paused. "Can we help?"

"There is a man who stands in my way. He will be in Paris soon."

"We shall be honored to remove that man from your way."

"Five million dollars."

"Excellency! Your friendship alone is a sufficient gift. But of course, we accept!"

"Good. I'll arrange to transfer half the amount. Call me on Wednesday morning for the details. The other half will be paid after you remove him."

"Agreed! And who is that dog, that filthy infidel, who dared to stand in your way?"

"Turn it off!" Prince Abusalim again struggled to sit up, but fell back, defeated, his own condemning words coming from the counter:

"That man is my father, Sheik Da'ood Ibn Hisham az-Zubayr."

"What did you say?"

"You heard me. My father will be in Paris next week. I'll let you know where he's staying. And I don't want him to suffer. A clean job, that's what I'm looking for."

"Your own father? Allah's mercy!"

"Can you do it?"

"Ah, well, for the freedom of Palestine, five million—"

The hajj's fingers tightened around Prince Abusalim's wavy mane, holding his head back against the headrest. He slid the blade down the prince's cheek, taking bristles and skin with it. "Stealing from your father to pay for his murder?"

The prince shouted, "Get your hands off me, *slave!*"

"I'm proud to serve." The hajj looked down at him. "Your father is a great man." He pushed up the back of the barber chair until Prince Abusalim was sitting up straight, the white cape around his neck, the hajj's left hand tightly clenched in his hair. The other hand held the blade to the prince's neck. "Your father is my master, not you!"

"And my father must have told you not to harm me!"

"*Do not raise your hand to my boy!* He did say that."

"Then obey! Or you'll pay dearly!"

"But I must protect my master, especially when his kind heart could cause his demise. I've known you since the moment you came out of your mother's womb. You won't wait for Allah to take your father in old age. You're a menace, and I'm your father's protector."

"If you kill me, my father will never forgive you!"

"All the same, I must do my duty. Now beg for Allah's forgiveness." The hajj's hand pulled hard on Prince Abusalim's hair, tilting his head back. With one quick movement, he slashed the prince's throat from ear to ear.

In the mirror, Prince Abusalim saw blood burst out of his slashed throat. At first there was no pain, but soon a fire spread from his throat to his chest and arms, and in another moment his whole body was burning. He tried to move but couldn't. The blood oozed down onto the white cape. He tried to talk, his jaw moving up and down without sound. The air that left his lungs never reached his vocal cords but slurped out through his severed trachea. He realized that this was the sound of his last breath. In desperation, his hands rose to stem the flow of blood, but he slumped, powerless. His head dropped forward, his eyes still open, seeing only red.

Gideon woke up as the jetliner crossed the coastline south of Tel Aviv. Hebrew music played on the speakers, "*We bring shalom upon you.*" The small TV screen above the aisle showed a video clip produced by the Israeli Ministry of Tourism, with flowers and sunshine and deep blue water splashed by a passing windsurfing board and a pretty woman on a grinning camel.

Down below, Gideon saw the cigar-like shadow of the plane on the blue water, the sandy Tel Aviv beach, and the strip of five-star hotels. The jetliner tipped its wings eastward. The roar of its engines drew up the tiny faces of fishermen on the rocky pier of Jaffa's old harbor.

They descended in a wide crescent over Ramla and Lod, touched down on a runway that bordered well-groomed fields, and came to a final stop a few hundred feet from the main terminal.

On the upper deck, a side door opened to welcome a hydraulic ramp. Men in El Al uniforms rolled out Bathsheba's coffin and Elie's hospital bed.

Gideon followed them onto the ramp, which descended to the ground. Feather clouds floated above, and the warm rays of the sun shone on Elie's face. He opened his eyes, and his hand felt about until it found the heavy bible, which rested on the sheets by his side. Gideon had placed it there last night, after helping Tanya and her Mossad agents clear out the suite at the Hilton.

Elie curled a finger.

Gideon leaned over the bed to listen.

"Call Zurich," Elie whispered. "Hoffgeitz Bank. Wilhelm Horch. Tell him to launch CFS."

"Tell him what?"

"Launch...CFS."

"Hey!" One of Tanya's agents ran over. "No talking!"

Gideon gestured dismissively. "He's confused. What did you give him?"

A plane was taking off nearby, and the ground quivered with the thunderous roar of its engines.

Screeching tires made him turn. Two white Subaru sedans, each with several antennas, let out men in civilian clothes. The leader was a smallish man in his thirties with dark complexion, rust-colored hair, and a blue blazer. He flashed an identification card at Tanya. "I'm Agent Cohen from the Shin Bet. We'll take over from here."

Tanya's team stepped forward, surrounding her protectively.

Gideon watched the confrontation with interest. Cohen was a generic last name that filled several pages in the telephone directory. His accent revealed a Sephardic background, probably from Iraq or Morocco. The Shin Bet, Israel's domestic security agency, primarily engaged in counter-terror and anti-spying activities. Many of its agents were Sephardic Jews, first or second generation immigrants from Arab countries, who were able to easily infiltrate Palestinian organizations and recruit informants.

"I am Tanya Galinski," she said.

"I know. An honor to meet you."

"What's your first name, Agent Cohen?"

"It's classified." He grinned.

"Do you know who this is?" She gestured at the hospital bed standing in the sun.

"Elie Weiss, Special Operations Department. Now retired."
Agent Cohen placed a hand possessively on Elie's bedrail. "As
you are aware, Shin Bet has jurisdiction over all clandestine
activities inside Israel."

"That's the law, but—"

"He's our responsibility now."

"But we need to question him about his activities overseas,
which is Mossad's jurisdiction."

"We'll make him available to you in a few days." Cohen
beckoned to his men. They rolled Elie's bed into an ambulance
marked with a red Star of David and loaded Bathsheba's coffin
into a hearse. Both vehicles drove off, disappearing around
the terminal building. The Shin Bet team got back into their
Subaru sedans.

Tanya walked over to Cohen's window. "What Shin Bet
department are you with?"

"Yehida Le'Avtahat Isihim."

Gideon was surprised. The VIP Protection Unit provided
bodyguards for senior government officials. Did it also conduct
investigative operations? Their sudden appearance here implied
that they did. But why were they interested in Elie Weiss?

Tanya tilted her head at the departing ambulance. "Are
you taking him into protective custody? Because I really need
access to him—"

"No problem." Agent Cohen's car began to move. "We'll be
in touch."

Tanya watched the departing cars. How did Shin Bet know she
was bringing Elie back? Perhaps someone at El Al Airlines
was on the lookout? It would have been better to question him
in Paris, find out about his network and how close he had come
to Klaus's fortune. The small, leather-bound ledger that Klaus
had entrusted to her in 1945, which she had given to Elie in
1967, was nowhere to be found in Elie's hotel suite or among
his belongings. Where was he hiding it? Without the ledger she
had no basis to approach the Hoffgeitz Bank.

And why was Shin Bet so eager to take custody of Elie before Mossad had a chance to properly question him? The Abu Yusef assassination clearly fell under Mossad's overseas jurisdiction. Something was up, and she was piqued. Did they know about the Nazi fortune? Everyone in the upper echelons of the small Israeli intelligence community envied the financial independence of SOD and its consequent freedom from bureaucratic budgetary constraints. But Elie's operation had always been tiny in comparison, too little for anyone at Shin Bet or Mossad to make a move to take over SOD. And as far as Tanya knew, only Abraham and Elie were aware of the plundered fortune her Nazi lover had deposited with the Hoffgeitz Bank of Zurich fifty years earlier. Had Elie managed to put his hands on it?

She turned to her agents. "I'll see you at headquarters tomorrow morning."

They departed toward the main terminal, and she held Gideon's arm, following behind. "Gidi'leh, how long have you worked for Elie?"

"Three years."

"Do you know where he got the money to finance SOD operations?"

"I know where he got the orders—from the prime minister."

"Elie was his own man. He took no orders."

"Why do you use the past tense? He's not dead yet."

There was no point in arguing. She stopped at the foot of the steps leading up to the terminal. "What are your plans?"

"I'd like to continue to serve."

"Well, SOD has just gone out of business."

"Don't be so sure. Elie believed in redundancy. He always had two tracks going on at the same time."

"Not when it came to himself. SOD was his show, and it's retiring with him. It's over. Would you like me to talk to Bira about a position for you at Hebrew University's archeology department?"

"In exchange for information?"

The sun was in her eyes, and Tanya used her hand as a visor. "I'll help you no matter what. But you care about Israel's security, don't you? Elie spent decades building a network of agents in Europe, possibly elsewhere. And he's got money for operations. Why should his agents and funds go to waste?"

"I can't help you. Elie traveled on his own, conducted hushed telephone conversations, and told us only what we needed to know. He kept things strictly compartmentalized."

"How about a notebook? A computer file? Any lists?"

"None that I saw, other than the files concerning Abu Yusef."

"We got those. Do you know names? Contacts? Locations?"

"Sorry."

She sensed that he was holding back. "Come by Bira's house later. Her vines have ripened late this year, red and juicy. I'll have her squeeze a pitcher for us, okay?"

Gideon smiled.

They passed through the wide doors into the main terminal and were greeted by the familiar air of impatience and excitement. The place was bustling with passengers and luggage carts. Loudspeakers played Hebrew music. They were home.

Tanya's team had tried to pry information from him in Paris the night before, but Elie had laughed at them. So they had put him to sleep, and now he was back in Israel. He held his bible, which gave him confidence that his plans would proceed despite this interruption. The switch at the airport had troubled him. It was all temporary, of course, until the deal with Rabin materialized. But why was Shin Bet so eager to take him in? He could hardly think with the drugs still in his system.

From the sights outside the window Elie could tell the ambulance was traveling east, across the Ayalon Valley on the Tel Aviv-Jerusalem Expressway. He glanced at the nurse, a plain, middle-aged woman, who sat on the bench with the patience of one used to long hours on the job.

The ambulance slowed down and took an exit ramp. A moment later it stopped on the side of the road. The nurse opened the rear doors and stepped out. Elie saw a gray Cadillac stop behind the ambulance.

A man in oversized sunglasses came out of the Cadillac and climbed into the ambulance. The doors closed, and a moment later they were moving again.

Prime Minister Yitzhak Rabin sat on the bench and took off his glasses. His face was wrinkled, his hair almost white, but his vital gruffness hadn't changed.

Elie cleared his throat. "Shalom, Yitzhak."

"Welcome home, Weiss." Unlike most of his generation, Yitzhak Rabin was a born Israeli, not an immigrant from Europe, and his Hebrew was free of any Diaspora accent. "How're you feeling?"

"In need of a major overhaul." Elie coughed.

"The doctors at Hadassah Hospital will put you back on your feet." Rabin leaned closer. "You've done Israel a great service by removing Al-Mazir, Abu Yusef, and their Saudi sponsor. Arafat can now proceed with the third phase of the Oslo process. And you can finally rest."

"Rest? I must get back to work. Great dangers ahead—"

"You've done enough." Rabin tilted his head sideways, signaling impatience. "It's the era of peace, my friend. Two states for two people."

"It'll never happen if your government falls. I told you. Everything is lined up."

"I can't accept your deal."

So that's what he came to say.

"Don't you want to stay in power? Don't you want Oslo to succeed?"

Rabin shifted on the hard bench. "I can't appoint you intelligence czar. Your agenda is too militant."

"Peace won't work without it. Carrots need sticks. Our enemies need deterrence."

"You're an old warrior. Me too. For us, peace is hard to believe in. But it's happening."

"All the more reason to eliminate anti-Semitic germs before they infect those willing to make peace with us. My network will launch—"

"Your time is over, Weiss. Retire, pass the torch, let other people do the job. We'll take care of your people, of course, once you tell us who they are."

Elie tried to speak, yet no voice sounded. He coughed again, and the burning in his chest blurred his vision. It was maddening that now, when he had finally managed to line up all his cards in a neat row, his own body was betraying him.

"Calm down, Weiss." The prime minister rested his hand on Eli's forearm. "Everything is taken care of."

Feeling Yitzhak Rabin's cool hand against his burning skin sent a shudder through Elie. It was a large hand, soft yet meaty, like a farmer's hand that had been away from the plow for too long. This unexpected gesture of affection told Elie that this was a farewell visit, not the bargaining among equals he had expected. "Not yet." He forced the words out. "There's work to be done."

Rabin smiled, his eyes creased. "Your life is a legend. I know better than anyone else that our victory in sixty-seven would have been a terrible defeat, a calamity, if not for your secret operation to destroy the UN radar. We owe you the glory of the Six Day War. And the Yom Kippur War, which could have been a second Holocaust if not for you. And now, our peace with Arafat would have been in peril if not for your decisive actions in Paris."

"There's more—"

"It's time to say *enough*. You must cooperate with the Shin Bet in winding down your operations. It's an order!"

Elie reached with great effort and grabbed the prime minister's shirt. "Don't you understand? I'm about to save you!"

"Save me?" Rabin laughed. "I have signed a peace agreement with Jordan, two interim agreements with the Palestinians—a dream come true! But when I come home at night, Orthodox hoodlums curse me and wave posters showing me in SS uniform. And to get Knesset approval for Oslo, I had to rely on the Arab members, and Shimon Peres had to bribe a member with a ministerial post and a staff car to get the tiebreaking vote. How can you help me? Get real!" The prime minister lit a cigarette, drawing on it a few times, filling the ambulance with smoke.

Elie extended his hand.

Rabin gave him the cigarette. "I don't need killers anymore. I need peacemakers—doctors, scientists, entrepreneurs, farmers, builders. Your time has passed, Weiss, and my time will pass soon as well. History will recognize us for what we've done for our people—you in secret, me in public."

The smoke filled Elie's lungs. He let it out slowly. "I've set things in motion. To help you regain popularity."

"I'm not making deals."

"Imagine. A right-wing assassin. Caught red-handed. In public." He drew from the cigarette and spoke while smoke came from his mouth. "In front of TV cameras. Your bulletproof vest shown to the world. The assassin's bullets still stuck in it. You'll bounce in the polls. You'll win!"

"I don't like to wear a bulletproof vest."

"You should. You must!"

Prime Minister Yitzhak Rabin got up, keeping his head bowed under the roof of the ambulance. He knocked three times on the partition separating the driver's cabin. "I'll win public opinion with peace, not with bullets."

"The wheels are already turning." Elie rose on one elbow. "You'll see! Each bullet's worth a million votes—"

"Shin Bet is dealing with local terrorists—Muslim Arabs, Orthodox Jews, whatever. They keep us safe. Keeps *me* safe."

"It's my expertise." Elie fought to keep his voice even. "Orthodox militants can bring down Israel. I still have assets."

"We have enough moles." Rabin knocked on the partition again. "You're very sick, Weiss. Make peace with the past. Take pride in what you've achieved. And share everything with the boys. Including your financial resources. We're all on the same side, you know?"

"Come on, Yitzhak." Elie tried to smile, feeling the ambulance slow down. "We go a long way back. Once I'm recovered, we can do great things together. Say the word, and the doctors will save me. They kept Golda alive for ten years with lung cancer!"

"Be well, Weiss."

"I have money for your campaign." Elie's voice was reduced to hoarse screeching. He grasped the heavy bible, lifting it. "Billions of dollars—"

The ambulance swerved to the side of the road, bumping over a pothole, and the bible dropped to the floor.

Rabin picked it up, put it on Elie's chest, and stepped down from the ambulance. A few seconds later, his chauffeur-driven Cadillac departed toward Jerusalem with a hiss of its powerful engine.

The nurse reappeared. She fixed the pillow under Elie's head. The ambulance continued on, shaking on the bumpy road.

He gestured at the small window. She opened it, and a soft breeze carried in the scents of Jerusalem pine. He watched the trees pass by, heard the whistles of sparrows, and contemplated his next move.

Tanya greeted the two soldiers at the entrance to the Mount Herzl Cemetery. She followed the path through the rows of rectangular gravestones, each bearing the name of a dead soldier. Elderly parents and a few young women tended to pots of flowers. An old man lounged in a beach chair, arguing with a headstone, his hands gesticulating in emphasis.

She reached Lemmy's grave and knelt beside it to brush off the dust and dry leaves from a recent storm. Her movements were almost automatic after years of practice—a ritual she had kept since 1967, stopping by every time she visited Israel. A few pieces of gravel rested on the stone—a mourners' custom. She counted six—one for each time Rabbi Gerster had visited his son since she had last cleaned the headstone. She sighed. *O, Abraham, what pain we've caused each other.*

With a handkerchief she cleaned the letters carved into the stone, shining each one patiently, and stepped back to look at the writing:

PRIVATE JERUSALEM ("LEMMY") GERSTER
KILLED IN BATTLE, JUNE 7, 1967
IN THE DEFENSE OF ISRAEL
GOD WILL AVENGE HIS BLOOD

Tanya brushed off an errant leaf. She noticed age spots on the back of her hand. So many years had passed. Such a loss. Unfair. Lemmy would have been forty-six now, a grown man with a family and a career. Successful. Happy. But no, he had been deprived of all the wonderful experiences of adult life. He was dead. Buried. Gone.

"Haven't seen you in a long time."

She turned, wiping her tears.

It was the old man with the beach chair, now folded under his arm. "Been away, eh?" His handlebar mustache moved with each word. It would have been comical if not for the wet lines down his creased cheeks.

Tanya nodded.

"I visit my son every day. I'm retired, wife's dead, so what else is there?"

"I work," she said, "to keep my mind busy."

He gestured at Lemmy's grave. "Your son?"

She hesitated. "Lover."

"Ah, well. That's a different kind of pain." The old man looked at Lemmy's inscription, likely trying to calculate their age difference.

"He was eighteen, I was thirty-seven."

"A boy with good taste."

"Thank you." She thought for a moment, and then told the stranger what she had not told anyone else. "I killed him."

He pointed to the stone. "Says here he was killed in battle. You don't look Arab to me."

"If not for me, he wouldn't have been on the Golan Heights. Or in the army."

"That explains it." The man put down the folded chair and leaned on it like a crutch. "The men of Neturay Karta don't enlist in the army."

"How do you know he was from Neturay Karta?"

"I see his father here every once in a while. The infamous Rabbi Abraham Gerster, leader of the ultra-Orthodox fanatics. But he's not the extremist the media made him out to be. A kind man, actually."

"True." Tanya sighed. "And I took away his only child."

"Do you have any children?"

Tanya hesitated. "A daughter."

"No husband?"

She shook her head. No one but Elie and Abraham knew that her daughter, Professor Bira Galinski, was the daughter of SS Oberstgruppenführer Klaus von Koenig, whom Abraham shot dead in the snowy forest one night near the end of World War II.

"Guilt is the worst pain." The man pointed at his son's grave. "Shalom was our only child. Our pride and joy. A handsome, smart, miracle boy. Our precious Shalom." He sighed. "An irony, isn't it? We named our baby for peace, and he grew up to die in war."

"Yes," Tanya said, choking on sudden tears. "An irony."

"As an only child, Shalom was supposed to serve in an office, far from the front. But I agreed to sign a consent form. He wanted to serve as a frogman. It was a matter of pride for him, to serve in a fighting unit, like his friends. And he had never asked for anything else. What could I do? Refuse his only request?" He stooped, as if all the air deflated from him. "*Ay, yai, yai.* Don't tell me about guilt. I hold a world record in guilt."

"I'm close behind you," Tanya said. "If not for me seducing him, Lemmy would have stayed in the yeshiva, studying Talmud, becoming a rabbi. I often think of what he lost—all those beginnings that make life worth it—a wedding, a first child's birth, a baby's smile, the joys of a full life—"

"Don't beat yourself up." The old man waved his hand. "Those black hats live in a kosher cocoon. At least you gave him a taste of real life before he died."

She remembered Lemmy on top of her, inside her, crying her name, possessed by passion and joy. The memory made her smile. "Thank you for putting it in perspective."

"My pleasure." He glanced at his wristwatch. "Got to see the wife before dark. She's at Sanhedriah Cemetery. So, shalom!"

"Shalom."

He turned toward his son's grave and yelled, "See you tomorrow, *Boychik!*"

Tanya sat on the ground by Lemmy's grave. His face came to her, tanned under the military haircut, his blue eyes squinted in laughter, his lips moist and sweet and warm. Despite what the old man had said, the guilt would forever fester in her. She had won Lemmy's heart, and his body too. But to achieve that, she had to tear him away from his world and put him on a path that took him to war and made him another statistic in the great victory of the Six Day War. And now, twenty-eight years later, Abraham was living as a monk among the ultra-Orthodox, and Tanya was working around the clock without a break lest her mind find the time to roam a regrettable past. And if she ever retired from Mossad, would she come here every day with a beach chair to carry on a conversation with a dead boy?

A while later she got up to leave. It was true, she realized, that the older you get, the fresher your memories become. Before she reached the gate, rain started to fall. She quickened her pace. The drizzle turned to a downpour. The guards hid under a canopy.

Bira leaned over and opened the passenger door. She held a pen between her teeth and a pile of students' exams in her lap. "You're soaked." She handed Tanya a box of Kleenex.

The rain drummed on the roof of the car, and the water formed streams down the windshield, giving the world a distorted, gray appearance.

When she wiped her face, the thin tissue paper fell apart, the pieces sticking to Tanya's skin. "Look at this. Who makes this junk?"

"It's not a bath towel, Mom."

They looked at each other and burst out laughing.

"Do you see these spots?" Tanya showed the back of her hand to Bira. "Like an old woman!"

Bira put the exams on the back seat and turned on the engine. "You're sixty-seven. What do you expect? Acne?"

"I expect nothing," Tanya said. "I had misery when I was young and beautiful, so why should I care about getting old."

"Why don't you retire and come live with us? The kids would love it. Eytan wants to build an extra bathroom to provide you with privacy. He's giving a new meaning to the Oedipal complex—he's in love with his mother-in-law!"

Tanya looked out the window at the passing views of wet sidewalks and people bent under umbrellas. "A man told me that he sees Abraham here often."

"Don't change the subject."

"I wish you didn't choose a career that runs so opposite to his people."

"You agree with what he said?" Bira quoted. "'Archeologists incite hate and violence between secular and Orthodox Jews for the sake of meaningless clay shards!'"

"Here we go again." Tanya sighed. "You could sympathize a tiny bit with his lifelong efforts to prevent fighting among Jews—"

"By appeasing those fanatical black hats?"

"Fine. You win." Tanya looked away. "Let's go home. I only have one night to spend with my grandkids."

"Only one night?" Bira glanced at her mother while changing gears. "Can't they leave you alone? You've done so much. Let others risk their lives."

"Don't be ridiculous. I'm not risking my life. I'm a government bureaucrat, a paper-pusher."

"I read the news, okay?" Bira drove slowly, staring forward through the mist left by the swishing wipers. "The Palestinian, Al-Mazir, killed in Paris. The attack on the synagogue. Abu Yusef's macabre departure. The Saudi prince's botched haircut. And the next day you suddenly show up in Jerusalem with a nasty bruise on your forehead, looking like you've been up for a week straight. I'm not stupid, and you're too old to dodge bullets."

"Rabin is older than me. And Golda Meir was even older when she took office. Maybe I'll run for prime minister? Shamir left Mossad to enter politics."

"You took over his job, didn't you?"

Tanya looked at her with surprise. "Shamir ran the Europe desk before me. But we are very different."

"I hope so. Had Shamir won another term as prime minister, we would still have no hope of peace. I couldn't wait for Rabin to beat him in ninety-two."

"Me too," Tanya said quietly. "Me too."

"Herr Horch?" Christopher was on the intercom. "There's a call for you. From Jerusalem."

"From whom?" A cold front passed through Lemmy's chest.

"He says his name is Grant Guerra."

"From Senlis?"

"It's the same name, but the call came from Jerusalem through the international operator. It's a collect call."

"I'll take it." Lemmy had seen the news of Abu Yusef's gruesome assassination and the ensuing firefight at the villa in Ermenonville, where most of his men were either killed or injured in a massive police raid. A clever setup, vintage Elie Weiss. But why would Elie's agent call from Jerusalem?

Christopher transferred the call, and it rang on Lemmy's desk.

"Yes?"

"Herr Horch?"

"Speaking."

"Have I reached the right person?"

"There is no other banker in Zurich with my name, if that's your concern."

"Good. Are we alone?"

"I'm alone in my office. As to the open international phone line you're calling on, we might as well be shouting at each other across Bahnhofstrasse." Lemmy switched his computer to the video portal.

There was hesitation, as if the caller was framing his sentences with great caution. "You saw the news from Paris?"

"I watch CNN like everyone else. How can I help you?"

"It's about E.W. You know who he is?"

"What is this about?"

"He's been confined."

"Yes?"

"He ordered me to call you, tell you to launch CFS."

"Say again?" Lemmy looked at his computer screen and saw Christopher at his desk, holding the receiver to his ear, his hand on the mouthpiece.

"E.W. wants you to launch CFS. I don't know what it means."

"Neither do I," Lemmy lied. "You called the wrong number. This is a bank in Zurich. We don't launch anything. Good day."

"Wait! You transferred the money—"

Lemmy hung up. On the screen he saw Christopher put down his receiver. Why was his assistant listening in on the conversation? Lemmy put the thought aside. The message from Israel was more important right now. Elie had looked sick at their last meeting, and his order to get rid of Herr Hoffgeitz and expedite the takeover of the bank had implied the urgency of a man whose time was running out. And then he had phoned Armande and scared him into a heart attack. And now this! The order was clear. *Launch CFS! Launch Counter Final Solution!*

How was he supposed to launch it? The money was within reach, but what about an organizational chart, detailed plans, lists of agents? Everything had been Elie's exclusive domain. He had hinted about sleeper agents, ready to activate at any time. But how was Lemmy supposed to find their names and contact information? Perhaps someone else would soon be activated, ordered to make contact. For now, it was clear that his task only was to penetrate Herr Hoffgeitz's veil of secrecy and take possession of the Koenig account. Perhaps that's what Elie had meant with his order.

B ira's home was in Ramot, a suburb of two-story homes built of roughly cut Jerusalem stones. Her oldest son, Yuval, was home on leave from the army. There were three other children—two girls in their teens and a nine-year-old boy who walked around the house wearing Yuval's red beret.

As they sat down for an early dinner, the doorbell rang. Bira went to the door and returned with Gideon. He was introduced to everyone. The girls giggled and whispered in each other's ears.

Tanya led Gideon to the small garden in the back, where they sat at a white plastic table. Three bicycles in different sizes leaned against the wall near a barbecue grill covered by a piece of stained gray cloth. A fence with climbing vines separated them from the next house, but the back of the garden was open to the east, where arid hills stretched all the way to the glistening lights of a distant Arab village.

Tanya rubbed her hands to warm up. "Isn't it good to be home?"

"Mom's happy."

Bira brought a pitcher of fresh grape juice and cookies. She poured the juice into plastic cups. "Why don't you stop by the university tomorrow? A Bedouin man has brought us a piece of clay with Aramaic writing. He found it near the Dead Sea. We'll start a dig as soon as I can find financing."

He watched Bira return to the house. She was tall and big-boned, with shoulder-length blonde hair. "She doesn't look like you," he said.

"More like her father."

"You did a good job raising her alone."

"We weren't alone. Mossad is like a big family. We moved often, different assignments, but she got a lot of love and grew up fine."

"That's an understatement"

"I always marvel," Tanya said, "how natural it seems to raise kids with a loving partner in a busy home, to pursue an interesting career and worry about soccer practice and monthly bills. To me it seems like a miracle."

"Thanks for the hint." Gideon sipped juice. "You didn't invite me here to discuss my love life or Dead Sea excavations, right?"

Tanya rested her elbows on the plastic table. "We have a problem with Elie Weiss. He didn't give us any info last night in Paris, and now the Shin Bet has him. We're trying to locate his human assets abroad so we can run them under Mossad. We're also curious about his source of funds. But we can't find anything."

"Elie never shares information. He doesn't trust anyone. Keeps it all in his head."

"Was there another safe apartment in Paris?"

"I don't know."

"How about a safe deposit box in a bank? Did you drive him somewhere or pick him up in a certain location?"

"Even if I knew, I wouldn't tell you."

"Listen, I understand. He's a scary man." Tanya looked at Gideon for a long moment. "After the war, alone with a small baby, I was so afraid of Elie Weiss that I joined the Mossad to hide from him." She gestured at the three bikes leaning against the wall. "It's a different world now. And Elie's locked up. Retired. You don't have to be afraid of him any longer."

"I'm not afraid of him," Gideon said. "I'm loyal."

"Your loyalty should be to Israel, not to Elie Weiss."

"I don't see the difference."

"There's a big difference! A long time ago, Elie Weiss was legitimate. He started under Ben Gurion, building up the Special Operations Department right out of the prime minister's office. The idea was to control homegrown insurgents, such as ultra-Orthodox fanatics and religious fundamentalists, by planting moles in every yeshiva and sect. But the law required all domestic-security operations to come under the Shin Bet. Elie was never a team player, so in sixty-seven he moved SOD operations to Europe."

"Serving the State of Israel."

"His agents think they work for Israel, but they—and you—work for a rogue outfit."

"Elie said that all SOD assignments come from Prime Minister Rabin personally. Did he lie?"

"Even the prime minister can't legitimize unauthorized assassinations!" Tanya took a deep breath, calming herself. "Mossad is the only government agency authorized to conduct secret operations abroad. We are entitled to his agents and resources."

"You're wasting your time. I work for SOD. Elie took me in, you didn't."

"But Elie is out," Tanya persisted, now that Gideon had implied being silent out of loyalty, not out of ignorance. "Why let his life's work go to waste—the agents, the funds, the contacts? You must do the right thing!"

"Will you hire me as a full Mossad agent?"

"You think Mossad is so glamorous? You'll spend the next thirty years in anonymity, in constant temporariness, away from family and friends, sleeping in cheap hotels and buying information from the slime of the earth. And you won't be able to tell your friends that you're sacrificing your life for them. That's what you want?"

"Yes."

"I won't do it," Tanya said. "I've ruined enough lives. I won't ruin yours."

"Mom?" Bira showed up with the phone. "It's for you."

Tanya listened as one of her subordinates in Paris reported on the investigation of Abu Yusef's murder, which headlined every news program in Europe. "Make reservations for me," she said. "I'll fly to Zurich first thing in the morning. Alone. No escort."

She put down the phone and looked at Gideon. "Our contact in the French police said that a man resembling Abu Yusef visited a bank in Senlis, supposedly for a meeting with a young business associate regarding a large cash payment. The money had come from the Hoffgeitz Bank in Zurich. Does it ring a bell?"

"*For Whom the Bell Tolls?*" Gideon stood up. "Shalom, Tanya."

Part Four
The Resurrection

Friday,
October 27, 1995

Lemmy reached the bank before seven a.m. and dialed a telephone number he had obtained from the international operator for Kibbutz Gesher in the north of Israel. A cheerful woman answered, "*Boker tov!*"

"And to you," he said in Hebrew, using his mother tongue for the first time in many years. "I am sorry to bother you. My wife and I are on a holiday in Switzerland."

"Good for you. How can I help?"

"We're trying to find an old friend who once worked at Kibbutz Gesher as a volunteer, and we're hoping you still have his contact information."

"We've had many foreign volunteers. When was he here?"

"Maybe five or six years ago. His name is Christopher Ditmahr."

"Oh, that name I do remember. Tall, skinny, always a happy smile?"

"That's him!"

"How devious they can be." She sighed. "He's not someone you want to be friends with."

"Excuse me?"

"You heard me. How did you meet him, anyway?"

Lemmy was ready for the question. "We were on a road trip, passed by your kibbutz, and he was hitchhiking. We gave him a ride to Tel Aviv. I think it was in eighty-nine or ninety, middle of the summer. We had a wonderful chat along the way, stopped for dinner in Haifa, and so on. He told us how much he loved Israel even though he wasn't Jewish. And he said something about going to work in a Swiss bank. That's why we thought of touching base with him now, since we're visiting his country." Waiting for her reply, he wondered if she believed his story.

"I don't think you want to *touch base* with this guy."

"Why not?"

"We kicked him out."

"For what reason?"

"We found out he was a skinhead. A Nazi aficionado."

"Christopher? That's impossible!"

"He fooled us also. But one of the girls saw it."

"*It?*"

"He has a tattoo—black swastika and the letters SS."

"Are you sure?"

"I saw it with my own eyes," the woman said. "As kibbutz secretary, I had to."

"And?"

"It was right there."

"Where?"

She chuckled. "When you see him, pull down his pants. You won't miss it."

Gideon thought of his father's photograph, hanging on the living room wall at home. It was a face filled with youth and hope. Would Joshua Zahav have wanted his son to serve Israel the same way as he had served? To risk death in a distant, cold land?

At the phone booth on the street corner Gideon asked the operator to dial collect to Paris. Dr. Geloux was in his office. He agreed to ship the cash-filled briefcase to the address Gideon gave him in Tel Aviv. He didn't ask any questions.

When Gideon put down the receiver, he found several men blocking his way.

The Shin Bet officer, who had introduced himself at the airport as Agent Cohen, pulled a sheet of paper from the breast pocket. "By authority promulgated by the emergency regulations, a decree has been issued to hold you in administrative detention for up to ninety days."

When Christopher arrived at his desk, Lemmy was still contemplating what to do with the shocking information from Kibbutz Gesher. Was his assistant a Nazi mole? It had been fifty years since Germany lost the war, but Nazi organizations continued to flourish in Germany, Austria, Belgium, and some of the Balkan countries. But here in Switzerland? He had always thought of skinheads as a bunch of frustrated racist youths trying to attract attention with shaven scalps and swastika tattoos. Their wrath was directed mostly toward poor immigrants and ethnic minorities, expressed with petty violence and street demonstrations. But obviously they were much more ominous. Was Christopher employed by such a group? Were they after the Koenig fortune?

He pressed the intercom. "Good morning, Christopher. Please come in."

His assistant entered the office and sat down.

"Have you thought about Herr Hoffgeitz's inactive accounts?"

"What else?" Christopher smiled. "It can't be anything illegal. I mean, Herr Hoffgeitz would never engage in criminal activity. It could risk the bank's future."

And you, Christopher? Are you engaged in criminal activity? Are you a risk to the bank's future? Lemmy suppressed the hostility that rose inside him. "Perhaps Herr Hoffgeitz knows facts that would protect the bank in case of exposure. But he's unconscious in the ICU, his recovery in doubt, and I don't trust Günter."

"He's very secretive. I don't think he has a life outside the bank."

"Günter is merely an employee. If there's trouble, they would look to the executive in charge for answers. That's me, and I'm concerned. Very concerned." In fact, Lemmy wasn't concerned at all. There was no risk of government interference in the bank's affairs, and according to Elie, the Nazi general had been dead since 1945. "What do you think they're hiding?"

"Maybe," Christopher said, "it's about Recommendation 833?"

Lemmy considered the idea. In 1978, the Council of Europe had adopted what became known as Recommendation 833, which required European countries to share banking information when clients were suspected of international money laundering and tax evasion. Switzerland was not a member of the European Community, and Swiss bankers enjoyed a surge in business.

"It doesn't make sense," Lemmy said. "This money isn't moving—no withdrawals, no deposits. Why? Tax evaders and criminals use their accounts. We know this from our own clients. Why is this account inactive? Maybe it's related to Clause 47b?"

"What's that?" Christopher shifted uncomfortably. He hated being caught unprepared.

"When Hitler came to power, Switzerland added Clause 47b to the 1934 Banking Act. It was aimed at reinforcing secrecy of bank accounts against the competition of bankers from Liechtenstein, in order to attract deposits from German Jews, who at that time thought the new Nazi government was only after their money."

"Wasn't there a big case about it?"

"Good memory." Lemmy gave Christopher an appreciative nod. The Interhandel case involved proceeds from a post-war sale of General Aniline and Film Corporation by the German cartel I.G. Farben, which employed slave labor during the war. The scandal had exposed the Swiss banks as Nazi profiteers.

"At least we're not like Banque Leclerc."

"No," Lemmy chuckled, "we're not. Our president is dying naturally." In 1978, the Swiss Banking Commission had shut down Geneva-based Banque Leclerc after the suicide of its CEO and the discovery of another executive floating in Lake Geneva. The investigation had revealed a deficiency of close to 400 million Swiss francs related to a shady resort project.

"I would have thought it's Jewish money from the war," Christopher said. "But the Banking Association has recently sent another survey."

"Only twenty-six banks responded to the questionnaires about dormant accounts."

"Didn't they find a lot of money?"

"Peanuts. In September they informed the World Jewish Organization that they had found eight hundred and ninety-three pre-war accounts with a total value of thirty-four point one million U.S. dollars and that they would continue to search. I assure you the Hoffgeitz Bank reported no such accounts."

"But Herr Hoffgeitz would not lie to the association, would he?"

"Not blatantly." Lemmy recalled watching his father-in-law rephrasing his response to the commission to fit the idea that the account was not completely inactive because of a single attempted withdrawal in 1967. But this wasn't something Christopher should know. "I need you to think creatively. Find a path around Günter's secrecy. We must find out what he's hiding and take control of whatever it is before it becomes a problem for the bank."

The El Al flight from Tel Aviv to Zurich was only half-full, and Tanya managed to sleep for most of the time. She travelled alone, her hair covered with a headscarf, her face behind oversized sunglasses. Passport control was quick at this early hour, and she had no luggage.

She bought a cup of coffee and wandered up and down the terminal, trying to shake off a feeling that she was being watched. The people around her seemed like the typical purposeful travelers, and she could trace no tail. It must have been her own unease, travelling without escort for the first time since she had taken command of Mossad's European operations a few years earlier.

Tanya found a bank of pay phones. She had committed to memory the telephone number for the Hoffgeitz Bank. There was little to go on—the name of the bank executive who had signed the wire transfer to Senlis, which ultimately resulted in Elie's successful elimination of Abu Yusuf and the Saudi prince. But she had a hunch that Elie must have planted a mole inside the bank. There was only one way to find out.

T he phone rang and Lemmy picked it up. "Wilhelm Horch here."

"I have a message for you." It was a woman, speaking German with a Bavarian accent. "From Elie Weiss."

"Excuse me?" Lemmy watched Christopher get up and leave the office.

"I have a message from Elie Weiss."

"You have the wrong number." He heard a click and noticed Christopher's line light up. Turning to his computer, Lemmy hit the keys for the video surveillance system.

"Aren't you Herr Horch of the Hoffgeitz Bank in Zurich?"

Lemmy selected the camera in Christopher's office. On the computer screen, his assistant was holding the receiver to his ear, listening. Lemmy hung up.

On the screen, Christopher put down the receiver.

Two minutes later, the phone rang again. The delay told him that she was probably dialing the general number of the bank and following the automatic directory instructions to reach his line.

He pressed the speaker button. "Yes?"

Behind the wall, Christopher picked up his receiver and listened.

"Don't hang up." She had a calm voice, almost familiar.

"You have the wrong person."

"Elie Weiss is incapacitated. You must talk to me now. Or would you prefer that I show up in your office?"

"We open at nine a.m., if you'd like to come in." There was something in her voice that interfered with his clear thinking. But with Christopher on the line, there was no time to hesitate. "Good-bye." He hung up, went to the door, and opened it.

Christopher's hand was still on the receiver. He looked up, blushing.

"Please go downstairs," Lemmy said, "and ask the account managers to search their client lists for the last name Weiss. Someone called me, and I thought it was a wrong number, but now I realize it could be a client of one of the others—"

"I can look it up on my computer. Other than Herr Hoffgeitz's accounts, we have all the account owners' names in the database."

"I already looked," Lemmy lied. "Perhaps the account is registered to a corporation. The account managers would recognize a name if it's the trustee or the executive related to the account, even if the name on the account is different."

The phone started ringing. Christopher reached to answer it.

"I'll take it in my office. You go downstairs and ask around." He waited, watching Christopher leave. Back at his desk, Lemmy answered.

"Don't play games with me, Herr Horch."

"Lindenhof Park," he said. "It's at the top end of Oetenbachgasse. Five thirty this evening."

"That's better," she said, and the line went dead.

Lemmy turned to the window. The sky was gray and bleak. He forced himself to think clearly. Elie's agent, Grant Guerra, had called yesterday with a message that could only come from Elie: *Launch CFS!* But the woman who had just called could not be speaking for Elie, who would never allow the use of his real name on a phone line. But how did she know Elie's name and that he was incapacitated? And if she wasn't part of SOD, who was she? Not an agent for any European law enforcement agency, that was certain, or she would have arrived at the bank for an official meeting, escorted by a Swiss detective, speaking politely and expecting no answers. And an official would not agree to meet at a public park on a drizzly evening.

Was she an agent for Mossad? No. There was no trace of a Hebrew accent in her speech, which he identified as purely native German from Bavaria. And Mossad wouldn't dare harass a senior Swiss banker in such a direct manner for fear of causing a diplomatic skirmish with Switzerland, which was highly protective of its banks. A Palestinians agent? Unlikely.

Judging by her speech and haughty, clipped style of interaction, she was German through and through.

Could she belong to the same Nazi organization as Christopher? Perhaps Elie had crossed swords with them, so to speak, or had even eliminated one of their Nazi elders years ago, causing them to follow him, trace him, and discover his connection to Lemmy. Had they planted Christopher at the Hoffgeitz Bank because of Elie? Was this German woman operating as Christopher's Nazi handler? That would explain how she knew that Elie was incapacitated: Christopher had told her after eavesdropping on the call from Grant Guerra!

But did it really matter how she knew about Elie or his connection to Lemmy? She endangered his cover as Wilhelm Horch, a successful, respectable banker. Therefore she endangered his life!

Paula and Klaus Junior looked back from the photograph on his desk.

What should he do?

That wasn't the correct question, which was: *What would Elie do?*

After almost three decades of working for Elie, Lemmy knew the answer, especially now, as they were finally nearing control of the Koenig fortune, about to launch the most ambitious secret program in the history of the Jewish nation—an end to centuries of anti-Semitic genocide. The order from Elie had been consistent with the mission. *Launch CFS!* But this German woman was an enemy. There was no doubt what Elie would do in this situation. *Eliminate her!*

Lemmy looked around his office—the wood furnishings, the Persian rugs, the soft leather chairs, the original paintings on the walls, and the family photographs on his desk. This was his world. The woman posed an existential risk. He must respond in kind. And then it would be Christopher's turn—force him to divulge his true identity and who he worked for, and then make him pay the ultimate price of betrayal. Perhaps that's what Elie had meant when ordering *Launch CFS!* Did Elie know that these modern-day Nazis were on his tail? Did he expect

Lemmy's first action in the Counter Final Solution campaign to be the elimination of Christopher and his cohorts?

Kneeling by the small safe, Lemmy turned the knob left and right until it clicked. He took out the box with the Mauser.

The vast plaza in front of the Wailing Wall was mostly in the shade now, as the sun descended behind the rooftops. A late-afternoon breeze picked up. Rabbi Abraham Gerster rocked back and forth in the rear of the group of Neturay Karta men.

Benjamin led the prayers, reading each sentence aloud, pausing for the men to recite the words. *"And we shall continue to mourn,"* Benjamin chanted, *"we shall dwell in sorrow, until God forgives His sheep, until He rebuilds His house on the mountain of His glory, on the ruins of Solomon's Temple."*

Repeating the words, Rabbi Gerster looked up at the tall wall of massive stones. Even after so many years, it was hard to believe they could stand so close to the focus of centuries-old Jewish longing. As the leader of Neturay Karta, he had started this weekly prayer tradition back in 1948, after the War of Independence had left Jerusalem divided, with the Old City in Jordanian hands. Every Friday afternoon, he had led the men to a hill by the border, where they had prayed in view of Temple Mount. In 1967, the Six Day War drove the Jordanians back across the Jordan River, and Rabbi Gerster had turned the Friday afternoon prayer of longing into a Friday afternoon prayer of gratitude at the Wailing Wall. And when Benjamin had taken over as the sect's leader, he had put his own stamp on this tradition, modifying it yet again into a prayer for the rebuilding of the temple.

But for Rabbi Gerster, this special time of the week—the hours before the commencement of the Sabbath—was a time of reflection about a past that had grown more painful with time. He thought of those early Fridays on the hill by the border, when Lemmy was a toddler, light as a feather, happy in his father's strong arms atop the huge boulder, with the

Jordanian-occupied Old City spread before them, the ancient walls and the Tower of David in reddish-brown, glowing in the twilight. The prayers had been mournful back then, but the days had been happy, Lemmy a blonde boy who loved his daddy with complete, unblemished adoration.

"Rabbi?" Benjamin took his arm. The prayer was over, time to walk back to Meah Shearim and receive the Sabbath. "Are you feeling all right?"

"Thank God, yes." He smiled at Benjamin. "And you?"

They followed the group up the ramp, away from the Wailing Wall.

"I'm worried," Benjamin said.

"Why?"

He helped Rabbi Gerster up a set of stairs. "Perhaps we can take you to a doctor?"

"There's nothing wrong with me, other than the fact that I'm getting old."

They reached the top of the stairs and followed the road that circled the Old City along the walls. A group of tourists surrounded their guide, who gestured at the firing slats in the ancient battlements, his Spanish rapid and melodic. A few of the tourists stared at the ultra-Orthodox group as if it were part of Jerusalem's quaint attractions.

"I'm worried, because you disappear for hours at a time, and Sorkeh complains that the food she brings for you is left untouched." Years ago, the rabbi had given his apartment to Benjamin and moved into an alcove off the foyer of the synagogue, which did not have a kitchen.

"Tell me something," Rabbi Gerster said. "As my heir, my successor in leading Neturay Karta, can you point to the primary lesson I have taught you, to the fundamental idea, the consistent thread of light in the chaos of faith?"

"That's an odd question."

"What is the single most important thing that I expect you to perpetuate as Neturay Karta's leader?"

"The value of shalom?"

"Go on."

"To maintain peace among our people," Benjamin said, "even when we see blasphemy, even when we see the secular Israelis breach the most sacred teachings of God—drive cars on the Sabbath or dig up sacred graves in search of archeological evidence of a past that we already know existed as written in the Torah. We pray, we show them an example of a life of virtue, and we protest loudly. But we don't raise a hand against a fellow Jew, albeit a sinner."

The curve in the road took them around a corner. To the west, only the top edge of the sun still glistened above the skyline.

Rabbi Gerster stopped and made Benjamin face him. "You are a good student. A good Jew. And a good rabbi. Now, do you trust me?"

Benjamin nodded.

"Then stop worrying. My efforts continue to be dedicated to this task of keeping Jews from hurting each other. That's all you need to know."

They turned into Shivtay Israel Street. Down by the gate of Meah Shearim, a woman stood by a car, waiting. Rabbi Gerster recognized Itah Orr. He would have stumbled, if not for Benjamin grabbing his elbow. She wore pants and a sweatshirt, and her hair was not covered.

The men murmured, "*Shanda! Shanda!*" One of them picked up a soda can from the gutter and raised it threateningly.

Taking a train from the airport to Zurich's main rail station, Tanya walked the streets, thinking of her next steps. After meeting Herr Horch, she would continue on to Paris tonight, where her team was engaged in tracking every piece of information related to the recent spate of Palestinian violence. Unlike the French police, Mossad wasn't interested in catching the perpetrators but in discouraging those who aspired to step into the shoes of Al-Mazir and Abu Yusef. Prime Minister Rabin had issued clear orders to prevent further terrorist attacks, which were turning a disillusioned Israeli public against the peace process.

The tip from the Mossad informant in the French police was intriguing, and she was eager to learn what Herr Horch really knew about Elie Weiss. It had been a stroke of luck that the bank manager in Senlis recognized the news photos of Abu Yusef's corpse and connected it to the large wire transfer signed by Herr Horch of the Hoffgeitz Bank of Zurich. She had also learned that Armande Hoffgeitz was recovering from a heart attack while Herr Horch ran the bank in his absence. She remembered Armande, who had been Klaus von Koenig's best friend. The last time they met, at the Swiss-German border crossing, Armande Hoffgeitz was a chubby thirty-four-year-old banker, lounging in the rear of his Rolls-Royce, congratulating himself for getting richer from a war that had destroyed most other people. It was odd to think of him as an old man with a bad heart. Should she visit him in the hospital? She chuckled. Seeing her would surely give him another heart attack.

But this was no time for nostalgia. Tanya was alarmed by the involvement of the Hoffgeitz Bank. This was a development she had to pursue herself. To her team she had reasoned that Herr Horch was more likely to open up to a woman than to a whole group of Mossad agents. Their time was better spent in Paris, tracking down the festering opposition to Arafat and the Oslo process. But the real reason she was doing it alone was the risk of exposure. No one at Mossad knew of her teenage relationship with the Nazi general or of the fortune he had left with Armande Hoffgeitz. There was little risk that Herr Horch would somehow make that connection, but even a small risk was too much for her to take. How could she justify to the chief of Mossad keeping such a secret throughout her decades-long career with the Israeli secret service? But even more crucial was her fear for Bira. It was one thing to grow up without a father, his absence justified with a fictional story of a brief relationship and a death in the war. But to be identified as the daughter of Himmler's deputy, Oberstgruppenführer Klaus von Koenig, a top Nazi whose hands were covered with the blood of millions of Jews? The ramifications of such disclosure were too horrific to consider. It would ruin Bira completely.

Tanya had taken a gamble by mentioning Elie Weiss on the phone, but the Swiss banker's rudeness in repeatedly hanging up revealed that he recognized Elie's name. And his suggestion to meet with her away from the bank was another indication that he knew the clandestine nature of Elie's business. He was clever to suggest a public park in a quiet neighborhood—a safe location for a rendezvous with a woman he didn't want to be seen with. Tanya would have preferred a café on a side street near Bahnhofstrasse, where she would be warm and dry. In general, it was safer to meet an informer in a public place, where the presence of strangers reduced the danger of outright violence.

It was unusual for her to wander around a European city without her escorts. But the vice president of an old Zurich bank did not pose a security risk. He was probably a younger version of Armande Hoffgeitz—overweight, bespectacled, and morally pragmatic. The only attack he was likely to engage in was a panic attack, and she had already planned the conversation to put him at ease. She had no intention of causing him or the bank any trouble—as long as they cooperated fully.

Her goals were simple. She had to assert the rights of the State of Israel in stepping into the shoes of Elie Weiss as a client of the Hoffgeitz Bank. She carried basic credentials—a power-of-attorney with Elie's forged signature and a letter from a physician at Hadassah Hospital confirming Elie's incapacitating emphysema. He might have used a false identity in his relationship with the bank, but Herr Horch's reaction proved he knew who Elie Weiss was. She assumed that Elie had also kept a safety deposit box with the bank. Finding a complete list of SOD agents would cut short an exhaustive investigation. And there was the issue of Klaus von Koenig and his fortune. Had Elie taken it over? Had he already spent much of it? Today she would have the answers. She expected Herr Horch to resist at first, but she would make him understand that he had to work with her rather than wait for a sick man in Jerusalem who wasn't coming back.

The rain intensified, and Tanya took shelter near a jewelry store. A tray of wrist watches and chained timepieces filled a whole window display. Inside, a jeweler in a three-piece suit noticed her through the window and smiled. There was something in his posture and blue eyes that reminded her of Abraham Gerster, and Tanya found herself searching his fingers for a wedding ring.

Don't be silly!

She turned and walked into the rain, following the directions she had memorized to Lindenhof Park.

"**S**top it!" Benjamin hurried over and took the empty Coke can from the man's hand. But Itah Orr had already drawn a canister from a belt holster and pointed it at them. "You want some pepper spray? Do you?"

The men lowered the brims of their black hats and entered the gate. But Rabbi Gerster approached Itah, holding his hands up in feigned surrender.

"Bastards!" She holstered her pepper spray. "They're lucky I have bigger problems right now."

"Rabbi?" Benjamin lingered at the gate. "Sabbath is about to start."

"Sabbath will wait another moment," Rabbi Gerster said. "Itah Orr, please meet Rabbi Benjamin Mashash, the leader of Neturay Karta and a man of peace, like me."

The reporter extended her hand, then pulled it back. "Sorry. I forgot women are too dirty to touch."

"It's not about cleanliness," Benjamin said, "but about preventing unnecessary temptation for men, whose self-control is poorer than women's."

"Thanks for the double compliment," Itah said. "I can see why you've been anointed."

"Go ahead." Rabbi Gerster patted Benjamin's shoulder. "I'll be a few minutes."

Benjamin obeyed, glancing over his shoulder as he walked away.

The rabbi gestured at her outfit. "Thanks for complicating my life."

"You took the words out of my mouth." Itah looked up and down the street. "They're after me. And they'll be after you if they find out we talked."

"Who's after you? The boys from ILOT?"

"Worse." She led him across the street and into a doorway of an apartment building. "I managed to give them the slip, but they'll find me again, I know it."

"Tell me everything."

"My friend works for the Commissioner of Banks at the Ministry of the Treasury. She has access to the database of every bank. I went to her office and we ran searches for Yoni Adiel. There were several people with that name, and we had to weed out the wrong ones by age, occupation, and so on. We eventually found the right one. He's paying tuition at Bar Ilan University out of his account, so we knew it's him. But we got screwed because it's a tripping account."

"What's that?"

"Like a trip wire. If someone steps on it—electronically speaking—an alarm goes off, and nasty people come after you."

"You're exaggerating the Israeli government's efficiency." Rabbi Gerster chuckled. "Maybe someone would call your friend to ask why she looked at the account, but there's no way they'll mobilize a surveillance team for something so benign."

"Obviously it's not benign."

A car engine sounded outside, and they peeked to see a white sedan with darkened windows cruise down Shivtay Israel Street, which was otherwise quiet in the minutes preceding the commencement of the Sabbath.

"Damn!" Itah pushed him back inside, where the darkness made them invisible to the people in the car. "They found me!"

"Impossible," Rabbi Gerster said. "How would anyone know you're here?"

"They must have put a tracer on my car. It's parked around the block." Itah stuck her head outside. "They're gone for now, but I can't go back to my car." She handed him a stack of papers held together with a rubber band. "That law student, Yoni Adiel, has an account at the Bank Hapoalim branch in Herzlia, which is where his parents live. Top three pages, here." She flipped through the stack. "His account gets a monthly transfer of funds from an account at Bank Leumi, which belongs to Freckles. Here." She showed him a sheet with numbers. "And Freckles' account gets frequent cash deposits, as well as a regular monthly paycheck from a multi-signature account."

Rabbi Gerster went through the stack, finding a page with tiny print that showed a copy of the signature requirements on an account. There were three sample scribbles. The account owner was listed as a series of numbers and letters. "What does it mean?"

"It's a government account. You remember the embezzlement scandal last year at the Ministry of Defense, with the fake acquisitions of light weapons?"

"So?"

"The Knesset passed legislation requiring each government agency to set up expenditure approval panels."

"Of three officials each."

"Correct. Freckles has been getting regular paychecks from a government account for the past ten years. And the fact that the agency's name doesn't appear on the account means that it's one of the secret services. Conclusion: Freckles has been a government agent for nine years!"

"Shin Bet?"

"Probably. Now look at this." She turned a few more pages. "Copies of checks Freckles gave to Rina Printing Ltd. It's a small shop in the Talpiot industrial area. Looks like nothing, but I sifted through the trash in the back and found leftover copies of some ugly right-wing propaganda."

"For example?"

"The poster that shows Prime Minister Rabin in Heinrich Himmler's SS uniform. Another shows him in a checkered kafiya. And a bunch of stickers: *Rabin = Rodef! Government of Traitors! Rabin is a Terrorist!* Do you understand?"

"There are several possible explanations. But I guess we have to assume that Freckles is an agent-provocateur. The Shin Bet gives him money to operate the fundamentalist ILOT group, print provocative anti-Rabin posters and stickers, and hand out money to activists such as Yoni Adiel. They're probably gearing up for the Likud rally on Saturday night."

"And look at this." She showed him a page listing deposits into Freckles' account. "He's enjoying not only the government's generosity, but some serious cash deposits."

"What's the *FF* next to each deposit?"

"French francs," Itah said. "Someone besides the Shin Bet is giving him tens of thousands in cash every couple of months, which he uses for the same right-wing provocations."

"It's probably the old sponsor that Yoni's girlfriend told me about. That's how Freckles explains the money to Yoni and the other ILOT members without telling them he's also in the pay of Shin Bet." Rabbi Gerster didn't say more, but he was certain now that the money was coming from Elie Weiss. The two knew each other—the stocky young man leading the demonstration by the prime minister's residence was Freckles, who had given Elie the thumbs up. Rabbi Gerster wondered if the dark-skinned youth with the sign 1936 Berlin = 1995 Oslo had been Yoni Adiel. And what was Elie up to with these young men anyway?

"This is explosive," Itah said. "The government finances right-wing militant activities, which taints the whole political right wing as anti-government fanatics!"

"It's not the first time a government used an agent-provocateur to delegitimize the opposition."

"But does the sponsor from Paris know that Freckles is also a government agent?"

"In other words, you think Freckles is a double agent?"

"Yes, but Yoni Adiel and the others have no idea that Freckles is anything but a fellow right winger." Itah showed him another paper. "And I found out how they met. This is an earlier statement from Yoni Adiel's account, and this is from Freckles' account, about the same time. My friend managed to pull out past history in both accounts. It's from a period before online banking and the advent of personal computers, so the government didn't bother to hide the agency's name. It appears that the two had worked together for another agency before going to the university, drawing regular paychecks. Look at these entries."

Holding the pages side-by-side against the dim light from the doorway, Rabbi Gerster saw entries that fell on the first or second day of each month for two years. The notations said: *Sherut Bitachon Klali,* Hebrew for *General Security Service,* otherwise known as Shin Bet. Smaller letters in parentheses read: *YLI.* "What's this acronym?"

"I also wondered, so I looked it up." She took a deep breath. "YLI stands for Yechida Le'Avtachat Ishim."

"The VIP Protection Unit?"

"Correct. Freckles and Yoni Adiel had worked for Shin Bet together, guarding VIPs for two years. Imagine the operational knowledge they accumulated, the familiarity with security procedures, even the lingo."

The VIP Protection Unit! Rabbi Gerster felt a sensation he had not experienced since hiding with Elie in the attic of the butcher shop while the Nazis slaughtered their families. It took him a moment to recognize the sensation, which resembled a flush of cold water through his veins: Fear.

Lemmy left the bank early, wrapped in his coat and a soft hat with a narrow brim. He had fitted the silencer to the Mauser, which he carried under the coat against his right hip. From Bahnhofstrasse he veered left into the Rennweg, then to Fortunagasse, a narrow, uphill alley lined with one-story, well-preserved medieval houses—a sharp contrast from the stately splendor of Bahnhofstrasse. The rubber soles of his shoes paced silently on the wet cobblestones.

At the top of the hill, a low stone embankment surrounded Lindenhof Park. Light rain curtained off the views. He passed among trees whose thin, bare branches simulated spider webs, spread wide to trap the unwary. Farther in, he zigzagged between black-and-white checkered squares and hip-high chess pieces, which waited in pre-game rows for springtime. Before marrying Paula, he had lived in an apartment building on the opposite hillside, which offered fair weather views of Lindenhof Park and its chess boards. Years later, he had brought Klaus Junior here to play a long and cheerful game on one of the giant boards.

But today the views were masked by rain and fog, which turned the park into a trap with a single entrance and limited opportunities for anyone seeking to hide. If the German woman attempted to bring reinforcement, Lemmy was confident he could pick them off as easily as ducks in a pond.

The ground under his feet was hard and bare, no grass or flowers. The fallen leaves had been cleared away, the lines of rake teeth drawn finely in the earth. He approached the edge, where a water fountain was topped by an armored statue. Far below, the Limmat River snaked between the hills of Zurich. Should he push the woman over the low wall at the edge instead of shooting her? The police would be less suspicious of foul play. But what if she didn't die? No. A bullet to the head would provide finality. The Mauser was tried and proven, a reliable tool that made him confident of the outcome, almost like a good-luck charm he had inherited—in fact, had stolen—from his father.

The wind picked up, the drops prickling his face like icicles. He slipped his hands into the coat pockets. His right hand touched the Mauser. His breath turned white from the cold.

He scanned the park. No one was around. A squat building was all that was left from the ancient Roman citadel. He imagined the steel-clad sentinels scanning the horizon, their alarm upon detecting invaders advancing from the distant, snowy peaks.

The gas lamps came on, shedding circles of yellow light on the ground. Lemmy sat on the low wall and looked down the cliff. He was not prone to height anxiety, but it occurred to him that his whole life was now teetering at the edge of an abyss.

A set of spotlights around the fountain illuminated the statue, and he realized it was a woman in black armor, a steel sword tied to her belt, a flag held up in her iron hand. A brass plaque told of Zurich's brave women, who had saved their city from the Hapsburg Army in 1292 by stripping the armor from their dead husbands and marching to Lindenhof. From across the Limmat, the enemy mistook the women for a reinforcement army and retreated. Lemmy saw in the steel face of the armored woman a determined expression, unafraid of the enemy gathered across the river. He heard marching, and it took him a moment to realize it was the real-life sound of a pair of advancing boots.

The woman's pace was fast and decisive. She was small, enshrouded in a long, buttoned coat, a dark scarf tied around her head. Her face was covered with large sunglasses despite the weather.

His fingers clenched the Mauser. Was she the caller, here to meet with him?

She passed in and out of the circles of light, approaching him in a manner that removed any doubt. She was not a casual visitor to the park. She was the target.

He tilted the weapon under his coat, the silencer aimed at the advancing figure. He scanned the park, seeing no one else. She was alone.

The rain intensified, drowning all other sounds, blurring his vision. The lower half of her face, under the sunglasses, stood out in its whiteness. He would start with a stomach shot—fatal, but not immediately—and after questioning her, complete the job with a bullet to the head. If she implicated Christopher, it would shorten the time Lemmy would need to interrogate his traitorous assistant.

His forefinger rested on the trigger.

The distance between them narrowed quickly.

He took a deep breath and stepped away from the water fountain, out of the pool of light.

The target kept walking.

He lowered the tip of the silencer, aligning it with her midriff.

Her pace slowed. Did she notice his hand in the pocket, the bulging coat over the pointed gun?

His finger began to press the trigger.

She made a quick move that brought her purse from the side to the front. He couldn't see her hand. Was she reaching for a gun?

The target entered the range of a gas lamp.

The Mauser in his hand adjusted slightly to account for the narrowing distance, lined up with her stomach. Lemmy exhaled, relaxing his muscles while his finger applied growing pressure on the trigger. At this point it became harder to press, a tiny steel bump to signal that the hammer was about to be released to knock on the pin, which would tap the base of the bullet. The exploding charge would shoot a cap of brass at high speed into her flesh. A stomach wound with this caliber would give her ten minutes of life, enough to reveal the information he needed.

The target stopped. "Herr Horch, I presume?"

Again, the same as on the phone, her voice unsettled him, like noticing a face on the street, reminiscent of someone he knew, like the target in Paris, who had Benjamin's smile.

Concentrate!

Lemmy's finger applied delicate force, avoiding an abrupt pull that would shift the perfect aim at her chest—

"The weather has turned against us, hasn't it?" She resumed walking toward him.

Her voice—closer, louder, clearer—hit him with shocking familiarity. It drew his gaze upward to the target's face, his hand instinctively following the sudden movement of his eyes, shifting the Mauser sharply just as his finger completed its travel backward. The hammer sprang, the Mauser jerked against his hip, the lapel of his coat blew sideways, and the muted pop of the shot tapped on his ears.

The woman collapsed. Her sunglasses fell off, her face suddenly visible, and Lemmy heard his own voice speak in wonder. "Tanya?"

Rabbi Gerster led Itah Orr up the stairs to Benjamin's apartment. When Sorkeh opened the door, he said, "A guest shouldn't bring a guest, but this friend needs a safe place to stay until after the Sabbath."

"Of course," Sorkeh said. "Come in, please, welcome. We love having guests for the Sabbath."

The little ones, clinging to her skirt, looked up with big eyes. Even they could tell that the woman in immodest clothes and exposed hair did not belong in Neturay Karta, that something out of the ordinary was going on even though the adults were pretending otherwise.

"Thank you." Entering the foyer, Itah's gaze rested on the single photo on the wall. She approached it, squinting at the small letters. "Your son?"

"Yes," he said, "that's my Jerusalem."

"A handsome soldier."

"That's nothing," Sorkeh said. "He was much more handsome in real life. And a brilliant Talmudic scholar. But God had different plans for him. How mysterious His ways are." She caressed her little daughter's head.

"Lemmy is with God now," Rabbi Gerster said. "Forever young."

Itah gave him a questioning look.

"I must hurry to the synagogue for evening prayers," he said. "You'll be fine here."

The two women, surrounded by the young children, went into the dining room to prepare the table for the Friday night dinner.

Heading back downstairs, Rabbi Gerster thought how good Sorkeh was for Benjamin, as she would have been a good wife to Lemmy. If not for Tanya's irresistible allure, which had drawn Lemmy away, this apartment would have passed to Lemmy, who would have filled it with his own children. How would it feel to have grandchildren, Rabbi Gerster wondered. Wonderful? Joyous? *Normal?* But it wasn't meant to be, and time had taken the edge off the pain and anger. He no longer blamed Tanya. She had taken Lemmy as a substitute because she couldn't have the man she truly loved, and when he did change his mind, it was too late. What if he had agreed immediately to leave his wife and son and this sect of misguided zealots for Tanya? What if he had agreed immediately to leave his wife and son and this sect of misguided zealots for Tanya? What if he had dropped everything on the day of her reappearance in October 1966 and joined Tanya, the woman *he* truly loved?

What if?

A hypothetical world of dreams. In reality, by his foolish decision to reject Tanya upon her reappearance from the dead, he had doomed his wife and son—practically sent Temimah and Lemmy to their death.

The bullet tore off her headscarf and knocked her down, but it didn't kill her, Tanya knew, because she could still see Herr

Horch. He approached her and stooped over, staring down. His next shot would be at point blank to ensure her demise. She managed to speak. "No need...for violence."

He knelt next to her and pressed a handkerchief to the side of her head. "Sit up," he said. "It'll reduce the bleeding."

She held his arm and sat up slowly, unsure of his intentions. Her decision to come here alone had clearly been a fatal miscalculation. But why would a respectable Swiss banker resort to shooting? It made no sense!

"It's just a scrape," he said. "You're very lucky. I never miss."

"Don't do...anything foolish." She closed her eyes to stop the world from spinning. "My colleagues...will come after you. They're big...on revenge."

"I know."

"Why did you...shoot me?"

"You don't recognize me, Tanya?"

He knew her name?

She opened her eyes and examined the man's face in the yellow light of the park lamp. He had a pleasant, handsome face, short, blonde hair with a few strands of gray, and blue eyes that radiated intelligence. She touched his face, her fingers feeling his wet forehead, the creases by his eyes, the strong jaw, the soft lips.

"You haven't changed much," he said.

"No!" She withdrew her hand from his face and tried to crawl away. "*No!*"

He smiled, and her remaining doubts went away. It was *him!*

She was cold. The world was dark and wet around her, not white like the hospital. But she had the same out-of-body feeling. "Am I dead?"

"That's right. We both died and went to Zurich." He put his arms around her and pressed her shivering body against his. "Or heaven. Who the hell knows anymore?"

Tanya was paralyzed. Her hands fell beside her body, her face buried in his coat.

He held her. "It's okay. It's really me. Your little Lemmy."

She began to cry.

When Rabbi Gerster entered the synagogue, the men were reciting the *Song of Songs*, a long poem that King Solomon had written three millennia earlier. *"How beautiful you are, my betrothed, how beautiful, your eyes like doves."*

On Friday evenings, the betrothed was the Sabbath, Solomon's verses recited to welcome the holy day. *"Like a rose among the weeds, my beloved among the women."*

He found Benjamin by a bookcase along the side wall, perusing a heavy volume. "I brought Itah to your apartment. She needs a place to hide. It's my fault. I asked her to look into things that were better left undisturbed. Now some people are upset with her."

Behind them, the men continued reciting. *"Your curls, a thick herd of goats, skipping down the slopes of the Gilead, your teeth, like scrubbed sheep, perfectly aligned, without a blemish."*

"With my family?" Benjamin closed the book. "Is it safe?"

"For now," Rabbi Gerster said, "it is safe."

Lemmy helped Tanya to a park bench by the water fountain. The rain had stopped, and she gazed at him through a curtain of tears. "I don't understand."

"It's simple. I work for Elie."

"But why?"

His eyes wandered away. "Why not?"

"You were a kid. Your whole life was ahead of you."

"I've been living my life, a great life, in fact. My mission has given me a meaningful existence—"

"To work for Elie Weiss is *meaningful?*"

He felt her trembling under his arm. "I was eighteen, and he offered me a chance to dedicate my life to our national survival, to fight for something I believed in."

"Do you still believe it?"

"I do. Elie's plan is the only way to end anti-Semitism once and for all. Eradicate Jew-hating with true finality."

Tanya saw the conviction in his eyes, still young and idealistic, the eyes she remembered from so many years ago. Young

Lemmy, the boy from Neturay Karta, the avid reader, with his endless questions, with so much passion. "But how?"

"You remember the UN radar at Government House in East Jerusalem?"

"In sixty-seven? Of course. That radar would have detected our planes as they took off, and the UN would have alerted the Arabs, cost us the element of surprise, probably the whole war."

Lemmy smiled. "I detonated the installation right under the UN chief's nose. But they later captured me and handed me over to the Jordanians for execution. Elie saved me, shipped me to Europe, and arranged a substitute corpse to be found on the Golan Heights with my ID tags but otherwise too mutilated for identification. Do you remember the aftermath of the Six Day War? Euphoria and a huge mess. No one knew what was going on."

"But what really happened?"

"I assumed the life of a German boy whose parents died in a fire. Wilhelm Horch had died too, but Elie had the records altered as if Wilhelm had survived. My German was pretty good already, having grown up speaking Yiddish. Elie had an old lawyer in Munich become my guardian and send me to Lyceum Alpin St. Nicholas, a boarding school in the Alps."

"It's not a coincidence that Elie sent you there. Armande Hoffgeitz and Klaus von Koenig studied there together, became friends."

"It's a great school, fancy old buildings, great facilities, and wonderful teachers. I was supposed to be sixteen, so I stayed there for three years, made friends, and during school holidays Elie trained me."

"While we mourned you."

"You rejected me, remember? Told me I was too young for you. Sent me to live with Bira and her friends."

"For your own good, yes, but—"

"But what? I was eighteen, alone in the world. *Eighteen!*"

Tanya sighed. "I remember how old you were. And even if you were older, you would have been no match for Elie Weiss. He's too clever, even for me."

"He taught me how to blend in, how to court the right girl, how to plan ahead. It has worked like a clock. I married and joined the Hoffgeitz Bank under the tutelage of my father-in-law."

"What did you say?"

"Armande Hoffgeitz is Paula's father."

"Oh, no!"

"And we have a son. Klaus Junior."

"Klaus?" A look of horror took over Tanya's face. "This is a nightmare."

"My work is very important. I've developed clients in the Middle East, oil-rich sheiks and so on. They give money to terrorist groups, I trace it, report to Elie, and—"

"I know how it works. But that's a red herring. Elie didn't recruit you to spy on Arab sheiks. Or to assassinate them. He recruited you with the single purpose of gaining control of the bank."

"Eventually." Lemmy shrugged. "Family relations are the only way to power in a Swiss private bank."

"So Elie told you to marry a Swiss sausage to get to the cheese."

"Initially it was a calculated move. But I didn't have to pretend for long. Paula is wonderful. I've grown to love her very much."

Tanya closed her eyes. "Jerusalem Gerster loves Armande Hoffgeitz's daughter. This is absolutely insane."

"Jealous?"

"You haven't lost your sense of humor." She searched his eyes for a long moment. "How could you do this?"

"What? Marry Paula?"

"Marrying for duty is in your genes. Your father made the same mistake."

"Say again?"

Tanya made a dismissive gesture. "How could you leave Israel, leave your life, your language, your friends? How could you turn into somebody else?"

Lemmy thought for a moment. "Elie saved my life. He offered me a great mission that will change the future of our people. And anyway, there was no one to stay for."

"No one?" Tanya looked at him incredulously. "Your father!"

"Rabbi Abraham Gerster? The saint who excommunicated me, made me into a pariah, drove my mother to suicide?" Lemmy sneered. "My father was a fanatical jerk, and he hated me."

"Don't say that." Tanya's voice broke. "Abraham loved you. He still does—"

"Oh please! He didn't even bother to attend my funeral!"

"That's what Elie told you?"

"Yes."

"Elie lied to you." Tanya rose from the bench. "Your father cried at your funeral. At least what we thought was your funeral."

"How do you know?"

"Because I was there with Bira and your paratrooper buddies. And your father fell on your grave, broken up. And he's been crying on your grave ever since, for twenty-eight years." She paused, her hand pressed to her chest. "And I've been crying there too." Her voice choked and her eyes became wet again. "I planted a few—"

"Shhh, it's okay." Lemmy hugged her. The rain had stopped, the clouds began to disperse, and patches of blue appeared in the darkening sky.

"You didn't die, but you did lose your life." Tanya blew her nose into a handkerchief. "It's my fault. All of it. Everything that happened to you and Abraham and your poor mother, all my fault. I'm a stupid, stupid woman!"

"You're making no sense. How could it be your fault?"

"It goes way back, long before you were born. If you knew the real Elie Weiss, you wouldn't follow him. He was raised to be a *shoykhet*, to slaughter livestock in the same village in Germany where your father grew up as the rabbi's son. The two of them watched the SS murder their families. They spent three years in the forests, coming out only to kill Germans and steal food."

"And you?"

"For me the war had started on a train ride to Dachau, where a handsome Nazi general plucked me out of the line before the gas chambers. It's a long story, but Klaus von Koenig loved me as truly as it was possible under those circumstances. He was Himmler's chief of finance—"

"Chief of looting."

"Yes, he also handled the valuables they stripped from the Jews. He deposited most of the gems and jewelry with Armande Hoffgeitz, his high-school buddy."

"But how did you connect with Elie and my father?"

"On the first night of 1945, my seventeenth birthday, I was in the car with Klaus, returning from the Swiss border. He was driving down a narrow, twisty Alpine road. They ambushed us. Your father shot Klaus." She pointed at the Mauser, which Lemmy still held in his hand. "But I had the only proof of the deposits—a ledger that Armande Hoffgeitz had signed. Klaus had given it to me for safekeeping." Tanya looked away at the Limmat River and the hills beyond. "That night, in the snowy Alps, while Klaus's body was still warm, I fell in love with your father—a different love, more like a tornado that swirled both of us into its epicenter. We spent three months together. But one day Elie returned alone and told me that Abraham was dead, that a group of Germans had sprayed your father with bullets until Abraham looked like a red sieve."

"And you believed him?"

"You've seen Elie work with his blade, so you know why I didn't question him. That night, when he fell asleep, I ran. And ran. I gave birth to Bira a few months later in a refugee camp—"

"Does she know?"

"What?"

"That her father was a Nazi general?"

Tanya smiled as if the question was a joke. "She didn't need a father. All the other Mossad agents missed their kids, so Bira was everyone's darling. You see, I joined the Mossad so that Elie wouldn't find me."

"But he did?"

"More than twenty years later. In sixty-six I was decorated for a successful operation, and he saw my name on a list at the prime minister's office. It was bound to happen. Bira was already grown, serving in the IDF, and I was no longer afraid of Elie. Big mistake, as it turned out."

Lemmy removed the handkerchief from the wound, which had stopped bleeding, and wiped the rain and tears from her cheeks. He noticed another bruise on her head, a week or two old, but didn't ask her about it.

"Abraham had somehow survived the Germans' bullets. Apparently, to explain my disappearance, Elie had told Abraham that I was dead—do you see a pattern here? And my purported death so devastated your father that Elie was able to convince him to dedicate his life to serving Israel secretly. Abraham had been groomed to be a rabbi, so he infiltrated the most fundamentalist ultra-Orthodox sect in Israel, where anti-Zionist ideology was the seed of future civil war among Jews. He joined Neturay Karta in nineteen forty-six and married your mother. Having a son named after the divided city of Jerusalem added to his mystic aura, and with his charisma and brilliant mind, Abraham Gerster ascended to the leadership of the sect."

"I don't believe it," Lemmy said. "My father was sincere in his fanatical faith. What you're saying is impossible. My father was a mole?"

"That's exactly what he was. Still is. Elie had recruited many other moles. That's his expertise. Look at you!"

"No." Lemmy stood up. "It can't be. My father was a real *tzadik*. Elie told me that my father banished me, sat shivah in mourning for me, because I rejected Talmud—"

"Elie told you? Elie *lied* to you! And to me! He broke our deal!"

"What deal?"

"In sixty-seven, I gave him Klaus's bank ledger in exchange for him ordering your father to let you leave Neturay Karta and become a normal Israeli." She bent over, as if about to be sick. "I made a deal with the devil. And I got my just reward. *Hell!*"

He helped her sit up. "I don't understand."

Tanya sighed. "When Elie found me, he told me Abraham was alive in Jerusalem. I came to your apartment—"

"I remember that Sabbath."

"Yes. It was on a Sabbath. I begged him to leave Neturay Karta, to shave his beard and payos, and return to me. It was nineteen sixty-seven, and we were still young, not even forty. We could still have a life together. But he refused. Your father was committed to his mission, feared that without him the sect would engage in fundamentalist violence. And he felt a duty to your mother and to you. I was devastated. And angry. So I—"

"Seduced his son?"

"It wasn't a rational process," Tanya said. "You looked exactly the way Abraham had looked back in nineteen forty-five. For me it was like going back in time, a chance to reunite with a young Abraham through you. I convinced myself I was doing you a favor, saving you from the ultra-Orthodox prison he had confined you to. And I succeeded! You saw the outside world and embraced it, and Elie got Klaus's ledger and instructed Abraham to let you leave the sect."

"Let me leave? He banished me in the synagogue, in front of the whole sect! They almost lynched me!"

"Your father had no choice but to publicly excommunicate you. It was necessary for his credibility in the sect. And you did fine, joining the army, becoming a healthy, happy Israeli paratrooper. I was so proud of you. But then—"

"I died heroically?"

"But then Elie played the same old trick!" She took his hands. "All those years, you were alive. I can't believe it. How could you do this?"

"What choice did I have? Under my circumstances, Elie's offer was enticing."

"You're right." Tanya's voice broke. "It's my fault. I caused this to happen."

"Don't blame yourself for my decision to serve—"

"You were a pawn!" Tanya stood, her voice suddenly filled with anger. "The three of us—Abraham, me, and Elie—we each had our own designs on you, young Jerusalem Gerster. We each had our own selfish agenda, cloaked in good intentions, to guard little Lemmy against the other two."

"But I made my own decision to read the books you gave me, to pursue you, to make love to you, to leave Neturay Karta—all were my choices! Mine alone!"

"Please, don't yell." She saw his anger and understood it. How could he accept that his life had been manipulated by three Holocaust survivors locked in a twisted triangle of love, hate, and misguided patriotism? How could he admit that he had paid so dearly for the sins of others?

"I chose to join Elie, and I don't regret it."

"It wasn't an informed choice. You were a naive adolescent. We played with your life. Your father intended to shelter you from reality, keep you in the sect, groom you to Talmudic stardom, but his selfish agenda was to install you as leader so he could become free from a life of lies. And me? I wanted to protect you from Neturay Karta's fanatical ideology, to set you free, to save you from a future of ignorance and enslavement to the tyranny of religious oppression, but my selfish agenda was to lure you into my orbit, to possess you because I couldn't have your father. And Elie's stated goal was to give you an opportunity to serve the nation heroically in a role that required a German-looking, bright youth to be planted as a mole in Switzerland, to chase the biggest Nazi loot, which in turn would be used for his grand scheme of *Counter Final Solution*. But Elie could have recruited someone else. His selfish motivation was to punish Abraham and me for loving each other, to separate us forever by guilt and grief, and he succeeded. I should have warned you about Elie. I can see it now so clearly, how he manipulated all of us!"

"I don't think you understand how incredible Elie's plan is. I've dedicated my life to its success, and we are very close to launching it."

"Nonsense. Elie is finished."

"Don't underestimate him again."

"That devil! He's a fanatic, dedicated to revenge, not to healing and building. Do you really believe anti-Semitism could be eradicated through mass murder?"

"Who's talking about mass murder? Our network of agents will conduct surgical assassinations of individuals—not only active terrorists and their sponsors, but anyone who perpetuates anti-Jew hatred, who instigates hostility toward Israel, who is like a cancerous tumor that would metastasize and spread unless excised with a slash of our scalpel. Imagine how history would have turned out if Hitler was eliminated in nineteen thirty-three? Or if Pope Urban II was dispatched to meet his savior before he called up the first crusade? Or if Ferdinand and Isabella died before they expelled the Jews from Spain? Or if the Roman emperor—"

"So you'll kill politicians and clergy. How about academics? Writers? Filmmakers? Cartoonists?"

"Their venom could be as deadly as an explosive belt. Eliminating them will save many Jewish lives. It's justifiable self-defense."

"Arbitrary execution without judicial process? That's murder!"

"We'll set up our own secret judicial process. Elie is right. The goal justifies all means. The very fate of the Jewish people is at stake." Lemmy shrugged. "Our personal feelings and sacrifices are irrelevant."

Tanya dropped his hands as if they had become too hot. "Then you too are a fanatic!"

"Excuse me." Elie Weiss removed the plastic oxygen mask from his face. "What day is it?" He knew the answer, but the young guard seemed gullible enough to play the role Elie had planned for him.

"It's Friday." He pointed at the window, where the sun was setting. "Beautiful, isn't it?"

"Friday?" Elie looked at the glowing view. "Then Sabbath will begin soon."

The guard nodded. Outside the door, the nurses were chattering at their station, and patients' relatives paced up and down the corridor. Elie had his own ICU room. A closed-circuit camera was monitored outside his door by two guards in three shifts of eight hours. Elie had engaged them in casual conversations, building rapport. They were not Shin Bet agents but students, who worked part-time in security after having finished their mandatory IDF service in combat units. They didn't know who he was, and their instructions were to keep him in isolation. He was not allowed to use the phone, and only medical personnel entered his room.

"The holy Sabbath." He pressed a button, and the bed rose to a sitting position. "My last Sabbath."

The guard's blushing discomfort was exactly what Elie expected.

"A person can feel the end. Do you know?"

The guard looked away. "Well, I'll be outside."

"Is there a synagogue here?" He knew the answer. Hadassah Hospital had a chapel on the lobby level, where a rabbi led services three times a day. "I want to pray before I die."

"We're not supposed to—"

"You can see." Elie tried to smile. "I can't run away."

The guard stuck his head out the door and exchanged a few words with his partner. They helped Elie out of bed and into a wheelchair. A short elevator ride took them down to the lobby, where they followed a sign to the synagogue.

It was a windowless room with a modest wooden ark. About fifteen men, most of them in hospital gowns, rocked over prayer books. The rabbi was a youngish man with a short beard and glasses. He read each portion of the evening service in a thin, pleading voice.

Once Elie's wheelchair was secured at the back of the room, one of the guards fetched a yarmulke and put it on Elie's head. The other gave him a prayer book. They went to the door and stood just outside, engaged in a hushed conversation.

When the service reached a quiet part, with each man murmuring the prayers, Elie caught the rabbi's eye. He came over and shook Elie's hand. "May God bless you with a full and complete recovery."

"I'm dying," Elie said, leaning forward, his lips close by the rabbi's ear. "I must get my own rabbi's blessing, but they're not letting me call him."

The rabbi glanced at the two guards. "I'm sorry, but this is not something I can help—"

"Rabbi Abraham Gerster of Neturay Karta. Have you heard of him?"

The rabbi's eyes widened. "Who hasn't?"

"Tomorrow night," Elie said, his voice masked by the praying men around them, "after the Sabbath, go there and give him this note." He pressed a piece of paper into the rabbi's hand. "God will reward you for helping a dying Jew."

The bench they were sitting on faced the low wall. As Lemmy stood up, his eye caught a movement among the trees by the giant chess board. "How many people did you bring?"

"None."

"The Israeli Mossad sends a woman alone on a mission?"

"I expected a business meeting with a nervous banker," Tanya said, "not a shootout." She started to turn around.

"Don't look." He pretended to tie his shoe. "Perhaps your superiors sent a backup team?"

"I run all Mossad activities in Europe."

He was impressed. "Could your subordinates have followed to watch your back?"

"Not without my knowledge."

"There's a man in a beige coat over there."

"Maybe he's a local getting some fresh air?"

"In this weather? Crouching behind a tree? I don't think so." Lemmy took her arm. "Are you armed?"

"No. I flew commercial from Tel Aviv this morning." She leaned against him as they strolled toward the chess boards and the only exit. "How many bullets do you have left?"

"Enough for another tragic mistake. Could it be a Shin Bet team?"

"No way. Only Mossad is allowed to operate outside Israel, and I'd know if another team was here."

"Elie operates outside Israel."

"SOD is independent. It's not a government agency. And Elie knows better than to interfere with Mossad." Tanya bent down, pretending to fix her boot. "Could be a remnant of Abu Yusef's group. Perhaps they followed you."

"Impossible."

"Didn't I manage to find you? The Arabs are no less sophisticated these days, and the money transfer to Senlis came from your bank with your signature."

They kept strolling. A chess board now separated them from the hiding man. The Mauser was ready in Lemmy's hand. "Get down!"

Tanya dropped, and Lemmy broke into a sprint. His first bullet hit the tree trunk, and the target leaped a short distance, hiding behind another tree, yelling something. Lemmy shot again, the pop of the silencer followed by the knock of his bullet on the side of the trunk and the splash of bark pieces. The target yelled again, still behind the same tree, coattail fluttering in the wind.

Lemmy closed in.

His next shot must have grazed the target, who lost his nerve and ran. Lemmy stopped, aimed carefully at the next gap between the trees, estimated the time to catch the target as he passed, and released the shot.

The target screamed and fell.

Holding the Mauser steady, Lemmy advanced, aiming at the head.

"*Al tirah*," the target yelled in Hebrew. "Don't shoot!"

Lemmy kept the Mauser aimed, finger on the trigger. "Are you Israeli?"

"Yes!" The man was short and bald and wore eyeglasses. "*Ai yai yai!* I'm wounded!"

"What Torah chapter did you read for your Bar Mitzvah?"

"*Ahhh!* My leg!"

"Answer me if you want to live."

"I don't remember! The story of the golden calf!"

"What happened to Korach and his men?"

"Shit! You're *meshugah!*" He moaned and curled on the ground, blood pooling under his leg. "They died, okay?"

"How?"

"The ground swallowed them! It should swallow you too!"

Lemmy reached under the man's coat, exposing a shoulder holster. He pulled out the gun, a standard Beretta, and tossed it far into the trees. "Why didn't you shoot back?"

Tanya reached them. "Identify yourself!"

The man shifted to look at her, causing his shattered leg to twist. "*Ahhh!*"

"He speaks Hebrew," Lemmy said. "Seems like your Mossad colleagues don't trust you."

"Plenty of Arabs speak Hebrew," she said. "Who do you work for? Abu Yusef?"

He groaned in pain.

"Okay," Lemmy said. "I'll shoot his other leg."

"No! My name's Tuvia Berr. Help me!"

Surveying the area, Lemmy said, "I don't see anyone else."

"He must be one of Abu Yusef's—learned Hebrew in a refugee camp."

"Right." Aiming the Mauser at the man's face, Lemmy said, "Say hello to Allah."

"No!"

"Tell us who you are," Tanya said, "and we'll get you medical help."

Rising halfway to a sitting position, the man uttered hoarsely, "Shin Bet."

"Impossible." Tanya patted the man's pockets, finding nothing. "You're lying."

"If you're Shin Bet," Lemmy said, "then tell us who to call for help."

The man recited a phone number.

"A Paris number?" Lemmy committed the digits to memory. "We'll try it, but if you're lying—"

"Make the call!" The man fell back, panting. "Ask for Number One."

Lemmy removed the man's belt and tied a makeshift tourniquet around the leg wound. He buttoned up the coat to keep the man warm. "By the way, which one of us were you following?"

The man pointed at Tanya.

They left him and hurried down the cobblestone street.

"He's lying," she said. "Shin Bet is limited to domestic security."

"Maybe they consider you a security risk?"

"*Domestic* security. It means within Israel's borders, which doesn't include Zurich, Switzerland."

"Not yet. And who's Number One?"

"Can't be the chief of Mossad. He's in Turkey. We spoke last night. This is a crucial time for Israel. We need support in each country for the Oslo Accords. We're enlisting various secret services to help us prevent attacks on Jewish targets. A couple of extravagant terrorist attacks could sway the Israeli public against Rabin and his peace policies."

"Could this Number One be the chief of Shin Bet?"

"In Europe? No way. And to put a tail on me? Only the prime minister has the authority to order an investigation of someone at my rank, and then only Mossad's own internal affairs division could do it, not Shin Bet."

"Maybe Rabin made an exception?"

"Send Shin Bet agents outside Israel? They'd be operating outside their immunity from criminal prosecution, outside their chain of command, and outside the law. It could be a cause for dismissal, possibly criminal indictment. That's the whole point of separating the secret services!"

"We'll soon find out." At a pay phone on the corner of Bahnhofstrasse, Lemmy inserted a phone card into the slot, punched in the number, and held the receiver near his ear so that Tanya could listen in.

"Hello?" It was a male voice.

"Tuvia Berr," Lemmy said, trying his best to imitate the injured man, "calling for Number One."

"This is Number One. Did you lose her?"

"The opposite."

"She's with you?"

"Aha."

There was brief silence on the other line. "Take her to your hotel room. Use all means to extract everything she knows about Weiss. And keep her locked up until I personally give you new orders. Understood?"

"Okay." Lemmy hung up. "Recognize the voice?"

She nodded, her lips pressed together until they bleached. "Chief of the Shin Bet?"

Another nod.

Lemmy glanced surreptitiously in both directions, detecting no irregular activity on the busy street. He called the police, informed the dispatcher about a wounded man in Lindenhof Park, and hung up before they asked any questions.

"They've gone rogue!" Tanya grabbed the receiver and punched in a series of numbers. "I must alert my team in Paris." She waited, but no one answered.

The prayers concluded with the singing of *Adon Olam*, praising the Master of the Universe for His creation, His oneness, and His mercy. Rabbi Abraham Gerster kept his eyes on the prayer book while the men of Neturay Karta departed the synagogue. When they were all gone, Benjamin came over and greeted him, "Sabbath Shalom, Rabbi."

"Sabbath Shalom, Benjamin. Why don't you send your boys ahead, so the two of us can talk?"

Benjamin complied, and Rabbi Gerster held his arm as they walked into the chilly night. The alleys were empty, lit by the glow from the windows of the apartments overhead, where families were gathering for the Friday night meal. Muffled voices came through, singing, *"Shalom aleichem, malachey ha'sharet.* Welcome, angels of peace, angels of heaven."

"You want to ask me about the woman journalist," Rabbi Gerster said, "but you hold back. A leader must not be timid."

"It's my respect, not timidity."

"Is there a difference?" Rabbi Gerster chuckled. "You know what Ecclesiastes said about the cycle of life, yes? Everything has a beginning and an end."

"He also said that there is a time for war and a time for peace."

"True. And a time to plant and a time to root out the planted." He squeezed Benjamin's arm. "All the sages interpret

Ecclesiastes as a serious philosopher, but I sometimes think he was writing comedy."

"Comedy?"

"You could read his pontification as joking about how our scriptures—everyone's scriptures, in fact—can be read to support contradictory agendas, how the righteous can find divine authority in the scriptures for anything one wants to preach—love and hate, forgiveness and revenge, peace and war. You can find words in the Torah or Talmud, in the Koran or the New Testament, to proclaim God's divine support of your agenda, whatever it is—and I say this from experience."

They reached the entrance to the apartment building where Benjamin lived. He leaned against the stone wall, as if feeling weak. "But Talmud is the absolute truth, right?"

"Absolute truth is in the eye of the beholder." Rabbi Gerster pointed upstairs. "Itah Orr is helping me investigate the truth."

"Here?"

"No. Outside of Neturay Karta. This community is now your responsibility. Should something happen—"

"To you?"

"To me. To others. Events might take unexpected turns. Our community includes some of the most feverish minds. In times of political upheaval, emotions tend to spike up. A few of our people might erroneously breach our tradition of insular Talmud studying and devout prayer. They might advocate political subversion and impious violence. As leader of Neturay Karta, you must face those hotheads decisively. You must smother each fire before it spreads."

"But you will help me, yes?"

"I know your strengths." He patted Benjamin's bearded cheek. "And I know your weaknesses. But this is a time for strength only. God is testing our community, while the secular society around us tears itself apart over the Oslo Accords. Israel is in the midst of political crisis of the worst kind."

"That's no surprise," Benjamin said. "Zionism has always been a rebellion against God, so how could it succeed?"

"There's time for gleefulness, and there's time for a clear mind. Do not heed your heart, even when it feels broken."

"By your absence?"

"Or by what people might say about me."

Benjamin's face was white against the darkness. "I don't understand!"

"All I'm saying is that, as a leader, your duty is to keep our men's noses in their books of Talmud and out of the news, no matter what happens to me."

Down in the bowels of Zurich's central railway station, they stood on the platform while the train to Amsterdam hissed with pressurized air. Tanya held on to him. "I don't want to lose you again. What if they come after you?"

"You're the one being hunted." Lemmy glanced at his watch. "There is a reason to this madness. Could it be the fortune hidden in my bank?"

"But no one knows about it except Elie, Abraham, me, and you."

"Maybe the Shin Bet is running a high-stake operation in Israel, and Elie somehow figured out what they're up to? Or the other way around—Shin Bet has stumbled on a rogue SOD operation?"

"But Elie is locked up. Why would Shin Bet engage in something so outrageous as going after me?"

"They probably suspect that, when you apprehended him in Paris, Elie told you what's going on. And we must assume they're not just speculating. Something triggered their extreme reaction. Try to remember. Did he say anything?"

"Not a word. But even if that's what they're worried about, I mean, for the Shin Bet to break the law by going to Europe, putting a tail on me and disabling my team—"

"To isolate you, they had to break your chain of command."

"They could go to jail for this!"

"What if they already broke the law? What if it's a big enough operation that, relatively speaking, this infraction is negligible, especially if they're afraid you'll expose their operation?"

"Pure speculations." Tanya gestured in dismissal. "For me to go to the media, it would have to be a revolution, a coup d'état."

The flow of passengers dwindled, and the conductors started slamming doors.

"This is wrong. I shouldn't run away." She straightened her coat. "I should call headquarters in Jerusalem, find out—"

"Didn't you hear what Number One said? *Use all means to extract what she knows.* That's not a vague aphorism."

"It's crazy. I'm too senior to toy with like that."

"Don't call anyone. We first have to find out why Shin Bet has thrown caution to the wind."

"I won't hide from my own government."

"Please, do it for me. For old times' sake."

Tanya sighed.

"When you reach Amsterdam, take a room at the American Hotel, near Leidseplein. I'll arrive tomorrow, and we'll plan our next move."

"I could call Rabin directly. We go back a long way."

"Don't fool yourself. Nobody is safe. Not even the prime minister."

She hugged him, and he put his arms around her narrow waist. He felt dizzy. *Tanya!* Almost unchanged but for a few wrinkles around the eyes and strands of silver in her hair. He had locked away the memory of her face a lifetime ago, banned it from his mind, yet here she was, green eyes glistening over high cheekbones, thinly drawn lips that curved into a worried smile.

A whistle blew.

He saw a man run through the doors leading to the platform. "Get on the train!"

A conductor reached to shut the last door, waiting as Tanya mounted the three steps.

"*Halt!*" The man ran along the train.

"I'll call you," Lemmy said. "What name will you be using?"

"Frau Koenig," she said.

The conductor noticed the advancing man and held the door while the train began to move.

"It's her husband," Lemmy said to the conductor. "He's very angry! Go! Quick!"

The conductor grinned and slammed the door.

The man tried to open another door, jogging beside the moving train toward Lemmy, who extended his leg and tripped him.

"*Ah!*"

"Oops!" Lemmy caught the falling man, and with a subtle, rapid jolt to the back of the head turned him unconscious. "So sorry."

Laying him carefully on the concrete floor, Lemmy glanced up and down the tracks, now deserted. He pulled the man's wallet and found a driver's license with a Zurich address and a business card of an office supply firm. The soft hands, genuine Tissot gold watch, and extended belly made it unlikely he was an Israeli agent. Or was he? Lemmy could take no chances. Tanya's life was on the line. Maybe even his own.

A moment later two railway employees showed up. He told them the man had tripped while chasing the departing train, and they called for help.

Christopher lived in a condo not far from the bank. Lemmy entered behind a cheerful group of young men and women on their way to a party. He carried a gift-wrapped box of Schmerling's chocolate. On the fourth floor, he rang Christopher's doorbell.

"Who is it?" His assistant's voice was muffled.

"Your boss."

"Herr Horch?" Three locks turned before Christopher opened the door. He was still in his work suit, but the tie was loose, the shoes unlaced, and the beer bottle half-empty.

"That's for you." Lemmy gave him the box of chocolate, forcing him to balance it in his left hand. "I apologize for surprising you like this, but as we approach a change of guard at the bank, I wanted to show my appreciation for your efforts."

"Thank you."

"And I also wanted to see how you live." Lemmy smiled. "After all, as my assistant on the top floor, you'll have access to a great deal of wealth. We don't want another strange Günter, right?"

Christopher put down the box of chocolate on a small table by the door. "Yes, I understand."

"So? Are you going to invite me in?"

"Oh. I'm sorry. Please."

"Unless you have company," Lemmy said. "I don't want to intrude."

Christopher shut the door and showed him into a living room. "I'm between girlfriends right now."

"Good." Lemmy drew his Mauser and aimed it at Christopher's chest. He removed the beer bottle from his hand and took a gulp. "Nice and cold."

The expression on Christopher's face barely changed. He obviously had strong nerves and good training. "Is this a real pistol?"

Lemmy sat on an armchair. "Toy guns have a red plastic tip at the end of the muzzle. And no silencer. But you already know that."

"Herr Horch, is this some kind of a test?"

"A test?"

"To see if I'm prepared for a bank robbery?"

"You're good," Lemmy said. "You're stalling for time, trying to figure out what I'm after and how you can retrieve your own weapon and reach parity here. Correct?"

"Weapon?" Christopher laughed. "You can't be serious. This is a joke, right?"

In response, Lemmy shifted his aim and pressed the trigger. The bullet hit the TV behind Christopher, blasting the screen.

"God!" Christopher jumped sideways. "What's wrong with you?"

"Pull down your pants."

"*What?*"

"Show it to me!"

Christopher hesitated.

Lemmy lowered the tip of the silencer until it pointed at Christopher's crotch.

"Don't shoot!" Christopher unbuckled his belt and lowered his pants and underwear. Along his circumcised penis was a tattoo of a black swastika and the letters *SS*.

"Regards from Kibbutz Gesher." Lemmy aimed the Mauser with both hands. "Tell me the truth or I will shoot it off."

His face red, his smile gone, Christopher pulled up his pants. Without asking permission, he sat down on the carpet. "My father did it. He was much older than my mother, served as an SS officer during the war. He was angry that she had allowed the doctor to circumcise me—there was an infection around my penis, and the doctor said it would help. Dad took me to an SS reunion in Munich when I was five or six. They got me drunk and had me tattooed."

"How touching," Lemmy said. "Father-son bonding. Only that I don't believe you. Tell me who you work for, unless you want to die tonight."

"I work for Elie Weiss," Christopher said. "Who else?"

"Don't lie!"

"I'm not lying. I didn't know his real identity when he first showed up, after my dad was killed in a ski accident."

Lemmy's curiosity was piqued. Paula's young brother had also died in a ski accident. "What kind of an accident?"

"When I was fourteen, we went on vacation to Unterstmatt in the Black Forest. My father didn't return to the lodge after dark. A rescue team found him in a crevasse off the slopes. The pathologist said that a sharp icicle penetrated his throat and punctured his brain. It had melted long before he was discovered, but the stab wound fit a long icicle. A freak accident, really."

The freakish part was that the exact same thing had happened to Klaus V.K. Hoffgeitz a few years earlier in Chamonix, a great distance from Unterstmatt!

"Go on," Lemmy said, struggling to control his voice.

"My father owned a factory, making chemicals for pest control and agriculture. After he died, the accountants told my mother that the business was bankrupt. We had nothing. Then a miracle happened. A little man with black eyes and a long nose visited us."

"Elie?"

"He introduced himself as Untersturmführer Rupert Danzig, an underling of my father from the good old days of the SS.

He offered secret help from a charity fund run by a group of veterans. The money started coming, enough to support my mother and send me to Lyceum Alpin St. Nicholas."

"Elie is a master in long-term planning."

"And in the summers I attended paramilitary youth camps to learn shooting and field work."

"Same with me," Lemmy said, "fifteen years ahead of you."

"When I graduated, Herr Danzig encouraged me to go to Israel for a summer. He said I must learn from the Jewish people about building a new life from nothing, a new nation from the ashes, putting all energies into constructive work, and so on. But I had a little thing with one of the girls in the kibbutz, she saw my tattoo, and all hell broke loose."

"They kicked you out."

"Right. Herr Danzig picked me up, and we drove to Jerusalem. We sat on a bench near the Wailing Wall, and he told me the truth. His real name was Elie Weiss, a Jew, a Holocaust survivor. He invited me to work for SOD, to prevent another Holocaust. I had nothing waiting for me in Europe. My mother had died the previous summer, and I didn't know any of my relatives, who had disliked my father and kept away from us. Also, the opportunity to serve the Jewish people was a chance to make up for what my father and his generation of Germans had done."

"You decided to work for a man who had lied to you and your mother?"

"When I learned his real identity, I realized that Elie must have extorted money from my father and others like him, threatening them with exposure. But I don't blame him. I've done my research. My father served at Treblinka. He killed countless innocent people. The SS motto was *Loyal, Valiant, Obedient*. It should have been *Loot, Victimize, Obliterate*." Christopher's voice rose in anger. "My father was a mass murderer. A monster!"

Lemmy secured the safety on the Mauser and holstered it under his coat.

"You believe me now?"

"It fits. Elie helped you get an MBA, intern in New York, and time your application to the Hoffgeitz Bank just when he told me to hire an assistant. But why?"

"To watch your back. There's a lot riding on you. Elie said that you are the key to the future safety and security of the Jewish people."

"That's all?" Lemmy stood up and buttoned his coat. "I'm just a middle-aged banker trying to survive the most confusing set of circumstances.

Christopher laughed.

"Anything else you want to share with me?"

"I'm the keeper of all SOD files—Elie's personal records, list of active and sleeper agents, files of former Nazis who pay Elie regularly to stay alive, and charts of tentative targets for Counter Final Solution. It's all kept on the bank's computer, encrypted, of course."

"What's the password?"

"JERUSALEM 1967."

"I should have guessed." Lemmy gestured downward. "That's some tattoo. Dating must be complicated."

"It's not so bad." Christopher grinned. "I tell them I'm too shy to fool around with the lights on."

"Do they buy it?"

"Oh, yes. Girls find shyness very endearing."

Saturday, October 28, 1995

"I'll be gone for a few days." Lemmy pulled away from Paula. "When I come back, I'll tell you everything, and you'll decide if you want me to stay."

"Very funny."

"I'm serious." He got out from under the covers and sat at the edge of the bed. "There are things I've kept from you."

"I know."

"Do you?"

Paula caressed his hand. "You spoke a foreign language in your sleep last night. It scared me to death. I thought there was a stranger in the room."

Despite the ominous implications, Lemmy burst out laughing, and Paula followed suit. When they calmed down, she threw a pillow at him.

He caught it. "Are you still scared?"

"Of you?"

"Yes."

"Are you nuts? I know how much you love me." She lifted her pinky. "I got you wrapped around this one like a slinky."

He leaned over and kissed her lips. "But there are secrets—"

Paula pressed her lips to his, silencing him, and they stayed locked in a passionate kiss until they both ran out of breath. "Wow!" She sighed. "That was nice."

He played with her hair. "There are parts of my work of which you might not approve."

"There's nothing you could tell me that would change how I feel about you. My father raised me not to ask questions. You think I don't know how Swiss banks serve dictators, drug dealers, and plain vanilla tax evaders from every country on earth? Those are the clients you must serve, because if you didn't, someone else would—here in Zurich or in Lichtenstein, Vaduz, or the Antilles. I don't need to know your professional secrets in order to trust you."

He put his hand under the sheets and caressed her flat belly. "We'll start working again when I'm back."

"Whether we need to or not."

"Really?"

Paula crossed her fingers. "My period is late. I'll give it another few days before doing a test."

"Wouldn't that be a treat?" Lemmy caressed her cheek. "I'll call you when I can."

"I'll be in the hospital every day. The doctors say my dad is showing signs of recovery. He's off the ventilator."

"Good. Call Christopher if there's any news. He'll know how to reach me."

Klaus Junior was still asleep when Lemmy kissed him good-bye. He drove the Porsche to the airport and parked it underground. KLM flight 312 to Amsterdam took off at 9:52 a.m., and ten minutes later the pretty attendant brought a breakfast tray and the *International Herald Tribune*.

Lemmy browsed the headlines. The first page contained the usual mosaic of news pieces from Wall Street and the financial markets in London, Hong Kong, and Tokyo. The second page was filled with photographs of toppled buildings in Beijing after an earthquake that killed hundreds of people. The third page contained summaries of international news, beginning with a report of the Philippine supreme court's decision to dismiss a challenge to Imelda Marcos's electoral victory. Another piece told of a brewing conflict in the Israeli parliament over the Rabin government's ban on construction in Jewish settlements in the West Bank. Likud leader Benjamin Netanyahu, whose poll numbers had recently surpassed Rabin's, declared: "The Labor government has betrayed Zionism and must be toppled."

The pilot announced the beginning of their descent. Lemmy watched through the window at the picturesque view of Rotterdam's harbor. From twenty-five thousand feet, Europe's largest harbor was a manicured line of fingernail docks on a blue canvas. As the plane descended, the groomed Dutch landscape grew larger, with its tiny canals, grazing cows, and robust green fields. A wide circle over the coastline brought the plane to Schiphol Airport. The weather was nicer than in Zurich—clear blue skies and a bright wintery sun.

The train took him to Amsterdam's central station, and from there he used the tram. He favored the Hotel de L'Europe on the River Amstel, where bankers and corporate executives walked the hallways in their tailored suits, consummating multimillion-dollar deals. But this time, Herr Wilhelm Horch of the Hoffgeitz Bank was not arriving to negotiate a major currency swap or to solicit a large deposit. There would be no dinners with wealthy clients, no rubbing elbows with colleagues. This time he was playing a different game altogether, a game he could not afford to lose.

"Herr Horch!" The front desk manager rushed to greet him. "Wonderful to have you with us again!"

"Good to be back," Lemmy said, forcing a smile.

The floor-to-ceiling windows of the high-rise apartment filled with the blue Mediterranean. Gideon watched the Tel Aviv beach, alive with bathers, joggers, and windsurfers. Behind him, the maternal housekeeper moved around the place stealthily with her broom and duster.

Agent Cohen showed up with two plastic bags. He took out pita breads stuffed with falafels, humus, and Israeli salad, topped with tahini sauce. He beckoned Gideon to the table. "How do you like this place?"

"I didn't know Shin Bet could afford such accommodations for its prisoners."

"We like our guests to be comfortable."

They ate while Arik Einstein sang on the radio, *"How did you leave me, friend?"*

"Here," Agent Cohen handed him a bunch of napkins.

"Thanks." Gideon wiped his lips and chin. "This is yummy!"

"Tastes like home, ah?"

"It does."

"My wife made it. She's from Yemen—they make the best humus. I told her it's for a friend who's been out of Israel for too long."

"It's delicious. Give her my compliments."

"I will." The Shin Bet officer put the last piece of pita bread in his mouth. He pushed the glass of orange juice across the table. "I squeezed it myself. Drink before the vitamins evaporate."

Gideon sipped the cold juice. "Good."

"Thought you'd appreciate it." Agent Cohen sat back and patted his belly. "I hear you want to join Mossad?"

"Who told you?"

"Mossad is a bunch of snobs. You're lucky they turned you down—you'd be away all the time, snooping around Europe, paying informants for worthless info." Cohen bunched up the food wrappings on the table. "Shin Bet is a different story. You could have fun right here in Tel Aviv."

"How do you know of my interest in Mossad? Have you eavesdropped on Tanya Galinski?"

"We do whatever it takes to keep VIPs safe."

"Including the arrest of agents of other secret services?"

"SOD is a one-man show, and the curtain just came down on its last performance. However, we could use your skills and experience."

"I'm flattered."

"So?"

"Why don't you tell me what's going on? Put everything on the table. I won't tell anyone, okay?"

"I'm not worried about that." Agent Cohen leaned forward, his elbows on the table. "Here's what we know: Your former boss,

Elie Weiss, has active assets in the extreme right wing, some kind of an agent-provocateur operation that has attracted a group of followers. They see themselves as Torah warriors under the acronym ILOT. We've had our eye on this SOD operation for a while."

"How?"

Cohen shrugged. "A few of them used to serve in our VIP Protection Unit. We've kept an eye on them. In fact, the ringleader still works for us—incognito, of course."

"How convenient."

"At first we liked this ILOT business. The roots of SOD, back in the sixties, were in planting moles in ultra-Orthodox communities, such as Neturay Karta, to watch for signs of brewing militancy against the secular Israeli society. In fact, we copied the methods Weiss had developed for the Shin Bet's own Jewish Department. But he wasn't supposed to continue operating in this area. We figured that he was so obsessed with the risk of Jewish civil war that he was keeping his eye on it, basically doing our job for us and paying for it from his secret stash."

"So what spooked you?"

"A couple of weeks ago, Elie Weiss met with Prime Minister Rabin."

"You guys eavesdrop on the prime minister also?"

"We're his bodyguards. We have video and sound surveillance on him at all times. Our operational assumption is that every meeting could turn into an assassination attempt. Anyone is a potential attacker. *Anyone!*"

"Including his wife?"

"Especially his wife."

They laughed, the tension released temporarily.

"Is Rabin aware of your exemplary diligence?"

"He's a big picture kind of a guy. He doesn't tell us how to protect him, and we don't tell him how to run the country." Agent Cohen smirked. "Anyway, Elie made a proposal to the prime minister."

"Tit for tat?"

"An exchange of favors. Big favors. We felt it was inappropriate and took steps to investigate. Do you know what I'm talking about?"

"No idea. I've been in Paris, chasing Arab terrorists."

"You don't know anything about Elie's grand plans? His political schemes?"

"No idea." It was the truth, but Gideon could tell that his interrogator didn't believe him. "You don't really know Elie Weiss, do you?"

"Only the myths," Agent Cohen said. "And our surveillance in the past few weeks."

That was shocking news. Had Shin Bet watched them in Paris? "Do you realize how dangerous he is?"

"Weiss? He is a pathetic old man. An archeological joke."

"A joke?" Gideon picked a crumb from the table and held it up as if there was something interesting about it. "Even now, as sick as he is, Elie Weiss could kill you before you had enough time to wipe the smirk off your face."

"Not anymore." Reaching under his jacket, Agent Cohen pulled out Elie's blade in its leather sheath.

"Without the blade he would only make your death more painful. You're better off giving it back to him."

The expression on Agent Cohen's face went from smug to wary. But the tone of his voice remained businesslike. "Have you trained with any of the local SOD agents? Have you met any of them?"

"I only knew Bathsheba. And I'd like to attend her funeral, by the way."

"Sorry. She was buried last night in Jerusalem." He raised a hand to stop Gideon's protests. "She received a soldier's burial. Family members attended, a representative from the defense ministry gave a moving eulogy, and six Shin Bet agents lowered the coffin. A very respectable ceremony, I assure you."

Gideon got up and went to the window. "A tragic ending to a tragic life."

"Elie mentioned to Rabin something about money. He claimed to have unlimited funds. Do you know anything about it?"

"Elie is a good liar."

"True," Agent Cohen said. "Have you been to Zurich with him?"

"Why Zurich?"

"He's got some business there, we're not sure what. Do you know?"

It was a trick question, Gideon realized. They must have followed him when he had made the call to the Hoffgeitz Bank. "I think he maintains an account there. It's standard procedure. Switzerland is a good place to keep money. Didn't Rabin's wife once maintain an illegal account there?"

"That was in New York."

"Oh."

"Which bank did Elie use?"

Now he was sure Agent Cohen knew the answer. So he told him. "The Hoffgeitz Bank. I've never been there, but Elie mentioned the name."

"Interesting. We'll follow up on it."

"In Switzerland? Aren't you limited to domestic investigations?"

"What do you want us to do? Refer it to Mossad?" Cohen laughed as if the idea was ridiculous.

"That's exactly what the law requires, doesn't it?"

"The law doesn't exactly permit the activities SOD has recently engaged in—shooting people on French roads, making people swallow explosives in seedy hotels, and so on. You could be prosecuted as a murderer, you know?"

"I know an unsubtle threat when it hits me in the face."

"That's right. And if you insist on an answer, it's simple. The VIP Protection Unit is tasked with pursuing any and all potential threats to the prime minister's safety. We may conduct our investigational operations anywhere."

"Including overseas?"

"Including outer space, if needed." Agent Cohen gathered the napkins and empty plastic cups into the bag and walked to the door. "Which is the reason my offer still stands. If you cooperate fully with our investigation, we'll sign you up as a Shin Bet agent."

"Right now?"

"As soon as our current operation is concluded successfully."

Rabbi Abraham Gerster had not given a sermon in Meah Shearim in over a decade. His extended retreat to the rear benches had elevated him to a *tzadik*, a man of mysterious righteousness, revered by everyone in the sect. Therefore, when he rose from his seat after the reading of the Torah and approached the dais, the men of Neturay Karta stood up in awe, and even the women in the upstairs mezzanine became completely silent.

"Good Sabbath!" He motioned for them to sit down.

The crowd murmured while sitting down.

"Some of you remember the days of the abortion debate, three decades ago, when the Zionist Knesset was preparing a law that was an anathema to us and to other God-fearing Jews." Rabbi Gerster smiled at Cantor Toiterlich, Sorkeh's father, who nodded knowingly in the front row. "And even the young among you know that we chose peace, shalom, rather than add internecine bloodshed to that of the unborn."

A wave of hushed exchanges went through the synagogue. For most of them, it was ancient history, yet the 1967 ruling had left its mark on every aspect of their insular, inward-looking life since then.

"Today the Promised Land is again torn by a political conflict over life and death. The so-called Oslo process promulgates a transfer of sacred parts of Israel to Arab control in exchange for their promise not to kill Jews anymore. The faithful must wonder: Are we allowed to give away God's land? Is there validity to the Arabs' promise to refrain from further terror and mayhem? And what of the deadly peril to Jews living in towns and villages in Judea, Samaria, and the Gaza Strip? Are they slated to live under Arab rule or be expelled from their homes?"

He let the silence linger, but no one broke it.

"Since the first Oslo Accord two years ago, Palestinian terror has taken more than one hundred and fifty Jewish lives. But the current Zionist leaders still believe that, in the long run, peace will bring security to our people. What else can the faithless Zionists believe in but brittle papers and human promises?"

The question lingered in the silent synagogue.

Rabbi Gerster glanced up at the women's mezzanine, where Itah sat with Sorkeh. "A schism threatens to tear apart our nation. A grave danger faces us, the Chosen People, who have returned to this sliver of land on the Mediterranean Sea, as God had promised to Abraham the Patriarch, *To you and your seed I give this land.* Our secular brothers and sisters are also Abraham's seed."

Many of the men followed his gaze upward at the women's section. Word had swept through the sect within an hour of Friday's encounter at the gate about the secular, immodestly dressed woman, who was granted shelter at the home of Rabbi Benjamin Mashash. And now she was attending Sabbath services among the families of Neturay Karta, while Rabbi Gerster was breaking his long silence.

"Handing over parts of the sacred land of Israel and risking lives of Jews are crimes under God's laws." He opened a tall book of Talmud that Benjamin had prepared for him on the lectern. "In the tractate of Sanhedrin, page forty-eight, Talmud discusses the murder trial of Yoav, King David's former military commander, who had killed Avner in revenge for Avner's killing of Yoav's brother, Asael. But Avner claimed that he had killed Asael because Asael had been pursuing him. In other words, Avner argued that Asael was a *Rodef,* a pursuer trying to kill him. According to Talmud, during Yoav's trial, King Solomon agreed that, if Avner had been justified in killing Asael in self-defense as a *Rodef,* a pursuer with the intent to kill, then he was in the right, and Yoav, who killed him in misguided revenge, was guilty of murder."

One of the men raised his hand. "But Yoav argued that Avner deserved to die because Avner could have disabled Asael by stabbing him, as the book of Samuel says, in the fifth rib, rather than kill him. The killing of a *Rodef* is allowed only if he cannot be disabled, only if his pursuit cannot be stopped with a strike that's less than deadly force."

"Exactly!" Rabbi Gerster closed the book. "I have heard that some rabbis now argue that Prime Minister Rabin is like a *Rodef* because his peace policies have led to terror and will cause even more loss of Jewish lives and handover of sacred land."

"That's right!" A young scholar in the back rose halfway from his seat. "He's a *Rodef*, and so are his heretical colleagues in the Zionist government!"

A few others voiced their support.

Rabbi Benjamin Mashash glanced up from his seat by the Ark of the Torah, but Rabbi Gerster shook his head. It was better to let hotheads blow out steam. Once they calmed down, they would listen to reasoned arguments.

Cantor Toiterlich raised his hand, which caused the younger men to quiet down. Not only was he one of the sect's elders, but as the cantor he was the person who led the prayers and represented every member of Neturay Karta in pleading for health and prosperity before the Master of the Universe. "An argument could be made," the cantor said, his baritone filling the hall, "that a person could only be considered a *Rodef* if he is in hot pursuit to kill another Jew, a physical chase with weapon at the ready. Therefore the *Rodef* concept doesn't apply to a political leader signing peace agreements with the goal of ending war, even if his well-intentioned actions could have indirect fatal ramifications."

"But what about the *Moser* concept?" It was the same young scholar in the back. "Just like *Rodef*, we have a duty to kill a Jew who is about to telltale or hand over another Jew to the Gentiles. There's no hot pursuit here, but still the same rule applies, right?"

"That's an excellent point," Rabbi Gerster said. "Can anyone offer a counter-argument?"

Jerusalem Mashash, Benjamin's eldest son, raised his hand. "*Soff ma'asse be'makhshava tekhilah.* Judge a deed by its motivation."

"Indeed!" Rabbi Gerster clapped. "Jerusalem, my boy, please explain what you meant."

"A person cannot be found guilty of a crime, or a sin, without having the intent to do wrong." The youth turned red, having found himself speaking in front of the whole sect in the middle of Rabbi Gerster's surprise sermon. But his eloquence wasn't hindered by his embarrassment. "In order for a Jew to be considered a *Rodef* or a *Moser*, we must prove his intent to cause deadly harm. Only with evidence of malicious intent can we judge him to be a criminal who deserved to be killed."

"Thank you, Jerusalem." Rabbi Gerster tugged at his beard. "You just reminded me of what the sage Hanina said: *I've learned a lot from my friends, even more from my teachers, but most of all I've learned from my students.*" He glanced at Benjamin, whose eyes glistened with fatherly pride. "Our learned youngster is correct. How could Rabin, or any political leader, be guilty of a crime when his intentions are to prevent more terror, to bring peace, and to save lives? From a Talmudic standpoint, a Jew is innocent if his intentions are pure, albeit tragically misguided."

Rabbi Gerster looked around the hall, filled with the bearded faces and the affectionate eyes of the men with whom he had spent half a century. "What is in a man's heart? What is on his mind? What is the primary motivation that guides him? Those are the questions we must ask in order to fairly judge another Jew." He paused, his eyes connecting with a few of the older men. "And I hope," he concluded, "that when the day comes for you to judge me, you shall apply this fair measure."

The men gasped, for the idea of judging the *tzadik*, the most righteous man in Neturay Karta, seemed implausible in the extreme.

"My life here, my achievements and my failures, should be taken as a whole. I implore you to find me innocent, for I have lived among you most of my days on this earth, working for this God-fearing community with love as my impetus and kindness as my inspiration."

The tone of finality, almost of a eulogy, did not escape the Talmudic scholars of Neturay Karta. They stared at him, up on the dais, and waited for an explanation.

But Rabbi Gerster only smiled. "And with that," he said, "I wish you Good Sabbath!"

The men stood up as he descended from the dais and returned to his seat. Cantor Toiterlich approached the lectern and commenced the last portion of the Sabbath prayer.

Gradually the men joined in chanting the Hebrew words. Moments later, when Rabbi Gerster glanced up from his prayer book, he found Jerusalem Mashash staring at him from among the swaying men. The rabbi winked at Benjamin's son, whose face broke into a bright smile.

A ccording to a brass plaque at the entrance, the Metz & Co. department store had operated on the same corner since 1740. Lemmy took the stairs up to the restaurant on the top floor. He sat by the window, which had a panoramic view of the southeast section of Amsterdam. Looking down, he saw the wide Kaizersgracht, its banks lined with houseboats of different sizes and ages, all meticulously painted, with garden chairs and potted flowers on the decks. A glass-covered motorboat, loaded with off-season tourists, cut through the oily water, passing under the arched bridge. On the street along the canal, a tram rattled on its steel rails, ringing its bell, while pedestrians and bicycle riders scattered out of the way. This was an ideal spot for tomorrow's meeting with Tanya.

The store was already decorated for the holiday season. Shoppers chatted in their throaty Dutch, eyeing the goods. Lemmy's mind went back to Paula and Klaus Junior. He had placed them in danger by the very nature of his work. The Shin Bet's aggressiveness in hunting down Tanya boded poorly for anyone associated with Elie Weiss. Was Shin Bet making a play for SOD's agents and resources? Was it about the Koenig account? And how long would it take for the capable Israeli agents to figure out that Wilhelm Horch was Elie's prime asset? How could he protect his identity—or his family? And then there was Tanya's story about his father. Had Rabbi Gerster been a mole within the ultra-Orthodox, working for Elie Weiss? Had his own decision to join SOD and serve Elie been based on lies? Had he wrongly hated his father all these years? It was hard to believe, but Tanya wasn't a liar. Or was she?

All the answers rested with Elie Weiss in Jerusalem.

Lemmy finished his coffee and left a generous tip. Downstairs, he used a pay phone by the glass doors to call the American

Hotel and leave a message for Frau Koenig to expect his call tonight at nine p.m. He hung up and punched in another number.

A familiar voice answered, "Doctor Mullenhuis Data Recovery."

"Oh, yes. I'd like to recover a crashed ego."

"Ego was too big?" Carl laughed. "You must be Swiss!"

"Why? You think we're self-important?"

"It's a fact. You Swiss are a bunch of pompous asses." The crunching of computer keys indicated Carl was securing the line from eavesdropping. He had obtained a doctorate in computer engineering five years after graduating with Lemmy from Lyceum Alpin St. Nicholas. But his career with IBM Europe ended abruptly after a competitor mysteriously obtained the code to revolutionary data storage software that Carl was working on at about the same time that Lemmy helped him buy a restored 1938 Horch 853 Phaeton, the only motorcar of its kind to survive WWII, for a huge sum in cash. Going independent, Carl had specialized in facilitating the acquisition of data in sophisticated yet unsavory methods, such as the surveillance system he had installed for Lemmy at the Hoffgeitz Bank.

"Okay," Carl said. "Safe to talk now. How's the system working? You have a problem?"

"The system is great. It helped me save my father-in-law the other day."

"The rule of unintended consequences. You want to install one at home too? Watch the little wife with the gardener?"

"You're sick. Listen, I'm in Amsterdam and need a favor."

"Shoot."

"In person. Meet me at the Begijnhof, inside the yard."

"What happened to the lobby at Hotel de L'Europe?"

"The Begijnhof, five thirty, okay?"

"I might be late. Have to finish up a project."

"A cheating husband?"

"Venture capital outfit. They're having a cocktail party tonight for all their competitors, with lots of booze and babes. They want every word recorded with full video, pick up all the secrets."

"You should be ashamed of yourself."

"Look who's talking!"

Tanya left the hotel briefly for a visit to a pharmacy. Back in her room, she spent an hour in the bathroom, cleaning the scratch left by Lemmy's bullet yesterday as well as the bruises from the attack at the synagogue. She thought of Andre Silverman and his son, the funerals she was unable to attend. And she wondered how Juliette could go on living without her precious Laurent.

The rest of the morning she spent scouting the newspapers for news of Israel—any political or other event that would explain why the domestic security agency had gone overseas in violation of its very charter. It was obvious that Israel was approaching a political crisis over Rabin's push to implement the Oslo Accords. Two major rallies were gearing up. The right-wing Likud planned a rally in Jerusalem tonight, and the Labor-led left wing was to hold a peace rally in Tel Aviv's central square next Saturday night. But political crisis wasn't unusual in Israel, even with such extreme accusations and counter-accusations. She still remembered the weeks leading to the 1967 Six Day War, the erosion of public confidence in the face of huge Arab armies supported by the Soviets, the digging of mass graves all over Israel in preparation for countless civilian casualties, and the bitter political acrimony around Levi Eshkol's government. Israel's fearful citizens had expected a crushing defeat at the hands of the Egyptians, Syrians, and Jordanians armies, reinforced by armored brigades from Lebanon, Iraq, Saudi Arabia, and Kuwait. Everyone feared a complete and fatal devastation of the young Jewish state.

But instead, Israel ended up celebrating an incredible victory, tripling its size, and cementing its right to exist in the Middle East. Still, that victory had planted the seeds of today's conflict over Israel's continued presence in the territories it had captured, a division that split Israelis along ideological lines. But a political crisis, severe as it was, could not explain the Shin Bet's criminal violation of clandestine boundaries.

She again tried calling the bookstore next to Andre Silverman's art gallery on Avenue Junot, where a member of her team always attended the phones, but got no response. A call to the gallery itself was answered by a woman whom Juliette had hired after the disaster. She informed Tanya that the bookstore had been closed since yesterday afternoon, when the staff left in the company of officious-looking people in two vans.

Out of options, Tanya decided to call Mossad headquarters in Tel Aviv. She had not checked in since yesterday, and for someone of her seniority, this should have caused alarm. By now they must be gearing up for a massive search, possibly worried about abduction.

"Research Department," a man answered. "How may I help you?"

"This is Tanya Galinski. Patch me through to the chief."

"Hold on."

The line was silent for a moment, then switched to music. Tanya listened to Israeli singer Boaz Sharabi serenade an old flame, promising to bring moonstones and sea treasures if she still loved him.

"Come on," she said, "what's taking so long—"

The music stopped, replaced by a dial tone.

She stared at the receiver in bewilderment. She punched the numbers again. The line was busy. But that was impossible! Mossad maintained multiple lines for incoming calls!

Tanya tried again.

Busy.

Was Shin Ben listening in on Mossad lines? Cutting off unwanted calls? Could they block this particular call? Or trace it back to Amsterdam?

The very idea seemed preposterous. Shin Bet wouldn't dare interfere with Mossad communications. This would cause open war between the agencies. On the other hand, perhaps its fear of Mossad was the reason Shin Bet was determined to isolate her, prevent her from telling her colleagues in Tel Aviv what was going on in Europe.

Tanya put down the receiver, more shocked than angry.

The message light was blinking. She called the front desk and learned that Herr Horch would be calling again at nine tonight.

L emmy walked the streets of Amsterdam for hours. Unlike other European capitals, its charm was unassuming, with arched bridges over murky water and absurdly-narrow houses along the canals. He repeatedly stepped aside to avoid bundled-up riders pedaling their way on bicycles. He thought about Tanya. Last night's events seemed unreal. Their encounter could have ended terribly. Instead it had turned into a reunion he had never expected. But the things she had told him also seemed unreal. His father—a mole? Elie Weiss—his father's handler? His own transformation from a young Neturay Karta Talmudic scholar to an IDF soldier—a deal between Elie and Tanya? And now he was risking everything in reliance on what she had said. But Tanya Galinski was no longer the woman he had made love to as a teenager. She was now a top Mossad official. Would she risk her position, maybe her life, for Lemmy Gerster, a boy she had long assumed to be dead?

A disturbing idea came to him. What if the man he had shot at the park was actually Tanya's agent. What if they staged the call to Paris to set him up? What if "Number One" was merely a playact for the purpose of deceiving him? What if Tanya wasn't in danger at all, wasn't anyone's target? What if *he* was the target? What if this whole thing had been staged to make him betray Elie's clandestine infrastructure and secret money sources so that Mossad could take over SOD?

It all came down to one question: Could Tanya be trusted?

He followed the Amstel River as it merged into the Singer Canal. Farther down, the row of houses seemed impenetrable until he came to an arched passageway. It led into a courtyard tiled in a colorful mosaic of the Holy Virgin. Each of the connected dwellings had a small garden, and Lemmy paused and took in the scent of freshly cut grass. A modest Catholic chapel on the left faced a stone-built English church on the right. He glanced at his watch. Carl was late.

Toward the corner he found a wall of icons. In the center, baby Jesus was cradled by Virgin Mary, while a burning candle cast golden light upon them. Below Jesus, a hand had written: *In de salvaeder.* Other icons had been carved into the stone wall by the loving hands of Beguine women over the centuries, biblical scenes whose colors had dulled from rain and wind. At the bottom was a drawing of an altar atop an arid hill, a young boy tied up, a bearded Abraham holding a long blade, ready to slay his son while a guardian angel stayed his hand.

"You believe in angels?" Carl threw his big arms around Lemmy.

"I need all the help I can get." He returned Carl's embrace, pounding his friend's back. "I'm up against very capable people."

"Government or private?"

"Government."

"Ah, bureaucrats!" Carl spat on the ground. "Incompetent fools, all of them."

"These are Israelis."

"Oops. They are the exception."

Lemmy laughed.

"How in the world have you antagonized the Israelis? I thought you Swiss vanillas are supposed to remain neutral."

"It's a long story. Can you get me a valid Dutch passport and a couple of credit cards with the same name?"

"Are you running away from them?"

"On the contrary. I'm going into the lions' den."

"To Israel?"

"Yes. My cover will be the car restoration. I hear there's a good selection of old Citroën models for parts."

"I'm sure they have plenty of Deux Chevaux wrecks, but your old Presidential will only take SM and DS parts. I'll run a search for you."

"Thanks." He handed Carl an envelope. "Snapshots for the passport. I'll meet you in front of Metz & Co. tomorrow at noon."

"I'll do my best. Anything else?"

"A friend of mine will be staying with you while I'm away. She's in danger."

"Is she pretty?"

"She's incredibly beautiful, considering she'll turn sixty-eight on January first."

They hugged, and Carl left. A few minutes later Lemmy headed back to his hotel. He walked quickly through the dark mist that descended on Amsterdam, his hands in his pockets, his head bowed against the cold.

From his room he called Christopher in Zurich and asked him to go to the bank the next morning and wait for his call.

Sabbath was over when three stars could be seen in the darkening sky. After the evening prayers and a light dinner, Rabbi Gerster and Itah Orr left Benjamin's apartment. Itah wore a long dress and covered her hair with a scarf. They walked to the center of Jerusalem. Along the way, she used a pay phone to call her neighbor and ask him to feed her cat and clean its litter box every other day until she returned.

"A cat," Rabbi Gerster said as they resumed walking. "You don't seem like a cat person."

"I hope you're not allergic," Itah said.

"I don't know. There are no pets in Neturay Karta." He hesitated. "I take it you're not married?"

"Three times widowed. First husband killed by Egyptian artillery on the Suez Canal, left me with a baby girl. Second saw his son born—thank God for small favors!—before he was hit by a Katyusha rocket near the Lebanese border. I actually have the casing and a bunch of fragments from the rocket. I put them together like a puzzle showing the Russian manufacturer's name, ink-stamps from Iranian and Syrian customs, and a Sharpie note from Hezbollah: *Jews are monkeys and dogs.*"

"Didn't Mohammed say that?"

Itah shrugged. "Even a great man can sometimes say foolish things. Didn't Moses tell God to go find someone else?"

"What happened to the third?"

"Johnny? He was Canadian—came to Israel too old to serve in the army so I thought we would be safe, grow old together, all that. Super guy. Helped me raise the kids like they were his own—though now they're both in Toronto, studying art on Grandma's dollar."

"And Johnny?"

"Run over while crossing the street. Can you believe it?" She chuckled to dispel the morbidity of her marital record. "The fourth would have to be suicidal."

"I disagree," he said, and left it at that.

On Jaffa Street, a line of police barricades blocked vehicle traffic, allowing thousands of pedestrians to march down the wide road toward the Zion Square. A building overlooking the vast square had been decorated with flags of the Likud party. A huge banner read: *Peace only with security!* Many held placards with photos of victims from recent terror attacks as well as skeletons of blown-up buses. A chorus of a few hundred people adapted the tune of a romantic Zionist folksong to crude lyrics: "Yes, Rabin is a homo…yes, Rabin is an SOB…'cause Rabin is a dog…and a murderer!"

The offensive crooning repeated again and again, with more voices joining. Rabbi Gerster felt Itah grip his arm. He turned to see an elderly man in a suit, who held a sign with a photo of a young woman and the words: I SURVIVED AUSCHWITZ, BUT MY DAUGHTER DIDN'T SURVIVE OSLO!

The long balcony across the front of the building was filled with political leaders of the right, led by Ariel Sharon and Benjamin Netanyahu. The banner under the line of Likud leaders read: THE MURDERER ARAFAT DESERVES CAPITAL PUNISHMENT!

Underneath, the plaza was dense with people, many of whom now chanted, "Death to Rabin! Death to Rabin! Death to Rabin!"

Arik Sharon started talking into a loudspeaker, barely overcoming the chanting crowd. "The murderer Arafat was brought into our midst by the collaborators. It's a government that forgets everything, forgets the victims of the war criminal Arafat!"

"Look!" Itah pointed at a stout young man wearing a white skullcap. "That's Freckles!"

Rabbi Gerster recognized him as the leader of the small demonstration in front of the prime minister's house. He was holding a placard with a life-size photo of SS leader Himmler in dress uniform, only the face was substituted with Prime Minister Yitzhak Rabin's face. Next to Freckles stood a few other young men with colorful placards on sticks, showing Rabin dressed as an Arab with a checkered kafiya, Rabin with a hangman's noose around his neck, Rabin shaking hands with Arafat under the headline: PARTNERS IN TERROR.

"Freckles is very creative," Itah spoke into Rabbi Gerster's ear as the noise around them was deafening. "But the money fuels everything. We need to find the old man in Paris!"

Rabbi Gerster nodded.

The crowd switched to another chant: "With blood...and fire...Rabin will expire!"

Next came Netanyahu, who managed to say, "Good evening," before the crowd roared, "Bibi! Bibi! Bibi!"

Rabbi Gerster saw other signs rise above the crowd's heads:

GOVERNMENT OF DEATH!

LABOR PARTY IS GOOD FOR ARABS!

GOVERNMENT OF TRAITORS!

YOUR DAY IS COMING!

Likud leader Benjamin Netanyahu declared: "Arafat is a serial killer whose rightful place is among war criminals. A wicked murderer who is now supported by the current Israeli government, which blindly enables him to implement the first phase in his plan to destroy the Jewish state!"

As the two of them advanced through the dense multitude toward Ben Yehuda Street, Netanyahu's voice faded, while the eerie serenade continued, "Yes, Rabin is a homo...yes, Rabin is an SOB..."

At nine p.m. Lemmy called the American Hotel and asked for Frau Koenig. He wondered if Tanya knew she was hiding in the same hotel where another beautiful spy had stayed, though he hoped Tanya's fate would be better than Mata Hari's.

She picked up after the third ring.

"It's your dead lover," he said, "calling from the great beyond."

"Not funny. Are you in Amsterdam?"

"Yes. How's your head?"

"Achy and confused. Can you come over?"

"I'll meet you at noon tomorrow in front of the Metz & Co. department store. You'll be staying with a friend of mine until I come back."

"Back? From where?"

"I'm going to Jerusalem. Elie holds the key to everything. I have to talk to him."

"They won't let you see him."

"You underestimate me."

"And you underestimate Shin Bet." She was silent for a moment. "What about the bank?"

"Swiss banks move slowly. I can handle most things by phone through my assistant."

"Especially inactive accounts."

"Exactly." Lemmy thought about the Mauser, which he'd left in Zurich, the writing engraved along the barrel. "Koenig was an Oberstgruppenführer in the SS, right?"

"Correct."

"That was the second-highest rank in the SS."

She hesitated. "He was an accountant by training, a genius really, when it came to budget allocations, financial administration, things like that."

"Things like calculating how many humans could fit in a cattle-train car? Budgeting for bulk-purchased Zyklon-B gas canisters? Valuating human hair as an industrial commodity?"

There was a long silence. "I didn't know about these things. I adored him."

"And he adored you back." An idea occurred to Lemmy. He sat on the hotel bed, pressing the receiver to his ear. "Enough to entrust the ledger to you."

"Klaus knew that my heart belonged to him." Then, as if an explanation was required, she added, "I was very young, barely fourteen, when he took me in."

"A fourteen-year-old girl." Lemmy paused. "Your birthday falls on New Year's, doesn't it?"

"I don't celebrate it anymore, but yes, I was born on January first, nineteen twenty-eight."

"I remember celebrating with you on the first day of sixty-seven. You bought a kosher cake so I could eat it."

"You were struggling to balance your faith with...what we had."

"It's odd how certain things get stuck in your mind forever."

"Please come over. We have so much to discuss."

"It's not safe," he said before temptation took over. "I'll see you tomorrow at noon in front of Metz & Co. There's a green phone booth across the street. Wait for me there." He was about to hang up, but the question just popped to his lips. "What's Bira doing these days?"

"My troublemaking daughter?" Tanya's voice softened. "She's an archeology professor at Hebrew University, digging up sacred grounds, pissing off the ultra-Orthodox, including Rabbi Abraham Gerster, unfortunately."

"A small world. Is she married? Has kids?"

"Yes. Her oldest is in the army already. Yuval. A wonderful boy, so smart and kind and idealistic. Just like Lemmy was...I mean...just like you were...back then."

"And now."

"But all these years." Her voice cracked. "If you only knew... how much grief."

"I'm sorry," he said. "Good night, Tanya."

Benjamin was waiting when Rabbi Gerster and Itah Orr returned to Meah Shearim. He had brewed fresh tea and set up cups on the dining table. "The chaplain from Hadassah

Hospital brought a note for you." He held it so they could read it together.

ABRAHAM, I'M IN THE ICU AT HADASSAH, 4ᵀᴴ FLOOR, LAST ROOM ON RIGHT. COME ASAP. LONG LIVE JERUSALEM! E.W.

Itah asked, "Who is E.W.?"

Rabbi Gerster sat down. He picked up the note and read it again, his hand trembling. "E.W. stands for Entirely Wicked."

"Wicked?"

"He's the devil himself."

"*God shall safeguard his sheep,*" Benjamin recited, "*from evil spirits and deadly debacles that frequent this earth.*"

"Amen," Rabbi Gerster said. "Did the chaplain say anything else?"

Benjamin offered Itah a jar of sugar cubes. "He said there were two young men guarding the patient, who appears weak, emaciated, and out of breath, yet in full command of his senses."

"That's an apt description." Rabbi Gerster stood, gulping the rest of his tea. "Benjamin, kindly call a taxi for us."

"At this hour?"

"Yes. Right now."

"But it's the middle of the night!"

"There's not a moment to spare."

"Then I'll go with you. They know me well at Hadassah Hospital." It was true. Every time a man, woman, or child from Neturay Karta was hospitalized, Rabbi Benjamin Mashash was praying at their bedside or helping feed them or comforting the distraught family members.

"I appreciate it," Rabbi Gerster said, "but you must stay here with your sleeping wife and precious children. Itah will join me."

"But—"

"Rest assured," Rabbi Gerster smiled, "that nothing inappropriate will happen."

Benjamin blushed. "I didn't mean to imply such a thing."

"Hey," Itah said, "why not?"

The taxi brought them to the military cemetery on Mount Herzl. Rabbi Gerster gave the driver a five hundred-shekel bill and asked him to wait. The guards were off-duty for the night. He used a flashlight to find a service shed and took two shovels.

Itah followed him through rows of headstones. "I thought we were going to Hadassah."

"The answer lies here," he said. After so many years of weekly visits, he could find his way around the cemetery with his eyes closed.

"Where are we going?"

"To pay a final visit." He pointed the beam at the headstone. "Here we are."

PRIVATE JERUSALEM ("LEMMY") GERSTER
KILLED IN BATTLE, JUNE 7, 1967
IN THE DEFENSE OF ISRAEL
GOD WILL AVENGE HIS BLOOD

When he inserted the edge of the shovel under the corner, Itah gasped. "What are you doing?"

"You saw the note." Rabbi Gerster used the long handle as a lever, lifting the stone.

"No!" She kneeled and held the stone down, preventing him from toppling it. "It was just a form of salute. *Long live Jerusalem!* Like a patriotic cheer or something."

"The man who wrote the note knows where to stab his victims for best results. I will be in pain until I find out the truth with my own eyes."

"E.W.?"

"Elie Weiss. He spends most of his time in Paris."

"You think he's the one giving money to Freckles?"

"I'm afraid so. And now he's trying to lure me to the hospital to facilitate his escape."

"By hinting that your son is alive?" Itah picked up the other shovel. "It's so transparent. Cruel!"

"But irresistible, right?"

"Surely you don't believe him, do you?"

"A bereaved father would grasp at any straw of hope."

"But you know the truth, right? Your son is long dead. No one can bring him back to life."

"If anyone can, it's Elie Weiss." Rabbi Gerster grunted as he lifted the headstone and rolled it over, exposing the dirt underneath. "That devil has a history of playing with life and death." He pushed the shovel hard into the soil.

"You can't actually believe this, can you?" But still, she joined him, and they dug until the top of the coffin was exposed. He got into the grave, stood wide so his shoes were off the coffin, and bent down to grab the cover.

"This is so wrong." Itah aimed the flashlight into the hole. "God will punish us."

"God is an illusion, remember?" Rabbi Gerster tried to pull up the side of the cover. "And so are ghosts, in case you're worried about the neighbors."

The coffin creaked, and the beam of the flashlight trembled with Itah's hand. "The body of your son is only bones now. How could you tell if it's really him?"

"Can't open it!" He straightened up, rubbing his hands. "Talmud forbids steel nails, only wooden nails are allowed in coffins. After all these years, it's bonded together."

"A chance to reconsider," Itah said with a tremulous chuckle.

He climbed out of the grave, turned, and jumped back in, landing hard on top of the coffin, which broke under his weight.

"Oh, shit!" Itah dropped the flashlight into the hole.

"Calm down. It's only bones." Rabbi Gerster pushed aside the shattered wood planks of the cover and reached in for the flashlight among the pieces of white cotton shroud. He shone the flashlight up and down the coffin interior, located the skull, and pulled it out.

The cranium emerged from the coffin with a length of the spine and a single shoulder, attached to an arm and a skeletal hand.

"Here," he said, "hold it."

"No, thanks. I'll hold the flashlight."

"At the time, they didn't let me see the body." Rabbi Gerster was breathing hard as he peeled strips of shroud from the skull. "They told me Lemmy had been hit point-blank by a grenade, that he was unrecognizable. I should have insisted."

The last piece of shroud came off the skull. He shook off the dust, and the bones rattled.

"Ouch!" Itah stepped back. "How can you mess with your son's remains?"

"I don't believe in life after death. I need to know if these bones belonged to Lemmy."

"But how?"

He turned the skull around. The grinning jaws, hollowed nose, and empty eye sockets faced them in eerie whiteness. "Point the light at the jaws."

Itah complied.

"Ah!" Rabbi Gerster probed the gaping mouth, toward the rear. "This guy has all his teeth!"

"So?"

"My Lemmy was missing this one." He tapped a tooth with a fingernail, producing knocking sounds.

"How can you be so sure? It's been decades!"

"I held his hand while the dentist pulled it—upper jaw, second molar from the back. Lemmy cracked it on an olive pit just before his Bar Mitzvah. You should have seen that boy. He didn't make a sound while that two-left-handed dentist labored with his pliers." Rabbi Gerster tossed the bones back into the grave. "This poor bastard is not my son."

"What now?"

"Now?" He began to shovel the dirt back into the grave. "Now we'll go back to Meah Shearim for a good night's sleep."

"And then?"

He leaned on the shovel. "In the morning, we're going to see an old friend and squeeze him until all the lies drain out of him."

Sunday, October 29, 1995

Lemmy had not expected Metz & Co. to be so busy on a Sunday morning, but shoppers kept coming in. Two female models dressed as tulips stood just inside the automatic glass doors, bowing their heads, adorned with red and yellow petals, and waving their green arms.

A security camera was mounted at the corner under the ceiling. It was aimed at the glass doors, but Lemmy estimated that the lens wasn't wide enough to capture him. At any event, with his fedora and winter coat, there was little risk of identification, even if someone bothered to examine the video footage.

Attached to the wall was a pay phone, which Lemmy could use while enjoying a clear view of the opposite street corner, where a green phone booth stood close to the arched bridge. Tanya had not arrived yet. He picked up the receiver and asked the operator to place a collect call to Zurich.

Christopher was at his desk. "Herr Horch?"

"Sorry to drag you to the bank on Sunday morning." Lemmy sheltered the receiver. "Regarding the inactive account, I want to try a few things."

"We first need an account number. Only then will the computer let me try a password." The sound of fingers hitting the keyboard came through the receiver. "I'm ready."

"Try this date: January one, nineteen twenty eight."

"One. One. One. Nine. Two. Eight." The keystrokes were quick. "No good."

"Try the opposite order: Eight. Two. Nine. One. One. One."

Rapid keystrokes. "Yes! It's asking me for a password!"

Lemmy breathed deeply. Tanya's birthday did the trick. Would her name finish the job? He glanced over the two tulips, toward the green phone booth on the other side of the street, by the arched bridge. "Try this: T-A-N-Y-A."

Again the keys clicked. "No good," Christopher said.

Lemmy bit his lips. A group of teenagers walked in, chatting happily. When they passed, his eyes caught sight of the petite figure across the street, her head held up, her hair flowing free now, casting a silky shadow over her shoulders.

"Try the reverse order: A-Y-N-A-T."

The rattling of the keyboard was followed by Christopher's cheer. "I'm in!"

"Tell me!"

"The account owner is Klaus von Koenig. First name is spelled like your son's name."

Lemmy wiped the sweat from his face. "What else do you see?"

"The entry page. It's asking for Günter's personal pass code."

"That's required if you wanted to conduct transactions in the account. There should be an icon for *View Only*. It'll let you see the history of the account, such as deposits, withdrawals, and balance."

"I'm clicking on *View Only*."

The keys rattled again. Then there was silence.

"Christopher? Are you there?"

A long whistle came through. "Jesus Christ Almighty!"

Lemmy turned to the wall, the receiver pressed to his ear.

Christopher's voice trembled as he read from the screen. "Client Name: Klaus von Koenig. Authorized Officers: Armande Hoffgeitz, Günter Schnell."

"Go on."

"List of deposits. The last one was received on January 1, 1945. That's fifty years ago!"

"The amounts?"

"Deposits are in goods. Primarily diamonds, rubies, pearls, and other gems. And expensive wrist watches. The goods were sold over the first two decades. Now it's all in financial assets, mainly stocks of large American corporations. There has never been a withdrawal."

"What's the current balance?"

"It's in U.S. dollars." Christopher cleared his throat. "Twenty-two billion, eight-hundred and forty-seven million dollars."

Rabbi Gerster waited for Itah in his alcove off the synagogue foyer. She had slept in Benjamin's apartment and arrived after morning prayers were over. She pointed at the narrow cot. "Did you have the best sleep in three decades?"

He laughed. "I couldn't sleep at all. And you?"

"Like a baby. And Sorkeh forced me to eat the biggest breakfast of my life." Itah burped. "Excuse me!"

"I wrote a letter to my son."

"Can I see it?"

"I've already hidden it in a place that only he would think of." Rabbi Gerster didn't mention the risk, of which they were both aware, that Shin Bet agents would arrest and interrogate them. It was safer for her not to know. "Are you ready?"

"Yes." She raised the plastic shopping bag in her hand. "Sorkeh lent me shoes, a headscarf, and a dress."

"You told her we might not be able to bring it back?"

Itah nodded. "What about the butcher shop?"

"They slaughtered a cow yesterday, so we got everything we need right here." Rabbi Gerster pointed to the icebox by the door. "It's a bit heavy."

They picked it up by the handles, one on each side, and carried it together. On Shivtay Israel Street they flagged down a taxi.

A half-hour later, they arrived at Hadassah Hospital. Itah left him at the entrance. She returned a few minutes later, dressed in a white coat, her hands in latex gloves, pushing a wheeled gurney.

They loaded the icebox on top of the gurney and rolled it through the lobby to the elevator. Up on the fourth floor, Itah lingered in the elevator with the gurney while Rabbi Gerster walked down the hall, past the nurses' station, the waiting area, and several ICU rooms. Next to the last door on the right, two young men in civilian clothes sat at a desk covered with books and papers, likely catching up on school work while making hourly wages. One of them glanced up, saw him, and nudged the other one, who whispered a comment that caused them both to snicker. Secular Israelis loved to poke fun at black hats for their odd garb and dangling side locks.

Rabbi Gerster didn't mind, especially today, considering what these two guys were about to experience. "Is the patient back from the operation?" He pointed at the closed door.

One guard lounged back in his chair, ready for fun. "What're you saying, *Hassid?*"

Ignoring the mocking tone, the rabbi smiled. "I was coming to pray with him after the operation."

"What operation?" The guard smirked. "A nose job?"

"Heaven, no!" Rabbi Gerster struggled not to laugh. "They had to remove most of his intestines—the AIDS is eating him up from within."

The mention of that dreaded contagious disease drained the blood from the guard's face. "Nobody told us he has *that!*"

Rabbi Gerster glanced over his shoulder. Itah was halfway down the hallway, approaching fast. "The poor *yid*. And he's not even forty."

"Oh!" The guard was relieved. "Our guy is an old fart."

"He sure is," the other one said.

Itah's gurney was rattling on the floor, closing in.

"I'm sorry," Rabbi Gerster said, pulling out a piece of paper. "Must be another room. You should have seen our patient. Not only his intestines. Also tumors from here." He gestured at his neck. "Big chunks. And here too." He tapped his buttocks. "His whole rectum had to be carved out. Riddled with AIDS. Practically rotting away."

"Yuk!" The two guards grimaced.

"Ah! Here's his nurse!" Rabbi Gerster half-turned toward Itah. "Where is he?"

"What's left of him," Itah said, "is in recovery." She patted the icebox. "And all this is going to the incinerator—lumps and lumps, chopped off, and all the blood he has lost, full of AIDS. Highly contagious!" She arrived fast, and at the last minute pretended to trip on something, yelped, and swiveled the gurney around, causing the icebox to tip over. Its contents emptied onto the guards' desk in a torrent of red blood, cascading fleshy chunks, and slithering intestines. The momentum sent much of the gory mess across their desk, over their books and papers, and onto their chests and into their laps.

"Almost twenty-three billion dollars." Lemmy took a deep breath. "One big account, inactive for fifty years. That's why Herr Hoffgeitz and Günter have been so anxious."

"It's incredible," Christopher said. "What now?"

"Sign out of the account and wait for further instructions from me. I'm going to Jerusalem to speak with E.W." He hung up and turned to watch Tanya. She looked up and down the street, searching for him. Was it a coincidence that she reappeared in his life just as he was gaining access to the fortune left by her Nazi lover in a dormant account for five decades? The account was larger than the annual budget of some countries. *Twenty-three billion dollars!* Was this just a twist of fate or was she lying to him?

Tanya stood by the arched bridge, observing the traffic of pedestrians and cyclists. Her composure didn't lend itself to coincidences. There was only one logical explanation for her sudden appearance in Zurich. She wanted Koenig's blood money. She had admitted to a long feud with Elie, and this was the final round—she had locked Elie up in Jerusalem and headed to Zurich to grab hold of the Nazi fortune! And if she had lied to Lemmy about the reason for coming to Zurich, she must have lied about the rest. The man hiding behind the chess board and the whole story about Shin Bet had been a show, put up for Lemmy's benefit, to confuse him, trick him into trusting her as they escaped together so that he would hand over Koenig's account to her.

Lemmy picked up the receiver and dialed. A tram rattled by, its bell tolling to ward off cyclists and pedestrians, hiding her from him. When the tram cars reached the next street corner, he saw Tanya step into the green phone booth and pick up the receiver.

"It's me," Lemmy said.

"You're late."

"I was on the phone with my assistant in Zurich. We managed to penetrate the most secret account at the Hoffgeitz Bank." Sweat dripped down his forehead, but he had to keep on his fedora, especially with the security camera so close. "It belonged to Klaus von Koenig."

"After all these years. Klaus was very good at his job, but he was also a romantic." Her tone was endearing, almost longing. "There must be an incredible amount of money in the account by now, after so many years of appreciation."

"You'd think." Lemmy stepped as close to the glass doors as the cord permitted and surveyed the street in both directions. If he was right about Tanya, there would be a whole Mossad team waiting to pounce on him.

"What do you mean?"

"Life's full of surprises." Sure enough, at the top of the arched bridge, a young woman in a knitted cap leaned on her bicycle by the railing, sipping from a coffee mug. Near her stood an older man, who wore sunglasses despite the cloudy day, pretending to watch the ducks in the canal. "I was also expecting a large balance."

"And?"

"It's disappointing." In the opposite direction, where the street leveled out, lined with small shops, Lemmy saw another couple, also pretending to ignore each other, both smoking as they examined window displays. "Seems like my father-in-law made some foolish investments in the seventies, then lost a great deal on Black Monday in eighty-seven."

"There must be a lot left though, right?"

"Less than a thousand dollars," Lemmy lied, watching Tanya for her reaction. "The account's practically empty."

The two guards screamed and sprang from their chairs. One of them doubled over and vomited. The other tried to shake off a length of intestine that had hooked on his belt. He moaned as if he'd lost the ability to speak coherently.

"Oh, my God!" Itah shoved the gurney against the wall and pointed at the staircase at the end of the hallway. "Run! Second floor! Biohazard showers!"

The two of them stumbled toward the double doors.

"Strip down and scrub everything!" Itah ran ahead of them and opened both doors. "Quick! Before the virus gets in your system!"

They were cursing as they ran down the stairs. Itah let the doors close. She grinned and motioned at Rabbi Gerster to get into the room while she dealt with the nurses, who were rushing over. "Don't worry," he heard her yell, "just a little accident."

Inside the room, Elie was already out of the bed. He removed the oxygen line from his nose and took off his hospital gown.

Rabbi Gerster emptied the plastic bag on the bed. "Put those on." He gestured at the long-sleeve dress, a woman's headscarf, shoes, and sunglasses.

Elie dressed and sat in a wheelchair, panting hard.

Itah distracted the nurses while the rabbi wheeled Elie out of the room and down the hallway. With all the commotion going on, no one paid attention to the little old woman in the wheelchair and the white-bearded man.

Downstairs, a line of taxis waited at the circular driveway outside the hospital's lobby. By the time Elie was settled in the back seat and the wheelchair was secure in the trunk, Itah showed up.

"Take us to the YMCA," Rabbi Gerster told the driver. "Near Agron Street."

As the driver began to ease away from the pavement, a white sedan raced down the access road and came to a screeching halt perpendicular to the pavement, blocking the taxi. Its doors flew open, and four men jumped out.

"It's impossible!" Tanya's voice was sharp, angry. "There's no way! How could he lose everything?"

"Armande likes to spend," Lemmy speculated. He noticed the man on the bridge speak to the woman while keeping his face toward the canal, his lips barely moving.

"It wasn't his money to spend."

"With Koenig gone, why shouldn't he?"

Tanya stood inside the phone booth, her hand pressed against her forehead. "I don't believe it. Israel needs this money."

"I'm sorry if you're disappointed."

"That's an understatement!" With the constant noise of people and bicycles around her, Tanya must have missed the sarcastic tone of his voice. "Did he move funds to another account? There must be a record!"

Lemmy was tired of lying to her. Tanya's reaction had already confirmed his suspicions. It was obvious she had come for the money. "Is your team ready to grab me?"

"What team?"

"Take me to a safe house? Drug me up for the interrogation?"

Her face was white through the phone booth glass. "What are you talking about?"

"It's all about the money, isn't it? You and Elie, the same—plotting, manipulating, using other people like pawns."

"No!" Across the street, through the pedestrians and cyclists, he saw Tanya pound her chest with a clenched hand. "It's not about the money!"

"I don't believe you."

"Lemmy, I beg you—"

"You set me up, didn't you?" He glanced up and down the street. Both couples were watching Tanya, barely pretending any longer. "There's no Shin Bet, no big secrets, no conspiracy. You came for the Koenig account." His voice rose to a shout. *"Didn't you?"*

The two tulips stopped greeting shoppers and turned.

"That's not true." Tanya looked around. "Where are you?"

"Where I can see you and your team."

"I don't have a team! I'm alone here!" Tanya noticed him across the street and through the glass doors. She dropped the receiver and ran out of the phone booth.

Lemmy's mind registered the rings of a coming tram while his eyes were locked with Tanya's eyes, wide and glistening. He dropped the receiver and held up his hand. "Stop!" But he was inside the store, and the glass doors silenced his warning.

Up on the bridge, the young woman tossed her coffee cup into the canal, mounted her bicycle, and pedaled down toward Tanya.

Emerging through the sliding glass doors, Lemmy saw the tram rushing at them from the right. Now holding both hands up, showing his palms to Tanya, he yelled again, "Stop!"

The woman on the bicycle gained speed, racing at Tanya from the left, while the tram arrived from the right, and they collided, the handlebar ramming hard at Tanya's left kidney, jolting her forward into the coming tram, which screeched and groaned, attempting to stop.

When the sedan blocked their way, Elie's hand went to his side, groping for the blade that wasn't there. All he had with him was the heavy copy of the Bible. He recognized the man who emerged from the front passenger seat. Agent Cohen yelled something at his subordinates, and the four of them sprinted across the pavement and into the hospital.

Elie let the air out of his lungs. It was time to instruct the driver to go, but he didn't trust his voice to sound like an elderly female.

The cabby cursed, maneuvered around the white sedan, and drove off.

"Maybe they had a medical emergency," Rabbi Gerster suggested. "One must assume good intentions."

"They seemed healthy to me," the woman said.

Elie recognized her. She was a TV reporter. Why was she here?

They travelled in silence. At the YMCA, Itah directed the driver to the parking lot. "My car is right there." She pointed. "The red Mitsubishi."

"Do you have enough gas to get to Haifa," Rabbi Gerster asked, "or do we need to fill up?"

"I have plenty," she answered, playing along. "Are you happy to go home, Mom?"

Elie nodded.

They got out of the taxi. Rabbi Gerster unloaded the wheelchair from the trunk while Itah paid the driver. They pretended to engage in discussion until the taxi was gone. Elie walked slowly toward the Mitsubishi.

"Where are you going?" She pointed at the King David Hotel across the street. "I arranged a room for us."

Realizing it was only a diversion, in case the cabby was later questioned, Elie nodded and sat in the wheelchair. "Let's go."

Itah looked at him closely. "Now I recognize you! You're the creep who came to my apartment to scare me off the story about Rabbi Gerster and his dead son."

"You have a long memory," Elie said.

"And you had a long knife!" She shoved his wheelchair toward the busy road. "I was hoping to catch you one day, throw you under a bus or something!"

"Calm down," Rabbi Gerster said. "You're getting a much better story now."

"You bet!" She stopped the wheelchair abruptly at the curb's edge as a bus rumbled by.

The tram stopped with an ear-piercing screech of metal brakes clamping on steel rails. Tanya lay on the cobblestones. Lemmy ran to her. A circle of spectators formed around them.

The right side of her body was covered with blood. Her arm was broken, and her leg pointed at an impossible angle. But her face was clear, and her thick hair spread around like a soft cushion.

"I'm sorry." He touched her cheek. "I thought they were your team."

Her lips parted and she tried to speak. He bent over her, his ear near her dry lips.

"Abraham." She struggled to push air through her vocal cords. "Abraham."

"I'm not Abraham. It's me, Lemmy."

Tanya's eyes had no confusion in them. He realized she had recognized him, that she was trying to tell him something else. "Abraham," she repeated.

"You want me to go to my father?" He kissed her forehead. "I will. I promise."

Peace settled into her eyes.

Medics shoved him aside and began working on her. He stood back and searched the faces of the spectators, trying to find the agents he had seen before. Rage swept over him. He thought he saw one of them in the back of the crowd and pushed through.

Powerful hands grabbed Lemmy from behind. It was Carl. "They're long gone," he said and practically carried Lemmy through the crowd and down a set of narrow stairs.

"There was another couple—"

"The smokers?" Carl pushed him along the stone dock. "They split. I watched the whole thing."

A speedboat was tied under the bridge. Carl untied the rope and hit the throttle. The boat's tail sank and its bow rose as it took off, raising waves that rocked the houseboats along the canal. Lemmy held on, his face turned into the cool wind.

After racing through a maze of narrow canals for fifteen minutes, Carl cut the engine, and the boat drifted to the wooden dock. "I found a Citroën for you in Israel. It's a DS, but most parts would fit your SM. It's been sitting outside a mechanic's shop in a small town near Jerusalem. The owner said you can stop by anytime. I wrote down the address and directions." He handed Lemmy an envelope. "There's also a passport, driver's license, American Express and Visa cards."

Glancing inside the envelope, Lemmy saw the name on the passport. "Baruch Spinoza?"

"You're going to Israel, aren't you? It's the first Jewish name that came to me."

"Are you out of your mind?"

"Wasn't he a brilliant philosopher? I thought you'd be flattered."

"He was excommunicated by the Jews of Amsterdam. Carrying his name would make me stand out like a pig in a kosher butcher shop."

Carl laughed. "But nobody would suspect your papers are forgery. I mean, who in his right mind would choose Spinoza as an assumed name?"

There was nothing he could do right now but plow ahead. "Can you check where they took Tanya and protect her in the hospital?"

"Fight it out with those Israelis?" Carl chuckled. "Her only defense would be anonymity. I'll play around with the computer records, make her disappear, so to speak."

"I leave it to you," Lemmy said. "Take care of Tanya for me."

"What if she dies?"

"Call the Israeli embassy and tell them. They'll take care of her remains."

They hugged for a long moment, and Lemmy climbed out. He stood on the bank of the canal and watched Carl's boat speed away. Again, he was alone.

"Long live Jerusalem?" Rabbi Gerster held up the note Elie had sent from Hadassah Hospital. "Where does he live?"

"I meant it metaphorically." Elie reclined in the large hotel bed, resting his head on the pile of pillows. "Kind of a salute to your son's memory."

"A bit peculiar," Itah said.

"I knew that Jerusalem's heroic sacrifice on the battlefield would prod you to act." Elie rubbed his hands. "I'm glad you understand. Surely you didn't think I would falsely imply that Lemmy really is alive. I mean, that would be too far-fetched."

They had checked into a suite at the King David Hotel and helped Elie into bed to ease his shortness of breath. He was still wearing the dress Benjamin's wife had lent them but had taken off the headscarf and glasses. As Itah had proposed, they didn't tell Elie about their visit to the cemetery the previous night or about their investigation of Freckles and Yoni Adiel. Her theory was that Elie's lies might reveal more about his agenda than anything he would tell them if he knew how much they had discovered already.

"No hard feelings," Elie said. "I hope."

"Even now," the rabbi said, "after so many years, any mention of his name hurts."

"Your son's death was a tragic loss," Elie said. "Such a promising young man. And what's most upsetting, I'm sure, is how unnecessary it was. Basically, if not for Tanya's seduction, he would never have left Neturay Karta. If not for that woman's irresistible allure, he would be alive today. That must make you very angry with her. It makes *me* angry with her!"

"Let my son rest in peace, would you?" Rabbi Gerster was barely able to conceal his rage. It was hard to believe he had once fought the Nazis with Elie Weiss, had served as his mole among the ultra-Orthodox, had followed his commands and trusted his idealism. By now it had become all too clear that this diminutive man was a colossal liar. "I got you out of Hadassah," he said. "Now tell me what's going on. Everything!"

"Of course." Elie smirked. He obviously thought that his manipulation had worked, that he was now in control. "Did you attend the Likud rally last night?"

"We did."

"I would have liked to have been there, see the action firsthand." Elie used the remote to turn on the TV. "They didn't let me watch the news."

On the screen, talking heads criticized Likud leaders Sharon and Netanyahu for tolerating the multitudes of placards showing Prime Minister Rabin in Nazi uniform and in PLO headdress, as well as the crowd's vicious chants, especially those calling for his death. But at the end of the program, as if in an afterthought, the moderator mentioned that opinion polls conducted on the morning after the rally show Netanyahu leading Rabin by nine points among likely voters.

"Everything's falling into place," Elie said quietly, almost in a whisper. "All according to plan." But before Rabbi Gerster could ask him anything else, his head slumped, and he began to snore.

———

Part Five
The Duplicity

Monday, October 30, 1995

The Mediterranean glittered with whitecaps as the plane began its descent toward Tel Aviv. Over the years, in moments of weakness, Lemmy had imagined visiting Israel. He knew he could never return as Jerusalem Gerster. That boy had died, and Wilhelm Horch had taken his place. He had a wife, a son, and possibly a baby on the way. And his position in Zurich was about to become even more powerful when he permanently assumed Herr Hoffgeitz's job. He had once considered taking Paula and Klaus Junior on a sightseeing vacation to Israel, but Elie had forbidden it, reasoning that someone might recognize Lemmy and blow his cover.

The coast appeared in the window, a strip of golden sand between the breaking waves and the towering hotels. Beyond the beach, Tel Aviv was an urban sprawl, stretching as far as he could see.

The KLM plane turned in a wide sweep over the southern outskirts of the metropolis and touched down with a healthy bump on a runway bordered by plowed fields.

The immigration control agent took one look at Lemmy's Dutch passport and laughed. "Baruch Spinoza!" She spoke loudly enough for her colleagues at the other counters to hear. "It's an honor to welcome you to the Jewish homeland!"

Lemmy voicelessly cursed Carl. "Thank you. Happy to be here."

"I've studied *Ethics* at the university. Clever how you questioned God's existence without actually expressing blasphemy."

"Appreciate the compliment. The late philosopher is my great-great-great-great-uncle. And I don't think he questioned God's existence, but rather suggested that God and nature could be the same, philosophically speaking."

"As I said, clever." She smiled. "And the purpose of your visit to Israel?"

"Shopping." He chuckled at the sight of her raised eyebrows. "Car parts. I restore classics as a hobby, always looking for missing pieces—doors, windows, handles, mirrors, a hood, this and that."

"Good luck." She handed him the passport. "There's a street bearing your name in Tel Aviv. Check it out, take a photo, lay a wreath, you know?"

"I'll do all three." He passed through to the luggage area, still smiling. That was the sabra spirit he remembered—direct and irreverent!

Itah went downstairs to thank the PR director, a close friend who had arranged for the suite the previous day. She returned with pastries, coffee, and clothes for Elie.

They sat on the balcony, the three of them facing the view of the Old City rather than each other.

Elie pointed. "The border used to run right under this hotel."

"Let me guess," Itah said. "You two worked together?"

"At the time," Rabbi Gerster said, "there was a concern that the ultra-Orthodox would rebel against the secular government. I worked with SOD to keep the extremists in check." He put down his coffee cup. "I used to take the men of Neturay Karta to pray within sight of Temple Mount every Friday afternoon. Over there. You see that huge boulder?"

"I was doing my mandatory service in the air force," Itah said. "I worked the wireless communications at Ramat David

Air Force Base. All our planes took off that June morning, heading to Egypt. I still can't believe they managed to reach all those enemy airfields undetected. The base commander told me that Mossad knocked down the only radar capable of early detection—that huge thing the Americans installed at the UN command over there." She gestured at the south of the city. "At Government House."

"It wasn't Mossad," Elie said. "My SOD did it. It's old history, but today's political situation is very similar. Back then, with the Arabs gearing up to destroy Israel, Prime Minister Levi Eshkol was losing the public's trust. Now, the Oslo Accords are failing to deliver peace and security, with terror attacks intensifying rather than declining, and Prime Minister Rabin is losing popularity. History repeats itself."

Suddenly everything connected in Rabbi Gerster's mind: Elie's financial support of the right-wing fringe ILOT as the opposition's firebrand, the insidious mingling of the extremists' virulent rhetoric into Likud rallies to paint the whole right as violent and lawless, the recruiting of former members of Shin Bet's VIP Protection Unit, and the grafting of Nazi and PLO garb onto Rabin's image to imply that he deserved to die. "Are you going to try it again? Are you?"

Itah looked from one to the other. "Try what?"

Elie lit a cigarette. "What is real wisdom but to succeed where one failed before?"

"Wisdom is to avoid repeating mistakes!" Rabbi Gerster sat back, shocked. "You're insane!"

"What's going on?" Itah asked.

"Back in sixty-seven, he tried to prop up Levi Eshkol with a fake assassination attempt."

"Not fake," Elie said. "A *failed* assassination attempt. Intentionally staged to fail."

"Now I'm confused," she said.

"Let me explain," Elie said. "There's a whole field of political science that supports this proposition—popularity through victimhood. For it to work, a politician must be the target of a real attacker with sincere murderous intentions, the weapons must be real and deadly, and the politician must be in the line of fire, in deadly peril. That's why President Ford gained nothing from two half-hearted attempts on his life in California while few today remember how unpopular and ridiculed Ronald Reagan had been before he survived Hinckley's nearly fatal gunshot. My plan in sixty-seven had been visionary, perfect, a real attack that was going to fail only because Eshkol was on the roof, briefing reporters, when the grenades were to explode near his ground-floor kitchen. The assassination attempt was supposed to be real in every respect, and it would have restored the prime minister's popularity."

"How?"

"Good luck is a political aphrodisiac," Elie said. "Voters love a plucky leader who laughs in the face of danger, who is steady in opposing the extremists, and who unites the nation after depraved assassins tried to divide it. The political situation today is perfect for such an operation. And that's how Rabin will win the next elections."

"It's madness!" Rabbi Gerster stood and grabbed the railing. "The Eshkol assassination failed because I discovered your scheme and stopped it! And by God, I will stop you again!"

"It's too late," Elie said. "The wheels are already in motion. Unstoppable."

Lemmy rented a zippy Fiat with a manual transmission. The wide, well-marked road out of Ben Gurion Airport wound through manicured flower beds and trim shrubs, which looked more like Switzerland than the dusty Israel he remembered. The buildings were large and modern, the cars new and abundant, and the road signs multi-lingual in Hebrew, Arabic, and English.

He glanced at the directions Carl had given him to the town of Bet Shemesh and turned onto the Tel Aviv-Jerusalem highway, heading east. The radio played edgy music, a mix of American pop and Middle Eastern crooning. He searched the stations for something more to his taste and happened upon the Voice of Israel, which announced the ten o'clock news.

Obeying the speed limit of ninety kilometers per hour earned him honks from the Israeli drivers, who tailgated him before passing. Some gave him angry glares, and others cut back in within inches of his front bumper. A couple of them actually hit their brakes as soon as they returned to his lane, forcing him to do the same. It was funny for a while, but eventually, as he approached the imposing monastery at Latrun, he decided that speeding was safer than driving legally. He swung into the fast lane and increased his speed to 130 kilometers per hour, which made all the difference.

The news started with politics, quoting Prime Minister Rabin: "The Oslo Accords are the only path to peace and security for Israel and its neighbors!" Opposition leader Bibi Netanyahu was quoted next: "The current government has placed our national security in the hands of Palestinian murderers!" Next came economic news, mixing impressive achievements by several exporters with pessimistic forecasts for the industrial and farming sectors should Palestinian terror attacks grow even more frequent and deadly.

Crime news came last: "A government spokesman announced this morning the exposure of a suspected ring of identity thieves. The group allegedly hacked into computers at the Central Bank and stole personal banking data, which was then used for illegal purposes. The suspects include a well-known ultra-Orthodox rabbi in Neturay Karta and a TV reporter."

Lemmy swerved across the left lane and came to a stop on the shoulder. *A well-known ultra-Orthodox rabbi in Neturay Karta!* No one in the insular sect, which banned television, computers, and all forms of entertainment, would have the means or inclination to engage in financial fraud, let along hack into computers at the Central Bank. And who beside his father could be described as a well-known rabbi in Neturay Karta?

The news ended, followed by a promotional jingle for vacations in Eilat. Lemmy turned off the radio. What was the meaning of this? Tanya had told him that his father, the great Rabbi Abraham Gerster, had been Elie's mole in Neturay Karta. Was Rabbi Gerster now in the crosshairs of Shin Bet, another casualty of SOD's collapse? Was Shin Bet busy arresting Elie's agents on trumped-up charges? And how long would it take for Shin Bet to pounce on Wilhelm Horch in Zurich? Or to track down the Dutch tourist Baruch Spinoza, who had ventured into Israel with neither contacts nor allies for support?

He looked over his shoulder at the moving traffic. No one stopped behind him or ahead of him. He rolled down the window and looked up at the sky, searching for a plane, a helicopter, or perhaps the Israelis' favorite—a drone.

Nothing but a blue sky and an endless chain of cars buzzing by his window. Were they waiting for him at Hadassah? Was Elie Weiss the bait in a Shin Bet trap?

The next exit off the highway took him to Bet Shemesh. The mechanic's shop sat on the main road. An elderly man wearing a greasy coverall and a colorful yarmulke had his hands deep in the engine well of a tiny Alfa Romeo.

"Shalom," Lemmy said. "I'm here to see the Citroën."

The man beckoned.

Behind the shop, twenty or so cars rested in various grades of disrepair. The DS was propped on blocks, but its space age, aerodynamic shape still connoted speed and sophistication. It was white, which would make painting any pirated skin sections easier. It was also rusty in all the suspect spots and was missing the rear seat. But otherwise Lemmy's meticulous inspection revealed it to be complete inside and out—a treasure trove of usable little parts that would otherwise cost a fortune to fabricate from scratch for the SM Presidential, which shared many of its components with the standard-body DS sedan.

The mechanic was back inside with the Alfa.

Lemmy found a sink and a bar of soap. Over the sound of the running water, he asked, "How much do you want for it?"

After a long silence, the mechanic said, "It was once owned by a lawyer in Haifa. He's now a minister in the government."

"That's quite a pedigree. I'll treat it well…except for taking off a bunch of parts."

That drew a chuckle.

"I can give you two thousand dollars. That's my only offer." Lemmy pulled a bundle of bills from his pocket. "I'll have it picked up in a couple of weeks."

The mechanic put on reading glasses and fumbled through a drawer. He produced a creased envelope with a title, which he and Lemmy signed.

He examined the signature. "Baruch Spinoza?"

"Guilty as charged," Lemmy said.

The mechanic gave him the title and took the money. "Wait a minute." He went into an adjoining space, which seemed like a combined kitchen-storage-hangout room, and reemerged with a small volume. "Sign this as well," he said, holding it forth.

Lemmy looked at the cover. It was a Hebrew translation of Spinoza's 1662 work: *On the Improvement of the Understanding.*

Elie tossed his cigarette over the balcony railing. "The problem with you, Abraham, is that your emotions drive your decisions. We're not theorizing over Talmudic esoteric quandaries here. We're dealing with reality. Don't you remember what we saw with our own young eyes? Don't you remember what happens to Jews who let misguided righteousness determine their fate?"

"I remember," Rabbi Gerster said. "They died like sheep in the slaughterhouse."

"You two might as well speak Chinese." Itah stood. "You better explain what's going on, or I'm going straight to the police. What's this talk of an assassination?"

"Calm down," Elie said. "Nobody is going to die." He lit another cigarette and puffed a few times. "It's very simple. The first stage of my plan required that I nurture a right-wing militia."

"The ILOT group," Itah said. "I've covered their activities for Channel One. Is Freckles your agent?"

"You know Freckles?" Elie looked at her with renewed appreciation.

"He's getting regular cash deposits in French francs. From you?"

For a moment, Elie considered whether she should be eliminated. But a TV reporter could be useful to his operation.

"Some of the ILOT boys are familiar with the VIP protection procedures. When opportunity comes, one will strike at Rabin."

"When?"

Elie shrugged. "They've shadowed the prime minister to major events, waiting for a lapse in security. The bullet will have low velocity, and Rabin will wear a bulletproof vest. A broken rib would be the worst he could suffer."

"That's your plan?" Itah gave him a doubtful look. "You're counting on a coincidence? You think Rabin's bodyguards will step aside for your assassin?"

"They're only human. The protective ring opens occasionally, even for a brief moment."

"And if this unlikely chance presents itself, how do you know the bullets won't kill Rabin?"

"Our rabbi here can explain why," Elie said.

"A religious man," Rabbi Gerster said, "especially one with a legalistic mindset, would follow Talmud to the letter. He will shoot at the fifth rib."

"The fifth rib?" Itah seemed bewildered. "Why not the fourth rib? Or the sixth?"

"Talmud is very specific about this. It's the prescribed method to stop a *Rodef* who is in deadly pursuit of another Jew, to disable the pursuer by striking him in the fifth rib. It's discussed in the tractate of *Sanhedrin*."

"Correct," Elie said. "Rabin will walk away from the shooting almost unscathed, but the Israeli public will have witnessed an honest-to-God assassination attempt. The political ramifications will be spectacular. The whole right wing will be swept off the map of legitimate politics and into the trashcan of fringe irrelevancy. Rabin's aura as an invincible warrior will be bolstered, making him undefeatable. He will win an absolute majority in the Knesset and use that mandate to push through the rest of his peace agenda."

"And owe you everything?" Rabbi Gerster tugged at his side locks thoughtfully. "What's your reward?"

"Everything I do is for our people," Elie said, looking at Itah, whose loyalty he wanted to win. "My work will not only end Arab terrorism, but will also prevent another Holocaust, another Exile, or another Inquisition. I'm determined to end the long chapter of suffering in Jewish history, to inoculate us against national disasters that have repeatedly stricken us."

"A lofty goal," Rabbi Gerster said. "You're still pursuing that phantom solution."

"The two of us are the same," Elie said while resting his hand on Rabbi Gerster's arm. "Since the day we hid in an attic and watched the Nazis slaughter our families, we have dedicated our lives to the eternal survival of our people, to the defeat of the next Final Solution, devised by another Führer, another Pope, or another Grand Ayatollah."

Rabbi Gerster remained quiet, which pleased Elie, who feared his long-estranged mole would rise up in opposition at this critical time.

"I've developed a comprehensive strategy," Elie continued. "*Counter Final Solution.* In short, we will reorganize the existing secret services—Mossad, Shin Bet, and my SOD—into a single worldwide force capable of performing all operational elements at top level. It will gather information, infiltrate government agencies, and worm its way into ideological organizations and academic institutions in order to identify, track down, and eliminate every enemy of the Jewish people at the outset of their hostile activity. The concept aims at preventing attacks on Jews or Israeli interests worldwide, thwarting all on-going anti-Semitic activities, and suffocating all anti-Jewish intellectual enterprises. Ultimately we will achieve a total and complete immunization of the Gentile world, a cure for all of its anti-Semitic tendencies. In other words, our Counter Final Solution will exterminate the anti-Semitic virus in its totality."

"By exterminating every human carrier?" Itah Orr shook her head. "Madness!"

Elie considered whether to say more. Recruiting a news reporter was like cultivating a pet wolf. She could become a formidable ally, but she could also turn on him and destroy everything. By sharing his plans, he had committed to playing for her support, which would be a major coup. But failing to recruit her would necessitate silencing her before she could blow the whistle. He asked, "Don't you believe in self-defense?"

"I do. But—"

"You think we should agree to again go into exile? Into the gas showers? Turn the other cheek for the convenience of our mortal enemies?"

"Of course not. But I also don't believe in killing indiscriminately."

"So you believe in self-defense as long as we're *discriminate* in our actions?"

"That's right."

"Me too," Elie said. "Join us, help us operate discriminately."

"Me?" Itah seemed intrigued rather than outraged. "I've been a TV reporter my whole adult life. What could I possibly do for you?"

"A lot of good. My plans include a media department, designated to deal with the global news and communications organizations vis-à-vis their anti-Semitic and anti-Israel agenda. You possess the skills to successfully run that department."

"I'm not into killing people."

"You can be the voice of reason. A leader of the alternative to physical elimination, which is a last resort anyhow. There are tremendous advantages in converting foes into friends, if possible."

"The term *Counter Final Solution* implies mass extermination. It suggests killing, not kissing and making up."

"If we can make supporters out of powerful enemies, what could be better?"

"Okay." Her dismissive hostility was gone, replaced by journalistic curiosity. "Is that part of your plan or something you just came up with to woo me?"

"Can you blame me for trying to turn you into a partner in the most exciting Jewish enterprise in our history?"

"Rather than exterminate me?"

"That's not an option," Elie lied. "We need an expert like you, capable of assessing the virility of mass communication personalities in various countries. You'll serve as director of the global media department. You'll apply the Counter Final Solution doctrine to journalists, authors, and entertainers. If the killing of an anti-Semitic demagogue could be avoided by converting him into a pro-Israel voice, then we gain twice!"

"That's a pipe dream." Itah's forehead creased, and she glanced at Abraham, who said nothing. She fixed her shoulder-length silver hair behind her ears. "No one has ever tried something like that."

"But you see the potential, yes?"

She nodded and shrugged simultaneously.

"Then help us change history!"

"To achieve this on a global basis would be prohibitively expensive. You'll need a huge staff of analysts ready to digest mountains of data, translators versed in every language, powerful computers connected to every media outlet, and agents on the ground in every country who are familiar with local culture and academic activities."

"Go on."

"And you'll need to buy off insiders, enlist them as pens-for-hire."

"Kind of intellectual moles?"

"Yes, major talents, capable of redirecting the political, religious, and emotional tone of newsmakers and scholars from anti-Israel to pro-Israel, from anti-Jewish to pro-Jewish, from warmongering to reconciliation. It's an enormous undertaking."

"But it's possible." Elie looked up at Itah, who stood up in excitement.

"In theory, anything is possible!" She laughed. "But in reality—"

"We'll need someone with extensive media expertise?"

"Of course."

"With creativity and vision?"

"Naturally."

"With guts and big balls. Someone like you?"

"Yeah, right!" Itah dropped into the chair. "It's a pipe dream."

"Why?"

"Because it would cost more money than God has!"

"How much?"

"I don't know." She was smart enough to know he was teasing her, but she couldn't resist the challenge. "A billion dollars, okay?"

"Is that your best estimate?"

"No, it's my wild guess."

"But you believe that you could do the job if this kind of money was available?"

"Oh, sure. If you give me a billion dollars, I'll build a media department for your Counter Final Solution that will change the tone of every news outlet. Israel would be more popular than Mother Theresa, okay?"

"Funny how things work out," Elie said. "A billion dollars is the exact budget I've allocated for the media department in my five-year plan." He extended his bony hand to Itah. "Partners?"

After a brief hesitation, Itah shook his hand. "You really have that kind of money?"

"A lot more," Elie said. "Welcome aboard."

Rabbi Gerster clapped his hands. "You're still the master," he said to Elie. "I'm impressed."

Lemmy stopped at a sporting goods store on the outskirts of Jerusalem and bought three baseball caps, three windbreakers, and three pairs of sunglasses, all in different colors. He followed road signs to Hadassah Hospital, which occupied a vast mountainside compound southwest of Jerusalem. Parking the Fiat in an overflow lot across the main road, he put on a yellow windbreaker, a matching cap, and sunglasses. He carried a blue set in a plastic bag.

The information desk was handling a long line. Eventually his turn came.

"I'm looking for a relative," Lemmy said. "She was admitted a couple of days ago, but we only got word this morning—"

"Last name?"

"Weiss."

The woman punched a few keys and looked at her computer screen. "Her first name?"

"Esther." Lemmy lowered his sunglasses and leaned forward to get a good view of the screen. "Esther Weiss."

She ran her finger down the list. "Don't have her. Did you check the Hadassah campus at Mount Scopus?"

"Not yet." Lemmy saw the name on the screen: *Weiss, Elie – Room 417.* "Thanks."

"Next!"

Lemmy headed toward the exit, circled the vast lobby, and found the gift shop. He selected a large bouquet and a get-well card, which he addressed to *Auntie Esther.*

"**B**illions of dollars?" Rabbi Gerster returned Elie's cold gaze without showing his anger. This was a dangerous moment, and the next step would determine whether he would ever see Lemmy again. "Have you finally put your hands on the Koenig fortune?"

Elie raised a finger to his lips, but Itah Orr didn't miss it. "Who's Koenig? What fortune?"

"Tanya gave you the ledger, but not an account number or a password." The rabbi kept his voice even. "There's no way you could reach that money without a mole inside the Hoffgeitz Bank."

Rising from the chair, Elie said, "Let's go inside. It's too chilly for me."

The rabbi blocked his way. "Answer me!"

"Yes," Elie said. "I have people inside. So what?"

"You needed a young, bright, adaptable agent—someone similar to what I had been when you convinced me to infiltrate Neturay Karta, unknown, unattached, totally dedicated, and capable of climbing to the top, becoming a leader, and reaching through the wall of secrecy to grab Koenig's funds."

"You know me too well."

"Such a mole had to look Aryan, speak German, and possess a flexible, sharp mind."

"Possibly," said Elie.

"Your candidate had to forgo his past life, forget his family and friends, and focus his whole life and future on this mission."

"In other words, an impossible criteria."

"Except for my son, who was a perfect fit."

"Theoretically, yes." Elie tried to squeeze by toward the glass door.

"It makes perfect sense. My Jerusalem spoke fluent German, had the looks and brains, and was alone in the world. A perfect recruit for such a long-term assignment in Switzerland."

"He was too dead for the job."

Itah groaned in shock at Elie's cruel response, but Rabbi Gerster didn't flinch. "What if he didn't die on the Golan Heights? What if he survived? It wouldn't be an unprecedented situation, considering your track record. Hadn't Tanya spent twenty years thinking I was dead? Hadn't I spent twenty years thinking she was dead?"

"I understand your pain," Elie said. "You excommunicated Lemmy, turned your only son into a pariah, and expected him to come back begging for your forgiveness. But instead he joined the army and found happiness among the paratroopers. Yes, his happiness was short-lived, and it's a tragedy. But don't try to relieve your guilt by pinning it on me."

With one hand, Rabbi Gerster grabbed the front of Elie's shirt and lifted him over the railing. The only thing that Elie's flailing hands could clench was the rabbi's white beard, but with a swipe of his free arm he knocked Elie's hands away.

"Stop it!" Itah stepped forward. "Killing him won't bring your son back."

"That's right," Elie said, glancing down over his shoulder, where a rocky garden rested eleven stories below.

"The body in the grave is not my son."

"It's true," Itah said. "We dug it up."

"Is Lemmy your mole at the Hoffgeitz Bank?" The rabbi tilted Elie farther back. "Answer!"

Elie closed his eyes. His limbs slumped as if he gave in—or fainted.

"Put him down," Itah said. "He knows you're not a killer."

Carrying the flowers in front of him, Lemmy stepped off the elevator on the fourth floor of the hospital. Three hallways led in different directions. A brass plaque credited donors who had helped construct each hospital wing. A directory pointed to rooms 400–420. The double doors were marked INTENSIVE CARE UNIT.

Beyond the doors he found a strange calm, as if the severity of the patients' conditions merited hushed voices and light steps. He glanced into the rooms while heading down the hallway. The buzzing of ventilators was constant, the sick lying immobile, connected to tubes and machinery. He kept his head turned sideways while his eyes surveyed the hallway from behind his dark sunglasses. Room 417 was near the end. A desk and two vacant chairs sat by the closed door.

He passed by the nurses' station, drawing no attention. The absence of guards was both a relief and a concern—either they were accompanying Elie for a test on another floor or they had moved him elsewhere. The last possibility, that he had died, was out of consideration. That would truly be a dead end.

A quick glance over his shoulder, and Lemmy slipped into Room 417, closing the door.

The bed was made. The side table was clear. No shoes, clothes, or personal effects. He opened the cabinets and found only medical supplies. Had Elie been moved to another room without changing the record in the computer? Was it an intended diversion? Turning back toward the door, Lemmy noticed a security camera bolted to the ceiling. A tiny red light indicated it was operating.

Three knocks came in quick succession, and the door flew open.

The satisfaction Elie had felt by turning the TV reporter into a potential member of his team was tainted by doubts. If she and Abraham had dug up Lemmy's grave, what else had they dug up? She was a professional investigator, and Abraham, despite decades of relative seclusion from the modern world, had clearly maintained both his incredible intellect and powerful physique. These two made for a dangerous pair. How much did they know?

Abraham pulled him back over the railing and lowered him into a chair. Elie kept his eyes closed and listened, hoping they would assume he was out and speak carelessly.

"He's so skinny and pale," Itah said. "Is he okay?"

"The shortness of breath is chronic emphysema." Abraham felt Elie's wrist. "But his heart is pumping well."

"Isn't he heartless?"

They laughed, and Elie heard them enter the suite. He needed to plan ahead. Abraham had guessed correctly that Lemmy was in Zurich rather than in the grave, but the time for their father-son reunion had not yet arrived, and maybe never would. They were more useful separately. As to the reporter, she seemed enamored with the rabbi and his mysterious life. They had worked well as a team, executing a clever rescue operation at Hadassah and choosing a perfect place to hide him. Elie knew that without their help he would be exposed to recapture by the Shin Bet. But he could not trust Abraham any longer. It was time to find another safe place to hide for the next few days.

All this trouble was temporary. Rabin's reluctance to make a deal in advance was nothing but the naïveté of a dignified career-soldier, who had not completely internalized the rigors of real politics. But after the assassination attempt, once Rabin saw how effective Elie's strategy worked, he would pull back Shin Bet and honor the deal. What choice would Rabin have while running for a certain victory over the discredited Likud? He would have to appoint Elie as intelligence czar—or risk a "leak" to the media of the true conspiratorial circumstances of the failed assassination, which would destroy Rabin's credibility.

Elie heard the TV blaring. He peeked inside and saw neither of them in the living room. The bedroom door was closed, and faint voices came through. Elie reached into Itah's purse, which rested on the table by the door. His fingers touched a few bills, which he pocketed, together with the suite's cardkey.

Downstairs he found a phone in the lobby and asked the operator for an outside line. Freckles answered immediately.

"It's me," Elie said.

"Hey! How's it going?"

"I need a safe house for a few days."

"Super! Not a problem!" The feigned exuberance must have been for the benefit of the people present in the room with Freckles. "It's a pleasure!"

"Pick me up at six tonight. The King David Hotel. I'll be in the restaurant."

"You got it!"

"Make sure you're not being followed."

"We're cool," Freckles said. "God bless!"

The door opened, and a nurse faced Lemmy. She was tall and broad, her white uniform ill-fitting, and her smile too wide to be sincere. "May I help you?"

"Oh, yes." He took a step toward the door. "I'm a bit confused."

She didn't move aside to let him out, but her smile remained fixed. "Are you looking for someone?"

"My aunt, Esther Weiss." He lifted the bouquet. "I was told she's in room three hundred and seventeen." He tilted his head at the empty bed. "It's not too late, I hope?"

"No, she's fine." Instead of stepping aside, the nurse entered the room and kicked the door shut with her heel. "Esther was taken downstairs for x-rays." She reached into her coat pocket.

He shoved the flowers in her face and used a chopping strike to disable her right arm. She raised a foot to kick him, which he dodged, taking advantage of her temporary imbalance to knock her other leg from under her, swing her around, and land a punch into her left kidney. She managed to elbow him hard in the chest, but a second fist to the kidney removed what was left of her fighting spirit. He pulled her coat off her shoulders, leaving the sleeves on, and used the loose ends to tie her hands behind her back. She was lying face-down on the floor, right under the video camera. He knew time was short before her colleagues showed up.

A sucking sound told him she had managed to fill her lungs for a scream. He silenced her with a knuckle-jolt to the side of the head.

The nurse was out cold. But not for long.

As he exited the room, a man was jogging down the hallway. Lemmy pretended not to notice and walked in the opposite direction, where another set of double doors was marked with a red exit sign.

He made it down one bank of stairs when the man yelled, "Stop or I shoot!"

Lemmy raised his hands and turned slowly.

The employee card that hung from the man's neck meant that he was part of the hospital security team, not a trained secret agent. His protruding belly confirmed it. And what he did next proved him an amateur. "Come back up here!" He stomped his shoe on the landing. "One step at a time! And keep your hands in the air!"

"What's the problem?" Lemmy took the stairs one by one, getting closer. "I don't understand. Is it illegal to take the stairs?"

"Come on!" The gun was pointing up at the ceiling now, the finger straight forward, not threaded in the trigger slot. "Now, over there!" He turned his head to the doors. "Walk through!"

That brief interval, when the security man faced the doors, was enough for Lemmy to deliver a hard chop to the back of his head. He collapsed, and Lemmy caught him before he rolled down the stairs. The gun was a small-caliber Beretta, and he pocketed it together with a spare magazine he found clipped to the man's belt.

A few slaps on the face, and the security guard came to.

"Where's the patient from four-seventeen?"

He shook his head.

Lemmy grabbed his hand and bent it backwards. "I'll break it in five, four, three—"

"In Haifa! They're in Haifa!"

"They?"

"The rabbi and the woman. They took the patient."

"How do you know?"

"The taxi driver is a regular here. He told Shin Bet. They'll catch them—"

"He drove them to Haifa?" Lemmy applied more pressure.

"No! Please!" The man's eyes turned to the door, praying for someone to show up.

"Answer!"

"To the YMCA in Jerusalem. They had a car there. They mentioned driving to Haifa—"

Holding the gun by the barrel, Lemmy knocked him unconscious.

On the way downstairs, he switched the yellow windbreaker and cap for the blue set. The ground-floor exit let him out on the side of the building. Pedestrians and car traffic seemed normal, and no one paid any attention to him. Across a large lawn was an outdoor cafeteria. He selected a seat that was partially hidden by the thick trunk of a eucalyptus tree yet provided a clear view of the main hospital entrance.

Moments later, a white Subaru with tinted windows and a few antennas stopped at the curb. The unconvincing nurse from room 417 emerged from the lobby, no longer smiling. She got in the rear seat. The security guard showed up soon after, pressing a pack of ice to the side of his head. He went around to the driver's side and leaned over the window, which was partially open. After a short conversation, the Subaru departed.

Lemmy waited twenty minutes before walking over to his Fiat. He took the road toward Jerusalem.

They argued in hushed voices over what to do about Elie Weiss. Rabbi Gerster wanted to threaten Elie with exposure of his secret dealings, but Itah objected. In her investigative experience, subjects volunteered much more information out of vanity and for shock effect than under duress. And the more urgent task was to stop the staged assassination plan. "It's political fraud on a grand scale!"

"What about my son?"

"Finding him must wait," Itah argued. "We should focus on the Rabin deal first."

"I have a feeling the two are connected."

"Perhaps. But the Shin Bet has also been paying Freckles. I can't wait to see Elie's face when we tell him that Freckles plays both sides."

"Maybe he already knows. With double agents you're never quite certain which side they really work for. It's possible that Freckles' first loyalty is to Elie. He could be taking Shin Bet's money and feeding them lies from Elie."

"You think Elie has outsmarted the Shin Bet."

"We'll soon find out." Rabbi Gerster took a deep breath. Deferring to Itah was difficult after spending the past fifty years in Neturay Karta, where women were relegated to household duties and obeyed their learned husbands on all substantive decisions.

"He's been out there too long," Itah said. "Let's check on him."

They found the balcony deserted. So was the bathroom.

"He'll be back." Rabbi Gerster picked up the phone and asked for the international operator, who gave him the number for the Hoffgeitz Bank in Zurich. When a receptionist answered, he spoke German. "*Entschuldigen sie bitte.* This is Herman von Klausovich from Bonn, general director of inter-governmental financial cooperation of the Federal Republic."

"Yes?"

"I met one of your top executives at a conference in Vienna a couple of years ago, but I cannot remember his name. In his forties, very handsome—Aryan, if you get my gist, *ja?*"

"That would be our vice president, Herr Wilhelm Horch."

"Yes, that sounds right. Is he available?"

"Unfortunately Herr Horch is away on a business trip. If you leave your number, I'll have him call you."

"I'll try again. *Auf Wiedersehen.*" He hung up and turned to Itah. "Wilhelm Horch. That's my son's name."

"Wilhelm?"

"I bet his wife calls him Lemmy."

Traffic was heavy on Herzl Road, which led into Jerusalem through dense residential neighborhoods, none of which had existed when Lemmy had last lived in the city. On his right, a restaurant on the ground floor of an apartment building spilled tables and chairs onto the sidewalk, most of them occupied by families. He remembered one of his father's sermons, given on the last Yom Kippur Lemmy had spent at home. Why was it, his father had asked, that every time the ancient kings of Israel had made peace with their enemies, the Bible went on to describe the elaborate feast that followed? The answer, according to Rabbi Gerster, was that feeding the body calmed the mind, including its fighting spirit. On Yom Kippur, on the other hand, fasting was designed to create a sense of urgency, intensifying reflection over one's sins and prompting repentance. The memory made Lemmy realize how hungry he was. As the light changed and traffic began to flow, he noticed a parking spot and veered right.

He chose a table that allowed him an open view while a wall protected his back.

A short, dark-haired woman began shuttling plates, not bothering to take an order. The pita bread was warm and slightly singed. The pickles were salty and crisp. And the humus was garnished with olive oil, chickpeas, and toasted pine nuts. Lemmy swiped a healthy load with a folded slice of pita bread and bit into it. The rich taste literally made him sigh with pleasure.

She rushed over. "Everything okay?"

Lemmy's mouth was full. He gave her a thumbs up.

She beamed and disappeared into the kitchen.

Lamb skewers came next, with couscous and chopped salad. He concluded with mint tea and baklava. While paying the bill, he asked her for directions to the YMCA.

Elie sat in a nearby park for a couple of hours. He enjoyed the unseasonal sun and watched a group of kids chase a ball. On his way back to the hotel, he paused occasionally to catch his breath and furtively search for suspicious persons lurking about. There was nothing but the usual bustle of Jerusalem on a busy afternoon.

When he returned to the suite, Rabbi Gerster and Itah Orr were watching a TV talk show, which pitted two Knesset members against each other. The raised voices and red faces were no surprise, but even the moderator seemed riled up when he asked the Likud MK: "Why is Netanyahu pouring oil on the fanatics' fire? Does he also wish to see Yitzhak Rabin burned at the stake?"

"Your plan is working," Rabbi Gerster said, pressing the remote control to lower the volume. "You must be proud."

"Indeed."

"I'm sorry for losing my temper."

"And I'm sorry for speaking harshly." Elie patted his shoulder. "Anger and grief go hand in hand, as we both know from our days of fighting the Nazis. Losing your son must be a never-healing wound. I wish I could ease your pain, my dear friend."

Abraham nodded, but the look on his face was too cryptic for Elie's comfort. Did he know more than he was saying? Had he and Itah really dug up Lemmy's grave? And even if they had, how could Abraham tell if the remains belonged to his son? Elie was about to ask him, but Itah grabbed the remote and increased the volume.

The TV screen showed two photos side-by-side, with a subtitle: RABBI ABRAHAM GERSTER & TV REPORTER ITAH ORR.

"The two suspects evaded police yesterday," the news anchor said, "when investigators sought them in connection with unauthorized hacking into financial databases and the theft of confidential bank records. The investigation revealed a criminal conspiracy with non-profit religious organizations, including Talmudic yeshiva institutions in Israel and New York, which have allegedly been utilized for money laundering." The two photos were replaced by a video showing several police cars at the entrance to the Meah Shearim neighborhood, and officers carrying boxes of evidence down the road from the Neturay Karta synagogue. A group of bearded men in black hats and coats held a prayer on the pavement nearby, swaying devoutly.

"Channel One," the anchor said, "announced it was suspending Itah Orr until the investigation is concluded.

Anyone with information on the suspects' whereabouts should contact the police."

Itah switched off the TV. "I don't believe this!"

"They're clever," Elie said. "You were identified on the security system at Hadassah, but they don't want to mention that scene, so they made up a criminal investigation. All you need to do is stay out of sight or change your appearance. Once my operation reaches its successful conclusion, Rabin will pull back Shin Bet, and we'll be home free."

"What if Shin Bet stops your operation?"

"They're groping in the dark," Elie said. "They know I'm up to something, but they don't know what. They're clueless."

"You're an optimist," Itah said, exchanging a glance with Rabbi Gerster. "Anyway, I can use Sorkeh's headscarf."

"Yes," Elie said, "but what about the famous leader of Neturay Karta?"

Rabbi Gerster stood up. "It appears that my rabbinical career is over."

Elie watched from the bathroom door. The scissors in Itah's hands were small but relentless. She snipped off the payos and worked through the bushy, gray beard that had masked Abraham Gerster's face for fifty years. The medicine cabinet was well stocked with shaving cream and disposable blades. She shaved him carefully.

Removing his black skullcap, Itah watered her hands and combed his hair backward. "My my," she said, standing back to examine her handiwork, "you're drop dead handsome!"

Elie felt a stab of envy. It had been the same with Tanya Galinski in 1945. Despite the deep snow and the warm corpse of her Nazi lover, Tanya had stared at Abraham Gerster the same way—enamored, enchanted. It was incredible to watch him now, at age sixty-nine, impact a woman the same way. Elie cleared his throat. "Shall we go downstairs for dinner?" He had decided not to warn them that Freckles would be arriving to pick him up. Their reaction would reveal how much they knew about the chubby agent-provocateur.

"I'm starving." Itah adjusted Sorkeh's headscarf over her hair.

"Why don't we order room service?" Rabbi Gerster absently rubbed his smooth cheeks.

"Don't worry," Elie said. "The restaurant here is too expensive for Shin Bet agents."

Traffic inched uphill while pedestrians threaded their way among the moving vehicles. Lemmy turned into the YMCA parking lot and found a spot for the Fiat. This was the last known stop in Elie's escape, and the mention of going to Haifa could have been a diversion for the benefit of the taxi driver's ears.

He stepped out of the Fiat, looked around, and immediately saw the solution.

Across the street, he strolled into the circular driveway at the King David Hotel and balked at the sight of two Subaru sedans with the familiar roof antennas. He kept moving along the circular driveway until he was back on the street, this time walking downhill. Was this the next trap? But how did the Shin Bet know he would be coming to the King David Hotel? Had they made the same assumption as he and were now searching the hotel?

A limousine passed by with small flags fluttering from the corners of its hood. It occurred to him that the King David Hotel was the preferred place for visiting foreign dignitaries. Shin Bet, or another government agency that used similar Subaru sedans, was probably at the hotel for reasons that had nothing to do with Elie Weiss, SOD, or the man travelling under the name of Baruch Spinoza. He almost laughed in relief. The world wasn't revolving around this single crisis! He turned back toward the hotel.

Rabbi Gerster felt naked without his black coat and hat, without the long beard and dangling payos. For decades, throughout his adult life, whenever he entered a public place, people recognized him, bowed their heads in respect, and made way for him. But as he entered the La Regence Grill, the only glances he attracted came from two middle-aged women, who smiled at him, and from a single man in a pink jacket, who looked up from his soup and winked. It took Rabbi Gerster a moment to comprehend that his new appearance was attracting a different type of attention, the type drawn by a handsome, mature man who radiated confidence and authority.

Elie ordered a cup of chicken soup. Itah and Rabbi Gerster ordered steak dinners.

Before the food arrived, a stout young man joined their table. His face was infested with the dotted pigmentation that had earned him his nickname. He was dressed inadequately in worn sandals, khaki shorts, and a white T-shirt that bore a quote from the prophet Isaiah: YOUR DETRACTORS AND DESTROYERS SHALL EMERGE FROM WITHIN YOU. The knitted skullcap sat askew on his head, jauntily contrasting with the nervous twitch of his mouth. At first glance, he seemed like a beggar who had slipped through the lobby to hit on gullible tourists before the maître d' threw him out.

Elie looked up from his soup. "You're early."

"Am I?" Freckles glanced over his shoulder.

"Three minutes," Elie said. "How uncharacteristic of you."

"Trying to get better at my job, you know?" He laughed nervously. "Ready to go?"

"Hungry, Freckles?" Itah nudged the basket of fresh rolls toward him.

He creased his eyes. "Do I know you?"

Itah pulled off the headscarf.

"Oh, God!" He stood, then sat back down, looked left and right. "No cameras, right?"

Itah laughed. "Not today. Hush hush. Like spies. You ever heard of Kim Philby?"

Freckles looked at Rabbi Gerster, and his eyes widened. "God, have mercy!"

"Amen." Rabbi Gerster's hand instinctively reached to touch his beard, which was gone. He realized that Elie had tricked them by summoning his agent to take him somewhere else. "How's business going for you? Money coming in steadily?"

"What's going on here?" Freckles got up again, glanced at the door. "I don't like this!"

"Sit down." Elie said it quietly, but the tone was icy. "You all know each other?"

"Freckles has been a great source," Itah said. "I've earned many kudos for my reports on ILOT. But lately I've come to doubt him a bit."

Elie's little black eyes focused on her. "Why?"

"Hold on." Rabbi Gerster noticed that Freckles kept looking toward the entrance to the restaurant. "I think we should—"

"I had a little peek," Itah said, "at his bank account. Regular deposits of French francs in cash, but also a monthly paycheck from Shin Bet, plus medical and pension. Did you know about that?"

"It's a trap," Rabbi Gerster said, rising.

Elie didn't answer Itah's question. His hand grasped the rabbi's toothed steak knife, rose unhurriedly, and stuck the knife upward into Freckles' chin just behind the bottom-front jaw. "Is that true? Do you work for Shin Bet?"

Freckles couldn't nod, and opening his mouth was also impossible. Only his lips moved when he squeaked, "I can... explain."

Rabbi Gerster grabbed Itah's arm. "We're leaving!"

Several of the patrons suddenly rose, including the man in the pink jacket, and surrounded their table.

"Step back," Elie said, "or I'll puncture his brain."

A man in a blue jacket jogged across the restaurant to the table, his hand held up. "Good drill, fellows. Excellent practice!"

"Agent Cohen." Rising slowly, Elie kept Freckles' chin impaled on the steak knife. "Call off your men and have a car ready for us outside."

"Let him go." The Shin Bet officer spoke too quietly for the other patrons to hear. "We can discuss our differences elsewhere."

"I think not." Elie headed for the door with Freckles.

Rabbi Gerster was determined not to allow Jewish blood to be spilled. "We're outnumbered. Let's live to fight another day."

"Follow me," Elie said, leading Freckles with the knife.

The rabbi saw Itah raise her eyebrows in a manner of someone accepting defeat. They had made a mistake not telling

Elie about the Shin Bet salary Freckles was earning, and Elie had kept from them the fact that he had summoned Freckles to the hotel. Now the game was over.

Rabbi Gerster could have pulled down Elie's hand to release the hapless Freckles, but the young man's double-crossing irritated the rabbi enough to make him choose a less-pleasant method. He swung his arm and hit Freckles on the forehead with the back of his hand. The agent's head flew backward, his face turned to the ceiling, and his chin tore off from Elie's knife. The strike's momentum caused him to fall backward, where he stayed sprawled on the carpet, too shocked to move.

Removing the knife from Elie's hand, the rabbi flipped it in the air and offered it to Agent Cohen with the handle first.

"Thank you." Agent Cohen clapped. "Great show!"

The other Shin Bet agents joined the clapping.

"It's only a drill," Agent Cohen said to the shocked patrons as his agents steered the group to the door. "Thanks for your patience. Enjoy your dinner!"

The clapping proved contagious, and the thirty or so patrons joined in, visibly relieved.

Wearing a burgundy windbreaker and a baseball hat, his overnight bag hanging from his shoulder, Lemmy approached the entrance to the King David Hotel. He had to go without the sunglasses, which would have raised suspicion at this hour. The two Subaru sedans were still there, and several idle men in civilian clothes stood along the driveway. He felt like a criminal entering a well-policed compound.

The tall doors were propped open to allow fresh evening air into the lobby. As he stepped closer, a large group was coming out, a tight circle surrounding an inner core of—he assumed— dignitaries that merited VIP protection. He stepped aside as the group emerged. Behind him, car engines came to life.

In the center of the group, one man was taller than the others, his thick mane of gray hair brushed back from a handsome face. He sensed Lemmy's gaze, glanced, and stopped in his tracks, causing the whole group to come to an awkward halt, bumping into each other.

It took a moment for Lemmy to recognize the blue, wise eyes. *Father!*

Lemmy was stunned, not only by seeing his father for the first time in almost three decades, but by the loss of his rabbinical manifestations. Yet years of honing his self-control in a life of clandestine survival kept Lemmy from expressing any emotions while his mind absorbed all the details within his field of vision: Elie, much shorter than the rest, looked frail. A woman, about fifty, wore a headscarf and an anxious expression. The men with the guns were alert, professional, focused on their three prisoners.

Lemmy reached into his pocket to draw the Beretta he had taken from the security man at Hadassah, but his father gave a quick shake of the head, turned in the other direction, and bellowed in the familiar baritone that Lemmy remembered so well: "Benjamin! Benjamin!"

Everyone turned in that direction. The agent in charge—blue jacket, thin lips, and rusty hair—recovered quickly and ordered them into the cars. A moment later they drove off.

"What a bunch of showoff girls," one of the bellmen said. "These guys think the world should stop for them."

"Come on," his colleague said, "they have to be ready if someone attacks a bigwig." He noticed Lemmy standing there. "Welcome to the King David Hotel." He reached for his shoulder bag.

"I'm fine," Lemmy said. But he wasn't. His hands shook and his knees threatened to buckle. His father's eyes had been surprised, but not shocked, as if he had expected to see his dead son show up alive. And his coolheaded diversion had prevented disaster. But had his father yelled "Benjamin!" only as a diversion, or also as a directive to go to Benjamin in Neturay Karta?

He entered the lobby and bumped into a chubby young man in sandals and shorts, who picked up his blue skullcap, which had fallen to the marble floor, and pressed it to his head. His freckled, sweaty face turned up to Lemmy for a second. There was blood on his neck and shirt. He mumbled something and sprinted to the exit, pausing to check that the circular driveway was vacant before running out into the night.

"What was that about?" Itah's lips were warm on Rabbi Gerster's ear. "Did you see Benjamin near the hotel? On the street?"

He shook his head.

"Then why did you yell his name?"

The rabbi smiled.

Agent Cohen, who sat next to the driver up front, glanced over his shoulder. "No more tricks, guys. We could be less polite, if you get my drift."

"Same here," Elie said. He was sitting by the window, looking out.

The Shin Bet officer sneered. "And I was told you're a dangerous man. *Ha!*" He faced forward and switched on the radio, filling the car with fast-paced Hebrew music.

Itah squeezed Rabbi Gerster's knee.

He leaned closer and whispered in her ear. "When we were leaving the hotel lobby, did you see the guy with the baseball hat?"

She nodded.

"That was Lemmy."

Itah jerked backward as if he had hit her. She mouthed, *No!*

Rabbi Gerster nodded and whispered, "My son!" And before he knew what was happening to him, his face crumbled, and hard, painful sobs burst from his chest. Itah put her arms around him, and he cried, rocking back and forth, consumed by joy and relief and by a terrible fear that this encounter, this brief, wordless eye-contact with Lemmy, would turn out to be the end, rather than a new beginning.

———

Tuesday,
October 31, 1995

Lemmy checked out of the King David Hotel in the morning. He left the rented Fiat at the YMCA and walked through the streets of Jerusalem, which bore little resemblance to the divided city of his childhood.

He crossed the point where the border had once cut an arbitrary north-south line and saw none of the bullet-scarred, half-ruined buildings that had abutted the no-man's land. Through the Jaffa Gate, which had been in Jordanian territory the last time he saw it, Lemmy entered the Arab Quarter of the Old City. He followed the market alleys, finding himself in the revived Jewish Quarter, home not only to Talmudic yeshivas and bearded scholars, but to artists' studios and galleries. Stone-built residences had been restored to original antiquity with meticulous details. Fenced-off archeological digs reached down through layers of sediment, unearthing physical remnants all the way back to King David's empire. Looking down into one of the deep holes, Lemmy could see the layers of Jewish life, each era settled atop the previous era, century after century, accumulated on this mountaintop citadel.

Reaching the vast plaza in front of the Wailing Wall, he found a marble bench all the way to the side. Religious and secular Jews, foreign tourists, and men in uniform stood at the wall shoulder to shoulder. The giant cubical stones piled up to immense height. The physical enormity and the weight of history gave the Wailing Wall an intangible spiritual aura. Lemmy thought of that early morning on June 5, 1967, when he had driven by this place, an eighteen-year-old IDF paratrooper, disguised in UN uniform, deep inside Jordanian East Jerusalem, tasked with blowing up the UN radar on Antenna Hill moments before every Israeli fighter jet took off for synchronized bombing raids against all of Egypt's airfields.

Only now, as he sat here in view of the Wailing Wall, in the center of Israel's modern capital, Lemmy realized that his own life's meaning really came down to that sunny morning twenty-eight years ago, which had changed Jewish history and saved his people from a second Holocaust at the hands of the Arab armies that were prepared to destroy tiny Israel with the best Soviet weaponry. The realization put things in perspective for Lemmy. Yes, he must expose the reason behind Shin Bet's illegal activities in Europe and protect Paula and Klaus Junior from the consequences of his secret life. But the current challenges were not beyond reach, considering what he had managed to achieve by age eighteen and the clandestine skills he had developed since then.

A notepad and a jar of pencils drew his attention. He tore off a piece of paper and scribbled: FOR TANYA'S RECOVERY. He didn't even know whether she was still alive, but he folded the note and stuck it in a crack between two stones. The wall was cooler than he expected, and he rested his forehead against it, closing his eyes. He thought of Tanya lying on the cobblestones in Amsterdam, looking up at him with eyes that were surprisingly peaceful. And he remembered her looking up at him almost three decades earlier, her black hair spread on a white pillow in the old house by the Jordanian border, her eyes not peaceful but burning with passion.

A man tapped Lemmy on the shoulder, startling him. "Are you Jewish?"

"Excuse me?"

He gestured at a group of black hats nearby. "We only have nine. We need one more to complete the minyan quorum for prayer."

"Oh."

"So? Are you Jewish?"

After a brief hesitation, Lemmy nodded. "Yes. I am a Jew." He accepted the prayer book and joined them in reciting the Hebrew words.

The previous night, the Shin Bet agents had brought the three of them to a top-floor apartment in Tel Aviv with enough bedrooms for everyone. It was quiet and peaceful, but Rabbi Gerster's mind was stormy and he couldn't sleep. He kept seeing Lemmy's face—a grown man, yet so familiar. Had he understood that he must seek Benjamin in the old neighborhood? Would Benjamin keep his cool and know what to do?

At dawn Rabbi Gerster tiptoed to the front door and tried the handle. It was locked. A female voice came from a hidden speaker. "Can I help you?"

"Looking for the bathroom," he said.

"That would be the little room with a toilet bowl. Down the hallway."

Later in the morning, they congregated in the kitchen. A young man with dark, curly hair and brooding eyes joined them.

"Gideon?" Elie glared at him. "Why are you here?"

"Same reason you're here."

Agent Cohen entered the kitchen, all smiles. "Here are your administrative detention papers." He tossed the documents in front of Elie, Itah, and Rabbi Gerster. The forms appeared genuine, with Ministry of Defense stamps and signatures at the bottom, authorizing Shin Bet to hold them without further proceedings and without a lawyer for up to ninety days.

The grandmotherly housekeeper cooked eggs to each person's liking, which they ate with slices of grainy bread and bowls of Israeli salad.

"Almost as good as the King David Hotel," Agent Cohen said as he poured olive oil on his salad.

"You're playing with fire," Elie said. A nurse had come in earlier and fitted him with a portable oxygen tank. A transparent plastic tube was held under his nose with a rubber strip that circled his head. "What has Freckles told you?"

"Question is, what has he told *you?*" Agent Cohen laughed and bit into a chunk of bread.

Rabbi Gerster wiped his lips and sat back in the chair. He had a hunch that the mutual antipathy between Elie and Shin Bet somehow involved Lemmy, but how? He sighed. Despite the bright light from the floor-to-ceiling windows and the endless span of the glistening blue Mediterranean, he was in the dark.

The synagogue was full of Neturay Karta men engaged in afternoon prayers. Lemmy's blue baseball hat and windbreaker stood out among the homogeneous black coats and hats. His clean-shaven face felt bare among the uniformly bearded men.

He sat in the rear and hoped that they would take him for another curious tourist who had wandered into the Meah Shearim neighborhood for its narrow alleys, old stone houses, and quaint inhabitants.

When the prayers ended, the men went back to studying. They swayed over open books of Talmud, arguing with each other, puffing on cigarettes. He felt a swell of longing, drawn to join them, even for a few minutes of reliving his youth. Their immersion in the study of Talmud was unlike any other scholarly endeavor—reciting, discussing, pondering, and debating every word and every subtlety in the sages' conflicting positions on every subject imaginable. Like their ancestors over countless generations, the men of Neturay Karta dedicated their lives to the study of Talmud as the ultimate way to glorify the Creator. At eighteen, Lemmy had broken away from the long chain of tradition. Until now, he had never doubted that decision.

But here, as the old synagogue enveloped him in the smells and sounds of his boyhood, with the palpable warmth and sense of purpose, with the joy of intellectual fencing in the worship of *Adonai*, the one God who had chosen us to receive His word,

Lemmy was struck by an overwhelming sense of loss, as if all the years of his adult life had been wasted away from his true destiny—*from his true self!*

With great mental effort, Lemmy shunned those nostalgic misgivings and focused his mind on the task at hand. One of these men was Benjamin—not the young and cheerful youth he remembered, but an older Benjamin, a man of forty-six with dark eyes and a laughter that was likely less explosive, yet still contagious.

Lemmy got up and paced along the book-lined side wall in order to better see their faces. Some of the men resembled what he imagined Benjamin would look like, but up close, none of them turned out to be his childhood friend and study-companion. Lemmy walked down the other side, examining more bearded faces, none of them Benjamin's.

Disappointment descended on him. Why had Father yelled Benjamin's name? Had Benjamin left Neturay Karta? Perhaps one of these men knew where Benjamin Mashash lived now?

Before he could ask, someone pounded on the lectern three times. Lemmy realized the lecture of the day was about to begin. He returned to the bench in the rear.

Rabbi Gerster's daily lectures had been the main event of each day of study, exposing novel, complex interpretations that none of the men had managed to reach independently. Superior intellect had long been the engine of rabbinical leadership, perhaps because Jews had lived in exile for two thousand years, lacking a political structure in which ambition alone could float a meritless man up to leadership. For Orthodox Jews, Talmudic scholarship had always been the sole criteria for prominence. And in the Neturay Karta of Lemmy's youth, his father, Rabbi Abraham Gerster, had reigned supreme with his incisive mind and powers of persuasion.

One of the men stepped up onto the dais and stood by the lectern, his eyes on the open book in front of him. "Two men grip a prayer shawl. Each one claims full ownership." His voice was soft and pleasant, intoning the words. He swayed back and forth, playing with his spiraling payos. "Talmud says that each one must take an oath that he owns at least half of the prayer shawl and shall accordingly receive one-half."

Lemmy raised his hand. "You call this justice?"

Many of the men turned their heads to see who spoke.

"One of them must be lying," he continued. "To split the prayer shawl between them means that the honest owner loses half. Is that fair?"

A man in a front bench responded, "These are not the original owners. They found the shawl in the street."

"Even then," Lemmy said, "the dispute is factual, not legal. One of them was the first to find it, and he's deprived of half of his new property while the other one walks away with plunder."

The man at the podium caressed his salt-and-pepper beard. "Plunder is not the issue here. These two are honest disputants. Each one believes he was the first to notice and grab the prayer shawl. Now—"

"So Talmud avoids the real issue," Lemmy said.

A murmur swept through the rows of men.

"What if one is lying? The honest one loses half to a thief."

Another man said, "Rabbi Sumchus and Rabbi Yossi discuss a similar scenario, with a banker who took deposits from two men. One deposited two hundred shekels, and the other only one hundred. When they came to collect, both claimed to have deposited the larger amount, and the banker couldn't remember. Rabbi Sumchus rules that each takes one hundred shekels, and the disputed one hundred remains until one of them admits that he had lied or until the Messiah comes and decides. But Rabbi Yossi says that neither should get anything so that the liar would lose his first one hundred shekels. Otherwise, there's no deterrence to lying."

"Okay," Lemmy said, "both Rabbi Yossi and Rabbi Sumchus agree that the disputed one hundred shekels should be held, not split, correct?" He swayed in the manner of a Talmudic scholar. "So why are we cutting the prayer shawl in half?"

"No one's cutting it," yelled another man from the opposite end of synagogue, "we split the value, not the thing itself!"

The rabbi on the dais closed his book and descended the three steps. He walked down the middle aisle toward the stranger in the back.

Lemmy stood up.

The rabbi stopped abruptly a few rows away and blinked, shook his head, opened his mouth to speak, but couldn't utter a word.

"Shalom, Benjamin."

"*Oy!*" Rabbi Benjamin Mashash pressed his hands to his chest as if experiencing a sharp stab of pain. "*Oy! Oy! Oy!*"

Rabbi Gerster was determined to find out what was really going on. He would not grope in the dark while his son, who had just come back from the dead, could unwittingly get entangled in a scheme to assassinate—or to pretend to assassinate—the prime minister! Squeezing Elie Weiss for information was pointless, even risky, with Elie's proclivity for sudden violence. But Agent Cohen seemed cocky enough to be susceptible to goading. Perhaps he would say something revealing.

"I was wondering," Rabbi Gerster said, holding up the detention order, "how many renewals you could obtain before the law requires you to release us or bring us before a judge?"

"I won't need renewals." Agent Cohen broke off another chunk of bread and smeared it with butter. "This whole thing will be over next week."

"Sounds good to me," Gideon said. "I'm going back to graduate school."

"You want us to believe that?" Agent Cohen laughed.

"I'm going back to Channel One," Itah Orr said with sudden venom, "and you'll watch me on TV telling the nation about you!"

"I don't think so," Agent Cohen said. "You'll be busy with criminal defense lawyers, trying to stay out of jail, fighting off computer hacking charges. Your friend at the treasury ministry has been very cooperative." Before she could respond, he turned to Rabbi Gerster. "And you? Will you go to Switzerland?"

The rabbi played with his fork, taking a moment to organize his thoughts. He had a feeling that the Shin Bet agent was fishing for information, that he didn't know the real situation. "Why Switzerland?"

"We know you called Zurich from the King David Hotel yesterday. Do you keep money at the Hoffgeitz Bank? Or is it SOD deposits?"

The rabbi exchanged a glance with Elie. Agent Cohen was assuming that the Zurich connection was merely about financial convenience and secrecy. His error must be reinforced. "God's work doesn't come free," he said.

The Shin Bet officer sipped from his orange juice. "Tanya Galinski was also in Zurich a couple of days ago."

"That's impossible!" The harshness in Elie's voice made everyone turn to him. "You're lying!"

Agent Cohen pulled a photo from his pocket and placed it on the table. It had been taken in the rain from a distance too great for detailed clarity. A man and a woman were sitting on a park bench under a bare tree. Her hair was loose, and he was pressing a handkerchief to the side of her head. Her petite size and pale face resembled Tanya, though it was hard to tell, especially as Rabbi Gerster had not seen her in many years. The man, however, he recognized from last night's encounter at the entrance to the King David Hotel: Lemmy!

"Shin Bet agents following Tanya Galinski?" Elie took a few shallow breaths. "It's illegal for you to spy on Mossad, and it's twice illegal to do it abroad!"

"Don't get technical with me." Agent Cohen beckoned the housekeeper to remove the dishes. "Who's this man Tanya met? Is he a bank employee?"

"She has many men," Elie said.

Rabbi Gerster was delighted. This photo confirmed that Lemmy was living in Zurich and working at the Hoffgeitz Bank. Also, it was obvious that Elie recognized Lemmy. And best of all, Shin Bet had not yet figured out who he was.

Agent Cohen turned to Gideon. "Do you know him?"

The young SOD agent shook his head. "Never been to Zurich."

Rabbi Gerster said, "Why don't you ask Tanya?"

Agent Cohen shrugged. "She's gone incommunicado at the moment." He pocketed the photo. "We have people in Zurich trying to identify the man she met. But it would be easier if you just told us."

Elie Weiss smirked. "Easier for whom?"

"Easier for him," Agent Cohen said. "My men are very upset. He'll suffer less if he turns himself in."

"Upset?" Rabbi Gerster struggled to keep his voice disinterested. "Why are they upset with this Swiss guy?"

"He shot one of our agents. When we find him, we'll make sure he *also* limps for the rest of his life—if he lives."

"Master of the Universe," Benjamin cried. "Blessed be His name for keeping us alive to celebrate this day!"

They held each other for a long time.

"Master of the Universe," Benjamin kept saying, "Master of the Universe!"

They wiped their eyes and stepped out to the foyer. Behind them, the men in the synagogue returned to studying Talmud, as wasting time was considered the worst of all sins.

They sat down, and Lemmy told Benjamin that the corpse of a Jordanian soldier had been buried in Mount Herzl under his name while he assumed a new identity and served Israel abroad. He gave no more details. It was safer for Benjamin not to know.

Benjamin told Lemmy about his life as Rabbi Gerster's heir, about his wife, Sorkeh Toiterlich, who had once been engaged to Lemmy, and his children, whom he listed by name and age, starting with his eldest, Jerusalem, born ten years after Lemmy's departure. Benjamin's wise eyes became moist again. Up close, Lemmy could see the wrinkles from age and responsibility, the paleness from the indoor life of a scholar.

"It worked out for the better," Lemmy said. "You're worthy of my father's place."

"Oh, no." Benjamin shivered. "Who could possibly replace Rabbi Abraham Gerster? We try to follow the path he has charted for us, that's all."

"He's not an easy man to please. I know from experience."

"That's true!" Benjamin laughed, his white teeth and squinting eyes instantly transforming him back to the youth Lemmy remembered.

Lemmy laughed too. "Crazy, isn't it?"

"It's wonderful! To see you alive…thank God for miracles!" Benjamin's face became serious again. "But your father is gone now. It's a terrible scandal. We're so worried about him."

"I saw him yesterday. He was arrested. We couldn't talk, but he communicated to me that I should come to you."

"To me? But I don't know anything."

"Perhaps he left papers or letters?"

"Government investigators came here and took all his belongings. Come, I'll show you."

A small alcove off the foyer held a cot, a desk, and Rabbi Gerster's chair. The bookcase was empty. The desk drawers were pulled out and turned over.

"They took everything, even his books."

Lemmy sat in the chair and gripped the carved lion heads at the ends of the armrests. "He committed no crimes. It's a diversion from what's really going on. That's what I'm trying to find out. Did he tell you anything?"

Benjamin shook his head. "A woman was here, the TV journalist that's also being accused. And the rabbi received a note from a patient at Hadassah hospital."

"What did it say?"

"Asked him to come to Hadassah. And it said: *Long live Jerusalem!* Now I understand what it meant!" Benjamin took a deep breath. "Did he recognize you last night?"

Lemmy nodded.

"He must be so happy! Every week he visited your grave. Your death continued to torment him. So when the note came, he rushed out with the woman in the middle of the night. He didn't tell me where they went, but there was mud all over their shoes the next morning, and he was happier than ever."

"Then he must have left me a note somewhere. Where could it be?"

Benjamin waved at the walls. "They took everything."

A memory came to Lemmy. On his last day here, back in 1967, his father carried *The Zohar*, the book of Kabbalah mysticism, which only the most righteous rabbis dared to study. "Go back into the synagogue and have the men search all the bookcases for my father's copy of *The Zohar*. It's bound in brown leather."

"I know how it looks." The hesitation confirmed Lemmy's assumption that *The Zohar* was the perfect hiding place for a note. Even an accomplished scholar like Rabbi Benjamin Mashash was wary of it. "Your father wouldn't leave it in the synagogue, where others could happen upon it."

"Please," Lemmy said. "Trust me."

Benjamin left, and a moment later his voice boomed from the dais inside the synagogue. Lemmy could hear the benches creak and the floorboards groan as the men fanned out to the walls of the synagogue to search the long shelves that carried thousands of books.

They were sitting in the living room on black leather sofas around a chrome-and-glass coffee table. Rabbi Gerster said to Itah, "Start moaning. I need background noise so they can't hear what I'm saying."

Itah complied, uttering a low moan toward the ceiling.

Rabbi Gerster leaned close to Elie. "I demand that you come clean with me!"

Itah kept going, interrupted only by a brief intake of air.

Elie gave him a cold, dark glare. "Tell her to shut up."

"The man in the photo with Tanya is my son. If you don't cooperate, Shin Bet will find and kill him!"

"Quiet, please," Elie addressed Itah directly. "This game could end badly."

Rabbi Gerster put his much bigger hand on Elie's. "If you don't level with me, I'll tell Agent Cohen everything I know—about Tanya, about you, and about the fortune left by Klaus von Koenig."

"You know nothing."

Itah raised her hand to quiet them and stopped moaning. She took a sip of water, gargled it, and resumed moaning. Meanwhile the housekeeper went to the phone and began punching numbers. Gideon leaped from the sofa and took away the receiver, hanging up. The woman shrugged and returned to the dishes in the sink.

"I won't sit idly," Rabbi Gerster said, "and let my son die again. Tell me the truth!"

Elie scratched his scalp. "The truth? You seem to know the truth already. Jerusalem Gerster died in sixty-seven, and a German teenager came to life in his stead. My Swiss agent might be living inside your son's physical body, but he's someone else. For him, you don't exist."

"That's a lie!"

"Can you blame him? When Jerusalem rebelled against the ultra-Orthodox lifestyle, you declared him dead and sat shivah for him—made your own son homeless and hopeless. And that was even before he became a soldier, before the war. You lost him forever when you excommunicated him."

"That's between me and Lemmy. You had no right to lure him into your spider web."

"Why? You had tossed him into the garbage, and I dug him out and made use of him. Why is it your business?" Elie's colorless lips curled, exposing teeth yellowed from smoking.

"Wilhelm Horch. That's his name, correct?"

The grin disappeared from Elie's face.

Itah ran out of breath, and the room quieted down. Instantly Gideon raised his head and howled, which made Itah burst out laughing and caused the housekeeper to smile for the first time.

Elie, however, was not smiling. He pointed at Rabbi Gerster's chest. "If you utter that name again, you'll cause Lemmy's death."

It seemed that Elie didn't know Lemmy was already in Jerusalem. "But Agent Cohen said they'll catch him—"

"Bravado. Kids playing spies." Elie sneered. "You have no reason to fear Shin Bet."

"I fear *you!*"

"For good reason." Elie raised two fingers, held together. "I have a backup agent, right next to him inside that bank. You disobey me one more time, and I'll have your son's throat slit. We understand each other, yes?"

Before Rabbi Gerster could respond, two Shin Bet agents burst into the apartment, guns at the ready. One of them was the nurse, a large, muscular woman, who aimed at Gideon. "Quiet!"

He stopped howling.

"What's going on here?"

"We're having a contest," Itah said, "a coyote-imitation contest. Would you like to try out?"

"We found it!" Benjamin rushed into the small room with the leather-bound book. "You were right. Rabbi Gerster hid it in plain view on the top shelf."

Lemmy opened *The Zohar* and browsed through the pages, which were yellow from old age. On page 67 he found a sheet of paper, folded in half, attached with a strip of tape. He peeled it off.

Jerusalem, October 29, 1995

My dear Lemmy,

Until a few hours ago, I had only grief, guilt, and regret to occupy my mind. Now I have hope—to hug you, to kiss you, and to beg for your forgiveness.

Much needs to be explained face-to-face, but just in case fate is again unkind to us, please know that I had deceived you and your mother. I don't believe in God, and so I'm not a true rabbi.

Why had I done that?

I have witnessed the Holocaust firsthand. No God stopped the Nazis, and no God will prevent future disasters and deaths. It's up to us to reduce Jewish suffering, each with the skills we possess. My skills are rabbinical by upbringing, and so I've dedicated my life to this job.

And what is this job?

As you have studied, civil wars and brotherly hatred typified the repeat demises of Jewish sovereignty in Israel. I came to live among the ultra-Orthodox as a mole, assigned to keep the extremists in check, lest they bring down this current iteration of the Jewish state, as they had destroyed all its predecessors since the empire of King David.

In the course of my duties, I caused you and my saintly wife much suffering. I condemned you to the loneliest agony—that of a son who hates his own father—because your innocent eyes saw in me only the cruelty of a devout fanatic. Was that the reason for your cruelty in rebuffing the pleading letters that your mother sent to you in the army?

But now I know how Elie had manipulated our lives to serve his fanatical ends. He caused me to become a deceiver, a hypocrite, a husband and father who cheated his family out of the love and loyalty which they deserved. And he made you repeat my errors in your own life. How ironic!

But Elie's malice does not diminish my responsibility. It's too late for either of us to obtain your mother's forgiveness, yet I hope you can find it in your heart to understand, and perhaps accept, that my choices were motivated by selfless idealism, foolish as it might be.

Now to the present. I am convinced that you will return to seek answers soon, as Elie's current scheme stinks more ominously than anything he tried before. This morning we'll try to pluck him out of the hospital and question him.

Stuffed into the binding of this book you will find a complete summary of my investigation, assisted by Itah Orr. The agent nicknamed 'Freckles' is the key. Seek him, and you'll find what Elie is up to, how to stop him, and how to free yourself from his web.

And for this—your freedom—I'm willing to lose my life. I'll do anything to bring you home, to give you a second chance to live a normal life.

I LOVE YOU, MY SON, MORE THAN ANYTHING IN THIS WORLD OR THE NEXT. I LOVE YOU MORE THAN I LOVE LIFE ITSELF, MORE THAN THE SUN AND THE AIR THAT I BREATHE.

YOUR FATHER,
ABRAHAM GERSTER

Lemmy held the letter before him, too choked up to do anything but look at his father's handwriting. He wiped his eyes and read the letter again, more slowly, from the beginning. One sentence especially made no sense: WAS THAT THE REASON FOR YOUR CRUELTY IN REBUFFING THE PLEADING LETTERS THAT YOUR MOTHER SENT TO YOU IN THE ARMY? Lemmy could not understand. What letters? He had received no letters from his mother during his IDF service!

"Jerusalem?" Benjamin touched his arm. "Are you okay?"

Lemmy tore off the book's binding and found a densely scribbled, three-page note that described everything Rabbi Gerster and Itah had uncovered about ILOT, Freckles, and Yoni Adiel. A copy of the table of contents of the *ILOT Member Manual* was also hidden there, together with bank statements showing the money that passed through the young men's accounts and old paychecks from the VIP Protection Unit.

A youth, about eighteen, came in and whispered in Benjamin's ear.

"My son tells me there are strangers in the neighborhood. They might be looking for you."

"Then I must leave." Lemmy folded everything and put it in his pocket. There was no point in breaking Benjamin's heart with Rabbi Gerster's blasphemous confession. "I don't want to put you in danger."

"Nonsense. You're not going anywhere." Benjamin took off his black coat and hat. "These should fit you."

Lemmy put them on.

"Now," Benjamin clapped his hands, "let's go home and have something to eat!"

Wednesday,
November 1, 1995

Lemmy woke up in a room he knew well. Sunlight came in through the window. Hushed voices filtered through the closed door. He lowered his feet to the floor. The bed screeched under him. His old bookshelves lined the wall, heavy with tall volumes of Talmud. He stuck his hand behind them, but there was nothing hidden there. He rubbed his face, chuckling at the memory of Benjamin's stunned expression at the sight of the novel he had pulled from behind the Talmud volume. They had been teenagers, budding Talmudic scholars in Neturay Karta, a sect dedicated to God's worship, where secular novels, like all forms of alien entertainment, were strictly banned. But Lemmy's secret relationship with Tanya, and the books she had lent him, had penetrated the walls of isolation, planted doubts in his mind, and eventually led to his blasphemous rebellion and his excommunication. He touched the first volume of Talmud—*Baba Metziah*—and wondered how things would have turned out if there had been no place to hide Tanya's novels in his room.

He washed and joined Benjamin's family for breakfast. His parents' old dining room had remained unchanged, the long table that left little room to get around, the portraits of famed rabbis that looked down from the walls. Like Rabbi Abraham Gerster before him, Benjamin sat at the head of the table, slurping tea from a tall glass. But unlike the old days, the other chairs were taken by children. They looked up at Lemmy, their chatter abruptly halted.

"Did we wake you up?" Benjamin stood, beckoning to a vacant chair.

"It's time." Lemmy smiled at the children. "Good morning, kids. My name is Baruch."

"Hi Baruch," they chorused as their mother appeared from the kitchen with a fresh cup of tea and toast with butter.

Last night, when Benjamin had brought him home, Sorkeh accepted his resurrection with surprising equanimity. "*Baruch ha'ba,*" she had said, which meant *Blessed be the newcomer.* "I never *felt* that you were dead. Now I know why."

The name Baruch stuck to him, and they agreed that Lemmy's return from the dead would remain a secret, not to be discussed with anyone.

The children resumed their busy chattering, the older ones getting ready for school. They breathed new life into his parents' old apartment.

After the meal, as he took his plate back to the kitchen, Lemmy thought of his late mother, bending over this very sink, cleaning a fish with a serrated knife. For a moment, he could smell the carp, hear his mother's scraping knife, and see the shining scales on the countertop.

After the children had left, Sorkeh brought him a black hat that had a fake beard and side locks attached to it. "Our kids have a treasure trove of costumes for Purim."

He put it on and looked at the mirror. That's how he would have looked had he stayed at Neturay Karta.

Benjamin summoned a few of his men, and they boarded a van. Driving through the narrow streets of Meah Shearim, Lemmy looked around, absorbing the changes and the things that had remained the same. He was surprised at the abundance of graffiti on the walls:

MEIR KAHANE LIVES! DEATH TO THE ARABS!

STOP OBSCENE ADVERTISING! BOYCOTT COCA COLA!

Digging up Jewish graves is sacrilege!

He who violates the Sabbath should
be stoned to death!

God's land is not for sale! Peace comes from God!

Zionism is blasphemy — we must wait
for the blessed Messiah!

They stopped to buy the morning papers, and Lemmy looked through the news pages. A brief report described the accusations against his father and Itah Orr, who were being interrogated at an undisclosed location. But there was no mention of Tanya Galinski or even a reference to an accident in Amsterdam involving an Israeli woman. It was the third day already, and nothing! He searched through the list of funeral announcements, relieved to find nothing there either. Tanya had run into the street because of his false accusations, and now she was lying in a foreign hospital surrounded by strangers. There was only one thing he could do to help Tanya right now, and it was worth the risk. "Let's get it done," he said to Benjamin, who nodded and spoke quietly to the driver.

"Enough with the games!" Agent Cohen stormed into the apartment. He slammed four photographs on the kitchen table in front of Elie Weiss. "Look!"

"You again?" Elie put down his knife and fork.

Itah said, "Here goes another good breakfast."

"If you don't give me answers, there won't be any more breakfasts—good *or* bad!"

Rabbi Gerster looked closely. The first photo was the one they had seen yesterday of Lemmy and Tanya in a Zurich park. The second photo showed him wearing a fedora, kneeling by Tanya, who was lying on a cobblestone street across rail tracks. The third photo was in a hospital room, Lemmy wearing a baseball hat. The fourth photo was grainy, likely enlarged from a wide-angle video lens. It showed Lemmy at the entrance to the King David Hotel, also wearing a baseball hat, but in a different color.

"A handsome fellow," Elie said. "Is he a hat salesman?"

"Don't!" Agent Cohen poked Elie's chest. "Tell me where to find him, because if I have to track him down myself—and I will!—then I'm going to shoot him in the head!"

Elie looked down at the poking finger. "Be careful where you stick it."

"I'm warning you! He'll be trapped and killed like a stray dog!"

"It's not good to be obsessed with revenge. All because he shot your guy in the leg?"

"And knocked out a nurse at Hadassah!"

"You should be grateful that your agents survived those encounters." Elie tapped the Amsterdam photo. "And how is Mossad's Europe chief doing?"

The mention of Tanya's official title caused Agent Cohen to exhale and drop into a chair. "We're not sure. She was picked up by an ambulance in pretty bad shape but doesn't appear on any patient list."

Elie chuckled. "It's not so easy to operate in Europe, is it?"

"We're learning."

"Let me speak to your Number One. I'll advise him to recall all his Shin Bet boys, send you back to chasing Arab stone-throwers in the refugee camps."

"She looks terrible." Gideon spoke for the first time. "Didn't you follow her to the hospital?"

"It's more complicated than that," Agent Cohen said. "There are sixteen hospitals nearby, a lot more within driving distance of Amsterdam. The Dutch emergency services and hospitals are connected to a central computer system, which is having some problems right now."

"That's odd," Gideon said. "What are they doing about patients' records, medical histories, prescriptions, operation schedules? People could die."

"No, no." Agent Cohen steered sugar into a tiny cup of coffee. "The problem is limited to records of hospital admissions. It also disabled the search module for patients' names, replacing it with numbers. Everything else is working fine, but for us it's a really bad coincidence—"

"It's not a coincidence," Elie said. "It's a taste of what's to come if you don't pull back and stop interfering in things that are way over your head."

Agent Gideon waved in dismissal.

"A surgical hacker," Itah said. "Impressive."

"That's good news," Rabbi Gerster said. "Someone's protecting Tanya."

"No one is protecting her," Agent Cohen said. "This computer problem will be fixed soon. We'll find her and we'll find *him!*" He pointed to the photos from Amsterdam, Hadassah, and the King David Hotel. "Based on the time each of these photos were taken, we know he entered Israel during a twelve-hour window— too brief for a boat ride, so he must have come by air through Ben Gurion Airport. We're scanning all video surveillance tapes. Once we have his name, it's over. We'll hunt him down."

Benjamin led the group of men through the paved campus paths. The Hebrew University at Mount Scopus covered the hillside with squat buildings constructed between wars in conflicting architectural styles. Students in flannel shirts and military-style winter coats glanced curiously at the ultra-Orthodox men.

The archeology department occupied a three-story structure that faced the descending desert hills to the east. The office on the top floor was marked: PROFESSOR BIRA GALINSKI – DEPARTMENT CHAIR.

In the small reception area, a young woman looked up.

"Good morning," Benjamin said. "I'm Rabbi Mashash from Neturay Karta."

"I know who you are. I heard your speech at our dig in Tel Gamla."

Benjamin smiled. "Did you like it?"

"It was better than throwing rocks."

"But you still won't leave our ancestors' bones in peace for the coming of the Messiah?"

"I don't think the Messiah wants to come while the bones of *live* Jews are broken with rocks."

"Excuse me," Lemmy said, "but can we see Professor Galinski?"

"She's not here."

"Where is she?"

"At home. Something happened to her mother. She got the news last night."

Lemmy was surprised. Other than he, only Shin Bet knew about Tanya's injury. Why would they tell Bira about it?

On their way back to the van, Lemmy asked, "Do you know where Bira lives?"

Benjamin smiled. "Last month, the Supreme Court rejected our petition against the digging of an ancient graveyard on the French Hill, north of Jerusalem. Our people were very upset, and there was talk of violence. Rabbi Gerster and I met with Professor Galinski at her home. No one knew about it. At Neturay Karta, she's considered an instrument of the devil."

"The devil?" Lemmy laughed. "She's just an archeologist."

"She's the leading archeologist in Israel."

"I see. How did the meeting go?"

Benjamin sighed. "It started well, she explaining how Israelis crave archeological evidence of our past national life here, and he explaining that Orthodox Jews believe that graves were resting places until the Messiah comes and resurrects the righteous. But soon their voices rose, she accused him of trying to enforce primitive religious rules at the expense of modern science, and Rabbi Gerster called her Bar-Giyorah."

"Bar Giyorah?"

"The uncompromising nationalist leader in the great revolt against Rome, which ended in the destruction of the Second Temple."

"I remember." Lemmy imagined his father with Tanya's daughter or, more strangely, with the daughter of SS Oberstgruppenführer Klaus von Koenig, confronting each other over an unbridgeable ideological gap.

The van followed Martin Buber Road, down the ridge connecting Mount Scopus with the Mount of Olives, past the Russian church spires of St. Mary Magdalene on the left, along the Valley of Kidron, where Lemmy noticed the hewn stone hand of Absalom's Tomb, King David's beloved, rebellious son.

Rabbi Gerster imagined Lemmy running, out of breath, a group of armed Shin Bet agents hot on his heels. There was silence around the breakfast table, and Agent Cohen repeated his threat: "We'll hunt him down like a dog!"

"A bunch of foxes," Elie said, "chasing after a dog."

"That's right!"

"Be careful. Sometimes the hunter becomes the hunted."

"Who's going to stop us? You?" The Shin Bet agent unbuttoned his jacket, reached inside, and pulled out Elie's sheathed blade. "Won't you need this?"

"In my time, Shin Bet was very selective." Elie flexed his yellow-stained fingers as if preparing for a delicate piece of manual undertaking. "No Sephardic boys were let loose running sensitive operations."

"Come on," Itah said, "that's below the belt."

Agent Cohen laughed, but his face was bitter. "Intelligence czar, ah? Exterminator of enemies?" He slammed the sheathed blade on the table. "You're a nobody, Weiss! *Nobody!*"

With a sense of pending doom, Rabbi Gerster said, "It's not worth it, Elie."

"You're a has-been," Agent Cohen kept going, "a nursing home candidate, a useless piece of broken machinery!"

Elie removed the oxygen tube from his nose and let it drop to the floor by the tank. "Sometimes a little pinky can bring down a mighty lion."

"Now you're a poet too?" Agent Cohen leaned over the table, his face up close against Elie's. "Everybody tells me to be careful with Elie Weiss. A dangerous man, they say." He poked Elie in the chest. "All I see is a pathetic old man. A sclerotic mummy. *A joke!*"

Rabbi Gerster suddenly realized that this was the culmination of Elie's calculated provocations, carefully staged in rising succession to build up Agent Cohen's rage and recklessness like a musical composition building up to a climactic crescendo. And there was nothing anyone could do to save the foolish agent.

"Again with the poking?" Elie looked down at the finger. "Is this some kind of a Moroccan custom? Iraqi? Egyptian? Where did your parents come from?"

"You have a problem with it?" Agent Cohen poked him harder. "Do you?"

With calmness that distracted from the speed of his movements, Elie's right hand clenched Agent Cohen's forefinger and twisted it sideways, producing the crunchy sound of a breaking bone.

"*Ahhhh!*"

Still holding the broken finger with his right hand, Elie's left hand rose to Agent Cohen's red face and threaded a pinky under his upper eyelid.

"Don't move," Elie said, "or you'll lose the eye."

Agent Cohen's cry was interrupted by a burst of vomit from his mouth.

Elie moved out of the way, let go of the broken finger, and collected his blade. He maneuvered around the end of the table, his pinky remaining inside Agent Cohen's eye socket. "That's a good fellow." From behind, he made the Shin Bet officer sit down. "Will you cooperate or do you want to look like Moshe Dayan?"

Agent Cohen bit down on his lower lip and moaned in pain.

"Take his gun," Elie ordered Rabbi Gerster. "His comrades will be here soon."

The boy who opened Bira's door wasn't crying, but his effort to fight back tears was endearing. He looked at their black coats and hats and started to close the door.

Benjamin blocked the door. "May we speak with your mother please?"

"She's not available now."

"It's important."

The boy disappeared.

Lemmy and Benjamin entered the foyer and closed the door, shutting out the sun. The rest of the men waited in the van.

Bira showed up a moment later. "Rabbi Mashash? What are you doing here?"

"We need to talk. It will only take a few minutes."

She led them through a narrow hallway, a kitchen, and out the back door to a patio bordered by climbing vines. They sat on white plastic chairs around a coffee table.

Lemmy remembered her as a twenty-year-old in an olive uniform, shouldering an Uzi machine gun. She had aged well, keeping an athletic build and lush hair, but her face was sun-beaten and her blue-gray eyes examined him with discomforting coldness. He asked, "Have you received any news from your mother?"

"You know my mother?"

"We know she's missing."

"That's what I heard." Bira's shoulders slumped. "Her boss called me yesterday."

"The chief of Mossad?"

She nodded. "I could tell he's worried. She's not a field agent. Why in the world would she be out there interacting with hostile—"

"It was a business meeting," Lemmy said. "She didn't expect any danger."

"And who told you that? God?"

He laughed.

Bira glared at him. "What the hell is going on?"

"I'm also wondering." Lemmy removed the hat with the attached beard and payos.

Bira wasn't amused. "What's this? Dressing up for Purim already?"

"We met once."

"I don't think so."

"It was way back, when your mother lived near the border and you were in the army."

She shook her head.

"I carried your duffle bag. It was bloody heavy."

"That boy died in the Six Day War."

"We argued. You dismissed faith, saying that Zionism is all about history, about proving who was here first, like establishing a legal ownership record. I countered that belief in the historical truth of biblical stories was a form of faith, which meant you were religious too."

She leaned closer to look at him. "That's impossible!"

"We said good-bye at the gate to Meah Shearim. I watched you go, and you waved at me from the corner."

She turned to Benjamin. "Is this some kind of a sick joke? My mother has grieved for Jerusalem Gerster for twenty-eight years, poured enough tears to refill the Dead Sea. I'm not going to accept this man—"

"It's me," Lemmy said. "It's really me."

Bira looked at him at length in the manner of a scientist examining a specimen that couldn't possibly exist. Then, without any warning, she leaned forward and slapped Lemmy across the face with such force that he fell off the chair and onto the floor.

Rabbi Gerster pocketed Agent Cohen's gun and pushed over the table, creating a barrier between them and the door. He crouched with Itah behind the tabletop and whispered. "Get away when nobody's watching. Find my son. Warn him!"

She nodded and pecked him on the cheek.

Gideon stepped over to the kitchen and stood with the housekeeper, who watched the whole thing with an open mouth. Elie positioned himself behind Agent Cohen, his pinky hooked inside the eye socket, his blade drawn, the sharpened edge resting nonchalantly on the trembling man's shoulder.

The door flew open and the two Shin Bet agents rushed in, guns ready.

"This feels like a déjà vu," Elie said. He was panting from the exertion, but no one mistook his thin voice for weakness. "Put down your weapons and slide them over, or Agent Cohen here will be shopping for an eye patch or a prosthetic arm. Or both."

The nurse hesitated while the other agent glanced at her. She aimed at Elie. "You know the drill—we're trained to kill hostage takers, not negotiate."

"You're trained to kill *Arab* hostage takers," Elie corrected her. "Not a Jew who's old enough to be your grandpa, who's been abused physically and mentally by this bully." He pressed a bit on the blade, which broke though the shirt and penetrated the shoulder slightly.

Agent Cohen groaned.

"Don't shoot," Rabbi Gerster said from behind the upturned tabletop. "We're all Jews here!"

Benjamin jumped up and stood between them. "No violence! Please!"

"Get out of my house!" Bira stood with her fists clenched, ready to hit Lemmy again. "*Out!*"

The boy who had opened the door for them came running, followed by a younger girl, who rushed to her mother's side. Their presence instantly soothed Bira's anger. Her hands fell by her side. "Everything is fine," she said. "Go back to your room."

The two kids looked at her and at the two men, unsure what to do. The boy pointed at Lemmy. "Where's your beard?"

Lemmy got up from the floor and showed him the hat and attached facial hair. "You want to try it?"

The boy put it on. His sister laughed, and they ran off.

"Just like my son," Lemmy said. "Klaus is ten, almost eleven. We're trying for a girl—"

"I don't want to know." Bira's anger flared again. "Son of a bitch! I could kill you for what you did to her—"

"Please," Benjamin said, "calm down."

"She's right," Lemmy said. "I deserve it."

"You deserve worse," Bira said. "Broke her heart, that's what you did. She blamed herself for your death—can you imagine living with this kind of guilt?"

"I never imagined how much pain my faked death would cause Tanya. She was my first love. Her rejection seemed like the end of the world to me. I was too resentful and too young. The last thing I considered was that she would grieve or feel guilty."

Bira sat down, still sulking. "All the grave-grooming and tears and self-deprivation. I can go on and on about the price my mother has continuously extracted from herself over that boy's death."

"I know. She told me."

"What? She knows you're alive?"

"Fate brought us together. We met, but she was being followed. She was hurt badly."

"Oh, no!" Bira sucked air, covering her mouth.

"Here." He handed her a note. "Call this number in Amsterdam. Ask for Carl. He knows me as a Swiss banker named Wilhelm Horch—Lemmy for short. Meet him there, and he'll take you to Tanya. But trust no one else. Your mother's life depends on it."

"What about your father?" Bira's eyes were no longer hostile. "The news reports are shocking."

Lemmy took out his father's notes, the bank statements and the *ILOT Member Manual*.

Bira read through everything while they watched her in silence.

"The strategy is working," she said. "There are a few of these fanatical groups. The fringe right is now setting the tone for the whole right wing, including Likud. But if the public learns that Shin Bet pays for these incitements, there's going to be a huge backlash. It will destroy Rabin politically, because no one will believe it was done without his knowledge."

"It appears that Shin Bet has let Elie plot the whole thing, pay for it from SOD budget, and then they shut him down at the last moment. They probably think that your mom was working with Elie Weiss."

Bira stood. "I can't worry about Israel now. I must take care of my mother." She left to prepare for her trip to Amsterdam. Lemmy picked a red grape and popped it into his mouth. He offered one to Benjamin, who recited a blessing and ate it.

"Amen," Lemmy said.

"I'm concerned." Benjamin pulled another grape off the vines. "What if those Shin Bet characters try to silence you?"

"I'm sure they're already trying."

"**O**kay." The nurse raised her gun, aiming at the ceiling. "But I won't surrender my weapon to you."

"Then give it to me," Gideon said. "I'm neutral."

Elie gave him a cold glance, but Gideon's offer was a clever face-saving way out. They put their guns on the counter, and Gideon collected them.

"Go over there," Elie said, pointing at the sofa against the opposite wall.

They obeyed.

He beckoned the housekeeper. "Bring the phone to the good nurse."

"Who do you want me to call?" The nurse's face was crimson, either from anger or shame. "The Red Cross?"

Rabbi Gerster stood up and pulled over a chair. He helped Elie sit down slowly, but the change of angle caused his pinky to shift, and Agent Cohen cried in pain.

"Call your Number One," Elie said.

The nurse opened her mouth to argue, but Agent Cohen yelled, "Do it!"

The call went though several secured connections before a man's voice sounded on the speakerphone. "Yes?"

"We have a problem," the nurse said.

"We have an opportunity," Elie said.

"Weiss? Is that you?"

"How's Paris treating you?"

"What's going on there?"

"Let's just say that…the tables have turned. Literally."

"Explain!"

"He's got Cohen," the nurse said from the sofa.

Number One was silent for a moment. "What do you want?"

"How's the wife and kids?"

"Skip the pleasantries, okay?"

"I'm upset," Elie said. "You had me arrested—twice. You detained my people. You invaded my territory and prospected for my financial resources. It feels like a hostile takeover."

"And who started it?"

"Ah. My meeting with Rabin?"

"That's right! You made a move on us!"

"Not exactly."

"Intelligence czar? Is that the mother of all takeovers or what?"

"I see your point."

"What did you think? You left us no choice!"

"If I may," Rabbi Gerster said, "this turf war is ripe for an armistice, so I propose—"

"*Excusez-moi*," Number One said, the speakerphone communicating his irritation, "but who the hell is this?"

"Rabbi Abraham Gerster of Neturay Karta."

"Holy shit! You work for SOD?"

"For the Jewish people," Rabbi Gerster said. "What about a ceasefire? Let's go back to the old détente. Elie calls off the deal with Rabin. SOD and Shin Bet return to peaceful co-existence. And we all live happily ever after."

"Too late," Number One said. "We already took over Freckles and shut down the staged assassination plot."

"Did you?" Elie's dark eyes focused on the bare wall across the room. "That boy, Yoni Adiel, is a free agent, real fanatic kind of a guy."

"We're watching him. He's in the bag. ILOT is history."

"Impressive," Elie said.

"Your deal with Rabin is off, Weiss—if there ever was a deal, which is in question."

"I accept my defeat," Elie said. "That's life. You lose some, you win some."

"Good," Rabbi Gerster said. "Let's all go home now."

"Not so fast," Number One said. "We've shut down your ILOT scheme, got you locked up, and are closing in on your financial sources in Zurich. Why should we give up a perfect set of cards?"

"What about your agents here?"

Number One chuckled. "You won't take another Jew's life."

"But I'll take another Jew's *marriage*." Elie slipped his pinky out of Agent Cohen's eye socket, making him cry out and cover his eye.

The line from Paris was quiet.

Elie wiped his pinky on a napkin. "How is Madame de Chevallier?"

Again, no answer.

"I hear she's satisfied with your new implant."

"*Weiss!*"

"But she complains that it makes you cocky."

Everyone burst out laughing, even the housekeeper in the kitchen.

"I guess the free rent balances it out for her."

"I'm warning you," Number One shouted, "shut up!"

"Don't take it personally, but I believe in wearing a belt *and* suspenders. To defend SOD's independence in any confrontation with our sister agencies, I've formed solid political bonds *and* collected sordid personal secrets about every one of my opponents. Push me any farther, and there's going to be a frightful surge in business for divorce lawyers, not to mention the media frenzy."

Number One's voice was deep with hate. "You wouldn't dare!"

"That's enough," Rabbi Gerster interjected. "Do we have an agreement?"

"I can't let you go," Number One said. "The peace rally on Saturday night is crucial for Rabin's government. We've detained hundreds of troublemakers and shut down provocative schemes, including yours. I won't risk setting you free to pursue your crazy plots again."

"Take me back to Hadassah," Elie said. "They were going to fix my lungs. I'm operating on reserves."

"Fine, as long as you remain in isolation. No outside contacts until after the rally."

"Agreed," Rabbi Gerster said in Elie's stead. "I'll stay with him at Hadassah."

"And I'm staying here," Gideon said from the kitchen. "The views are breathtaking."

"Excuse me," the nurse said, "but where's Itah Orr?"

There was a long silence as everyone looked around.

"She's not my agent," Elie said. "Feel free to send your dogs after her."

"Wait." Agent Cohen was pale as the wall. "What about the Zurich shooter?"

"There's new information," the nurse said. "He arrived on a KLM flight yesterday. We traced his entry record. He is travelling under the name Baruch Spinoza."

Rabbi Gerster barely managed to suppress a smile—Lemmy had assumed the name of another young Jew who, over a century earlier, had been excommunicated by his congregation.

"Only a matter of time," the nurse said. "His name will pop up somewhere, and we'll take him down."

The comment made Rabbi Gerster cringe. The powerful Shin Bet was chasing after his son with the intent to kill! He cleared his throat and asked, "Doesn't the stand-down agreement extend to *all* SOD agents?"

But the phone line had already gone dead.

Itah Orr changed taxis three times before reaching the central bus station in southern Tel Aviv. The evening rush was peaking, thousands of office workers and day laborers heading home. She lingered at shop windows, but no one was following her.

At a secondhand clothing store, she exchanged her outfit for a long-sleeved dress that reached down to her shoes and a dark-gray headdress, which she tied in the ultra-Orthodox style, hiding all her hair. She bought basic toiletries at a pharmacy, as well as a note pad, sunglasses, and a fresh can of pepper spray to replace the one confiscated by Shin Bet.

She paid cash for a room at a seedy motel. Against the background noise of hookers and their eager customers, she sat at a rickety desk and wrote down the events of the last few days.

Part Six
The Understanding

Thursday,
November 2, 1995

The van left Meah Shearim after morning prayers with the same dozen black-garbed men whom Benjamin had brought along yesterday. They obeyed him without question, treating him with a reverence that astonished Lemmy. His childhood study-companion had come a long way.

As they had planned, the van parked in front of a phone booth on a busy street, and Lemmy stepped out. He placed a collect call to Zurich, and Christopher accepted it.

"Any news?"

"Yes," Christopher said. "I received a call from Prince Abusalim's father, Sheik Da'ood az-Zubayr. He demanded full accounting of his late son's dealings with the bank. I explained that you're away on business."

"Call him back and extend my deepest condolences. Tell him that I plan to personally travel to the az-Zubayr oasis at a time of his convenience to assist him with the transition of the account and any other service that he would require."

"Understood. Also, Herr Hoffgeitz regained consciousness last night. He asked for Klaus V.K. and had to be reminded that his son had been dead for a long time. He then asked for Klaus Junior. Paula brought your son, and Herr Hoffgeitz told him to learn from you how to run the bank."

"He said that?"

"Yes. The doctors decided to sedate him again, give his heart a chance to heal."

"Anything else?"

"A personal message from Paula. I don't understand it. She said to tell you that she's still late."

"Still late?" Lemmy laughed. "That's good! That's *very* good!"

Itah Orr took the bus from Tel Aviv to Jerusalem. On the way to Meah Shearim, she stopped at a vegetable stand and filled up two shopping bags, paying in cash. On Shivtay Israel Street she joined a group of ultra-Orthodox women.

A white Subaru sedan parked on the pavement near the gate. As the cluster of women approached, two men emerged from the car and ambled over. Their presence, though impolite, achieved the desired effect. The women stopped, afraid to risk even accidental body contact with the strangers, which would constitute a sin under Talmud's strict chastity rules.

"Shalom!" One of the men held up a silver, feline-shaped keychain. "Any of you girls lost this?"

Itah recognized the spare keys to her car, which she had parked nearby last Friday. The thought that these men had invaded her home and rummaged through her personal possessions made her see red, which was probably what they were hoping for. She kept her head up, her eyes hidden by the sunglasses.

"Anyone?" He dangled the keys. "Come on, ladies!"

None of the women responded.

"How about this?" The other agent held a short piece of gray, hairy rope. "Anyone?"

It took Itah a moment to realize it wasn't a rope. It was her cat's tail. As the agent shook it, she could see the clipped end, red with blood.

Biting her lips to block a scream, she reached into her purse for the pepper spray.

With Elie Weiss and Rabbi Gerster gone to Hadassah Hospital, the apartment felt big and empty. Gideon settled to watch CNN while the housekeeper set the breakfast table for two.

Agent Cohen showed up with warm pastries and a bandage over his eye. He held up his finger, which was taped to a short stick. "I'm filing a disability claim, maybe an early retirement." His joviality didn't mask the jittery tremor at the corner of his mouth.

"You shouldn't feel embarrassed about what happened yesterday," Gideon said. "Even your Number One is no match for Elie Weiss."

The housekeeper served coffee and set the pastries on a plate.

"Fact is, I failed," Agent Cohen said. "I underestimated him, and this debacle will haunt me for the rest of my career. Especially if the situation turns into a real disaster."

"What do you mean? I thought it's over. Didn't SOD and Shin Bet agree to a truce?"

"That's the least of our worries." The agent bit into a chocolate-filled croissant.

"What else is there to worry about?"

He swallowed and sipped coffee to chase it down. "Spinoza."

"Isn't he part of the deal? Surely Elie will send him home now."

"We don't think Elie controls Spinoza." Agent Cohen pulled photos from a thick envelope and set them on the table. The first group showed Arab sheikhs in settings that varied from formal dinners to car races and camel rides. "That's him, with the red kafiya. His real name is Wilhelm Horch. A German national, married to a Swiss woman. He's vice president at a Zurich bank, and his personal assistant is a member of a Nazi group."

"How do you know?"

"Mossad has files on every significant businessman with ties to the Middle East. We have access to those files. Horch has extensive Arab clientele. No one knew of his connection to Elie Weiss—we're still not sure of the nature of this relationship. When Tanya Galinski met Horch at a Zurich park a few days ago, we happened to be tailing her because we suspected she's involved with Elie's assassination scheme."

"What's Horch's game?"

"He's been playing Elie," Agent Cohen said. "Look at these photos from the Galeries Lafayette."

The same man, wearing a coat, a fedora, and a fake goatee, stood inside the glass doors of the Galeries Lafayette. Other photos showed him on the stairs and in the menswear section. "These are from the security cameras, recorded during the thirty seconds preceding the shooting of the Arab kid in the dressing room."

"That shooting was a disaster," Gideon said. "Police descended on the place, and Bashir drove off too fast for us to follow him back to Abu Yusef's hiding place. Elie was certain the Arabs killed Latif in some kind of an internal feud."

"We believe the Saudis paid Horch to do the job."

"Why would they?"

"Latif's killing—supposedly by Israel—provoked Abu Yusef's attack on the synagogue."

"But why would the Saudis do this?"

"To derail the peace process. Every Mideast dictator is terrified of an Israeli-Palestinian peace, even if they pay lip service in support of peace. Israel is their scapegoat. Peace would allow their masses to focus on the real culprits behind their poverty and suffering."

"So they sent their Swiss banker to kill Abu Yusef's boy toy to throw us off his tail and provoke another attack? It seems like a big risk for a small gain."

"Not so small. Terror attacks are the main reason for Israelis' loss of faith in the peace process. Our data shows that Abu Yusef's attack on the Paris synagogue—just that one attack alone—caused public support for the Oslo Accords to drop four points among Israeli voters. In fact, Abu Yusef was getting ready to launch simultaneous, multi-target attacks all over Europe, which would have dealt a fatal blow to the peace process. Only thanks to Elie's two-prong method, which allowed you to find Abu Yusef through his sponsor, this disaster was averted."

He placed more photos on the table, showing the Swiss at the Metz department store in Amsterdam. "You see the pattern—he loves crowded retail venues. We think Tanya Galinski approached him in Zurich, and he agreed to meet her again in Amsterdam, where he pushed her under the tram."

"Horch did that?" Gideon sipped coffee and examined the photos, which covered half the table. The theory made sense, but one aspect nagged him. Elie was not an easy man to fool. Hadn't the Swiss banker provided Elie with good information on Prince Abusalim, which led them to Abu Yusef?

"Double agents," Cohen said, as if reading Gideon's mind, "have to prove their loyalty by giving useful, true information to both sides. But in the end, a double agent is loyal only to himself and therefore must choose one side. And a double agent who fears exposure will kill you unless you kill him first."

The van rattled on the cracked asphalt of Shivtay Israel Street. As it approached the gate, Lemmy saw a group of women, their way blocked by two secular men in civilian clothes, one of them holding up something in front of the women.

"Hit the horn," Benjamin told the driver. "Quick! Hit the horn!"

The driver pressed down, releasing a long, drawn out beep. It startled the women, and Benjamin stepped out of the van. Lemmy watched him speak with the two men, who returned to their Subaru. The women entered the neighborhood carrying their grocery bags. One of them glanced back over her shoulder, and Lemmy recognized her as the woman who had left the King David Hotel under guard with his father and Elie Weiss.

At Benjamin's apartment, Sorkeh prepared an early lunch for them. She hugged Itah Orr. "This outfit looks good on you—like a beautiful Neturay Karta woman. We have several learned widowers. We can find you a perfect *shiduch!*"

"I think I've already found my match," Itah said, and Lemmy noticed redness spread to her cheeks. Was she talking about his father?

Benjamin and Sorkeh left the room, and Itah said, "Your father sent me to warn you. Shin Bet is after you. They claim you shot one of their agents in Zurich."

"It's true," Lemmy said. "But it was an honest mistake. Tanya knew he wasn't Mossad, and since Shin Bet is not authorized to operate outside Israel, we assumed the man was an Arab."

"Shin Bet sees it differently. And knocking down the nurse at Hadassah didn't help. They know your assumed name—Baruch Spinoza." She chuckled. "Nice touch."

"Wasn't my idea."

"Did you find your father's letter?"

"Yes. Have you discovered anything new since he wrote it?"

Itah pulled off the headdress. She described in detail what had occurred at the apartment in Tel Aviv. "All they care about," she concluded, "is to ensure that nothing interrupts the Saturday night peace rally in Tel Aviv. It's supposed to launch Rabin's reelection campaign. Labor strategists are working hard to bus in supporters from all over Israel, and Shin Bet is locking up every potential troublemaker. They shut down ILOT and Elie's fake assassination operation."

"What about you?"

"They're confident that my credibility is ruined and my nerves are shot by the criminal accusations. They're wrong. None of it will stop me from going public with everything I know, except that I'll have to find a way around exposing your father."

"Where does it leave me? Should I let Shin Bet shoot me in the leg to get even?"

"Don't be ridiculous."

Lemmy pulled the gun from his coat pocket and dropped it on the table. "I'm good at what I do, but I can't fight the whole Israeli secret service."

"You won't need to," Itah said. "I have an idea. There's a crucial debate in the Knesset today. We'll approach Rabin and ask him to order Shin Bet to leave you alone."

"That's bold. Can you get us in?"

"It's open to the public. But we'll need to find a way to meet him."

"I can do that," Lemmy said. "He owes me one."

"The prime minister?" She laughed. "What does he owe you?"

"Oh, just his victory in the Six day War."

Agent Cohen lined up a series of photos on the table, showing the Swiss banker at passport control at Ben Gurion Airport, at an Avis counter, and at Hadassah Hospital.

"The plot thickens," Gideon said. "What reason did he give at the airport for his visit?"

"Car restorer shopping for parts. Original, isn't it?" Agent Cohen sneered. "We found his rented Fiat at the YMCA. No fingerprints. He's a professional."

"Are you watching departures at the airport?"

"Yes, but only as a precaution."

"Why? He saw Elie being arrested at King David. Without access to Elie, he won't stick around to get caught."

The agent collected the photos, slipping them into the envelope. "He has a job to do."

"What job? To kill Elie Weiss?"

"That too, as a defensive move, to get rid of someone who can identify him. But his primary target is not Elie Weiss."

"Then who?"

"Our Shin Bet analysts believe the Saudis are paying this assassin a fortune, enough for him to disappear afterwards, retire to some island for the rest of his life. They want him to do something that will destroy the Oslo Accords once and for all, a decisive hit that will end this whole effort to reach a permanent co-existence with the Palestinians in the foreseeable future."

Gideon waited for him to continue, but he remained mum, as if the answer was too shocking to be pronounced out loud.

"Kill Arafat?"

"Worse," Agent Cohen said.

"Who could be worse?"

"We believe this Horch-Spinoza guy has come here to kill Prime Minister Yitzhak Rabin."

Lemmy left the gun in Benjamin's apartment, and Itah did the same with her pepper spray. Equipped with borrowed Israeli identification cards from a lookalike Neturay Karta couple, they received visitor tags at the entrance to the Knesset building, passed by the giant menorah, and crossed the vast forecourt. Inside, the three giant Chagall tapestries reminded Lemmy of the stained-glass windows at the Fraumünster church in Zurich, though here Chagall had brought to life biblical Jewish figures other than Jesus Christ. But the colors and flair touched Lemmy with warm familiarity.

The legislature was in session. The public gallery was filled with school children and tourists. Itah and Lemmy found room in the last row. A thick Plexiglas partition offered open views of the assembly hall below, filled with Knesset members of all parties. The government ministers, including Yitzhak Rabin, sat up front near the podium.

A Knesset member from the government coalition was arguing for censure of the Likud Party over the events at the right-wing rally last Saturday night in Jerusalem. "Is there no shame? Are there no limits to verbal violence? When is it too much? Tell me!"

Someone from the opposition benches yelled, "Rabin broke his promises!"

"He's a liar," another member shouted.

The speaker hit the podium. "Is name calling acceptable? Cursing the prime minister? Slandering him? Chanting sexual innuendo? Urging his early death?"

No one responded to that.

"Democracy and free speech don't make it kosher to call for the prime minister's murder!"

The speech was interrupted by the grave voice of Prime Minister Yitzhak Rabin, emerging with an odd echo from the rear benches: "I will never, never give up land that provides Israel with a security buffer against Arab attacks!"

Knesset attendants in uniform ran down the aisles, looking for the source of the recorded speech.

"I will never," Rabin's voice roared, "never give back the Golan Heights—"

Among widespread laughter, the attendants grabbed a young Knesset member who had smuggled in a cassette player and portable loudspeakers to play Rabin's old speech—an embarrassing reminder that the prime minister's current policy contradicted his past promises.

Surrounded by his ministers, Yitzhak Rabin appeared amused by the prank, glancing back at the struggling attendants.

"Our Labor leaders changed their minds," the speaker continued, "because our enemies changed their hearts and agreed to peace. But Likud leaders are sticking to unrealistic policies. At Zion Square on Saturday night, they acquiesced to their supporters' chants, adopted their murderous demagoguery, and poured oil on the fire of violence that's consuming our democracy. The Likud Party is trying to topple the government by inciting a mob! I therefore move for a censure of the Likud Party!"

Benjamin Netanyahu, twenty years younger than the prime minister and an eloquent speechmaker, climbed the steps to give his party's response. "It's unfair," he said, "to indict a large portion of the population because of the unsavory acts of a handful of hoodlums."

Prime Minister Rabin stood and walked away from his front-bench seat, up the aisle, to the exit doors.

Netanyahu paused and turned to the Knesset chairman, who pounded his gavel and said into his microphone, "I ask the prime minister to return to his seat. Please!"

Rabin lit a cigarette, his back to the Knesset plenum. An elderly secretary in a beige pantsuit brought him a file with documents, and he browsed through, ignoring the noise.

The chairman pounded his gavel again. "Please! I ask the prime minister to return and hear the opposition's reply! Please!"

Several Knesset members went to the door and spoke with Rabin. Netanyahu waited at the podium.

Itah leaned over and said, "They're like children!"

"Worse," Lemmy said.

Down below, Prime Minister Rabin stubbed his cigarette and returned to his seat. The Knesset chairman pounded his gavel.

"As we can see," Netanyahu said, "extreme behavior happens on both sides of the aisle—even on the government side."

"Let's go," Lemmy said.

The Labor Party had offices on the second floor, reached via a wide set of stairs. The elderly secretary took one step at a time, holding the thick file to her chest. They caught up with her.

"Excuse me," Lemmy said, "would you kindly ask Mr. Rabin to spare a moment for a quick hello?"

"You'll have to send a letter requesting an appointment—"

"Please tell him that I was the soldier who blew up the UN radar at Government House in sixty-seven. My name is Baruch."

The secretary scribbled in her notepad and pointed to a decorative, wooden bench under a bronze sculpture representing the killing fields at Babi Yar. "Wait here. I'll ask him after the vote."

A gent Cohen returned to the apartment an hour later. He handed Gideon a wallet. "Here's money, credit cards, and identification as special agent assigned to the prime minister's office, with top security clearance. It will allow you access to every government agency, full cooperation from officials, and total immunity in the line of duty."

Gideon collected the wallet. "Why me? Don't you have enough Shin Bet staffers to chase this guy?"

"I don't have anyone from SOD." Agent Cohen handed him a Beretta 22. "You've worked in Europe, you trained with Elie Weiss, you understand Spinoza's way of thinking. It's your case now." Agent Cohen saluted with his stick-taped finger. "From now on, I'm at your service. We can't afford to fail."

"No, we can't." Gideon pocketed the wallet and stuffed the gun in his belt. "But where do we start?"

"I have agents checking out every hotel in Jerusalem and the vicinity for anyone resembling Spinoza. Also, we've copied all the security tapes from the King David Hotel, where he spent the night after running into Elie at the entrance."

"Were you there?"

Agent Cohen nodded. "I arrested them."

"Did you notice Spinoza?"

"No. Our agents found him on the security camera tapes later."

"Do you think Elie noticed him?"

Cohen hesitated. "You know, there was an interruption just when we were leaving the hotel."

"Did Elie act up?"

"No. Weiss was as cool as a rotting cucumber." Agent Cohen sat back, struggling to remember. "It was odd. I think Rabbi Gerster tripped. We all stopped, and he yelled something. But later, in the car, a strange thing happened."

"What?"

"That rabbi is a tough one." Agent Cohen shook his head. "I can't explain it, but as we drove off from the hotel, he burst out crying."

"*Crying?*"

Prime Minister Yitzhak Rabin waited in a large conference room reserved for government meetings held while the Knesset was in session. Two bodyguards frisked Lemmy and Itah at the door, which remained open. Music came from speakers in the ceiling, a Hebrew folksong from the early days of Zionism.

"You chose an interesting day to visit," he said, shaking their hands.

Itah said, "Are there any boring days here?"

"Yom Kippur used to be boring," the prime minister said. "What's this about the UN radar? Were you that kid Elie Weiss sent in?"

"That was me," Lemmy said, removing the black hat with the attached beard and side locks. "Sorry about the disguise."

"I'm sure there's an explanation for this." Rabin chuckled. "You know, all these years people have called me a military genius, but if not for what you did that morning, they would be calling me an idiot."

They laughed.

"So tell me what I don't know," Rabin said, lighting a cigarette.

Lemmy quickly retold the story of his recruitment by Elie Weiss in 1967, the destruction of the radar just before Israel's jets took off, his faked death, and training in Europe as an agent for SOD. He skipped the Koenig account, but described the events of the past week.

Rabin listened without interrupting. He showed neither surprise nor alarm. When Lemmy finished, he asked, "Your father's papers?"

"Here." He handed the note and documents.

Rabin read through quickly and removed his glasses. "Interesting, but misguided. I was briefed by Shin Bet last night. Freckles and his right-wing rabblerousing was never authorized by Shin Bet. It was all part of the scheme Weiss cooked up to taint the Likud, culminating in the staged assassination attempt to boost my popularity. Shin Bet confronted Freckles last week and scared him enough to switch his loyalty. They shut down this SOD operation, locked up Elie Weiss, and broke up the ILOT group—I'm told they're a bunch of kids, boy scouts."

"Boy scouts," Itah asked, "with guns?"

"With blanks," Rabin said. "Shin Bet confirmed there were no live bullets. It was all a game to make noise in the media, to prime it for the final act of trying to shoot me, also with blanks. But it's all over now. Finished."

Lemmy was taken by his gruff charisma, which radiated the confidence of a man certain of his goals. "Knowing Elie Weiss, I suggest you still wear a Kevlar vest to the peace rally."

Rabin chuckled. "What can he do from a hospital bed?"

"If anything was supposed to happen on Saturday, he must have set the wheels in motion long ago. That's how he operates."

"Listen, Weiss is a hero of Zionism, a defender of the Jewish people. I respect his achievements. But his time has passed. I can't indulge his grandiose ideas, especially not in today's world. We're making peace, but he acts as if we're still in the middle of the Holocaust."

"He's a very capable man," Lemmy insisted, "despite his age and emphysema."

"Unfortunately," the prime minister said. "I'm told he's dying."

"Even if that's true, what about Tanya? I saw Shin Bet agents try to kill her."

"How do you know they were Shin Bet?" Rabin lit a cigarette. "The report I received states that, as part of the VIP Protection Unit's investigation of Weiss's fake assassination plot, they followed Tanya to Zurich, but lost her there. She apparently travelled to Amsterdam, where she was hit by a tram."

"I was there," Lemmy said, "and I didn't push her."

"Perhaps Weiss had other agents in Amsterdam? Some kind of a redundancy?"

Lemmy had no answer to that.

"And since you mentioned Tanya, would you know by any chance where she is?"

"No, but I know she's in good hands. Someone I trust."

"I'm pleased to hear that." The prime minister smiled. "She's the most senior woman we have."

"In Mossad?"

"Probably in the whole Israeli government service."

"Then why were your agents following her?"

Rabin stood up. "Listen, those Shin Bet boys are entrusted with my personal safety. They do their best to keep me alive. How can I question their loyalty?"

"Maybe they're acting out of misguided loyalty. As the saying goes, the road to hell is paved with good intentions."

"Touché." He got up and went to a large board pinned to the wall. "Come, look at this. Maybe it'll help you understand what I'm dealing with here."

The color-coded graph showed the political spectrum. In the center, the tallest bars stood for Labor and Likud. The other parties were listed on the left or the right according to their affiliation.

On the left were: Meretz, Hadash, Democratic Front for Peace-Communists, Arab Democratic Party, Progressive List for Peace, Hatikva, Movement for Democracy and Aliyah, New Liberal Idea.

On the right, following Likud, were: Advancement of the Zionist Idea, Tzomet A, Tzomet B, Moledet, Golan Loyalists.

Below the graph was a list of the religious parties: UNITED TORAH JUDAISM, SEPHARDIC RELIGIOUS PARTY/SHAS, NATIONAL RELIGIOUS PARTY, MEIMAD, GEULAT ISRAEL, TORAH AND LAND.

Next was a list of non-partisan groups: GUSH EMUNIM, YESHA (SETTLEMENTS OF JUDEA AND SAMARIA), KACH/KAHANA KHAI, NETURAY KARTA. The third list was of the parties-information for the next elections: RUSSIANS' PARTY, PENSIONERS' PARTY, TALI, WOMEN'S PARTY, ON WHEELS, MORTGAGE VICTIMS, NATURAL LAW PARTY, TZIPOR, MOTHERS IN BLACK, PARENTS AGAINST SILENCE, OFFICERS AGAINST OCCUPATION, CITIZENS FOR THE GOLAN HEIGHTS, PIKANTI.

Lemmy asked, "What's *Pikanti*?

Itah answered. "Salad dressing factory's workers believe they have a good shot at a seat in the Knesset to fight against income tax."

"I see."

Fourth was a list of Arab groups: PLO, PLO HAWKS, PFLP, AL FATAH, HAMAS, ISLAMIC JIHAD, AND HEZBOLLAH.

"Do you realize why I don't have time to worry about Weiss or micromanage my own protection unit?" Prime Minister Rabin pointed to the board. "Israel is boiling, and I have to sit on the lid. And every group of radicals spawns another one, even more idealistic, more pious, more righteous, more extreme. So we have to use administrative detentions and other methods to stay the course."

"Stay in power, you mean," Itah said.

"I didn't come here to sit in the prime minister's chair," Rabin said sharply. "Or to win favor with X, Y, or Z. I see this as the crowning achievement of my life. I started in the Jewish underground, fighting the British. I commanded the army in battles and served as ambassador in Washington. I was prime minister once before, but was too inexperienced in politics. And I've served for over five years as defense minister. Now I'm here again at a unique point in time. I feel there's a real chance to fundamentally change the relationship between Israel and the Arab world, our neighbors, and the Palestinians."

"A noble cause doesn't sanctify all means." Lemmy waved at the board with all the parties' names. "Does it mean nothing that leaders who represent half the population oppose your Oslo Accords?"

"I despise them! Who are they? Did they fight like me? Are they responsible for our defense achievements, like me?"

"Aren't they?"

"The positive elements in the nation stand with me. Come to the peace rally on Saturday night. You'll see the huge support for peace!"

"We'd love to attend," Itah said. "But the goons from the Shin Bet are after us. And they got the police after me on fictional charges."

The prime minister waved dismissively. "By the time you reach the Knesset exit, I will have ordered them not to bother you again." He accompanied them to the door and shook Lemmy's hand. "You should visit the new promenade at the Government House area. You won't recognize the place."

"Great idea," Itah said. "Let's go there right now."

The phone rang, and Agent Cohen picked it up. "Yes?" He listened. "With Itah Orr? Are you sure? Then get a team over there!" He slammed the phone and ran to the door.

"What's happening?" Gideon followed him.

"Spinoza met Rabin at the Knesset."

"You're kidding!"

"What chutzpah this guy has!" Agent Cohen hit the elevator button repeatedly. "*Shit! Shit! Shit!*"

The door of the next apartment opened, and the nurse peeked out.

"We're done here," Agent Cohen said. "Pack up."

"But I don't understand," Gideon said. "Did Spinoza try to—"

"No. Visitors are searched at the entrance to the Knesset. No weapons allowed."

"If Elie trained him, Spinoza doesn't need a weapon."

"Rabin is watched constantly." The elevator arrived, they rushed in, and Agent Cohen hit the lobby button. "We're not dealing with someone suicidal. Spinoza is a professional killer who wants to get out safely."

"Then why would he risk going into the Knesset to meet Rabin?"

"Scout the target? Establish rapport? Who the hell knows?"

"What did they discuss?"

"I don't know yet. Itah Orr was with him."

"Why is she helping Spinoza?"

Agent Cohen shrugged. "She probably doesn't realize what she's dealing with. For all we know, Spinoza might be disposing of her as we speak."

Itah and Lemmy strolled across the forecourt to the main exit, pausing to look at the views of the Israel Museum and the Supreme Court. There was no sign of trouble as they exited though the visitors' gate and flagged down a taxi.

"To the Old City," Lemmy said.

Traffic was slow in the city's center, and the cabby dropped them off near the Jaffa Gate. They stopped at a store filled with knickknacks and bought pocket-size binoculars. Passing by David's Tower, Lemmy found stairs leading up to the top of the ancient wall surrounding the Old City. He led the way to the southern ramparts and found an archer's slit that the wind and rain had widened over the centuries.

Across a wide gulch, the opposite ridge was dominated by the massive whitewashed structure of the old Government House, where the British high commissioner had resided until Israel's independence in 1948, followed by the UN Mideast Command until 1967, when Israel captured East Jerusalem from Jordan. There was no trace of the giant radar receptor, which Lemmy had destroyed with a bomb on the first morning of the war.

The most striking view was a long promenade, which crested the ridge all the way to the right, across what used to be the border, and connecting with the main road to Hebron. He trained the binoculars on the boardwalk and scanned it slowly. The parking area at the eastern end was sparsely used by a few cars and three tour buses. But suddenly two white sedans sped up the access road and let out a group of men. He switched his focus to the parking lot at the western end of the promenade.

A similar group arrived there in a hurry. They advanced from both directions, like pincers. They stopped visitors, checked papers, and held up photos to compare faces.

Itah took the binoculars. She scanned the view across the gulch. "Unbelievable. The prime minister lied to us!"

"I don't think so." Lemmy took the binoculars and headed back toward David's Tower.

"What are you saying?" She followed him. "Shin Bet won't act against Rabin's explicit orders!"

"Why not? VIP protection is a tricky business. They have to ignore the wishes of the individual VIP. A public figure cannot dictate the terms of his own protection. On the contrary. Everything must be done to remove a threat, even against his orders."

"But you're no threat to Rabin." Itah held his arm as the narrow path atop the ancient wall turned right.

Lemmy stopped and turned to face her. "What makes you so sure?"

Itah looked at him.

The dry wind picked up, stinging them with dust. A muezzin chanted nearby.

She glanced at the edge of the wall and the long drop to the bottom.

"See what I mean?" Lemmy chuckled. "Even you aren't completely sure. As far as they're concerned, I could be a turncoat. As long as I'm walking around, I'm an unacceptable risk."

Friday, November 3, 1995

After midnight, the hospital quieted down. But Elie waited another hour before getting out of bed. In the soft light from the window, he saw Rabbi Gerster rise from his cot and follow him into the bathroom. He pressed the lever to flush the toilet. "Abraham," he whispered, "are you still committed?"

"To what?"

"Preventing another Holocaust."

"Counter Final Solution?"

Elie nodded.

"I'm committed. But first I must save my son."

It was the response Elie had expected. "Lemmy needs no saving. He's capable of saving himself. He came here to help you. Leave the country, and he will follow you. I'll make sure of it." Before Abraham could argue, he added, "Tanya is the one who needs your help."

"I know. But how can I leave the country?"

"I've prepared papers for you, only I didn't think you'd need it so soon. Go to Hapoalim Bank, Herzl Boulevard branch. Manager is David Abulafia. He has an envelope for you. Cash, credit cards, German passport under the name Abelard Horch."

"Abelard Horch?"

"Lemmy's father."

In the darkness, Rabbi Gerster gripped Elie's thin forearm. "You were planning to reunite us all along!"

"I'm not a monster," Elie said. "Tomorrow, take a flight to Amsterdam. Look for the Mullenhuis Data Recovery Company. The owner, Carl, will know where to find Tanya."

"How do you know?"

"That Dutchman is the only person Lemmy would trust. They're true friends."

His breathing belabored, Elie lay back under the covers in the elevated hospital bed. He watched Abraham get dressed and bunch up the blankets on his cot in the shape of a sleeping person. His shadow bent over Elie's bed. "Shalom," he whispered.

Elie grabbed his shirt and made him lean closer. "Tell her." He struggled for air. "Tell Tanya."

"Tell her what?"

"That I sent you to take care of her. To be with her. Tell her!"

"I will." Rabbi Gerster tiptoed to the door, put his ear against it, and waited. A while later, the soft sound of the guard's snoring came through. He cracked the door and slipped out.

The Kings of Israel Plaza was a vast concrete square in the center of Tel Aviv. Gideon looked up at the massive, Soviet-style city hall, which towered over the plaza on the north side. In its shadow, carpenters were assembling the stage for tomorrow night's peace rally. He had already briefed the director of security on the need to empty the building at the end of the workday and keep it secured until after the rally tomorrow night.

Around the plaza, teams of laborers unpacked audio equipment and placed loudspeakers at regular intervals. Ibn Gevirol Street ran along the east side. It was a six-lane artery that connected north and south Tel Aviv and was due to be shut down to vehicle traffic hours before the event. They waited for a lull in traffic and ran across.

The sidewalk teemed with pedestrians, who patronized the retail stores on the street level. Above the stores, the buildings had six or seven floors of residential apartments, many sporting balconies that enjoyed unobstructed lines of fire at the stage, as did the hundreds of apartments along King Saul Boulevard on the south side of the plaza.

"This is unacceptable," Gideon said. "We have to remove the residents and secure all these apartment buildings before the rally."

"You can try," Agent Cohen said.

"Why not?"

"You've obviously spent too much time away from Israel." He gestured at the buildings. "You think these Israelis would just pack a bag and leave their apartments? Every one of them has already invited his friends and relatives to come up and sit on the balcony during the rally. They'll drink lemonade and crack sunflower seeds, spitting the skin shards on the poor schmucks below, who will stand on their toes to catch a glimpse of the dignitaries, get squeezed by total strangers, and gag on body odor and cigarette smoke, because they don't know anyone who owns an apartment overlooking the plaza."

Gideon laughed.

"That's why we have to count on sharpshooters, about a hundred of them, on the roofs all around."

"They should pay special attention to empty balconies," Gideon said. "I don't think Spinoza would try shooting from a populated apartment, even if he can somehow get invited."

"He won't be able to bring a rifle to the area. We're setting up roadblocks. Anyone carrying a package or a bag will be searched. Israelis are used to being searched at the entrance to every mall and movie theater, so no one would mind."

"We have to assume," Gideon said, "that Spinoza knows those facts, that he has a plan that's not vulnerable to a roadblock, a search, or a pat-down."

At Lemmy's request, Benjamin had called the chaplain at Hadassah Hospital and asked for his assistance in accommodating a group of Neturay Karta men, who wished to visit the sick before the Sabbath, comfort them, and pray for their salvation. It was a common enough occurrence, and the chaplain was happy to oblige.

Twenty minutes later, the van dropped Lemmy, Benjamin, and eight other men at the hospital entrance. The chaplain waited for them with visitor stickers, which they placed on the lapels of their black coats.

The hospital rooms held six beds each. Benjamin conducted a brief service in every room, his men following his lead, praying with the patients, some of whom were too sedated to notice.

"What is Spinoza's plan?" Gideon shaded his eyes with his hand as he looked up at the buildings surrounding the King of Israel Plaza. "Without a long-range rifle, he could try a handgun with a silencer. Could he enter the area behind the stage and ambush Rabin on arrival or departure?"

"Impossible," Agent Cohen said. "Our VIP Protection Unit always sets up a sterile area to prevent such attempts. It's standard procedure for public events. No one but the VIPs and our own guys can enter a sterile area. But he could shoot at the stage from the front, standing among the crowd."

Gideon turned and looked across the plaza toward the half-constructed stage. "Even if he's up front, aiming up at the stage, he would still be pretty far. And let's say he can manage a perfect shot, how does he plan to get away?"

"There's going to be panic. He could slip through the crowd and disappear."

"What if the guy next to him is a kibbutznik? Or a reservist from an elite commando? Spinoza knows that almost every Israeli is an IDF veteran. They won't panic. They'll jump him!"

"Only if they notice the gun."

Gideon wasn't convinced. "It's too chancy. This guy is calculated, careful, Swiss. He won't risk a wild shot at the prime minister while surrounded by thousands of aggressive Israelis."

They strolled to the middle of the vast plaza. A couple walked a dog nearby. A woman rode her bicycle toward King Saul Boulevard. And a teenager dribbled a basketball, jogging with oversized headphones. The sun was up now, its warmth building up.

"A diversion," Gideon said. "He could use a few small bombs, even firecrackers, to create mayhem. He'll shoot Rabin and disappear."

"Dressed up as a policeman, he could easily slip away."

"For all we know, he might have a collaborator, ready with uniform and appropriate IDs."

"There could be a rifle hidden someplace on one of the roofs or in an apartment, waiting for Spinoza." Agent Cohen waved at the surrounding buildings. "There are a thousand spots he could have chosen."

"That's right. And tomorrow night, he would walk through a checkpoint, get to his prearranged position, prime the rifle and shoot at his leisure."

"And walk away while Rabin bleeds to death."

Despite the fresh morning air, the image made Gideon break into a sweat. "Would Rabin agree to speak via video instead of attending the rally in person?"

"Yeah, right!" Agent Cohen rolled his eyes. "The peace process hinges on this event. Labor Party officials expect a record number of supporters—two or three hundred thousand, possibly more. Rabin's political career depends on this event. If it's successful, they expect an upswing that will last through the elections."

"Will he at least wear a bulletproof vest?"

"He considers it a sign of chicanery."

"An old soldier." Gideon sighed. "Then we must find Spinoza before tomorrow night."

"And eliminate him," Agent Cohen said. "A final solution."

Gideon followed Agent Cohen into the Shin Bet mobile unit, a box truck that was parked in the designated sterile area near the stage. It was packed tight with electronic equipment, operated by several technicians in civilian clothes. A number of monitors showed video input from various sections of the Kings of Israel Plaza.

"Let's watch the video from the King David Hotel." Agent Cohen loaded a cassette into a player connected to a TV set. "Maybe you'll see something I've missed."

The black-and-white picture showed the main entrance to the King David Hotel from above, with two bellmen, guests coming and going, and car horns in the background. A man in a baseball hat appeared on the right, just as a group came out of the lobby.

"Here!" Agent Cohen paused the player and used the stick taped to his broken finger to indicate each person on the screen. "That's Spinoza, standing aside with the baseball hat. That's me, with my four agents around Itah Orr, Elie Weiss, and Rabbi Gerster without his beard and hat." He restarted the video.

The group proceeded through the wide exit doors. Rabbi Gerster's head turned, and he stopped in his tracks as if he hit an invisible wall. The agent behind kept walking and bumped into him, and the group stopped with grunts of surprise.

"Did you see that?" Agent Cohen paused the video again.

"Rabbi Gerster didn't stumble," Gideon said. "He stopped walking when he noticed Spinoza."

"But why?"

"They're both SOD agents, right? Maybe they trained together."

"The Neturay Karta rabbi and the Swiss assassin? Come on!"

"Clearly they know each other."

"And now they're both missing. The rabbi slipped away from the hospital before dawn this morning." Agent Cohen pressed play. On the TV screen, Spinoza's hand went into his pocket. Rabbi Gerster shook his head once, turned the other way and yelled, "Benjamin! Benjamin!" Everybody followed his gaze, and then Agent Cohen barked an order, and the group moved forward, exiting the video frame at the edge of the driveway. Car doors slammed, engines rumbled, and tires screeched. Spinoza and the bellmen exchanged a few words, and he entered the hotel.

"Did you notice," Gideon said, "Rabbi Gerster's quick head shake? Spinoza was about to draw his gun."

"It's not his gun," Agent Cohen said petulantly. "He stole it from our agent at Hadassah."

"You're lucky he didn't use it."

"He's the lucky one. There were five of us, guns in hand."

"You still don't get it, do you?" Gideon stepped out of the mobile unit and turned his face up to the sun, his eyes closed. The tape presented more riddles rather than clues. Who was Spinoza, or Horch? An agent of SOD, or a Saudi agent spying on SOD? Or was he a gun for hire? And how could a Neturay Karta rabbi control such a coldblooded assassin with a quick shake of the head, saving the lives of five Shin Bet agents? The only known connection between them was Elie Weiss. He held all the answers.

Gideon heard Agent Cohen come out of the mobile unit and turned to face him. "How quickly can you get us to Hadassah?"

The agent pointed up, where a helicopter was hovering. "Fifteen minutes, give or take."

It took the better part of an hour until they completed a series of prayers with patients and reached Elie's room. A guard sat outside the door. He put aside his newspaper and stood up. "Sorry. This room is off limits."

"Off limits to God?" Benjamin placed a hand on the guard's shoulder. "Did you say your prayers this morning, my good friend?"

The guard blushed and said something about taking his kids to Friday night services. Benjamin blessed him with good health and longevity and opened the door. The guard didn't stop him.

The room had not changed since Lemmy's previous visit, except for a TV set on a shelf, tuned to a news channel. The night table carried a plate of untouched food and metal utensils—possible weapons, but low grade—and a thick book bound between carved wooden plates. Benjamin and his men gathered near the bed, shielding it from the surveillance camera above the door, as Lemmy had instructed them earlier.

Elie's black eyes watched them. An oxygen tube run from a wall outlet to his nose. The sheet over his chest rose and sank, accompanied by a squeaky sound.

Lemmy removed the black hat with the attached beard and side locks.

"Nice outfit," Elie said.

Benjamin and his men chanted the "Prayer for the Sick."

"Where is my father?"

"Flew out of the cuckoo's nest."

"Where did he go?"

"Back to the field." Elie pressed a button, and the head of the bed rose, lifting him halfway to a sitting position. "Why are you here? Haven't you received my orders?"

"Tanya came to Zurich. I almost eliminated her by mistake. She told me about my father's real job, about your manipulations."

"Ah." Elie looked toward the window. "Tanya."

"I know what you've done." Lemmy kept his voice lower than the praying voices behind him. "You manipulated my father into a life of lies. Then you deceived me, an eighteen-year-old kid, to give up my life and become someone else." He took a deep breath, controlling his rage. "It's monstrous!"

"You feel sorry for yourself?" Elie breathed a few times. "You suffered?"

"Yes!"

"You don't know what suffering is. Go back to your job!"

"All your schemes are for naught. Shin Bet has shut down your ILOT. You'll never become intelligence czar."

A weary grin appeared on Elie's gaunt face.

"I tried to protect Tanya, but they got to her in Amsterdam. I had to leave her, broken and bleeding, surrounded by strangers, abandoned. Is she suffering enough? Are you pleased with the consequences of your games?"

The grin faded away. For a moment there was no other reaction, but then Lemmy saw something that stunned him. In the corners of Elie's eyes, tears bubbled up.

There was a knock on the door, and the guard peeked in. "Are you done praying?"

"You see this road?" Agent Cohen had to yell over the racket of the rotors. He pointed down at the narrow blacktop that slithered up the Judean Mountains. "It's the Burma Road. Back in forty-eight, when Rabin was a young commander, he tried to save Jerusalem from the Jordanian siege, but the main road was blocked by Arab terrorists. Someone found this goat path and broke through with supplies for the Jewish civilians. But it was too late to win the battle."

The helicopter was flying low, the tree summits almost within reach. Gideon rested his forehead against the window, looking down at the landscape of planted pine forests and deep ravines, an occasional boulder breaking through the green with the bleached white of sandstone.

"He never forgave himself," Agent Cohen yelled.

"Who?"

"Yitzhak Rabin, for losing the battle for Jerusalem, leaving it divided for nineteen years. That's why he insisted on winning it back in sixty-seven."

Gideon nodded. These historic details seemed trivial now, as he was flying to Hadassah Hospital to confront the man who had hired and mentored him. Despite his misgivings about Elie's methods, joining with Shin Bet against the old man felt like a betrayal.

"Three minutes." Agent Cohen pointed at a distant cluster of buildings among the green mountains. "There's Hadassah Hospital."

"We're almost done," Benjamin told the guard, closing the door. "Psalms, seventy-nine. *Lord, how the Gentiles invaded your domain, contaminated your Holy Temple, turned Jerusalem into wreckage.*"

While the men of Neturay Karta repeated after Benjamin, Lemmy leaned closer to Elie. "Shin Bet is hunting us down. I fear for my family. I must make a trade with them. Offer them something they can't refuse."

Elie grimaced.

"I'll give them Koenig's money. It's a king's ransom—they won't turn it down. I already know the account number and password."

"You do? That's good. Very good."

"Where's the ledger?"

"What ledger?"

"The record of all deposits that Armande Hoffgeitz signed in forty-five. Where did you hide it?"

Benjamin recited, "*They fed the carcasses of your fallen faithful to the circling vultures, the flesh of your disciples to the earthly scavengers.*"

"I gave you my orders." Elie's head rose from the pillow, trying to show himself to the surveillance camera over the men's black hats. He gave up and lay back. "Counter Final Solution. That's your job."

"Tanya told me she gave it to you, and you presented it to Günter Schnell in sixty-seven. Where's the ledger?"

"Go back to Zurich and serve the cause, or your cute little Nazi namesake will die—"

"In a ski accident? Like Christopher's father? And Paula's brother?"

The gaunt hand gestured in dismissal. "Gentiles."

"I want the ledger!" He placed his hand on Elie's neck. The skin was cold against his palm. He closed his fingers and squeezed.

From above, Hadassah Hospital looked like oversized Lego blocks, positioned among the pine trees in cascading order on a moderate slope, adjacent to the Ein Shemen village. A heliport was marked with a crossed circle and an orange windsock. The pilot descended slowly, balancing the chopper against a gust of wind from the north.

Elie's weak hands clasped the bedrails, rattling the frame. His mouth opened and closed, his yellow teeth clinking.

Lemmy let go. "Where is the ledger?"

His breathing fast and shallow, Elie reached under the sheets. His hand came out with his sheathed blade, which he offered to Lemmy. The gesture was more than a sign of capitulation, of a lifelong killer expressing his readiness to be killed by his successor. It was meant to symbolize a passing of the torch.

But Lemmy had no interest in carrying Elie's torch or in trying to figure out if this was yet another manipulation, another clever signal intended to achieve the opposite result of what its plain meaning would suggest. He grabbed the blade and tossed it to the floor. "Answer me!"

Elie turned his face to the window.

Lemmy applied pressure again, shutting off the wind pipe.

Elie writhed, his legs kicking the mattress.

"They spilled your chosen's blood around Jerusalem," Benjamin chanted, *"and no one to bury the dead."*

The men of Neturay Karta repeated the verse, their voices louder to drown out Elie's noisy struggle.

"Where is it?" Lemmy's grip tightened. He leaned so close that his face almost touched Elie's aquiline nose. The squeaky breathing had stopped. Elie's legs kicked once more. His hands feebly pulled against the rails.

Benjamin stepped closer to Lemmy and chanted, *"Be forgetful, Lord, of our early sins, put forward your compassion, for we are pitiable."*

Elie's eyes opened wide, focused on Lemmy, who released the pressure.

The chest under the white sheet heaved abruptly, air shrieking as it filled the sick lungs.

"We are your chosen," Benjamin recited, *"your sheep, Shepherd, our gratitude is eternal, from one generation to the next, forever we shall praise your glory."*

Lemmy put his hand on Elie's chest, weighing down. "For the last time, where is the ledger?"

"Let's…make…a deal." Elie's sallow face twisted into a grin, and he coughed hard.

Lemmy's right hand clenched into a fist and rose up, ready to hit the demon in the bed. But Benjamin gripped his forearm while the men repeated, *"Forever we shall praise your glory."*

Elie looked away, the black eyes focused not on the window, but on the night table by the bed, the tray with untouched lunch, utensils, and the thick book. Lemmy pushed the utensils out of Elie's reach, more out of habitual caution than of real concern that Elie would attempt to attack him. The balance of power was too tilted, and even in his current state Elie would not be suicidal. He wasn't the type.

Lemmy picked up the book, surprised by its weight. The top cover was a wooden plate carved with a Star of David and the Hebrew word for *Bible*. He noticed the unusual thickness of the cover and opened it. The back of the wooden plate was lined with a mesh material that connected it to the book's spine. He gripped the front cover and tore it away from the bible.

A sigh came from the men.

With a knife from the food tray he separated the wood from the back lining. Loud cracking sounded as the two parts separated, and something fell to the floor.

Lemmy picked it up.

A small booklet, bound in black leather, stamped with a red swastika. He browsed through the pages, noting enormous quantities of precious stones, categorized by clarity and carats. On the last page was an acknowledgment: DEPOSIT OF ABOVE-LISTED GOODS WAS RECEIVED 1.1.1945 BY HOFFGEITZ BANK OF ZURICH. The handwriting and the signature below belonged to Armande Hoffgeitz.

For a moment, Lemmy was Wilhelm Horch again, a meticulous Swiss banker holding an important financial document. He examined each page. It was an undeniable evidence of a horde of blood money, which his bank had kept secret for fifty years. The ledger, if exposed, would subject the Hoffgeitz Bank to the worst scandal in the long history of Swiss private banking. Or, better yet, it represented access to almost 23 billion U.S. dollars, which could be traded with Shin Bet in a bargain that would save him and those he loved.

No one waited for them at the rooftop landing pad. Gideon got out first and helped Agent Cohen, who shielded his bandaged eye with his injured hand. They jogged to the end of the helipad and went down a steel staircase to the actual roof of the building.

"There!" Agent Cohen pointed to a sign: STAIRS – EMERGENCY ONLY.

They entered an enclosed stairway and headed down.

"Weiss is on the fourth floor," Agent Cohen said. "You can do the talking. I'll do the finger breaking and eye poking, okay?"

Benjamin beckoned his men to the door. Lemmy was ready to leave, but he noticed Elie reaching for the torn bible, which rested on the bed. Lemmy picked it up and ripped off the bottom cover. He used the knife again to separate the lining from the wood and pulled out a few pieces of paper hidden inside. He unfolded the brittle sheets.

Letters.

Familiar handwriting.

Mother!

He picked one letter, dated March 22, 1967, addressed to him in the army:

My Dearest Jerusalem,

You haven't responded to my previous letter. Perhaps you are away on exercises. Today is Thursday, and I went out of the apartment for the first time since that terrible day, when your father, in his understandable anger, excommunicated you. Everyone was very happy to see me at the synagogue, and most of the donated clothes are gone. I asked Benjamin to take the rest to Shmattas to be exchanged, and he did it well. He also misses you very much and prays for your return. Please write a few words to let us know how you are. Your father agreed that you may come home to celebrate Passover with us, provided that you respect our traditions. Please, I beg you to come, even if you have to go back to the army. Maybe you don't understand what it means for me. When you have a child one day, God willing, you will understand my agony. So please come home for Passover. I pray for your safe return.

Your loving mother,

Temimah Gerster.

She had written to him three more times, the last letter filled with anxious, urgent pleas. At the bottom, under Mother's signature, his father wrote:

JERUSALEM,

PLEASE RESPOND TO YOUR MOTHER, WHOSE HEART IS BROKEN. CRUELTY IS THE GRAVEST SIN, WHILE FORGIVENESS IS THE FINEST VIRTUE.

YOUR FATHER,
RABBI ABRAHAM GERSTER.

"I had to...intercept your mail," Elie said, his voice thin. "These letters...would have interfered...diverted you...from your destiny."

Lemmy was weak with a shattering sense of loss and grief. WHEN YOU HAVE A CHILD ONE DAY, GOD WILLING, YOU WILL UNDERSTAND MY AGONY.

"They rejected you...sat shivah for you...and you hated them."

"Because I didn't know about these letters, which show that my parents had a change of heart, that they loved me still, even without my black hat and side locks." Lemmy shook the letters in Elie's face. "You've read these! You saw her pain! How could you let her suffer like this?"

Elie rose on his elbow, his face twisted in sudden fury. "We are soldiers! We have a war to win! If we indulge there will be real suffering! There will be another Holocaust!"

"These letters," Lemmy pressed them to his chest, "are my Holocaust."

On the fourth floor, Gideon stood aside as several bearded men in black coats and hats stepped out of Elie's hospital room. "What's this? Who let them in?"

The guard smiled sheepishly. "They just wanted to pray with the patient. I couldn't refuse."

Agent Cohen pushed his way in. Gideon followed him and froze at the sight of the man standing by Elie's bed. Unlike the others, he had removed his hat, which rested on a chair with the attached fake beard and payos. His face was unmistakable: *Spinoza!*

Gideon drew his gun in a single, fluid motion, pulled on the barrel to slip a bullet into the chamber, and aimed at the assassin.

Spinoza raised his hands and said in perfect Hebrew, "*Ani sochen Israeli.* I'm an Israeli agent. Just like you."

"Shoot him!" Agent Cohen maneuvered to the side of the room. He tried to draw his gun with his injured hand, but the gun dropped to the floor. "Kill him!"

"In God's name!" It was the last of the black hats, who was still in the room. "I'm Rabbi Benjamin Mashash and I know this man. He's a Jew. We grew up together!"

"Get out!" Agent Cohen pushed him through the door and slammed it.

"I'm unarmed," Spinoza said. "I'm not a threat to anyone."

"End this now," Elie Weiss said, and while Gideon assumed the order was addressed to him, he heard Spinoza reply, "Be quiet. You've caused enough damage already."

Gideon stepped closer, aiming, "Identify yourself!"

"My name is Jerusalem—"

"Shoot him!" Agent Cohen picked up his own gun from the floor with his left hand and tried to cock it. "He's an assassin!"

"I'm part of SOD," Spinoza said. "My cover is Wilhelm Horch, vice president at the Hoffgeitz Bank in Zurich. Look at this." He held forth a small, black booklet. "I'm offering you a trade. I can transfer a huge—"

"Your father," Elie said from the bed, "went to see Carl. You should follow him."

Gideon's finger slipped into the trigger guard. "I'm calling for reinforcement." With the Beretta aimed at Spinoza, he moved toward the nightstand by the bed, but there was no telephone there.

"Shoot already!" Agent Cohen pounded Gideon's back, and a shot exploded in the room.

But the Swiss wasn't standing where he had stood a second before. And while Gideon was momentarily stunned by the blast of his unintended gunshot, a blurred figure rolled across the floor and kicked his legs from under him. Gideon spun in the air, the hard tiles coming at his head. He heard Agent Cohen scream in pain and felt a heavy body collapse on top of him. Then something very hard thumped the back of his head, and the world went dark, accompanied by the eerie laughter of Elie Weiss.

Benjamin had the presence of mind to rush downstairs with his men, start the van, and drive it to the front of the hospital, arriving just as Lemmy ran out, his hat askew, his fake beard covering his mouth.

They drove in the opposite direction from Jerusalem along winding mountain roads in a circular path that led them eventually back to the city through its northwest suburbs. Lemmy used the time to digest the changed circumstances. If Elie had spoken the truth, Rabbi Gerster had left Israel to be with Tanya. But following his father would not be possible as long as Shin Bet continued the chase. For some reason, Agent Cohen was determined to eliminate him, which made any deal unlikely.

Lemmy asked Benjamin to stop at a post office, where he mailed Koenig's ledger to Christopher with instructions to keep it locked in the safe until his return to Zurich. He also sent the signed title for the Citroën DS with a note to arrange its shipping from Bet Shemesh to Zurich. The old letters from his mother he kept folded in his pocket.

Back in Meah Shearim, the white Subaru was still parked near the entrance, the two agents leaning against the hood, smoking. They had been checking women, obviously under orders to locate Itah Orr, but they ignored men entering the neighborhood. This would change now, Lemmy knew. His safe haven was no more.

Benjamin sent his men to the synagogue to resume their Talmud study, but not before instructing them to keep mum about the events at Hadassah Hospital. Sorkeh was ready with lunch, but Lemmy had no appetite. He told Itah what had happened.

"It's obvious," she said, "that they think you intend to kill Prime Minister Rabin."

"That's illogical," Benjamin argued. "They saw Lemmy with us at Hadassah, so they now know we're giving you shelter here. Why would we, a religious community, hide an assassin?"

"Come on, this is Neturay Karta, the most anti-Zionist Jewish sect in the world. You're an enemy of Israel!"

"We have no enemies," Benjamin protested. "Our Talmudic theology dictates that only God, through his Messiah, may collect the Chosen People from exile and rebuild our homeland. Therefore we are ideologically and religiously opposed to Zionism and the establishment of the State of Israel. But we're not its enemy in a physical, worldly sense."

"Really? Don't you preach against Israel?" Itah counted on her fingers. "First, that modern Zionism caused the collapse of Jewish observance. Second, that Israel's secular nationalism and emphasis on material land possessions contradicts spiritual Judaism? Third, that the promiscuous Israeli society is a menace to the future of the Jewish faith?"

"Yes, we contend that—spiritually speaking—modern Zionism has cost this nation more Jews than the Holocaust. But we don't advocate violence. We would never condone killing of another Jew!"

"Even of a Zionist politician who's a danger to others? Even a *Rodef*, a pursuer of Jews, who must be struck down according to Talmud?" Itah knuckled the table. "From Shin Bet's perspective, your support of Rabin's assassin is perfectly logical."

Benjamin shook his head. "The only possible explanation is that Shin Bet thinks Lemmy is fooling us into hosting him, that we don't realize who or what he really is."

"Then I must leave," Lemmy said. "It's only a matter of time before they come here. I don't want to put you at risk."

Benjamin gestured at the window, painted red with the setting sun. "Sabbath is about to begin. They won't dare to invade our community."

"Why?"

"This is the City of Jerusalem, home to over two hundred thousand ultra-Orthodox Jews, many of whom are prone to religious protests. Our Neturay Karta community is small, but visible. The government will not risk inciting a riotous explosion in Jerusalem on the eve of the peace rally. I think you're safe within Meah Shearim, at least until after the rally."

Gideon and Agent Cohen spent a couple of hours in the emergency room. A series of tests revealed no concussions, fractures, or internal injuries for either of them, which was surprising as they had been unconscious for almost an hour. Spinoza clearly knew his business.

A report came from the Shin Bet desk at the airport. The name Horch had popped up on a KLM passenger list for that morning's flight to Amsterdam. The individual had been dressed in a sport coat and khaki slacks, eyes shielded by gold-rimmed Ray-Ban sunglasses. He presented a valid German passport that identified him as Abelard Horch, age 69. Carrying an overnight bag though security, he bought a Sony Walkman at the duty free store and a German translation of an Ira Levin novel, *Sliver*. Despite the identical last name, the German tourist did not match the age and physical description of Spinoza. He was allowed to board his flight, which had taken off before noon, passing over Tel Aviv and the Mediterranean coast toward Europe.

Agent Cohen tossed the report. "The real Horch was here at Hadassah Hospital at the same time. It's a good thing we're not looking for a guy with my last name, or we would get a thousand reports a day."

"We're running out of time," Gideon said.

"It's your fault. I told you to shoot him!"

"How could I put a bullet in a man who raises his hands and speaks Hebrew?"

"He's a chameleon, don't you get it? For what the Saudis can pay, they hire the best. This guy is probably the top assassin operating in the world today. He can pass for a Frenchman, a Russian, or a Hungarian for all we know. You should have eliminated him at first sight, like I told you to."

Gideon nodded thoughtfully. "I'm impressed with how he disabled us so quickly. But why didn't he kill us?"

"Do I have to repeat myself?" Agent Cohen rolled his eyes in exasperation. "Spinoza is a professional. He won't kill unless he's being paid to kill you, or if you represent mortal danger to him, which obviously you weren't. Next time, I suggest that you shoot, not talk, okay?"

"First we have to find him. An ultra-Orthodox man in Jerusalem is like a needle in a haystack."

"There's a way to deal with those *schvartzehs*." Agent Cohen used the derogatory term *blacks* for the ultra-Orthodox. "They know each other's business like there's no tomorrow. Watch this." He curled his good finger at the hospital chaplain, who was waiting just outside the ER.

The chaplain rubbed his hands nervously while explaining how Rabbi Benjamin Mashash, the leader of the Neturay Karta sect, had arranged with him to bring a minyan of men to pray with patients. "This is a Jewish hospital," he said, "how can I refuse when a righteous rabbi offers to spend time here, provide spiritual healing to the—"

"That's why Rabbi Gerster yelled *Benjamin!*" Agent Cohen spat on the floor. "He was telling Spinoza to go to Rabbi Mashash in Neturay Karta!" He waved off the chaplain, who scattered away before they changed their minds.

"But what's the connection between Rabbi Gerster, Rabbi Mashash, and Spinoza?"

"Maybe the Saudis are paying Neturay Karta to help Spinoza. That sect hates Israel as much as the Arabs do."

"I doubt it. But let's assume he's still with them. Neturay Karta has hundreds of families, and each one would do the rabbi's bidding and hide Spinoza, no questions asked. How are we supposed to find him?"

"Break down their doors one by one until we get him!"

"Not so simple." Gideon pressed on the bruise at the back of his head. "Going door to door would require lots of agents, together with police support, roadblocks, armored vehicles. There's going to be resistance, barricaded doors and windows, stone throwing. And as soon as word gets around Jerusalem about police invasion in the middle of the Sabbath, thousands will flood the streets. Neturay Karta is a core of fundamentalism, but the rest of the other ultra-Orthodox neighborhoods aren't exactly bastions of patriotism. Unless we're ready to deal with a city-wide riot, we must come up with a better plan."

The ICU doctor appeared. "I checked Weiss. His vitals are fine, but we can't wake him up. I don't know what's going on. It might be neurological."

"We need him awake," Gideon said. "He possesses information that's essential to our investigation. It's a matter of national security."

The physician shrugged. "You'll have to wait."

"He's pretending," Agent Cohen said. "Stick a needle in his foot, and he'll wake up."

"We tried pricking his toe."

"And?"

"No response. Not even an eyelid twitch."

"What did you expect?" Gideon chuckled. "You're not dealing with a normal human being."

"Try breaking his finger," Agent Cohen said. "Or poking his eye."

Saturday, November 4, 1995

Sabbath morning at Benjamin's small apartment was different than any other morning. A huge pot of meat, potatoes, and pinto beans had been simmering on the stove since sundown on Friday, filling the apartment with the unique smell of *tcholent* that Lemmy remembered from childhood. He was looking forward to Sabbath lunch after the services.

Everyone was up early, preparing to go together to the synagogue. Rather than a full breakfast, Sorkeh had put out slices of pound cake and a pitcher of milk. Benjamin sang to the youngest while changing his diaper. Lemmy helped one of the boys lace up his shining Sabbath shoes, while Sorkeh brushed her teenage daughter's hair and tied it with a red ribbon. Itah borrowed a flowery headdress from Sorkeh, which went well with a taupe dress she had found in a box of donated clothes. The oldest boy, Jerusalem, was lying on the living room sofa, his face rosy with fever. When everyone was dressed and ready to go, they wished Jerusalem Good Sabbath and a speedy recovery, and went to the synagogue.

Itah walked with Lemmy behind the large Mashash family. "I used to hate them," she said. "Their black coats and hats, their beards and side locks, and their holier-than-thou isolationism, as if we, secular Israelis, were not really Jews."

"And now?"

"Now that Neturay Karta is the only place I'm safe?" She laughed. "Your father cares for these people, and I understand why. They're like a Jewish microcosm, a biosphere of Talmudic life, unchanged and uncontaminated since before modernity. Look at them—like shtetl dwellers in Poland three centuries ago."

At the forecourt of the synagogue, hundreds of Neturay Karta members congregated to exchange greetings and share news of recent engagements, new babies, and illnesses. Everyone was dressed in their best clothes, the men in tailored black coats and wide-brim felt hats, the women in colorful headdresses, and the kids in miniature outfits resembling the adults, except that the unmarried girls wore their hair uncovered.

"One day," Lemmy said, "I'll bring my wife and son to visit, see how I grew up, what gave me a solid foundation in life."

"And what is that?"

"Talmud," Lemmy said. "Everything you see here is the direct result of a communal, lifelong devotion to the study of Talmud, which is a boundless intellectual world spanning ten thousand pages of debates over right and wrong. A student of Talmud spends his days agonizing over what constitutes an ethical behavior in every aspect of one's life—worship, family, business, politics. There's nothing like it."

"Do you miss it?"

"Yes, I miss Talmud. I miss it terribly. But I don't miss the insular lifestyle. And I couldn't live without cars."

Itah laughed. "Cars?"

"Love them," he said. "Have you ever fooled around with a Porsche? Made out with a classic Citroën?"

"Shhh!" She gestured at the people around them. "It's Sabbath!"

They made their way between the people of Neturay Karta into the foyer of the synagogue. At the foot of the stairs leading to the women's section, Itah said, "You could have been their rabbi."

Lemmy looked at the animated faces of bearded men, the kind smiles of untimely aged women, the cacophony of Yiddish and Hebrew, and the little boys with kiddie black hats and dangling side locks, running around, squealing in joy. It was so familiar, yet so alien. He tugged at his fake beard. "I guess... it wasn't meant to be."

Rabbi Gerster spent the night in a small hotel overlooking a muddy canal. When he checked out, the Dutch proprietor said, "Good-bye, Herr Horch." It took him a moment to remember this was his last name—same as his son's, yet again.

According to the phonebook, Doctor Mullenhuis Data Recovery operated out of a warehouse in the southern outskirts of Amsterdam, on the road to Leiden. He didn't have much hope of finding the office open on a Saturday morning, but to his surprise, a man opened the door as soon as the taxi stopped in front of the building. Rabbi Gerster asked, "Are you Carl?"

"It depends."

"My name is Abelard Horch."

Carl's eyes lit up, but he didn't volunteer anything.

"I'm Lemmy's father." He put down the bag and patted his chest. "Back from the dead."

"Yes," Carl said, "I can tell by the sense of humor!"

They went inside, where floor-wide workrooms were filled with computer terminals and bundles of color-coded wires. If there was a method to the madness, it was well concealed. Carl collected his keys and led the way to an underground garage, a large space occupied by about twenty cars. He went for a red Ferrari. "This is a real sport car," he said, holding the door open for Rabbi Gerster, "not like your son's wimpy Porsche."

He sat with his bag on his lap as Carl maneuvered the grunting Ferrari out of the garage. "I don't know my son as an adult. Do you like him?"

"He's the best." Carl drove fast through the deserted industrial area toward the highway. "And if I ever marry, it will be someone like his Paula. Body and soul, that woman is perfect. Delicious!"

A map of the neighborhood was pinned to the wall, and within it, an area was marked with a red border that started and ended at the gate on Shivtay Israel Street. "This is our area of activity." Gideon tapped the map with his pointer. "The vehicles will drop us at the gate. We'll have sixty seconds to run up the alley to their synagogue. We must place a tight ring around the building before they notice what's happening. Neturay Karta is a fundamentalist sect, and the men are accustomed to evading police during demonstrations. We don't want them running out of the synagogue and alerting other neighborhoods. Surprise and speed are the keys to our success today."

The briefing room at the Jerusalem central police station was almost full. In addition to Agent Cohen's four subordinates, there were forty police officers and two medics.

"Our intelligence," Gideon continued, "indicates that all the members of Neturay Karta attend Sabbath morning services, including women and children. This is our only chance. A door-to-door search would incite a full-scale riot here, possibly spreading to the rest of the city." He tapped on the enlarged photos beside the map, showing Spinoza and Itah Orr. "Former TV reporter Itah Orr, accused of banking fraud and identity theft. The man with her uses the name Baruch Spinoza, but is also known as Wilhelm Horch, a Swiss national. He's probably dressed as an ultra-Orthodox man. Study his face in the flyer you're about to receive. Be alert and careful. He's a professional assassin."

Each of them had been given a printout of a photo from Hadassah Hospital's security cameras, which had captured Spinoza's bearded face as he had entered the hospital on Friday with the other Neturay Karta men.

"The plan is simple," Gideon continued. "We'll enter through the main synagogue doors and run up the side walls to surround the congregation. Two of you will go upstairs to the women's section." He selected them with his pointer. "As soon as we surround the crowd, I will explain to them that we have no hostile intentions other than to apprehend the two criminals. At this point, either they'll hand the suspects over to us or we'll search the rows in the prayer hall and in the upstairs mezzanine until we find them. Questions?"

One of the police officers raised his hand. "What are the engagement rules? Should we have guns at the ready, or keep them holstered?"

"Holstered," Gideon said. "We won't give him a reason to shoot. He's a professional, not a fanatic. He doesn't want to die. As soon as he realizes he's trapped by an overwhelming force, he'll surrender."

"What about the rest of them. How can we defend against them?"

"Are you afraid of a bunch of Talmudic scholars? The worst they can do is spit on you. Do you carry a handkerchief?"

Everybody laughed, and another officer asked, "What if the two suspects aren't in the synagogue?"

"They've taken cover inside a sect with strict rules of behavior, which include mandatory attendance at Sabbath morning prayers. We expect them to adhere to their hosts' customs in order to blend in."

"That's correct." Agent Cohen stepped forward. "However, we have identified Rabbi Mashash's apartment as an alternative hideout. My team will raid it. We're experienced in urban warfare from our work in the West Bank and Gaza. If the suspects are hiding there, I'm confident we can apprehend them easily. Or eliminate them."

An hour into the service, the Torah scroll was carried up to the dais and rolled open on the table for the reading of the weekly chapter. The men stood in honor of the sacred scroll. They all wore striped prayer shawls draped over their heads and shoulders, providing each man with spiritual privacy.

The reading was divided into seven portions, and one man was honored to come up to the dais and make a blessing over each portion. Lemmy followed the verses, his finger proceeding under the Hebrew words in his book as Cantor Toiterlich read them from the scroll on the dais. The familiar ritual calmed him, taking away the worries that had plowed his mind all night.

He felt at home, yet this wasn't home. Zurich was home, Paula and Klaus Junior were home, and the coming baby was home.

An hour later, for the last portion, Rabbi Benjamin Mashash announced, "Ascend and rise for the seventh Aliya, our guest, who took the name Baruch."

A murmur passed through the congregants. Normally a person was called up to the Torah by his first name and his father's name. Lemmy hesitated. Everyone in this hall, except Benjamin, knew that Rabbi Gerster's only son, Jerusalem, had been dead for almost three decades. What if someone recognized him?

Benjamin beckoned him to the dais.

Raising his prayer shawl to cover his head and most of his face, Lemmy paced up the aisle and onto the dais. Cantor Toiterlich, Sorkeh's elderly father, used the silver pointer to mark the spot on the parchment. Lemmy placed the corner of the prayer shawl on the words and kissed it. His face hidden by the edge of the shawl, he bent over the scroll and recited. *"Blessed be He, Master of the Universe, who chose us from all the nations and gave us his Torah."*

As Cantor Toiterlich bent over the parchment to read the quill-scribed ancient words, a loud bang sounded in the back of the synagogue.

Lemmy turned to see a group of police officers burst in, spreading left and right and along the side walls. The last to enter was Elie's young, curly-haired agent from the Galeries Lafayette, whom Lemmy had knocked out cold at Hadassah Hospital yesterday.

Gideon was pleased. The operation has commenced smoothly. While Agent Cohen and his Shin Bet team headed to the rabbi's apartment, he led the police team to take control of the synagogue. As expected, it was filled with men and boys, while the women of Neturay Karta gazed down from the mezzanine in rapt silence.

"Good Sabbath!" Mounting the dais, Gideon held up his laminated ID. "This is an official search by the police and the security services of the State of Israel. Stay where you are and nothing will happen to you!"

"And Good Sabbath to you." Rabbi Benjamin Mashash smiled. "Nice to see you again. Would you like to join us for the reading of the Torah?"

Gideon stood among the handful of men on the dais, all draped in their prayer shawls. "I apologize for this interruption," he said. "You should be able to continue with the service as soon as we complete our business here."

"God will be pleased," Rabbi Mashash said.

"Could you instruct your people to cooperate with us?"

The rabbi gestured at the police officers along the walls. "Do we have a choice?"

"Exactly." Gideon pulled a copy of the flyer. "We are searching for this man, who uses the name Baruch Spinoza."

The name provoked angry muttering. The excommunicated philosopher, though long dead, was not a popular figure among ultra-Orthodox Jews.

The elderly cantor started saying something, but the rabbi interrupted him. "If we had such a troublesome Jew among us, we would have excommunicated him right away."

The congregation exploded in laughter.

Gideon put his lips to the rabbi's ear. "Your actions yesterday at Hadassah suffice to justify your arrest as well. Cooperate, or else!"

Rabbi Benjamin Mashash turned to his men and spoke in a sonorous voice that reached every corner of the large hall. "Our sages said that the laws of the land should be respected, even when they contradict the laws of Talmud."

Gideon breathed in relief.

"It follows, therefore, that the lawmen of the Zionist government, who have just interrupted our Torah reading, should be respected." The rabbi pulled off his prayer shawl. "Respect means forgiveness, which we will express by including them in our prayers."

"Thank you." Gideon turned to glance at the front section of the synagogue, making sure the officers guarded the front rows.

"To be thus included," the rabbi said, "a Jew must drape himself in holiness, like this." He tossed his prayer shawl in the air, holding on to one end, and shook it as a maid would shake linen over a bed in order to expand it to its full size. He swiveled sideways, forming an overhead canopy, which softly descended onto Gideon, engulfing him completely.

W hen Benjamin covered him with the prayer shawl, the young agent uttered a muffled shout and tried to free himself. Lemmy pulled off his own prayer shawl and wrapped it over him as well. Cantor Toiterlich, with impressive swiftness for his age, did the same, and the agent's struggle turned helpless. The cantor laughed, but when his eyes landed on Lemmy, he froze, his mouth agape.

"It's a long story." Lemmy gave him a quick hug. "Benjamin will explain later."

The hall turned into a madhouse. The men followed their rabbi's example and shrouded each of the policemen in prayer shawls. Soon Neturay Karta's frail scholars were doubled over in laughter while all the policemen were struggling to find their way out of multiple layers of striped cloth.

"Thank you," Lemmy kissed Benjamin's cheek and ran off. "I'll be back one day!"

"God bless," Benjamin yelled after him.

Itah was already in the foyer, her headdress loose, her sleeve torn from the wrist up to the armpit. "Don't ask," she said as they ran out. "We didn't have prayer shawls upstairs, but there were only two of them."

They reached the gate, which was blocked by several police vans and a few white Subaru sedans, one with a half-open window. Lemmy reached inside and opened the door. It took him thirty seconds to rip off several plastic pieces from under the steering column, strip a few wires, and start the car.

"I'm impressed." Itah held on as he made a sharp turn. "They teach hotwiring in Swiss banking school?"

"I just finished re-wiring an old Citroën. They're all the same, basically."

"And your buddy Benjamin—he's something else! That agent didn't know what hit him!"

"My clever, wonderful Benjamin." Lemmy changed gears. "It's like we're teenagers again."

What struck Gideon more than anything else during the few minutes of his confinement was that no one tried to hit him or push him off the dais or hurt him in any way. On the contrary, when he stumbled after failing to free himself, the ultra-Orthodox men pulled off the prayer shawls, helped him sit on a bench, and served him with sweet wine in a plastic cup. Similar scenes took place around the synagogue, where the frazzled police officers, their hair messed up, their faces red, were nevertheless smiling as the men catered to them with wine and good cheer.

Rabbi Benjamin Mashash was gone, and suddenly Gideon remembered that Agent Cohen was about to raid the rabbi's apartment. Was Spinoza hiding there? Gideon ran out and headed down one of the alleys, trying to recall the map he had pinned to the briefing room wall. He took the turns from memory, catching up with the rabbi, who was older and in the physical shape of one who spends his days studying.

"He's not there." The rabbi panted badly. "Only my son... ill...stayed home."

Gideon sped up. "I'll stop them," he yelled over his shoulder. But he knew he was too late.

"Slow down," Itah said. "Nobody is chasing us."

"Are you sure?" Lemmy opened the storage bin between the seats, finding a bottle of water and loose change. There were two sets of communication devices—a CB radio and another unit he wasn't familiar with. He made sure both were turned off. "Search the glove compartment."

She did. "Registration papers and manuals. A pen."

"What kind?"

"The pen? Ballpoint."

"Good." He took it and stuck in his shirt pocket. "Where are we?"

"The French Hill neighborhood. It was built after the Six Day War."

"That's why I don't recognize it." Lemmy stopped on the side of the road. "We need to figure out what's going on."

"The raid?" Itah unscrewed the cap from the water bottle. "I thought they'd wait for you outside the neighborhood, but obviously they're impatient."

"Why? How can I hurt Rabin if I'm holed up in Meah Shearim?" Lemmy took the bottle from her and took a sip. "Maybe they're worried about something else."

"Other than Rabin's safety?"

"Elie would know. I should have squeezed him harder."

"There's someone else you could squeeze." Itah found a roadmap folded between the seats and spread it open.

"Who?"

"Freckles." Her finger traced a road on the map. "He's the only agent serving both SOD and Shin Bet."

"He's a low-level provocateur. Why would they tell him?"

"Freckles doesn't need to be told. He's a born sniffer. He would know." She tapped the map. "The settlement of Tapuach. That's where he lives."

"In the West Bank?"

"No. In Switzerland." Itah laughed. "You've never been to a settlement, have you?"

"I left Israel one day before the IDF captured the West Bank. Other than my radar sabotage foray into East Jerusalem and a recent visit to the Wailing Wall, I've never been across the sixty-seven border."

"How bizarre. Our worst political problems in the past decades—the vicious rift between left and right, the loss of international support, and the Intifada—all came after the Six Day War." Itah punched his arm. "If not for your pyrotechnics at Government House, Israel's first strike would have failed. Even if we had somehow survived the Arabs' overwhelming forces, we would have never captured the West Bank. If not for you, the Middle East would have gone in a different direction."

"You blame me?" Lemmy merged back into traffic, speeding up. "Don't you believe in God?"

Smoke petered out of the windows on the second floor of the apartment building. Gideon ran up the stairs. The door was broken, hanging from a single remaining brass hinge. He yelled, "Abort! Abort!"

"Stay back!" Agent Cohen's voice was muted by the gas mask. "We got Spinoza!"

The teargas had immediate effect on Gideon. His eyes watered and his nose began to burn. The apartment was wrecked, with bullet holes and broken furniture. "Abort, I said!"

Agent Cohen was crouching in the hallway. "He's cornered!"

"It's not him!"

Down the hallway, the nurse lifted her leg to kick in a door to one of the bedrooms, while another agent stood with his back against the wall, gun ready.

"Go," Agent Cohen shouted. "Shoot to kill!"

"No!" Out of time and breath, Gideon sprinted forward. The nurse kicked in the door and released a first shot. Gideon collided with her, and together they fell on the other agent, who yelled in pain.

Agent Cohen ran toward them.

Inside the room, Gideon glimpsed a bookcase that fell over on its side. A choked cough came from behind the makeshift barricade. A hand rose and tossed a book at them.

"Give it to me!" Agent Cohen grabbed the gun from the nurse and aimed it into the room with both hands.

Gideon lifted his leg and kicked him in the crotch.

"It's my son!" Rabbi Benjamin Mashash ran into the apartment, his face pale, his black hat pressed over his mouth and nose. "Jerusalem! *Jerusalem!*"

Agent Cohen sat against the wall and moaned.

The youth emerged from behind the makeshift barricade. He was badly bruised, and his torn pajama shirt hung from one shoulder. Half-blinded by the tear gas, he fell into his father's arms. "Don't worry," he said, "the stupid Zionists didn't get me."

As soon as they left Jerusalem, the trees disappeared, giving way to the barren hills of the West Bank. The occasional Arab village welcomed them with odors of smoke, a mix of small and large homes in no particular order. The stark absence of vegetation was broken only by the Jewish settlements with their tidy red roofs, green fields, and fruit orchards, cut off from the surrounding parched land with tall fences.

Half an hour later, the settlement of Tapuach—*Apple* in Hebrew—welcomed them with a massive steel gate across the access road. A sign read: NO VEHICLE TRAFFIC DURING SABBATH!

Lemmy parked the car, and they walked to the guardhouse. A man in a white shirt and a knitted skullcap shouldered his machine gun and opened the gate.

Up close, Lemmy realized that most houses were nothing more than rickety prefabricated trailers, covered with ivy and painted white. Cracked concrete paths meandered between young trees and makeshift vegetable gardens. A woman pushing a double-stroller gave them directions.

Freckles opened the door, wearing a blue tank top, shorts, and sandals. A small bandage was taped to his chin.

"Hey, partner," Itah said.

Behind him, a woman with a Russian accent yelled, "Who is it?"

"I'll be right back," he replied and joined them outside, closing the door.

"Good Sabbath," Lemmy said. "Do you remember me?"

Freckles shifted his knitted skullcap back and forth on his head, as if he had a bad itch. Then his eyes lit up. "King David Hotel. You wore a baseball hat, right?"

"Good memory. I can tell Elie Weiss trained you."

He nodded.

"Interesting," Itah said. "Then why did you betray him?"

"Not here." Freckles walked fast, his sandals slapping the concrete path. He led them to a playground, where a bunch of kids climbed ropes and pushed the limit on creaking, steel-chain swings. "I've served both SOD and Shin Bet for years. There was no conflict—it was like doing one job for two employers and twice the pay. But Agent Cohen forced me to choose, told me

Elie Weiss was dying and that I could go to jail for many years for a conspiracy to shoot the prime minister."

"Are you guilty?"

Freckles smiled, showing crooked teeth. "It was Elie's idea, you know, to have a religious guy use low-velocity bullets, shoot Rabin once in the ribs over a bulletproof vest. I mean, it has to look real to convince everyone that the right-wing crazies actually tried to kill him, right?"

"Let me see if I understand," Itah said. "The Shin Bet discovered Elie's staged assassination plot, gave you an ultimatum, and forced you to betray him."

"There's no betrayal!" Freckles got red in the face. "I work for them, so I report my whereabouts."

"Meeting Elie at the King David Hotel?"

He shrugged.

"And they shut down the operation and arrested Yoni Adiel?"

Freckles looked away. "Something like that."

"Don't lie to me."

He folded his arms on his chest. "Maybe you should leave."

Lemmy patted his shoulder. "Do you know who I am?"

"I don't care." Despite the height difference, it was clear that Freckles felt that his youth and muscular build gave him advantage over the middle-aged man Itah had brought with her.

"Let's say," Lemmy said, "that while you got a baccalaureate degree from the university of Elie Weiss, I went on to earn a doctorate."

"Congratulations." Freckles grinned. "But I still don't care."

"Perhaps you should. You see, I kill people for Elie Weiss. Traitors, for example."

Standing by the kitchen table, Gideon helped Sorkeh clean up and bandage Jerusalem's scrapes and bruises. The news of the apartment raid had spread quickly, drawing a large crowd of Neturay Karta men, who filled the alley below, waiting for Rabbi Benjamin Mashash to come out. But he had shut himself in his small study off the foyer, and his praying voice filtered through the closed door.

"There," Sorkeh said to her son, "all done. You go back to bed, and I'll bring you some tea." She went over to the dining room, where Agent Cohen was having a hushed conversation with his team, and said, "You should be ashamed of yourself!"

He turned to her, his injured eye covered with a beige patch, his red face still marked by the straps of the gas mask. "Shut up, woman, before we arrest you."

"Is that so?" Sorkeh went to the window and looked down at the crowded alley, which went quiet immediately. "Men of Neturay Karta," she yelled, "come up here and remove these Nazis from your rabbi's home!"

A roar came from below, and the drumming of shoes on the stairs gave the whole building a tremor.

"*Shit!*" Agent Cohen retreated with his subordinates into the corner, drawing their weapons, while Sorkeh returned to the kitchen.

Gideon ran to the study and pounded on the door.

Rabbi Benjamin Mashash emerged just as the first few men appeared at the entrance, pushed from behind by the crowd. He stood in front of the door leading to the dining room.

The foyer filled with men in black coats and hats, their hands clenched into fists.

"Sabbath is a holy day of reflection and prayer." Rabbi Mashash gestured. "Pass it down."

"Sabbath is a holy day of reflection and prayer," the men repeated. Others did the same, and the sentence could be heard making its way down the stairwell to the alley.

"We will allow these misguided Jews to leave our community in peace."

Again the words echoed repeatedly until they faded away.

He beckoned Agent Cohen. The Shin Bet agents holstered their weapons and trotted warily through a narrow path among the men of Neturay Karta. Gideon nodded at the rabbi and his wife and followed the Shin Bet team downstairs and through the alleys to the gate.

Freckles recovered quickly, but he was smart enough to know they had seen the look of fear on his face. "You don't scare me," he said, trying to sound defiant. "Everyone here is my friend. We all carry guns."

Itah turned to Lemmy. "I guess we're screwed, ah?"

"I guess so." He smiled at Freckles, placed an arm on his shoulder, and made him turn away from the playground.

"Hey!" Freckles tried to free himself. "Let go!"

But Lemmy's arm was already bent at the elbow, forming a tight collar around his neck. With his left hand Lemmy pulled the pen from his pocket and shoved the ballpoint tip into the double-agent's ear. Itah was ready with her crumpled headdress, which she pressed to his mouth to silence his scream.

They led him into a cluster of trees nearby. None of the playing kids noticed anything unusual, and their chatter continued uninterrupted.

Freckles moaned as he tried to force away Lemmy's hand.

"That was your eardrum. It will heal. But any deeper than this, and my pen would demolish your middle ear, destroy your auditory system and your balance. After that, I'll be autographing your brain. I'd rather not, but I need to know that you'll cooperate and not scream. Is it safe now?"

Freckles froze, lowering his hands.

"Is it safe?"

He made a sound that indicated a positive response.

Lemmy pulled the pen out of Freckles' ear and held it up. "Too much wax."

Itah removed the gagging headdress.

"They took over Elie's operation," Freckles said rapidly, his voice thinner, as if his vocal cords had narrowed. "Wasn't my idea!"

"I thought they shut it down," Lemmy said, aiming the pen at the ear.

"Don't! Please!"

"Keep talking."

"Rabin won't wear a vest. They had me load Yoni's gun with blanks. He doesn't know. He thinks they're regular bullets."

"When will he shoot Rabin?"

"Tonight. At the rally. Yoni will be allowed to enter the sterile zone. After the rally, near the Cadillac, the bodyguards will leave Rabin's back exposed for a shot."

"My God," Itah said. "Does Rabin know about this?"

"No."

"But why would Shin Bet get involved in politics? Domestic security priorities don't change, whether it's Rabin or Netanyahu, Labor or Likud!"

"It's not about politics." Freckles tried to shake his head, but it was still held in the vise of Lemmy's bent arm. "It's about making their life easier."

"It makes no sense," Lemmy said.

"Actually, it does," Itah said. "With the two-state solution, which seems inevitable, Israel will leave the West Bank and Gaza, and the Palestinians will want their future state to be *Judenfrei*. That means evacuation of all the Jewish settlements." She waved her hand around. "Including this one, which is growing every week. From a domestic security standpoint, speeding up the process is a necessity—the longer it takes, the larger the settlements, the harder it will be for Shin Bet and the IDF to remove all the Jews from the territories. The staged assassination will strengthen the Rabin government, demonize the right, and legitimize harsh measures against the settlements with a view to total evacuation. Shin Bet is thinking ahead, that's all. Security considerations, not politics."

"That's right," Freckles said. "Planning ahead. An assassination attempt by a right winger is a perfect excuse to come down hard on the whole settlement movement, arrest leaders, shut down support organizations, and deflate public sympathy for the settlers ahead of the eventual evacuation."

"It's risky," Lemmy said. "Is Yoni willing to go to jail?"

"Yes," Freckles said. "He's sincere about shooting Rabin pursuant to the *Rodef* doctrine."

"But what if he checks his ammo? He could switch to live bullets. This could end up being a *successful* assassination—by mistake!"

"It's a blessed gun." Freckles tried again to free himself, but stopped when Lemmy's pen slipped into his ear canal.

"Do you want gray matter seeping out of your ear?"

"Ouch!"

"What's a blessed gun?" Lemmy pulled the pen back, but not all the way. "Explain!"

"After loading Yoni's gun with blanks, I arranged for a rabbi to hold a little ceremony." Freckles grinned despite the pain. "He recited a prayer over the gun, wrapped it in a sacred parchment, sealed it with kosher wax, and instructed Yoni to open it only when the condemned *Rodef* is within range."

At Atarot airfield north of Jerusalem, Gideon, Agent Cohen, and the other Shin Bet agents boarded a helicopter. The mood was grim. Not only they had driven Spinoza out of the confined area inhabited by Neturay Karta, but the attack on Rabbi Mashash's apartment had been a complete disaster.

The discovery that one of their vehicles had been stolen was embarrassing, but its built-in tracking device provided the best possible hope of catching Spinoza before the commencement of the peace rally. The device worked only when the engine was on, and tracking was spotty in areas of poor cell coverage. So far, since its disappearance had been noticed, the car had not shown up on the monitors at Shin Bet headquarters.

After takeoff, the passengers' headphones were tuned to an all-news radio station, which carried a live report from the Kings of Israel Plaza in Tel Aviv. In the early afternoon, dozens of buses arrived from all over the country, unloading cheerful revelers, who swarmed the surrounding city blocks with provincial excitement. The tight security arrangements included multiple checkpoints, traffic barricades, bomb-sniffing dogs, and horse-mounted riot police. A small contingency of anti-peace demonstrators had already been arrested for gathering without the appropriate license.

The helicopter followed the main highway to Tel Aviv, descending the Judean Mountains over the string of rusting skeletal trucks and buses, preserved as memorials to the fallen soldiers of the 1948 War of Independence. But soon the Ayalon

Valley stretched before them, with open fields of honey-colored wheat and straight rows of vines.

Agent Cohen, who sat up front next to the pilot, suddenly turned and motioned at Gideon to change the channel on his headphones. "The car has just been traced," his metallic voice came through. "Somewhere in the West Bank. We're changing course."

They took Freckles' FN Browning handgun and warned him to remain mum about their visit. Ten minutes down the road, Lemmy stopped at an intersection: Left to the border crossing over the Jordan River, right to Tel Aviv.

"A fork in the road," Itah said. "No pun intended."

"The mother of all puns." Lemmy pointed to the east. "We could cross the border and go to Amman. I have several clients among the king's courtiers, and the Swiss embassy will take care of the paperwork and fly us back to Zurich."

"Nice for us," Itah said, "but the Israeli electorate will be left to watch a spectacle of corruption, deceit, and manipulation, leading to unearned election victory for Labor and a witch hunt against the political right."

"It would seem less important from distant Switzerland. My father will join us, and we'll spend Saturdays on the lake, eat and drink, and get to know each other."

"Tempting." She smiled. "But even your Swiss chocolate will taste bitter to me. I'm a reporter, and this is the story of my career. And I can't sit back and let such fraud go through." She reached for the door handle. "Let me go by myself. I can hitchhike from here, get to Tel Aviv, and call on a few media colleagues. We'll expose the staged assassination, either before or after the rally." She opened the door. "You go home to your family."

Lemmy reached over and shut her door. "I'm going with you."

"Why?"

He engaged first gear and waited as a convoy of three IDF jeeps reached the intersection and turned east toward the

Jordanian border. "Because a piece of parchment and a glob of kosher wax won't stop a determined assassin."

"How do you know?"

"It wouldn't stop me." The Subaru's rear wheels screeched as he accelerated in mid-turn, heading west toward Tel Aviv. "And it won't stop Yoni Adiel."

"New information," Agent Cohen said. "They've been to a settlement. Tapuach." He gestured at the pilot, who banked to the left in a wide sweep.

Gideon adjusted the mouthpiece. "What about sending a ground unit to set up a roadblock and arrest them?"

Agent Cohen gestured to the nurse, who unzipped an elongated package and took out a long rifle, equipped with a scope. She cocked the weapon and glanced through the scope. Satisfied, she gave it to Gideon to hold while she changed places with the agent sitting by the sliding door.

"Why Tapuach?" Gideon gave the rifle back to the nurse.

"Freckles lives there."

"Ah." Gideon could see through the front windshield the barren hills of the West Bank. "Did he tell them anything?"

"Of course." Agent Cohen used binoculars to inspect the narrow roads below. "He told them a bunch of bullshit. It's his specialty."

"Why would Spinoza risk capture? What did he expect Freckles to know?"

"Information about tonight! What else?" Agent Cohen's tone grew impatient. "Freckles knows all the details of SOD's fake assassination plan, which he helped us shut down. Spinoza needs every detail he could gather about tonight's security arrangements. That's why he went to see Freckles, and that's why we have to stop him. Do you get it now, or do I have to spell it out for you?"

"I get it," Gideon said, though he wasn't completely convinced.

"Good, because I'm counting on you to bring down Spinoza before tonight. The peace rally must go peacefully!" Agent Cohen chuckled at his clever pun. "Peace...fully!"

The pilot adjusted direction again, heading west, down from the watershed toward the coastal plain and the Mediterranean. The nurse grabbed the handle and pulled open the sliding door, letting in the roar of wind and engines.

Other than the Dutch signage and abundance of tall nurses of both genders, the VU Medisch Centrum in Amsterdam wasn't much different from Hadassah Hospital. The recent computer glitch had forced the staff to pay close attention to each patient, making sure the correct treatment was provided to the right person. Many beds carried cardboard signs with patients' names, and family members stayed around the clock to guard against mistakes. Carl joked with a pretty nurse in the elevator, who seemed disappointed when he stepped off with Rabbi Gerster on the fifteenth floor.

Carl led him to a room across from the nurses' station. "Best location," he explained. "From such proximity, the nurses are motivated to empty the bedpans."

Rabbi Gerster was still chuckling when he entered the room and saw Bira, holding a moist cloth to her mother's forehead. Tanya's eyes were closed. Her arm and leg were in a cast, attached to a steel-wire apparatus. Her face was impossibly white. He stared at her, unable to breathe.

"Can I help you?" Bira didn't recognize him.

He removed the sunglasses.

Her eyes opened wide and she hurried around the bed. She stopped before reaching him, holding back, unsure of his reaction.

He stepped forward, opened his arms, and took Bira into a tight embrace. And to his great surprise, Tanya's daughter, the tough archeology professor who had defied him repeatedly, buried her face in his chest and sobbed like a little girl.

The Cross-Samaria Roadway followed a moderate decline through the West Bank hills toward the Green Line and the Israeli city of Kfar Saba, a large bedroom community at the edge of the Tel Aviv metropolis. "Look at this view," Itah said. "On a clear day you can see every Israeli city from Ashdod in the south to Hadera in the north. Basically, sixty-percent of Israelis live within sight of here."

"And within range."

Itah looked at him. The resemblance to his father was striking, but so were the differences. Where his father was a thinker, a deliberate leader who used words and gestures to influence others, Lemmy spoke and acted like a man of action—decisive, showing no hesitation. "Range is a relative term," she said. "In sixty-seven, we worried about King Hussein's artillery positions on these hills, and in fact he bombed our cities before the IDF destroyed his army and pushed him back from the West Bank. But in ninety-one, Saddam Hussein's Scud missiles easily hit Tel Aviv from Baghdad, and the Americans forbade us from responding in kind."

"And in a few years, we'll be within range of Teheran's ballistic missiles." Lemmy sped up to pass a station wagon.

"That's the reason Yitzhak Rabin decided to make peace," Itah explained, "even if the Palestinians get to sit here and aim Katyusha rockets at us. He wants to create a ring of peaceful Arab countries around Israel—Egypt, Jordan, Syria, Lebanon, as well as a Palestinian state—together forming a buffer against Iran, Iraq, and Saudi Arabia."

"It's a risky gamble." Lemmy crossed into the opposite lane to pass a motorcycle, ridden by a couple who both wore black helmets and gray ponytails.

"Rabin is a strategic thinker. He looks at the whole region as a single battlefield, which is the reason he really believes in this peace. Only he could inspire so many Israelis to support reconciliation with the PLO—"

The shots came one after the other, blowing both tires on the left side of the car. Lemmy struggled with the steering wheel, but the car veered to the shoulder, flipped over, and landed upside-down in a ditch.

In the sudden silence, Lemmy heard the rattle of a helicopter. "Are you okay?"

No response from Itah.

Bullets knocked on the car.

The seat belt buckle took several tries to yield. He crawled out through the shattered window. A cloud of dust lingered from the car's tumbles. Freckles' FN Browning was already in his hand. He cocked it, advanced up to the edge of the ditch, and waited for the dust to settle.

The helicopter was somewhere to his right, hovering low. Lemmy traced the sound with the barrel of the FN Browning. A gust of wind cleared the dust. A sniper hung out of the open door as the helicopter slowly descended toward a flat piece of desert. More shots hit the car.

Lemmy aimed at the most vulnerable part of the craft—its rear rotor. He released one, two, three shots.

At first there was only a brief burst of steam-like vapors, but then the sound level changed. The sniper managed one more shot, hitting the dirt by Lemmy's head, but the helicopter began to spin around, showing its other side, which gave Lemmy direct visual line to the pivot holding the rear rotor. He pressed the trigger three more times. There was a popping noise, and the helicopter turned again, tilting sideways, and hit the ground.

No explosion. Must have been low on fuel.

Lemmy crawled back into the wrecked Subaru.

He didn't need to check Itah's pulse to know she was gone. The car's gyrations must have tossed her upper body sideways through the window. Her head was crushed.

Someone was yelling.

The motorcycle riders.

They had been close behind when the first shots hit the car. The bike was lying on its side, and the man was crouching by his female passenger in the middle of the road. Lemmy ran over. She was conscious, crying softly.

A car was approaching. It was the station wagon he had passed earlier. "There's your ride," Lemmy told the biker. "Get her to a hospital."

The motorbike was an old Triumph Bonneville, its few chrome parts shining, a testimony to pride of ownership and, Lemmy hoped, good repair. He lifted the bike, scanned the controls, slipped the gear into neutral, and stepped on the kickstand. The engine fired up immediately.

The owner yelled something.

Lemmy shoved the FN Browning in his belt and straddled the bike, revving the engine.

Another shout, this one closer.

He turned.

The biker held forth a helmet. "Don't leave the bike idling too long—it'll overheat."

Slipping on the helmet, Lemmy rode off, surprised by the engine's smooth response. A moment later he was speeding down the hill, his eyes squinting against the sun, which was descending toward the Mediterranean. As he breathed deeply, the adrenaline rush subsided, and anger flooded him. Itah was dead, and with her died the feelings she had developed for his father and the knowledge she had accumulated to help him in his quest to uncover the truth and secure his family's safety. Again he was alone.

Part Seven
The Redundancy

Saturday, November 4, 1995, Sunset

Gideon found himself in a daze, engulfed by smoke and groans of pain. He was upside down, the safety harness cutting into his shoulders. It was hot, and he thought, *I don't want to burn!* Bracing his head with one arm, he unbuckled and dropped to what was left of the ceiling. He helped the other agents get free and edge out of the wreckage. The nurse was gone.

They cleared off the shards from the front windshield and helped Agent Cohen and the pilot get out. The nurse's body was sprawled on a boulder a good distance up the hill, having flown out during the crash landing.

A few minutes later, an IDF jet flew low overhead. Two military helicopters followed, landing in a swirl of dust and tumbleweed. Army medics ran over.

Agent Cohen had lost his eye patch, exposing a black eye. His broken finger was off its stick, and he cursed as one of the medics fixed it.

Touched by the last rays of the sun, the first helicopter took off with the wounded agents and the dead nurse, heading to Hadassah Hospital in Jerusalem. Gideon and Agent Cohen boarded the second one. As they ascended into the air, the rolling lights of ambulances could be seen on the road nearby.

A report came through the wireless. The wrecked Subaru contained one dead woman, who fit Itah Orr's description. Her notebook was on its way to headquarters. Spinoza, however, had apparently stolen a motorcycle and disappeared down the road. By now he was already in a dense, urban area, impossible to detect until he reached the center of Tel Aviv.

"Put out an alert," Gideon said. "Every police officer, every sharpshooter on the roofs, every soldier manning a checkpoint. We have less than one hour until the rally begins, and Spinoza is halfway there already. We have to catch him!"

Agent Cohen radioed in the description of the Triumph Bonneville and its rider to the chief of the Tel Aviv police, who commanded all the perimeter checkpoints and roadblocks around the peace rally. A flyer with Spinoza's photo had been distributed already, with a warning that he might be disguised as a black hat. Anyone fitting his description was to be stopped, searched thoroughly for weapons, and released only if his Israeli identity was established without doubt.

As they flew over Tel Aviv, the giant square appeared below in glorious lights, already filled with people. The helicopter circled above, and they could see the IDF sharpshooters on the roofs, the gathering spectators on balconies around the plaza, and the traffic barriers on every incoming street and avenue.

The pilot put down on the helipad at Ichilov Hospital, a short distance from the Kings of Israel Plaza. They ran to a waiting car.

Tanya opened her eyes to see Bira in the arms of a tall, gray-haired man in an elegant jacket and a gentle manner. He looked at her and smiled—*Lemmy's smile!*—and she recognized him. She tried to speak, but her throat was dry. She swallowed, and said, "You're free."

Abraham Gerster rubbed his clean-shaven cheek. "Yes, at last, I am free."

She looked at the two of them, her daughter and the man she loved, standing by her bed, holding each other. "If I knew…it would take this." Tanya moved her broken leg, shaking the wires. "I'd have done it…sooner."

They laughed.

"What about…Lemmy?"

Abraham hesitated. "I think he's in Meah Shearim with Benjamin, hiding from the Shin Bet."

Tanya sighed. "Your son isn't…the hiding type."

"That's what I'm afraid of."

She watched Abraham's face, as handsome as the first time she had seen him, kneeling beside her in the snow, wiping the blood from her forehead. "Elie trained him," she said. "Lemmy will prevail."

"We can't lose him again."

"*No!*" Speaking so sharply hurt her chest, where three of her ribs were fractured. Tanya shut her eyes. She felt Abraham's warm lips on her forehead. For a moment, it took away the pain.

The address Lemmy remembered from Yoni Adiel's bank statements took him to a two-story house on a busy street in Herzlia. The first floor was all windows under an unlit sign: *Adiel & Sons – Kosher Meat and Fish*

Lemmy pushed the Triumph behind the corner of the house and took the stairs up. He smoothed his hair and tried to brush off the dirt from his white shirt and black pants. There was nothing he could do about the scratches and bruises from the rollover.

The woman who opened the door was heavy, with dark skin and a wide smile. "Shalom! How can I help you?"

"I am Professor Baruch." Lemmy smiled. "From Bar Ilan University."

"Oh!" She opened the door wide and beckoned him. "Please, come in. It's an honor!"

An older man with a black skullcap and a gray beard was sitting in the living room, swaying over a book.

"This is Professor Baruch," she explained, "from Yoni's law school."

The man extended his hand. "I am Yaakov Adiel, Yoni's father."

They looked at Lemmy's soiled clothes.

"I ride a motorcycle," he explained with an apologetic smile. "Today, gravity reminded me what a foolish hobby it is."

"*Oy vey!*" Mrs. Adiel cradled her cheek in her hand. "Did you get hurt?"

"Only my pride." He turned as a young man entered the room—dark, skinny, frizzy black hair, and intense, dark eyes under a colorful knitted skullcap.

"That's Yoni's older brother," the mother said. "Haim, please say hello to Professor Baruch from Bar Ilan Law School."

The brother didn't smile. "Yoni never mentioned you."

"Is he home?"

"He just left," she said. "As soon as Sabbath was over. He's going to visit friends at a settlement—four different buses, a long trip."

"No taxis?"

The parents laughed, and Mr. Adiel said, "We're raising seven children, Professor. They use public transportation."

"Which settlement?"

The brother said, "Why do you want to know?"

"Haim!" She smiled apologetically. "Yoni went to Tapuach. He will be so disappointed to have missed you."

But Lemmy wasn't listening to her any longer. He returned the brother's hostile glare without blinking. Did Haim know Yoni's real agenda?

She said, "Would you like a cup of tea?"

Haim turned and walked out of the room. Lemmy followed him down a hallway, past a kitchen, which seemed to be in the midst of a major cleanup after the Sabbath, and into a bedroom with two sets of bunk beds against opposite walls.

Haim kicked the door shut. "What do you want?"

On the desk Lemmy noticed a clean ashtray that held several bullets. He picked one. Twenty-two caliber. A blank. "He switched the bullets?"

"The Arabs ambush our people in the West Bank. Blanks won't help him."

"Help him with Arabs or with something else?"

Haim came closer, his fists clenched. "Stay out of my brother's business—"

Lemmy grabbed him by the neck, hooked a leg behind his knees, and slapped him down on the floor, knocking the air out of him. "Where is Yoni?"

The young man tried to push away the hand from his throat, but Lemmy landed a knee on his sternum and pressed a thumb onto his Adam's apple.

The bravado was gone, the eyes wide with fear.

Lemmy lifted his thumb. "Answer!"

"He took the bus."

"Which one?"

"Number 247. To Tel Aviv."

"The bus route?"

"Ayalon Avenue. All the way."

Lemmy let go of Haim. "What color skullcap is Yoni wearing?"

"I don't know. Blue and white, I think."

The immensity of the crowd surprised Gideon. Israelis of all ages, ethnicity, and economic status stood shoulder-to-shoulder, straining to see the stage. The mayor of Tel Aviv, a retired IDF general, spoke about his dream of peace with the Arabs, his voice booming from hundreds of loudspeakers. "And that's why I'm honored, on behalf of the people of Tel Aviv, to host this peace rally and to support my courageous comrade and brother-in-arms, Prime Minister Yitzhak Rabin!"

A deafening cheer came from the crowd, and Rabin could be seen in the front line of the public figures on the stage, waving at his supporters.

Agent Cohen stopped and listened to a report on his walkie-talkie. A man fitting Spinoza's description was stopped on King Saul Avenue. He was carrying a licensed pistol. His ID had an address of a kibbutz in the south, and he claimed to be a veteran major in the IDF. "I don't care! Arrest him!"

More people were arriving. Many waved Israeli flags on little sticks or held up placards in support of Labor, Meretz, or Shalom Now! As expected, the hundreds of balconies overlooking the plaza were filled with spectators. Near the stage, a bunch of youths jumped into the reflecting pool, splashing each other to the delight of the TV cameras.

A singer took the mike, his hair long, his face heavily made up. He broke into a familiar tune with lyrics that Gideon couldn't follow. The crowd went crazy, clapping, dancing, squealing at the top of their voices.

Gideon smiled, then remembered the reality of Spinoza on the loose. This happy night could still end in tragedy.

Behind the rear of the stage, Agent Cohen entered the sterile area, which was guarded by police officers and Shin Bet agents in civilian clothes. "Wait here," he told Gideon and consulted quietly with a few colleagues who, Gideon assumed, were also members of Shin Bet's VIP Protection Unit.

At the far end of the sterile area, the prime minister's official car—a gray Cadillac—waited with its doors open, the driver standing by, smoking a cigarette.

L emmy rode the Bonneville as hard as he dared. He cut in front of cars, passed in narrow spaces between lanes, bypassed stationary traffic on the shoulder, and took chances at busy intersections. After the restful Sabbath, when most businesses were closed and families spent time together at home, Israelis flooded the streets, especially teenagers and young professionals, patronizing restaurants, bars, and movie theaters. Many were young and inexperienced drivers, though it took nothing away from their confident aggression at the wheel.

But the risk paid off when Lemmy saw bus number 247 ahead, ascending the bridge over the Yarkon River at the entrance to Tel Aviv. The motorbike sputtered a bit on the upswing, but caught up on the downward stretch of the bridge. A pickup truck separated him from the bus, but the street lamps briefly illuminated the interior. Through the rear window

Lemmy could see the head of a young man with black hair and a knitted blue-and-white skullcap.

He leaned into the opposite lane to pass the pickup truck, catching a glimpse of the side of the bus, which bore an ad showing a swimsuit model lounging in the curves of a giant green pepper. The pickup truck accelerated, the youths in the cabin hollering. Lemmy downshifted and pulled the throttle all the way. He barely had time to cut in, avoiding an oncoming car whose headlights beamed into his eyes with intensity that left him momentarily blinded. As he struggled to regain focus, his vision concentrating on the rear of the bus, Lemmy failed to notice the lights turn red above the next intersection. He approached it at full speed just as a woman and a child stepped down from the curb.

An elderly nurse came in to plump up Elie's pillows. She raised the head of the bed and brought a cup of apple juice to his lips. On the TV screen across the room, a live broadcast from the peace rally showed happy faces singing in Hebrew. Colorful banners swayed in the gentle breeze:

PEACE NOW!

YES TO PEACE!

WE LOVE RABIN!

KIBBUTZ MOVEMENT SUPPORTS PEACE!

LABOR STUDENTS FOR PEACE!

The anchor described the unprecedented high attendance—possibly half a million people.

The singing ended, and the mayor of Tel Aviv invited Prime Minister Yitzhak Rabin to speak. The crowd cheered.

Rabin's face filled the screen. He smiled sheepishly at his perennial political rival, Foreign Minister Shimon Peres, who stood beside him.

When the crowd finally quieted down, Rabin spoke. "I was a soldier for twenty-seven years. I fought as long as there was no prospect of peace. But I believe that there is now a chance for peace. A great chance! And it must be seized!"

More cheers while Rabin leaned on the podium with a lopsided grin. Elie wondered if his posture meant that Rabin had relented and put on a bulletproof vest, its weight causing him to lean on the podium. He watched Rabin's familiar yet aged face. They had both spent a lifetime in the service of the Jewish people. Elie wondered what was going through Rabin's mind, how it felt to receive such explicit adulation, to be embraced by the loving masses, to bask in the glow of popular gratitude, rather than lie alone in a starched hospital room.

"I have always believed," Rabin continued, "that most of the nation wants peace and is prepared to take risks for peace. You, by coming here, are taking a stand for peace. You prove that the nation truly wants peace. And rejects violence!"

The last word generated booing through the plaza, and the TV camera captured individual faces, mouths open, hands waving.

"Violence is undermining the foundations of Israeli democracy." Rabin's voice grew angrier. "Violence must be rejected! Condemned! And contained! Violence is not the way of the State of Israel! Democracy is our way!"

"Exactly," Elie said quietly. "Exactly!"

Lemmy knew that the old brakes wouldn't manage to stop the motorcycle in time. The woman gripped her daughter's hand, both of them paralyzed in his path. Paula's face flashed in his mind, the girl she may be carrying. His foot pressed the rear-brake pedal, locking the wheel, and he shifted his weight left, leaning the Triumph as it slid sideways, both wheels now perpendicular to the direction of travel, sliding rather than turning. The tires uttered a hiss as they scraped against the road, slowing him down. Just before hitting the two, he straightened up, swerved right, and hit the curb. The bike became airborne. In slow motion it flew over the street corner, into the main cross street, bounced a few times without falling over, and reached the median, where the front wheel lodged into thick shrubs, throwing Lemmy off.

He lay on his back for a moment, only the dark sky filling his view.

People ran over and helped him up. They asked him questions, their voices indistinct. He didn't reply.

Traffic was stationary. A siren sounded in the distance. He checked himself. Each of his limbs worked fine, nothing broken.

More questions. Someone held Lemmy's arm.

He pulled the Triumph out of the bushes, off the median, and mounted it. The people around him stood back, stunned. He stepped on the kick start, the engine roared, and he took off, using the pedestrian crossing to return to his original direction.

Despite pulling the throttle all the way, the bike rewarded him with meek acceleration. Possible causes flew through his mind. A failing cylinder? A cracked fuel line? A misaligned sparkplug? Anything worse than that and the bike would croak!

As his speed increased, he noticed a wriggle in the handlebar. Was the front wheel bent?

Yoni's bus was out of sight.

Elie Weiss watched Prime Minister Yitzhak Rabin waiting for the applause to quiet down. He stood straight now, an old soldier's proud bearing. *So much for a bulletproof vest.* "Peace is not just a prayer," Rabin declared. "It starts with a prayer, but it's also the primary aspiration of the Jewish people. Peace has its enemies. They are trying to harm us. Torpedo the peace."

A few catcalls sounded in response.

"We have found a partner for peace," Rabin said. "The PLO, once an enemy, has now forsaken terrorism."

He paused, but there were no cheers. Even after signing the first two Oslo agreements, the murderous PLO and its scruffy, arch-terrorist leader were perceived as necessary evils rather than friends.

"There is no painless way forward for Israel," Rabin said. "It is our fate. And the way of peace is painful also. Filled with sacrifices. But better the pain suffered along the way of peace than the way of war. Anyone who served like me, who has seen the grieving families of the IDF, knows it. We must exhaust every possibility. Every opening. Bring a comprehensive peace!" He paused and watched the applauding crowd, indulging them like a father.

"This rally sends a message to the Israeli public," Rabin announced. "To Jewish people everywhere. To the multitudes in the Arab lands. And to the world at large. The nation of Israel wants peace and supports peace! And for this, I thank you!"

Elie watched a blonde woman take the microphone, Rabin and Peres at her side. She had a clear, sonorous voice, as she broke into an old, familiar tune of Israel's lingering hope: "*Let the sun rise, the morning brighten up, and the purest of prayers, shall not disappoint us....*"

The camera caught faces in the crowd, singing, waving flags, throwing flowers at the stage. Rows of men and women clasped hands and swayed from side to side, lips moving with the words, eyes bright with hope, some with tears of joy.

Back on Prime Minister Rabin, the camera showed him singing, his eyes on a piece of paper, scribbled with the lyrics. "*So let's sing a song for peace, no whispered prayer, sing for peace, cheer it loudly!*"

Elie closed his eyes and listened to the singing from Tel Aviv. He knew that soon the singing would give way to screaming.

Police had set up detours in the center of Tel Aviv, the roads clogged with stop-and-go traffic. Lemmy threaded the bike between cars. His elbow hit a side-view mirror, and the driver shouted an expletive. He passed several buses. None was number 247. He scanned the road ahead. He was not familiar with the streets, unsure where the peace rally was taking place.

Pedestrian traffic was getting denser. He heard music from loudspeakers and recognized the tune as an old song from his army days—something about giving peace a chance.

Farther ahead a bus took a left turn, and Lemmy recognized the swimsuit ad on the side of Yoni's bus. But in the moment before the bus disappeared, he saw the vacant rear bench. There must be other buses displaying the same advertisement! On the other hand, the proximity to the peace rally could mean that Yoni had disembarked.

On the right, Lemmy saw a bus stop, now empty. The passengers who had stepped off the bus were walking away, melting into the crowd. He proceeded slowly down the road, searching. Many bare heads, a few skullcaps, none blue-and-white.

A side street was blocked off to vehicle traffic with steel barriers. At the far end Lemmy could see the bright glow of the Kings of Israel Plaza, the throngs of people, the banners, and huge flags. He stood on the pegs, holding on to the handlebar, and from that higher perch scanned the forest of heads that filled the side street between him and the plaza.

Blue-and-white skullcap! Halfway down!

His finger on the horn button, Lemmy steered the Bonneville around and jumped the curb. He rode between two barriers, speeding up just as a policeman noticed him and blew his whistle. People heard it and turned. Others were startled by the engine noise and moved aside.

He was halfway down when the pounding of horseshoes made him glance back. Two policemen mounted on huffing beasts bore down on him. With one hand, Lemmy pulled off the helmet and tossed it over his shoulder. It hit one of the horses on the snout, causing it to neigh, swerve, and bump the other horse. Lemmy returned his gaze to the front while the noise behind went from huffing and trotting to cursing and shouting.

The blue-and-white skullcap was near the end of the blocked-off street, close to the plaza and the mass of people at the peace rally. Lemmy maneuvered around a group of elderly ladies bearing flags of the Workers Union and circled back, stopping in front of a young man who resembled Haim Adiel. He bumped into the bike, but as Lemmy reached to grab his arm, he stepped back. His face was covered by a film of sweat, which the mild winter night did not merit.

Yoni Adiel turned and ran.

Lemmy rode after him.

He turned into a path that led to the entrance of an apartment building, where the Bonneville leaped over the front step and roared into Yoni, pinning him to the wall. Lemmy leaned forward over the handlebar and punched him hard in the right kidney.

The two policemen showed up, batons at the ready.

"Sorry about the horses," Lemmy said as he lowered Yoni to the floor. "This guy is armed and dangerous. Call for reinforcement!"

"They got Spinoza!" Agent Cohen broke into a run down Ibn Gevirol Street, shoving people aside, and turned right into a dense, pedestrian-only street. Gideon followed him close behind. A few policemen were running from the opposite direction.

A narrow path led to an apartment building.

Inside the small lobby, Agent Cohen pushed between the policemen.

Gideon saw a motorcycle. Behind it, a dark-skinned youth was being held facedown by Spinoza, who smiled and said, "There you are. The beauty and the beast."

Gideon drew his gun, cocked it, leveled it at the Swiss, and pressed the trigger. But the man again acted with swiftness that belied nature as he dodged out of the line of fire and somehow kicked up the motorcycle. The bullet must have hit the gas tank, which burst out in flames and sent everyone running outside.

Agent Cohen yelled, "Don't let him get away!"

"Not going anywhere," Spinoza said in perfect Hebrew, appearing next to them, his skinny captive dragged along by the neck. "Your patsy here has switched his blanks for hollow-point bullets. He would have killed Rabin."

Gideon was already raising his gun, but noticed Agent Cohen's expression turn into fear as he turned and yelled at the policemen, "Get all the civilians out of here!"

They started pushing back the spectators.

"Hey!" Gideon pointed to the dark youth Spinoza was holding. "Who's this guy? What bullets?"

"It's his accomplice!" Agent Cohen pointed. "Shoot them both, idiot! Now!"

"He's framing you," Spinoza said. "Shin Bet wants to pin everything on SOD in case the assassination scheme goes badly."

"What scheme?" Gideon turned to the Shin Bet agent. "Didn't you shut it down?"

Agent Cohen drew his own gun with his left hand and aimed it at Gideon. "Shoot, or I'll shoot you!"

With a casual flip of the hand, Spinoza knocked the gun from Agent Cohen's hand. "Shin Bet kept Elie's operation going," he said. "But Rabin won't wear a vest, so they loaded Yoni's gun with blanks." He shook the young man, causing his skullcap to fall off. "Right?"

The assassin reached behind his back. "I'm just getting my wallet." He pulled it and showed them a laminated card. "I have a license to carry a gun everywhere, including into secured zones."

Spinoza patted him down and found a package stuffed under Yoni's shirt. "You always carry it like this?" The gun was wrapped in a parchment, but the wax seal was broken in half. He handed it to Gideon. "They had a fake rabbi load it with blanks, recite a blessing, and seal the parchment. But this kid outsmarted them, switched the bullets back to deadly hollow points. Did you recite another prayer over it?"

"Of course," Yoni Adiel said.

Gideon turned to Agent Cohen. "Is it true?"

"Don't worry about it." The Shin Bet agent pointed at Spinoza. "This is the real assassin!"

Drawing a large pistol, Spinoza held it up with two fingers. "This is the only weapon I have—took it from Freckles earlier. It's an FN Browning, nine millimeters long. No silencer. If I try to shoot Rabin with this, it will make more noise than a Howitzer. I'll be lynched."

"But you were in Paris!" Gideon tried to think straight. "You killed Abu Yusef's boy, caused us to lose Bashir, provoked the synagogue attack—"

"Elie sent me on that job. You know how he operates. Belt and suspenders. I also shadowed you when you were chasing Al-Mazir—those BMW bikes were fast!"

"The blue Porsche?"

Spinoza nodded.

Agent Cohen beckoned a group of men in civilian clothes who appeared out of nowhere. They circled the group in a tight ring.

Gideon lowered his gun. "Who are you?"

"My name is Jerusalem Gerster," Spinoza said. "Lemmy, for short. I'm the rabbi's son. Been working undercover for Elie Weiss in Zurich for years."

"Take him," Gideon said to the men, pointing at Yoni Adiel. "Only him!"

"Wait a minute," Agent Cohen protested, "I'm giving the orders here!"

"Not anymore." Gideon raised his gun and slapped Agent Cohen with the barrel right on the mouth, causing him to fall backwards, blood splattering from his mouth.

Yoni Adiel turned, connecting his wrists behind his back for the handcuffs. He smiled at Gideon—a cold, arrogant smile. As they took him away, he yelled, "Redundancy!"

Elie watched as the TV camera followed Prime Minister Rabin. He shook hands with the long-haired singer, who also won a kiss from Mrs. Rabin. Going down the wide stairs to the sterile area, the camera caught Foreign Minister Shimon Peres linger by Rabin's car on the opposite side.

A reporter asked the prime minister whether he intended to accept opposition leader Benjamin Netanyahu's invitation to discuss the rising level of political violence. Rabin's smile disappeared. "It would be stupid, naive, for me to meet with him. Why should I? I'm tired of the hypocrisy of the Likud. They speak against violence, but support it. One day Netanyahu leads a rally while his supporters are calling for my death, another day he wants to meet with me. It's the epitome of hypocrisy!"

The camera backed away as the silver-haired mayor came over to introduce one of the organizers. The prime minister's wife, Leah Rabin, effusively thanked them for the most successful political rally in the country's history.

Meanwhile Rabin paused and extended his hand to the cameraman. "And thank you as well," the prime minister said. The picture jittered with their handshake.

Lemmy almost felt sorry for Elie's young agent. Gideon's face reflected utter confusion as he began to realize how Agent Cohen had used him to further a devious agenda that could have led to an unintended *real* assassination of the prime minister. "Can you believe their stupidity," Gideon said, "trusting the prime minister's life to blanks and parchment?"

"It could have worked," Lemmy said.

"He wanted me to shoot you," Gideon said, "one SOD agent killing the other, or better yet, we shoot each other simultaneously, providing a perfect cover story in case something went wrong with their scheme—which it would have! That's why Yoni said—"

"Redundancy?" Lemmy considered it for a moment. "No. I don't think he was talking about us."

"What else?"

Suddenly Yoni's departing comment seemed ominous. "Could there be another assassin?"

Following him down the path to the street, Gideon said, "But Elie supported ILOT. Why would he...you mean, a parallel operation?"

"Exactly!" Lemmy pushed through the remaining spectators and broke into a sprint toward the plaza. "Another ILOT-like group, another *Rodef* verdict, another religious extremist! The same thing!"

"Redundancy!" Gideon yelled the word like a man discovering the key to heaven—or hell. "Belt and suspenders!"

They ran across Ibn Gevirol Street, against the flood of departing revelers, toward the massive city hall building that overshadowed the empty stage.

Many well-wishers had lingered around the sterile area behind the stage, pressing against the waist-high police barriers. Lemmy and Gideon pushed through, shoving people aside. The music was still playing from the loudspeakers, making it useless to yell any warnings.

Prime Minister Yitzhak Rabin was walking across the sterile area toward his Cadillac, circled by bodyguards.

Lemmy scanned the area. "There!"

A lone man, dark and skinny, with a knitted skullcap and intense face, stood near a fountain, smack in the middle of the sterile area. He bore an uncanny resemblance to Yoni Adiel, except that he was slightly shorter and wore dark clothes. He watched Rabin and his entourage approach.

Gideon and Lemmy jumped over the barriers, and immediately a group of policemen was all over them.

"Protect Rabin!" Lemmy pointed. "Stop this man!"

But as Rabin neared the Cadillac, the assassin took three steps, reached with one arm through a gap that opened between two bodyguards, and shot the prime minister in the back.

On the TV in Elie's room at Hadassah Hospital, gunshots sounded. Someone yelled, "Blanks! Blanks!" A scuffle erupted around the prime minister. Cries of fear. Sirens whined.

Elie watched the confusion on the screen, people running back and forth.

A few minutes passed.

A woman was being interviewed. "No," she said, "I saw him enter his car. There was no blood. Rabin was fine!"

Elie sighed. All according to plan. He closed his eyes, dozing off.

A little while later, someone yelled—not on TV, but outside the door. Another voice responded, anxious, fretful. Then an anchor on the screen said, "We now go to Ichilov Hospital in Tel Aviv for a live news conference."

A man stood with a stained sheet of paper, his eyes red. "With horror, grave sorrow, and deep grief, the government of Israel announces the death of Prime Minister Yitzhak Rabin, murdered by an assassin."

Elie Weiss heard a wail from the television—or maybe from the hallway outside his room. The words repeated in his mind. *Yitzhak Rabin, murdered by an assassin.*

Laughter erupted from Elie's dry lips. He fought for air, and another screeching laugh cut through his chest. He sat up, choking, as the nurse ran into the room. She was yelling for help. His hand pulled off the hospital gown, his fingernails plowing the flesh of his chest, digging to reach the fire inside.

Someone outside his room cried. More voices down the hall, filled with horror.

The nurse pressed a button on the wall. An alarm went off.

The man on the TV held up the paper and said, "Rabin's blood spilled all over his copy of the Song of Peace."

Drawing a last breath, Elie convulsed in laughter and pain. He rolled off the bed to the hard floor.

———

Part Eight
The Aftermath

Sunday, November 5, 1995

Lemmy entered the house, using his own key. He surprised Paula in the kitchen. They hugged and kissed. "What happened to you?" She touched his face, then took his hands and caressed the bruises. "Have you been in an accident?"

"Sort of." He smiled. "It's a long story, but I'm fine."

She pressed his hand to her tummy.

He laughed. "*Really?*"

"Really. And I have another surprise for you. Father woke up yesterday and dictated instructions to the board of directors. They approved your appointment last night." Paula smiled. "My husband, the president."

Lemmy nodded. The seeds that Elie had planted decades earlier were finally bearing fruit. With the power to direct every aspect of the bank's business, combined with control of the enormous Nazi fortune, the time had come for the Final Counter Solution.

"Papa!" Klaus Junior ran down the stairs and jumped into Lemmy's arms. "What did you bring me?"

"Actually, I brought something very special."

Paula's forehead creased. "Not another old car?"

"An old man, actually." Lemmy smiled to ease the shock. "Not too old, though."

"Who?"

"My father."

Klaus Junior said, "I have another grandpa?"

"Is this one of your jokes?" Paula seemed ready to laugh.

"No." Lemmy kissed her again. "I'll explain later. Right now, he's anxious to meet you."

They went to the foyer.

"Father," Lemmy said, his voice choking, "please meet my wife, Paula."

The hand that shook hers was large yet soft.

"Welcome to our home," Paula said. "It's a wonderful surprise."

"And this is Klaus Junior," Lemmy said.

"Hi." The boy looked up at the clean-shaven face, the gray hair, and the large blue eyes that smiled down at him. He beckoned. "Want to see my room?"

"Calm down," Gideon said, holding his mother, "I'm here, okay?" But she clung to him silently, not letting go. He led her to the kitchen, sat her down, and made tea for both of them.

The apartment smelled the same—fried chicken schnitzel and detergent—the smells of his childhood. She had aged since he last saw her, almost a year ago, and her hands shook as she held the saucer and sipped tea. Seeing her like this made him realize how much pain his career had caused her.

"I'm staying home," he said.

"Until when?" She put down her tea.

The correct answer would be: *Until the investigation is over.* But he couldn't say that. "My department is going through some changes. I'll hear in the next few days."

"Changes? Because of the tragedy?"

"Not directly. My boss is very sick."

The *Ma'ariv* newspaper was on the table. Most of the first page was dedicated to the assassination, the responses from world leaders, and the accusations against the Likud and other right-wing parties for creating a murderous environment.

The Jerusalem Assassin 465

Gideon turned to the second page and saw the headline: ITAH ORR, VETERAN TV REPORTER, DEAD IN CAR ACCIDENT.

"It's the end of the Zionist dream." His mother sighed. "A Jew killing the prime minister? It's a nightmare! All the right-wing leaders should go to jail, every last one of them!"

"It's more complicated than that." Gideon took off his shoes.

"What happened to your boss?"

"He's in a coma. I just visited him."

"I'm sorry to hear that. At least he's not lying alone in a foreign country like your father, his memory be blessed. A man should be surrounded by his family."

"He doesn't have a family. The Nazis killed them. He dedicated his life to preventing another Holocaust."

"Oh." She shook her head. "How sad."

Gideon knew what she was thinking. "Don't worry. I plan to have a family one day."

"Of course you will. When I'm too old to enjoy it."

He laughed. "I'll give you grandchildren. It's a promise, okay?"

"I should live long enough to see them." His mother went to the fridge. "I'll fry some chicken for you. Do you want potato latkes with it or blintzes?"

Tanya watched them enter her hospital room, three solemn men in ill-fitting suits. The oldest one she had known for decades. He was her direct commander, the chief of the mighty Mossad. He was a lifelong agent who had risen through the ranks, surviving countless clandestine operations in a morbid process of elimination that left him alone at the top.

He hugged Bira. "Sorry, kid. We screwed up, letting your mom get hurt like this."

"Is this a get-well visit," Tanya asked, "or an execution?"

"A little of both." He smiled and pulled a chair while his two companions left the room with Bira. "How are you feeling?"

"Physically or mentally?"

"Mentally, we're all sick. The worst day in Israel's history."
He sighed. "A watershed event. A breaking point. We'll never
be the same."

"What really happened? How *could* it happen?"

He rubbed his tired eyes. "The witch hunt has started. Finger
pointing. Heads rolling. The works."

"Then why are you here?" Tanya felt sudden anger. "You
should be in Jerusalem running the investigation."

"I'm a Rabin man. And today there's a new king in Jerusalem."

"Shimon Peres is smart enough to know that no one but you
has the credibility, the experience, the tools to investigate this
as deep as it gets—"

"Shin Bet will investigate itself."

"That's ridiculous!" Tanya explored his poker face. "Are you
teasing me?"

He shook his head.

"But they've gone rogue! There must be an external
investigation!"

"Not going to happen. Peres wants this whole affair wrapped
up quickly. We must concentrate on healing the nation, and so
on." The chief of Mossad patted the cast on her arm. "We have
enough external enemies, don't we?"

"No! I won't go along with this!"

"Don't make it personal."

"But they're criminals!"

"Misguided men, even incompetent, but with good
intentions." The chief pulled out a piece of paper. "Last night,
shortly after chairing his first cabinet meeting, the interim
prime minister signed this order. I flew here especially to deliver
it to you."

"What is it?" She reached across her broken body with the
left hand, the IV lines swaying with it. "An order to shut up and
play dead?"

"Something like that."

Tanya looked at the sheet of paper. It bore the menorah
emblem at the top and the letterhead: STATE OF ISRAEL – OFFICE
OF THE PRIME MINISTER

Above a scribbled signature, the page carried a single sentence: BY AUTHORITY GRANTED TO ME UNDER A UNANIMOUS RESOLUTION OF THE GOVERNMENT OF ISRAEL, I HEREBY APPOINT TANYA GALINSKI AS CHIEF OF MOSSAD, EFFECTIVE IMMEDIATELY.

THE END

Author's Note

While the characters populating this novel are fictional, the assassination of Prime Minister Yitzhak Rabin on November 4, 1995 is a historic fact, and so are the political figures, public events, and the social unrest portrayed in this story.

In an effort to remain true to the historic record, I relied on newspaper and magazine articles, several books, the unclassified sections of the Shamgar Commission Report, and available video footage of the violent political rallies in Israel in the months preceding the assassination and of the actual shooting, which was captured by a lone cameraman.

It is now a matter of public record that the real-life, right-wing militant group EYAL played an active role in events leading up to the assassination. EYAL resembles the fictional ILOT group described here.

Yigal Amir, the law student who shot Rabin, was a member of EYAL. He told his interrogators: "I would not have done what I did if not for my religious duty to defend the people of Israel, based on the law of *Rodef/Moser*, which applied to Rabin, as was decreed by many rabbis." He was convicted of murder by an Israeli court and is serving a life sentence. He has since married and become a father.

The Israeli attorney general also indicted a Shin Bet agent who, according to the Shamgar Commission and various news reports, was a mole inside the Israeli right-wing activists and the leader of EYAL. He was fully aware of Amir's assassination plans. His trial (for allegedly failing to report Amir's concrete plans to Shin Bet) was postponed repeatedly, eventually resulting in an acquittal.

Shortly after the investigative commission chaired by retired Supreme Court President Meir Shamgar submitted its report to the Israeli government, the chief of Shin Bet resigned. No explanation was given, and the report remains largely classified.

The historic record leaves many questions unanswered. Why had Shin Bet taken no action despite having Amir identified as an extremist by Shin Bet's own informant inside EYAL? Why did Shin Bet allow Amir to hang out in the secure sterile area behind the stage while Rabin was departing the rally? Why did Shin Bet bodyguards violate routine protocol by leaving Rabin's back exposed to an easy shot just at the moment they passed by Amir? And why did a bodyguard yell "They're blanks! Blanks!" immediately after the shooting, preventing Amir's elimination by Rabin's guards?

In a *New York Times* piece, published days after the assassination, Likud leader Benjamin "Bibi" Netanyahu wrote that "*the most outrageous charge is that we are guilty because we share with the assassin the idea of opposing the Oslo agreements. This is McCarthyism at its purest.*" Less than a year later, Netanyahu won the general elections, beating Shimon Peres, who had inherited the premiership from Rabin. In one of its first acts, the Likud government fulfilled Israel's commitment under Oslo to hand over control of Hebron, another West Bank city (and the resting place of the Jewish patriarchs), to Arafat's Palestinian Authority.

Did the assassin achieve his goal of derailing the Oslo peace process? As always, history is prone to conflicting interpretations. But the fact is that the Oslo process followed Rabin to the grave as disillusionment grew deeper with each deadly terror attack on Israeli civilians. Nevertheless, when Israelis elected Rabin's protégé Ehud Barak, who in 2000 offered Arafat at Camp David practically all of the Palestinians' territorial and political demands, Arafat declined and incited another intifada. And when Arafat died in 2004, he left a divided Palestinian population and a Mideast conflict dominated by Iranian-sponsored Hamas, Hezbollah, and myriad other militia groups sworn to the destruction of the Jewish state.

Against this grim reality, it is worthwhile to recall the hopeful 1993 White House ceremony for the signing of the first Oslo Accord, where Prime Minister Yitzhak Rabin said: "We, like you, are people, people who want to build a home, to plant a tree, to love, to live side-by-side with you in dignity. We are, today, giving peace a chance." Alas, like other Mideast leaders who gave peace a chance, Yitzhak Rabin paid with his life.

Acknowledgments

My research has benefited from the works of many scholars and biographers, particularly those who participated in the political and military events surrounding the Oslo Accords, Palestinian terrorism, and the Rabin assassination. For readers interested in further exploration, a list of my primary bibliographical sources appears next.

In writing this book I relied on the warm support of family members and close friends, whose thoughtful input, critical comments and enthusiastic encouragement were instrumental and invaluable to this work. Special thanks to editor Renee Johnson, as well as the professional staff at CreateSpace.

Bibliography

Ross, Dennis. *The Missing Peace: The Inside Story of the Fight for Middle East Peace.* New York: Farrar Straus and Giroux, 2004.

Indyk, Martin. *Innocent Abroad: An Intimate Account of American Peace Diplomacy in the Middle East.* New York: Simon & Shuster, 2009.

Gold, Dore. *The Fight for Jerusalem: Radical Islam, the West, and the Future of the Holy City.* Washington, D.C.: Regnery Publishing, 2007.

Beilin, Yossi. *Touching Peace.* Tel Aviv: Miskal – Yedioth Ahronoth, 1997 (Hebrew ed.).

Rabin, Yitzhak. *The Rabin Memoirs.* New York: Random House, 1979.

Harris, Bill (Director). *Yitzhak Rabin – Biography.* New York: A&E Television, 1995 (VHS).

Dallas, Ronald. *King Hussein – A Life on the Edge.* New York: Fromm Int'l, 1999.

Wallach, Janet & Wallach, John. *Arafat – In the Eye of the Beholder.* Secaucus, NJ: Birch Lane Press, 1997.

Lewis, Bernard. *The Crisis of Islam – Holy War and Unholy Terror.* New York: Modern Library, 2003.

Dawidowicz, Lucy S. *The War Against the Jews – 1933-1945.* New York: Bantam, 1986.

Raviv, Dan, and Melman, Yossi. *Every Spy A Prince – The Complete History of Israel's Intelligence Community*. Boston: Houghton Mifflin, 1990.

Raviv, Dan, and Melman, Yossi. *The Spies: Israel's Counter-Espionage Wars*. Tel Aviv: Miskal – Yedioth Ahronoth, 2002 (Hebrew ed.).

Katz, Samuel M. *Soldier Spies – Israeli Military Intelligence*. Novato, CA: Presidio Press, 1992.

Gutman, Yechiel. *A Storm in the G.S.S. (Shin Bet)*. Tel Aviv: Yediot Ahronoth, 1995 (Hebrew ed.).

Netanyahu, Benjamin. *Fighting Terrorism: How Democracies Can Defeat Domestic and International Terrorists*. New York: Farrar Straus and Giroux, 2001.

Carroll, James. *Constantine's Sword – The Church and the Jews – A History*. New York, Boston: Houghton Mifflin Company, 2001.

———

Also by Avraham Azrieli

Fiction:

The Masada Complex – A Novel

The Jerusalem Inception – A Novel

Christmas for Joshua – A Novel

Non-Fiction:

Your Lawyer on a Short Leash

One Step Ahead – A Mother of Seven Escaping Hitler

www.AzrieliBooks.com

CPSIA information can be obtained at www.ICGtesting.com
Printed in the USA
LVOW01s0226130315

430391LV00025B/508/P

9 781460 906552